A Sweet Historical Western Romance
by
USA TODAY Bestselling Author
SHANNA HATFIELD

Aundy

Copyright © 2013 by Shanna Hatfield

ISBN-13: 978-1484966280
ISBN-10: 1484966287

For permission requests, please contact the author, with a subject line of "permission request" at the email address below or through her website.

Shanna Hatfield
shanna@shannahatfield.com
shannahatfield.com

Special thanks to Keith F. May. The books you shared about Pendleton's history, as well as the answers you provided to my many questions, were invaluable. Thank you!

To those who take a leap of faith,
even when they can't see
where their feet will land...

Books by Shanna Hatfield

FICTION

CONTEMPORARY

Grass Valley Cowboys
The Cowboy's Christmas Plan
The Cowboy's Spring Romance
The Cowboy's Summer Love
The Cowboy's Autumn Fall
The Cowboy's New Heart
The Cowboy's Last Goodbye

Rodeo Romance
The Christmas Cowboy
Wrestlin' Christmas
Capturing Christmas
Barreling Through Christmas

Silverton Sweethearts
The Coffee Girl
The Christmas Crusade
Untangling Christmas

Women of Tenacity
Welcome to Tenacity - Prelude
Heart of Clay
Country Boy vs. City Girl
Not His Type

Stand Alone Titles
Love at the 20-Yard Line
Learnin' the Ropes
QR Code Killer

HISTORICAL

Hardman Holidays
The Christmas Bargain
The Christmas Token
The Christmas Calamity
The Christmas Vow
The Christmas Quandary

Pendleton Petticoats
Dacey
Aundy
Caterina
Ilsa
Marnie
Lacy
Bertie
Millie
Dally

Baker City Brides
Tad's Treasure
Crumpets and Cowpies
Thimbles and Thistles
Corsets and Cuffs
Bobbins and Boots

Hearts of the War
Garden of Her Heart
Home of Her Heart

NON-FICTION
Fifty Dates with Captain Cavedweller
Farm Girl | Recipes of Love
Savvy Entertaining Series

Chapter One

Clickety-clak. Clickety-clak. Clickety-clak.

The sound of the train kept perfect time with the runaway thumping of Aundy Thorsen's heart. Each beat took her closer to an uncertain future and she wondered what madness possessed her to make such a rash decision.

"Miss?" A gentle tap on her arm brought Aundy's head around to look into the friendly face of the porter. "We'll be in Pendleton soon. Just wanted to let you know."

"Thank you," Aundy said with a smile, nodding her head. The porter had been helpful and kind, answering her many questions and making two rowdy salesmen intent on bothering her relocate to a different car.

Aware that she was asking for trouble traveling alone, Aundy figured since she was taller than most men and not considered beautiful, she wouldn't have any problems.

The persistent salesmen had been the only nuisance in an otherwise uneventful, yet exciting, adventure.

Growing up in Chicago, she'd never traveled any farther than her aunt's stuffy home across town. Aundy tried to commit to memory each detail of her trip that would soon end in Pendleton, Oregon. Once there, she would marry Erik Erikson, a farmer who wanted a Norwegian bride.

Her betrothed, a man she had yet to meet, offered to travel to Chicago so they could wed there then make the trip to Pendleton as a married couple. Aundy assured him she would be safe traveling alone, although she was grateful for the train ticket and generous sum of money Erik provided to cover her expenses. Aundy had saved most of it, accustomed to living frugally and making each penny count.

However, she wished she'd purchased something to eat at their last stop. She willed the rumbling in her empty stomach to discontinue.

Suddenly overcome with the thought that she would soon meet Erik and become his bride, nerves replaced her hunger.

Although Erik wasn't the first man to whom Aundy found herself engaged, he would be the first she married. Not willing to think about the affectionate glances and gentle smile of the playful boy who had stolen her heart, she instead focused her thoughts on the man awaiting her.

Six months ago, desperate to make a change in her life, Aundy happened upon a discarded newspaper and her gaze fastened on an advertisement for a mail-order bride.

Normally one to ignore such nonsense, Aundy felt drawn to the words written by a farmer named Erik Erikson.

Wanted: someone to build a future with and share in my dreams. Seeking loving wife with a tender heart and gentle spirit. Must be willing to move to Pendleton, Oregon. Hard worker, good cook, and Norwegian ancestry preferred. Farm experience helpful, but not essential. Outward beauty irrelevant. Please reply to…

Intrigued, Aundy ripped the advertisement out of the paper and carried it around in her pocket for two weeks, debating if she should send a reply. Finally, she sat down and composed a letter to Erik Erikson of Pendleton, Oregon, a place she'd never heard of and certainly never dreamed of seeing.

She wrote about her life, how she worked as a seamstress at a factory during the day then helped cook and clean at a boardinghouse in exchange for her room and board. Not considered beautiful by any sense of the word, Aundy assured him she had a strong constitution, a tender heart, and a willingness to work hard. She described how her parents, both from good Norwegian families, made certain their three children knew their heritage.

Convinced she'd never receive a reply, Aundy was surprised when a letter arrived from Erik. He invited her to correspond with him so they could get to know one another better before making any decisions or commitments.

They wrote back and forth, sharing bits of information about themselves, their families, their hopes and dreams. Aundy came to like the man in the letters penned with a confident hand.

Erik wrote he wasn't much to look at, had never been married, and owned a farm that was on its way to being prosperous. He shared how lonely his life seemed and how much he wanted to have a family of his own.

When he wrote saying he was in love with her letters and asked if she'd agree to marry him, she quickly replied with her consent, changing the course of her future. Bespoken for the second time in her young life, Aundy had no delusions about being in love with Erik. Love died along with her beloved Gunther two years earlier.

Nonetheless, she had plenty of admiration and respect to share with Erik along with her devotion and loyalty.

Even if she never brought herself to love the man, she would be a caring, gentle wife.

Forcefully returning her thoughts to the present, Aundy took a shallow breath in the train car filled with the mingling odors of stale food, unwashed bodies, and smells from the washroom.

She longed to press her warm cheek against the cool glass of the window. Instead, she tipped her head so she could see over the sleeping woman beside her to admire the brilliant blue sky, pine-dotted mountains, and snow-covered ground outside.

The train chugged through the rugged Blue Mountains of Eastern Oregon. Aundy realized she was farther away from her familiar world than she ever imagined possible.

Tamping down her fears of what waited ahead, she pulled a handkerchief out of her reticule. Carefully rubbing her cheeks, she hoped to remove the worst of the soot. Grime covered every inch of her being from the long trip. She couldn't wait to soak in a tub of hot water, wash her hair, and dress in clean clothes.

She sincerely hoped Erik wouldn't mind if she did that before she put on her wedding dress and exchanged nuptials with him. He didn't mention his plans for when they would wed, but she assumed he would want to do so as soon as possible. If her assumptions proved true, she supposed she would most likely be Mrs. Erik Erikson before the end of the day.

That thought made her grip the reticule so tightly in her hands, her fingers cramped inside her soft leather gloves.

A light touch on her arm drew Aundy's gaze to the woman who sat beside her for much of the trip.

"You'll be fine, dearie," Mrs. Jordan said, her kind brown eyes twinkling. "Nothing to worry about at all."

"Thank you, ma'am." Aundy patted the hand resting on her arm and offered the woman a small smile. With mile upon mile of nothing to do but stare out the window and watch the incredible changing scenery, Aundy and Mrs. Jordan discussed their individual reasons for being on the train. The elderly woman traveled to Portland to live with her only daughter.

"You're a smart, brave girl," Mrs. Jordan said, sitting straighter in her seat. "I have no doubt that everything will work out for the best. If it doesn't, you know how to get in touch with me."

"I'm sure all will be well." Aundy was grateful she had a slip of paper in her possession with Mrs. Jordan's new address. If she ever needed somewhere to go, at least she had one friend on this side of the Rocky Mountains.

Aundy adjusted her hat, brushed at her skirt and the sleeves of her jacket, and moistened her lips. Although Erik said looks didn't matter to him, she certainly hoped he wouldn't be terribly disappointed when he met her. Perhaps she shouldn't have refused when he asked for her photograph.

Afraid he would break off their commitment once he realized she was no beauty, she figured he would take her as she was or she'd be in an even bigger mess than the one she left behind in Chicago.

She gathered her belongings along with her courage and glanced out the window. The snow had disappeared, leaving random patches covering the ground as the train made its way out of the mountains. The sky was so blue and wide open, she wondered if she could see up to heaven.

Would her father and mother look down and give their approval to what she was about to do? She prayed if Gunther could see her, that he wasn't disappointed with her for marrying someone she would never love.

Aundy trapped a sigh behind her lips, brushed at her skirt one last time, and sat back to wait as the train rumbled to a stop, willing her pounding heart to slow as well.

The porter finally announced their arrival and stood outside the car, helping the women disembark.

After giving Mrs. Jordan a quick hug, Aundy slipped on her coat, grabbed the Gladstone bag that had been her mother's, and stepped outside into the bright sunshine and brisk February air.

"Best wishes, Ms. Thorsen," the porter said as he helped her down the steps.

"Thank you, sir." Aundy tipped her head at him before turning her attention to the platform where a sea of people churned back and forth. How was she ever going to find Erik?

Cowboys and farmers, businessmen and miners, Indians covered with colorful blankets, Chinese men wearing long braids and strange hats, and women dressed in everything from plain calico to ornately festooned dresses milled together, all blending into a mass of varied colors.

Aundy filled her lungs with the clean air and wished, again, she had exchanged photographs with Erik when he asked. His description said he was tall, blond and plain. She'd written him a similar portrayal of her own appearance.

She looked around and counted four men who were several inches taller than the majority of the crowd. One had dark hair that fell down to his shoulders, one was an extremely handsome cowboy, one wore a nice suit, and the last one appeared to be a farmer in mud-splattered overalls who was not only dirty, but had a mean look about him. She certainly hoped he wasn't her intended.

When the man in the suit removed his hat, clutching it tightly in his big hands, his white-blond hair glistened in the mid-day sun. Flecks of mud on his boots and the hem of his pants didn't detract from his crisp shirt, attractive vest or well-made tie.

Discreetly studying him a moment, Aundy hoped he was the man she was about to wed. Despite his obvious nerves, he had a kind face, even if it was older than she anticipated. Erik never stated his age, never asked hers.

While she was considered a spinster at twenty-one, she guessed Erik's age closer to forty from the lines time and life had etched on his face.

Although not handsome, he had a gentleness about him that held Aundy's interest. If this was, in fact, her betrothed maybe she hadn't lost her mind after all.

Determined to make the best of her situation, she squared her shoulders and straightened her spine. She marched up to the man as he continued to search the faces around him.

"Mr. Erikson?" Aundy asked, stepping beside him. The surprised look on the man's face when he turned his attention her direction made her smile. "Erik Erikson?"

"Yes, I'm Erik Erikson." He studied Aundy with undisguised curiosity. "May I assist you?"

"I certainly hope so." Her jaunty grin made him smile in return. "You did say you needed a bride and asked me to marry you."

"Oh! Ms. Thorsen? Is it really you?" Erik cradled Aundy's gloved fingers between his two work-roughened hands.

"It is, indeed."

"I had no idea… I didn't think…" Erik attempted to chase his thoughts back together. "You said you weren't comely and when I saw you get off the train, I thought you were much too lovely to be my bride. It's a disservice, Ms. Thorsen, saying you are plain. You look like one of the Viking queens in the stories my mother used to read me at bedtime - tall, strong, and beautiful."

His comments made her blush. No one had ever called her lovely or compared her to a Viking queen, although her father used to tell her she had the tenacity of her ancestors running through her veins.

Erik took her bag and escorted her off the platform over to a wagon hitched to a hulking team of horses.

"Meet Hans and Henry," Erik said, setting her bag in the wagon then giving her a hand as she climbed up to the seat. "I would have brought the buggy, but I assumed you'd have luggage. If you wait here a moment, I'll get your trunks."

"Thank you." Aundy warily studied the horses. With a childhood spent in the city in an apartment, she had no experience with animals, other than two kittens that belonged to her sister, Ilsa. She told Erik from the beginning of their correspondence he'd have to teach her about his farm and livestock. As he wrote about his day-to-day activities, she gleaned information about his horses and Shorthorn cattle, as well as the pigs and chickens he raised.

Although she wanted to crane her neck and stare at everything she could see, Aundy instead glanced around inconspicuously, taking in a variety of interesting faces and places. Erik wrote the town was growing and was one of the largest cities in Oregon. She hoped to have time to explore her new home another day.

She watched Erik walk with his head and shoulders above much of the crowd as he collected her trunks.

He soon returned, easily carrying one of her trunks while two younger men struggled to carry her other trunks. He set them in the back of the wagon, tossed each man a coin with a nod of his head, and climbed up beside Aundy.

"I let the pastor know to expect us as soon as the train arrived," Erik said, turning the horses so they began lumbering down the street.

"The pastor?" Aundy worked to keep from swiveling her head back and forth as Erik drove past stores and business establishments. There were so many interesting buildings and fascinating people.

"Pastor Whitting." Erik forced himself not to stare at Aundy. She was young, tall, and much prettier than he'd anticipated. Not that her looks mattered, but her smooth skin, dusted by a few freckles across her nose, golden hair, and sky blue eyes made him glad he'd placed an advertisement for a bride.

Although most of his friends thought he had lost use of his mental faculties, Erik was tired of being alone and didn't have time to find a wife or properly court a woman.

He vowed to make it up to Aundy by spending the rest of his life showing her she was special to him. He'd fallen in love with the girl in the letters she wrote. It was easy for him to see he'd love the woman beside him even more.

Erik grinned at her. "I thought we could get married, have lunch, and then head out to the farm. I wanted to have time to show you around the place before it gets dark."

He laid out his plans so plainly, as if getting married was an ordinary occurrence, that Aundy needed a moment to absorb his words. It looked like her mother's wedding dress would stay packed in the trunk and a bath would have to wait. Resigned to exchanging vows with Erik in her current state of disrepair, she smiled at him and put a hand on his arm. "That sounds fine."

"Good." Erik grinned at her in such a way he resembled a happy boy as he turned the horses down a side street. Aundy could see the church ahead and tried to calm her nerves. The warmth of the sun beating down, despite it being February, forced her to remove her coat. Erik tucked it behind the seat, placing it on top of one of her trunks.

After he stopped the horses close to the church steps, Erik walked around the wagon, and reached up to Aundy. When she started to put her hand in his, he gently placed his hands to her waist and swung her around, setting her down on the bottom step.

The breath she was holding whooshed out of her and she looked at Erik with wide eyes. She'd never been handled so by a man and wasn't sure if she liked it or not. Part of her thought a repeat of the experience might be in order for her to make up her mind.

"Shall we?" Erik asked, offering her his arm as they went up the church steps.

Before she could fully grasp what was happening, she and Erik exchanged vows. He slid a plain gold band on her finger then the pastor and his wife offered congratulations on their marriage. They exited the church into the bright afternoon sunshine. Aundy had to blink back her disbelief that she was finally a married woman.

"We can eat just around the corner, if you don't mind the walk," Erik said, gesturing toward the boardwalk that would take them back toward the heart of town.

Aundy nodded her head as Erik placed a hand to the small of her back, urging her forward.

Soon, they were seated in a well-lit restaurant, enjoying a filling, savory meal. Several people approached their table, offering words of congratulations. Aundy smiled when a few of the women invited her to stop by for a visit sometime soon.

It appeared that Erik was a well-liked member of the community and for that, Aundy was grateful. She'd never lived in a rural town, but assumed getting along with your neighbors spoke well of a man's character.

Aundy watched Erik finish his piece of pie and hoped this marriage would be a blessing to them both. She didn't know what had prompted her to act so boldly, writing to a stranger, but right at this moment she was glad she sent Erik that first letter.

"Well, Mrs. Erickson, are you ready to go home?" Erik asked as she took a last bite of cherry pie and wiped her lips on a linen napkin.

"I suppose so." Realization that she was no longer Aundy Thorsen but Erik's wife struck with a sudden force.

Erik left money for their lunch along with a tip on the table. He stood and put on his hat, offered Aundy his arm, and escorted her back to the wagon.

Although Aundy expected him to help her into the wagon, she was surprised when he pulled her into his arms, right there in front of the church for any and all to see as they passed by.

"Thank you for coming, Aundy. For marrying me." Erik kissed her quickly on the lips. He seemed unable to stop himself from giving her an affectionate hug. "I promise to be a good husband to you."

She looked into his eyes and saw the questions there. Aundy tamped down her unease at having a man who was still a stranger kiss her. She placed a hand to his cheek and patted it with a growing fondness. "I know you will be. And I'll do my very best to be a good wife to you."

"You could start by giving me a kiss," Erik teased, waggling a blond eyebrow at her.

Aundy smiled and kissed his cheek, grateful that Erik seemed to have a fun, playful side. "You'll have the town gossiping about me and I haven't even been here two hours."

"Everyone knows I came into Pendleton to marry you today and I can't see a thing wrong with a husband kissing his lovely new bride."

Cheeks filled with bright color, Aundy accepted Erik's help into the wagon and sat down, pleased at his words.

Once they headed out of town, she relaxed as the noise and activity of Pendleton fell behind them, and the rolling fields opened before them. She released a sigh, gazed up at the sky, and breathed in the fresh air.

"Anything you want to know? Any questions?" Erik asked, watching Aundy as she settled against the wagon seat.

"I don't think you ever told me how old you are." Aundy studied Erik's profile, trying to guess his age.

"I'll be thirty-nine next month," he said, turning to look at Aundy with a soft light in his eyes.

"And you've never been married?"

"Never. I got so busy building the farm after my parents died, I kept putting off finding someone to court. I woke up one day and realized if I wanted to have a wife and a family, I had better do something about it. So I placed the ad and you know the rest of the story."

"I guess I do." Aundy looked with interest at the fluffy clouds drifting across the azure sky overhead and the fields that surrounded both sides of the road. If the land had been flat, she was sure she could have seen for miles. Instead, the gently rolling hills provided their own unique perspective to the landscape. Unfamiliar with wide-open spaces and such clean air, Aundy breathed as deeply as she dared and soaked up the sunshine.

"How old are you?" Erik asked, breaking into her thoughts.

"Twenty-one, although people often mistake me for someone older." Aundy laughed as a memory surfaced. "Someone once asked if Ilsa, my sister, was my daughter. I didn't know whether to be insulted or pleased."

Erik chuckled. "Pleased, I would think. People can't help but see the way you carry yourself with confidence and strength. That's a good thing."

"It is?" Aundy liked the sound of Erik's laugh. Although she'd only just met the man, it wasn't hard for her to imagine spending her future with him. Since stepping off the train, what she'd seen and experienced led her to believe Erik was gentle and mannerly. He might not be handsome or young, he might not make her heart pound or butterflies take flight in her stomach, but she thought he would treat her with respect and care. If they were fortunate, they might even come to love one another someday.

"Certainly, it is. I wouldn't want some flighty young thing, so wrapped up in herself that she wouldn't take proper care of a home or her husband. It's easy to see that you'll be a good wife, Aundy. You're a sensible girl and I appreciate that." Erik looked at his new bride with a teasing smile. "I also appreciate your fine figure, beautiful eyes, and that sweet smile."

Her cheeks turned pink and felt exceedingly warm from Erik's words of praise. Aundy lifted her gaze across the fields, dotted with a few skiffs of melting snow.

She heard Erik chuckle again before she felt his fingers on her chin. He gently turned her face toward his.

"I didn't mean to embarrass you, but I want you to know I think this marriage is going to work out just fine." Erik leaned over and pressed another quick kiss to her lips.

Aundy closed her eyes and waited to feel something, anything. Instead, Erik pulled back and she opened her eyes to find him studying the road ahead.

"Do you think… if it isn't… what I…" Aundy stammered, trying to figure out a way to ask if she could take a bath when they reached his farm.

"What is it? Go ahead, Aundy. Don't be afraid to ask me anything."

"May I please have a bath? I feel like I'm wearing dust from way back in Wyoming and half a train car of soot."

"Yes, you may," Erik said, bringing his gaze back to his bride with an indulgent smile. "You can do that while I take care of the evening chores, after I show you around the farm. How does that sound?"

"Wonderful," Aundy said, excited at the prospect of being clean. "As soon as I'm finished, I can fix the evening meal."

"No need. One of the neighbors said she'd have a basket waiting on the table for a cold supper so you wouldn't have to cook on your wedding day."

"How thoughtful." Aundy decided Erik must have nice neighbors. "I'll have to thank her later for her kindness."

"It's Mrs. Nash. She and her husband and son live on the farm to the south of us. They're good folks. Ol' Marvin Tooley lives on the farm to the west but he's cantankerous on a good day, so stay away from him if you can."

Aundy nodded her head, wondering what made Mr. Tooley crotchety.

When they passed a lane that turned off the road, Erik inclined his head that direction while the horses continued onward. "That's the Nash place. Been here for many years. Raise mostly cattle and wheat. Good folks and good friends as well as our closest neighbors."

Aundy again nodded her head and gazed up the lane, catching a view of the top of the barn over a rise in the road. Pole fences ran along a pasture down to the road and she could see dozens of cattle grazing lazily in the sun.

"Are those…" A sharp crack resonated around them, spooking the team. The horses lunged forward and the wagon began flying down the muddy road.

"Whoa, boys! Whoa!" Erik called, pulling back on the reins, frantic to get the team under control.

Aundy clung to the side and back of the seat, praying for the runaway horses to stop.

"Get down, Aundy," Erik yelled, motioning for her to climb beneath the wagon's seat. She followed his orders, wedging herself into the space as she listened to the thundering of the horse's hooves and Erik's shouts for them to stop.

The wagon veered sideways then slid back before hitting the side of the ditch bank and flipping over, sliding in the mud.

Aundy's screams mingled with Erik's shouts before everything went black.

Chapter Two

Cautiously opening her eyes, Aundy tried to recall where she was, what was happening.

She remembered the runaway wagon and shifted her gaze upward. The floor of the wagon loomed above her head while her back rested on the base of the broken wagon seat. Swiftly realizing the wagon was upside down, she felt grateful the seat had kept her relatively safe.

After taking a quick inventory to make sure she could feel her toes and fingers, she discovered her left arm throbbed painfully, but everything else seemed to be in working order.

Carefully turning over, she hoped Ilsa would forgive her for completely ruining the travel suit she had painstakingly remade from some of their mother's clothes.

Mud oozed through the fabric of her skirt and into her petticoat as she scooted forward over the front end of the wagon. Cold and slimy, it made her shiver as she climbed from beneath the wagon and pulled herself upright.

The horses were both still on their feet, hooked to the wagon. Blood trickled down the hindquarters of the one nearest her. Nervous and antsy, each time they moved, the wagon creaked and shifted. Afraid of them spooking again, Aundy looked around, wondering where Erik had gone.

Two of her trunks sat upended in the road, a little muddy but none the worse for wear. The third rested at an odd angle with the lid hinges broken. A pile of frothy white unmentionables floated in the mud near her bedraggled coat. Hastily gathering her soiled clothes, she rolled them in her coat and set the bundle on top of one of the unbroken trunks.

Upset, she craned her neck, hoping to catch a glimpse of Erik, when she heard a deep moan. She walked around the end of the wagon and drew in a sharp intake of breath. A corner of the wagon bed rested on her husband's chest, pinning him in the mud with his head twisted to one side.

"Erik," she whispered, hurrying to him. Aundy dropped to her knees and lifted his head to her lap. "Erik, can you hear me? Please, Erik. Please wake up."

Another deep moan answered her pleading. Pulling a handkerchief from her pocket, she wiped at the mud on his face and begged him to wake up. His eyelashes fluttered and he finally opened his eyes.

"Aundy?" Erik raised his eyes to hers. Pain and despair filled their blue depths.

Tears rolled down Aundy's cheeks. "Erik, what can I do? How can I help you?" She had no idea what to do. Nothing helpful came to mind. She certainly couldn't move the wagon herself and was afraid to get near the horses.

"Unhook the horses," Erik said, clenching his teeth as the animals moved nervously and the wagon shifted on top of him.

Aundy carefully lifted his head from her lap. She spied Erik's hat lying a few feet away and slid it beneath his head to keep him out of the mud.

"I don't know how. What do I do?" Aundy straightened her spine and turned to look at the horses as they took another nervous step, dragging the upended wagon across Erik, causing him to gasp for air.

Finally regaining the ability to speak, Erik gave her instructions using as few words as possible while Aundy swallowed down her fear. She unhooked the horses, just as

Erik told her, and hurried back to him. The team took a few forward steps then dropped their heads to graze on the side of the road, unaware of the havoc they created with their wild run.

"Get Garrett," Erik whispered as she bent down beside him. His voice grew weak and he squeezed his eyes shut.

"Who's Garrett? Does he work on your farm?" Aundy wracked her brain for the name Garrett. Had Erik mentioned anyone named Garrett in his letters? Not that she could recall.

"Neighbor. Garrett Nash." Erik slowly turned his head in the direction of town.

"Garrett Nash," Aundy repeated. Erik had pointed out the Nash farm about a half-mile down the road. "I'll be back as soon as I can."

Erik didn't answer but he opened his eyes and blinked.

Aundy grabbed her mud-soaked skirts in one hand while she held her injured arm close to her side and started running down the road, sending a steady stream of prayers heavenward for Erik to be fine. By the time she reached the turnoff to the Nash farm, her lungs burned and she was convinced she'd accumulated so much mud on her shoes and clothes, it added an extra twenty pounds of weight.

She topped the little rise in the Nash's lane and took in a massive barn and corrals. A big two-story farmhouse offered a welcoming porch that wrapped all the way around. She hated to go to the front door in such a state, but she didn't know what else to do. After racing up the steps, she rapped sharply on the door, trying to catch her breath.

The door swung open as she raised her hand to knock again. She looked into the cheery, round face of a small woman with dark hair and silvery gray eyes.

"My gracious, dear. What brings you to our door? I don't think I've seen you around these parts before."

"Wagon wreck," Aundy managed to say as she struggled to draw air into her lungs. If she hadn't been wearing her hated corset, she'd have been able to run to the house with no trouble.

"Wagon wreck? Where? On the road?" The woman stepped out on the porch and gazed in the direction of the road.

"Yes, not far." Aundy moved back, mindful of getting mud on the woman's spotless white apron or lavender dress.

"Is anyone hurt?"

"My husband. He's pinned beneath the wagon." Aundy tamped down her growing sense of panic.

"What's your name?"

"Aundy. Aundy Thor… Erickson." Aundy corrected herself at the last moment, remembering her name was now Erickson.

"Are you Erik's bride?"

When she nodded her head, the woman bustled across the porch and picked up an iron bar. She beat it against a triangle hanging from the porch eaves.

Aundy breathed deeply as air filled her lungs. "The pastor married us earlier today. The horses spooked and the wagon flipped over on Erik."

"Oh, my gracious. The boys will be here soon and they'll take care of everything." The woman motioned for Aundy to sit on a chair by the door. "I'm Mrs. Nash, but I hope you'll call me Nora. I'll run in and telephone the doctor. You're welcome to join me."

"Thank you, Nora, but I'll just…"

Nora disappeared inside the house, unable to hear the last of Aundy's words. She was gone only a moment and returned to the porch just as Aundy heard pounding feet racing toward them.

"What'd you ring the bell for, Ma?" An extremely tall, incredibly attractive man took the porch steps in one long stride and stopped next to Nora. He noticed Aundy standing off to the side and gave her a brief perusal before turning to his mother with a quizzical expression.

"Aundy, this is my son, Garrett." Nora made a brief introduction. Turning her attention to Garrett, she pointed her finger toward the road. "Erik Erickson was in an accident. According to his new bride, the wagon is just down the road on top of him. I think you better get down there and see what you can do. I tried the doc but no one answered my call, so we should send someone to fetch him."

"Yes, ma'am." Garrett jumped off the porch and ran in the direction of the barn.

"Why don't you come inside, dear, and we'll see about getting you cleaned up." Nora reached out to grasp Aundy's mud-covered hand.

Aundy pulled back and began moving down the steps. "Oh, no, ma'am. I couldn't bring this mess inside your home and I promised Erik I'd be right back."

"I wouldn't mind, honey. You'll catch your death all muddy and cold like you are," Nora said, taking a step toward her. Before her hand could reach out to the wide-eyed girl, Aundy turned and started running down the lane.

Garrett hustled out of the barn on his horse, accompanied by Tom, one of the ranch hands. Stopping at the porch to speak with Nora, Garrett motioned Tom on down the driveway.

"Go on and get the doc and the pastor if he's home," Garrett instructed then turned his attention to his mother. "I asked Jim to hook up the wagon. Maybe you could bring some blankets and whatever medical supplies you can round up. I don't know what kind of shape we'll find things in, but it might be a help."

"I will, son. Go on, now, and see what you can do. I'll be there as quick as Jim's got the wagon hitched and I let your father know where we're going." Nora gave Garrett's leg a pat before he urged the horse forward.

Garrett hurried his big bay horse down their lane to the road. Caught off guard when he answered his mother's summons, he never expected to see a woman standing on the front step covered in mud from head to toe.

A hat that had probably been the height of current fashion perched on her head like a dead bird and mud-streaked blonde hair fell down around her ears, trailing along her back. The dress she wore was finely made, but he doubted she'd ever get all the mud out of the burgundy wool.

He tried not to think about her eyes, the same shade of blue as the sky overhead, or her extraordinary height. Under all that mud, he would bet that Erik's new bride was quite striking in appearance.

She certainly didn't rattle easily, since she hurried to their house for help even though they were all strangers to her.

Near the end of their lane, he spotted Mrs. Erickson doing her best to run in the mud. It sucked at her feet and pulled her off balance but she continued at a brisk pace. He watched as she glanced over her shoulder at him then came to a stop.

"How about I give you a ride?" he asked, holding out his hand for her to mount behind him.

"I don't want to get you or the horse dirty," she said, shaking her head. "But thank you for the offer."

"Come on, we're wasting time discussing it." Garrett wiggled his gloved fingers her direction, motioning for her to take his hand.

She walked over to the horse and looked up at him, noticing his eyes were the same silvery shade as his mother's. "I've never been on a horse, so tell me what to do."

Garrett recalled Erik saying his bride-to-be was a city girl, so he offered her an encouraging smile. Since her skirt wasn't full enough for her to ride astride, she'd have to sit in front of him. He had no doubt she'd think the proximity to him highly inappropriate.

"Just stick your foot in the stirrup and I'll pull you up." He was impressed that she didn't put up a fuss, instead showing a strong, practical nature when she nodded her head.

Garrett held her left hand to steady her while she gathered her skirts out of the way with her right. He caught her wince.

"Why didn't you tell me your arm was injured?" he asked, leaning over and grabbing her around the waist, lifting her in front of him. The mud-flecked feather on her bedraggled hat smacked him in the face and he fought the urge to grin.

"It's fine." Aundy swallowed back a moan. The throbbing in her arm made her feel lightheaded, or maybe it was the impropriety of riding across a stranger's lap. With Erik injured, what society deemed proper no longer seemed very important. She stiffened her posture and tried not to think about Garrett's arms around her as he urged his horse through the mud.

"Sure it is. If I was a betting man, I'd wager it hurts like the dickens." Garrett observed the woman possessed an obvious obstinate streak. He studied the road in front of him, attempting to ignore the feel of the woman held so close to him as he kept an eye out for the wagon. After rounding a little bend, the wagon was easy to spy, turned over in the middle of the road. It was hard to miss Erik trapped under the back of the wagon, his face a ghostly shade of white beneath the mud coating his head.

Garrett stopped Jester, his horse. He gently held Aundy by the waist and set her feet on the mud-slicked road. Easily swinging a leg over the back of his horse, he dropped to the ground.

"Erik? Can you hear me?" Garrett knelt by his neighbor and friend. Although the man was more than ten years his senior, they often talked over the fence about farming, ranching, and life in general. Erik had been a guest at the Nash dinner table many times over the years and they were all pleased for him when he announced his plans to wed.

Erik didn't move and appeared to be barely breathing. Garrett took off his glove and felt along the man's neck finding a pulse, although the beat was faint.

"We need to move the wagon." Garrett stood and pulled on his glove. He looked around, expecting to see Erik's team. "Where are the horses?"

"Erik made me unhook them before I went to get you," Aundy said, sitting next to Erik, holding his head in her lap again. "He said they'd find their way home."

"They're probably already at the barn, waiting to be fed." Garrett had no idea how badly Erik was injured but getting the weight of the wagon off his chest needed to happen immediately. Taking stock of the situation, Garrett noticed for the first time Aundy's trunks scattered on the ground near the wagon. He strode to where they rested in the mud, picked up the first one, and carried it to the back corner of the wagon. He did the same with the second, placing it next to the first trunk.

"We're going to have to work together to do this, Mrs. Erickson," Garrett said, looking into her scared face. He surmised she was much younger than he first guessed. She wore confidence in an easy manner, but currently looked very young and frightened.

The accident was a terrible way to welcome Erik's bride to Pendleton.

When she nodded, he motioned her to stand at the end of one of the trunks. "I'm going to lift this corner of the wagon. When I do, push that trunk beneath it to hold it up. We'll do the same thing with the second trunk. As soon as it's secure, I'll pull Erik out."

Aundy nodded her head, frightened by the thought of the wagon falling back on Erik or trapping Garrett as well.

"Don't you dare use that arm." Garrett stared at her left arm, still held tightly against her side. "Get down like this and push with your back and shoulder."

He demonstrated how he wanted her to move the trunks and she got into position, lifting her sodden skirts out of her way as best she could by placing the hem in her injured hand.

Garrett grunted and strained, putting all his strength into lifting the wagon. Finally, he hefted the corner of the wagon off the ground high enough the trunk would fit beneath it. "Now!" The muscle in Garrett's jaw worked as he bore the weight of the wagon. Aundy quickly slid the first trunk into place, followed by the second.

With a speed borne of fear, he hurried to take Erik by the shoulders and move him from beneath the wagon.

"Get back from there, please, Mrs. Erickson. I don't know if the trunks will hold it or not and I don't want you to receive more injuries," Garrett said, pulling Erik a safe distance away.

If Aundy had two good hands to work with, he would have had her pull Erik out from beneath the wagon when he lifted it. Her injured arm, combined with Erik's deadweight, meant there was no possible way she could have moved her husband using one hand, no matter how hard she tried.

Curious as to what kept his mother and their hired hand, he turned to mount Jester and ride back to the ranch. The jingle of harness let him know his mother approached.

Jim drove Nora right up to where Garrett and Aundy kept watch over a motionless Erik. Prepared to jump down into the muddy mess, Jim's restraining hand on Nora's arm kept her from leaving her seat. "Just stay here, Mrs. Nash," Jim said, setting the brake and handing her the reins.

"My gracious, Garrett! We've got to get that poor man home," Nora said as Jim and Garrett carefully carried Erik to the back of the wagon and gently laid him on some old blankets she'd spread in the wagon bed. Jim climbed up to the seat while Garrett tied Jester to the back of the wagon then swung Aundy into his arms, setting her close to Erik.

She glanced at Garrett, uncertain his behavior was appropriate, especially since she was now a married woman. His touch made a jolt zing through her from the top of her head to her mud-covered feet. Surprised by his strength, Aundy thought Garrett acted like she weighed no more than a bag of flour and she knew for a fact she was taller and sturdier than many men.

Carefully cradling her left arm against her chest with her right, Aundy continued her prayers on Erik's behalf while Jim urged the wagon toward Erik's farm. Only by staring intently at her husband's chest could she see it barely rise and fall. That had to be a good sign, at least she hoped it was.

The wagon turned and she looked up to see a house in the distance along with a big barn and several outbuildings. While not as big or impressive as their neighbor's abode, Erik had what appeared to be a solid one-story home with a porch across the front and back, and a yard with a nice fence. His horses stood at the barn dragging the reins of the harness behind them, waiting to be relieved of their burden.

Jim pulled the team to a stop at the edge of the front walk and hurried down to help Garrett carry the injured man.

Nora hustled out of the wagon and ran inside the house before Jim and Garrett made it to the porch steps. Aundy trailed along behind, uncertain what she could do to help.

"Bring him in here," Nora called from a room off the large living area.

Heedless to the mud dripping from all their clothes, the men carried Erik into the bedroom and carefully placed him on an oilcloth Nora had yanked from the kitchen table.

"That should keep the bedding from being ruined," Nora said, watching as Garrett and Jim removed Erik's boots and the outer layers of his muddy clothing. Erik groaned. Though still unconscious, his hands tightened into fists. When he coughed, drops of blood dripped from the corner of his mouth.

Nora grabbed a rag from the basket of supplies she set by the bed and wiped Erik's face. Shaking her head, she left the room and took Aundy along with her while Jim and Garrett removed the rest of Erik's muddy clothes. After stoking the stove in the kitchen, Nora filled a big pot with water and set it on the stovetop to heat. She returned to the sink and began filling another large pot.

Nora moved the teakettle to the front to heat faster. When Garrett and Jim entered the room, she filled a bucket with water.

"I'm afraid to do too much more until the doc gets here," Garrett said, nodding toward Aundy. "Maybe you can help her get cleaned up, Ma, and see about setting her arm. Looks to me like it's probably broken."

"What?" Nora spun around. Aundy held her arm against her side, her face pale and pinched with pain. "Why didn't you say something earlier? I would have set your arm before we ever left my house."

"We need to see to Erik first." Aundy's legs felt weak beneath her and dizziness started to overtake her. "I'll be fine."

"My lands, child," Nora said, taking control of the situation. Gently placing her hand on Aundy's muddy shoulder, she directed her to sit in one of the kitchen chairs. "Garrett, you and Jim take this water and these rags and see what you can do about cleaning Erik. Just be careful. We don't know what might be injured." Nora handed Garrett the bucket full of water while Jim took a stack of rags and a couple of towels.

Aundy began to shiver, whether from the shock or her cold, muddy clothing she didn't know. White-faced, she sat in the chair and pinched her lips together in an effort to keep from fainting. Other than being knocked out when the wagon wrecked, she didn't plan to lose consciousness again.

Anxious to focus her attention on anything other than her arm and Erik lying injured in the other room, she noticed a basket packed with food on the counter. It was most likely the cold supper Erik mentioned Nora prepared.

"It was nice of you to provide supper for us." Aundy used her good hand to motion to the basket.

"My pleasure. It's not every day a new bride moves into the neighborhood. Erik was so excited about you coming, he nearly burst his buttons." Nora smiled as she filled yet another kettle then set it on the stove. "We hope you'll enjoy being a part of our Pendleton community. The town is definitely growing and we need good families to help lead it in the right direction."

"I didn't have the opportunity to see much in town, but it looks like you have a nice variety of shops and stores."

"Yes, and if there's something you want that's not available in town, the mercantile can order just about anything." Nora decided Aundy had to have a bath before she could do anything with her arm.

Garrett and Jim returned with a pile of dirty rags and damp towels. Quietly opening the kitchen door, Garrett stepped off the porch and dumped the water on a nearby bush then rinsed the mud out of the bucket before setting it on the end of the counter.

"How is he?" Nora asked, watching Garrett.

"Same. I think we got rid of most of the mud. We wiped down the oil cloth and put one of your old blankets over him." Garrett leaned over and whispered something to Nora, causing her to nod her head with a grim expression.

Nora rolled up the sleeves of her dress to her elbows. "Can you boys run back down to the wagon and get Aundy's trunks? She'll need clean clothes to wear and I doubt Erik has anything here fit for her to put on. You had better take care of Erik's horses, too. We'll pray the doc shows up soon."

"Yes, Ma," Garrett said, opening the door. "I think Erik gave all the hands orders to stay away from the house the rest of the day, so I don't know that any of them will be around to offer assistance. Once we get the horses cared for, I'll see about rounding them up."

"Good." Nora pointed toward the back door, indicating it was time for Garrett to get out of the kitchen.

"Let's get you cleaned up, honey. Garrett helped Erik put in a bathroom recently, once he knew you were coming. Not too many farm wives have indoor plumbing, but Erik wanted to make sure you had every convenience he could provide. He thought it might be hard for you to get used to country life and wanted to do what he could to make you feel at home."

Astonished by Erik's thoughtfulness, Aundy couldn't speak. She nodded her head mutely and blinked back her tears.

"I'll run the bath water then we'll get you out of those muddy clothes," Nora said, bustling out of the kitchen and down a short hallway. Aundy heard water running and looked forward to getting out of her filthy clothes and scrubbing away the mud.

Nora returned to the kitchen, carrying one of the old towels she brought from home.

"Take off your muddy clothes, honey, and wrap this around yourself, that way you won't be dragging all the mud along with you." Nora set the towel on the table while Aundy got to her feet and tried unsuccessfully to unbutton her dress with one hand. Nora helped remove her clothes and wrapped the towel around her.

Embarrassed to be in need of assistance, and from a complete stranger, Aundy's pink cheeks flamed through the mud splattered on her face.

"Go soak a while and by the time you're ready to get out, the boys should be back with your things." Nora pointed toward the bathroom.

As the woman hurried down the hall, Aundy glanced at her arm, glad to see the bone didn't poke through the skin. Maybe it was just sprained.

Eyeing the wonderful bathtub, Aundy closed the door behind her and used the old towel to wipe off as much mud as she could before sinking into the steaming water.

While the hot water relaxed her sore, abused muscles, she continued to send up prayers on Erik's behalf. She couldn't hear what Garrett whispered to Nora, but by the looks on both their faces, it had to be bad. She felt guilty soaking in a tub of hot water with a bar of fragrant rose soap Erik had no doubt purchased for her scenting the air while he lay unmoving in his bed. As soon as she was clean, she'd go sit with him and hold his hand. It was the least she could do.

33

Frustrated by her attempts to wash her hair one-handed, she was relieved when Nora knocked and stuck her head around the door. "Need any help?"

"If you don't mind, I could use some with my hair," Aundy said, looking chagrined.

Nora soaped Aundy's hair, maintaining a running conversation while she worked. "Did Erik say you were from Chicago?" Nora busied herself massaging Aundy's scalp.

Aundy didn't think anything had ever felt so good and closed her eyes to savor the experience. "Yes, ma'am."

"He said something about you being a seamstress. Is that correct?"

"I worked as a seamstress in a factory that made ready-made clothing. Our mother taught my sister and me to sew when we were quite young."

"Did your sister work in the factory with you?"

Aundy shook her head. "No, thank goodness. Ilsa has a rare talent with a needle. She works for my aunt, creating gowns for some of Chicago's most elite clientele. I would not have allowed her to work in the factory."

"Oh? Why not?" Nora asked, unfamiliar with what factory work entailed.

"The hours are long, the pay is poor, and the working conditions are less than pleasant," Aundy said, managing to suppress a shudder.

Her beautiful, delicate younger sister wouldn't have lasted a week in the factory. Some of the male supervisors weren't above making life miserable for the pretty girls who turned down their attentions. On top of that, the work was backbreaking, sitting in front of a sewing machine for hours on end with insufficient lighting. Aundy never had any problems because she wasn't perceived as one of the young, attractive girls. Instead, she was lumped in with the matrons who went unbothered, for the most part.

Determined to make a better life for herself, and eventually her sister, Erik offered Aundy the opportunity when he asked her to marry him.

Educated and intelligent, Aundy hadn't been able to secure any suitable work when she found herself desperate to earn an income, which was why she took the job in the factory. Her family needed the money and didn't have the luxury of waiting for a good job to come along.

"Does your sister still work for your aunt?"

"Yes, she does." Aundy's tone took on an edge as she thought about the cruel woman who held her sister's fate in her hands. "I was hoping to eventually bring Ilsa out here to live on the farm. Erik mentioned in one of his letters that he wouldn't mind. He just asked that I wait a few months to give us time to get used to being married. Now, I…"

Nora placed a gentle hand on Aundy's head as the girl struggled to keep the tears filling her eyes from rolling down her cheeks. Erik's bride seemed to be a levelheaded, capable girl who took things head-on and without a lot of fuss. She would make any rancher or farmer a good wife, especially someone like Erik who was older and somewhat set in his ways. "Everything will work out just fine, Aundy. Don't you worry."

"Thank you, Nora," Aundy whispered, squeezing the woman's hand in her right one.

Nora laughed as she noticed Aundy's fingers looked shriveled from the water. "Let me see if I can find something for you to wear until Garrett and Jim get back with your clothes. We need to get you out of there before you melt into the water."

In a rush, Nora left the room but soon returned with a warm flannel robe in a dark shade of blue. She handed Aundy a towel then turned her back, giving the girl some privacy.

"I appreciate your help," Aundy said as she briskly rubbed her skin dry with a rough towel then pulled on the robe. A masculine scent clung to the fabric and she knew it must belong to Erik.

After watching her struggle to dry her long, blonde tresses, Nora took over, using the towel to squeeze out the excess water.

A noise from the front room sent Nora scurrying out the door while Aundy waited in the bathroom. She heard the clomping of boots in the hallway, going past the bathroom door, and the sound of something heavy being set on the floor in the next room.

The men's footsteps thudded toward the front of the house as a knock sounded on the bathroom door. Nora opened it and motioned Aundy to follow her to the bedroom next door, where her trunks sat against one wall.

"The boys used some burlap at the barn to get your trunks clean, although I think that one," Nora pointed to the trunk with the broken lid, "is sadly beyond saving. I've got your dirty clothes soaking so we can get that nasty mud out of them."

Nora unfastened the straps and latches on the trunks, pushing up the heavy lids and watching as Aundy dug inside, taking out clothes. The sensible girl chose a dark green dress she could wear without a corset. Although wrinkled, it was clean and serviceable.

Nora smiled, admiring the fine stitching that made the dress unique. "Did you or your sister make this dress?"

"Ilsa made it for me. As I said, she's the one who's talented with a needle. I can run a sewing machine with the best of them, but Ilsa makes things lovely," Aundy said while Nora helped her dress.

Nora studied the bruising on Aundy's injured arm. She didn't like the looks of a knot that formed under the skin. "Where's your hairbrush, honey? I can help you with your hair."

Aundy pointed to a bag sitting next to the broken trunk.

Nora took out the hairbrush and a length of black ribbon. "Come sit here and I'll brush it for you."

Aundy quietly sat in the chair Nora indicated while the woman brushed her long hair. Although not curly, it wasn't exactly straight either, and most often took on a life of its own. Nora brushed until she was satisfied with her efforts then pulled it back and tied a ribbon at Aundy's nape to hold the hair out of her face. Enjoying Nora's efforts at pampering her, Aundy couldn't think of the last time someone brushed her hair. It was probably Ilsa back before their parents died.

"Your hair is lovely, honey. So long and thick, and such a pretty color."

"Thank you, ma'am. I appreciate you helping me." Aundy rose to her feet and dug in a trunk for a pair of slippers. She slipped them on, instantly warming her cold toes. "May I sit with Erik, please?"

"Certainly," Nora said, smiling at Aundy and patting the girl's cheek. Traveling across the country to marry a man she'd never met had to be frightening. To have the horses spook and wreck the wagon before they even got home from the wedding must be terrifying. She was very impressed with Erik's bride. Although it must hurt, she didn't complain.

Together, they walked down the hall to the front room. Aundy looked up when Garrett opened the front door.

"Ma, I thought…" Garrett lost his ability to focus as he noticed Aundy, clean and fresh, with her blonde hair hanging in golden streamers down her back.

"You thought what, son?"

"Um… I… we might need a couple of sticks for a splint for Mrs. Erickson's arm." Garrett handed Nora two thin but sturdy sticks, recalling why he'd come to the house. He hadn't counted on Erik's bride being so young, tall, or attractive. Garrett gave himself a mental shake and reminded himself the woman just married one of his very good friends.

"I was hoping to wait until the doctor arrives, but maybe we should go ahead and set it," Nora said, eyeing Aundy's arm.

"I can wait." Aundy wasn't anxious to have anything done to her arm. She'd seen plenty of accidents at the factory. It was going to hurt like everything to pull her arm back into place if that was, in fact, what needed to happen.

Still carrying the sticks, Nora led the way to Erik's bedroom where he rested, pale and unmoving, on the bed.

Aundy stood at the door, listening to his labored breathing. His chest rattled with every effort he made to draw in air. Although a blanket covered him to his waist, she could see Nora tried to bandage the multiple scrapes and open wounds that were bleeding. A red spot soaking through the blanket on his thigh indicated more wounds. Aundy hoped the doctor would soon arrive.

She approached the bed and gratefully sank down on the chair Garrett placed behind her. Gently, she picked up Erik's hand.

"Erik, it's Aundy." She lightly rubbed her fingers on the back of his hand. Garrett and Jim did a good job of removing the mud that covered him from head to toe. Even his fingers were clean and he smelled faintly of soap. "Please wake up. Please?"

Aundy felt a hand on her right shoulder and lifted a teary gaze to meet Nora's. The woman nodded her head, indicating Aundy should keep talking to Erik.

"If you'd told me you were going to plan so much excitement for my first day here, I might not have been so willing to come." Aundy tried to add a touch of humor to her voice, although she fought down her tears. "Next time, I'd appreciate a little warning before the horses run off like that, if you please. I'd at least take off my best hat before it ended up looking like a plucked chicken."

Garrett chuckled and took his mother's arm, pulling her out of the room.

"Let's leave her be until the doc comes," Garrett whispered as he and Nora returned to the kitchen. Jim rode out on Jester to see if he could find any of Erik's hands. The ranch foreman, an older man everyone called Dent, didn't usually get too far from the home place.

Nora prepared a cup of tea for Aundy when they heard the jingle of a harness. Garrett greeted the doctor and pastor at the door. Tom took the doctor's buggy and horse to Erik's barn for a little feed and rest after the trip out to the farm. The sun was nearly set and the night looked like it would be dark and cold.

The doctor removed his coat and hat, hanging them on the hall tree near the front door as he spoke. "Tom wasn't sure what happened, just there had been an accident."

"Erik's horses spooked, flipped the wagon over on him," Garrett said as the pastor shook his hand and followed the doctor to Erik's bedroom. "This is Aundy, Erik's bride. We think she's got a broken arm, but haven't been able to talk her into letting us set it yet."

"Mrs. Erikson, it's nice to meet you, although I'd prefer to have done so under other circumstances. I'm Doctor Reed, but everyone calls me Doc." The doctor set his bag on the end of Erik's bed and rummaged inside.

When she got to her feet, the doctor looked at her in surprise, not expecting her to be taller than his average height.

"Thank you for coming," she said, stepping aside so the doctor could get close to Erik.

Pastor Whitting put his hand on Aundy's shoulder, giving it a gentle squeeze. "Why don't we wait in the front room while Doc takes a look at Erik? Garrett will help him."

Aundy nodded her head and followed the pastor to the front room where Nora set a tray laden with cups of tea and a plate of cookies on a low table. Aundy accepted a cup and sipped the flavorful brew. For the first time since she walked inside the house, she noticed the nicely furnished room, done in shades of brown and tan. Although masculine, the space was inviting and welcome heat filled the room from a large fireplace.

Pastor Whitting and Nora chatted while Aundy waited for the bedroom door to open and the doctor to give her some good news.

From the moment she realized Erik was hurt, a gnawing sense of foreboding clawed at her mid-section and filled her with dread. She had no idea what she would do if something happened to Erik. He wasn't just a man who'd sent for a mail-order bride. Through their letters, he had become a friend. One she cared for even if she couldn't profess to love him.

When the door opened and the doctor stepped out, followed by a grim-faced Garrett, Aundy set her cup on the low table in front of her and stood.

"Mrs. Erikson, perhaps you should sit down," the doctor said, taking her right hand in his. When she shook her head, looking at him wide-eyed and fearful, he took a deep breath. "I'm terribly sorry, but Erik isn't going to make it."

Chapter Three

Garrett watched Aundy's face turn white and her knees give way as she sank onto the chair behind her. Hearing her quick intake of breath, he saw her press her lips together, as if she could hold back her grief.

The pastor stepped beside her, awkwardly patting her shoulder while the doctor took the chair next to hers.

"I wish I had better news for you, Mrs. Erickson, but the accident crushed several vital organs and resulted in internal damage that is beyond healing. Erik's lungs are filling with liquid and soon he won't be able to breathe. In addition, his right leg is broken, but I'm not going to put him through the agony of resetting it," Doc said. He rubbed a weary hand over his tired eyes. "I don't know how long Erik will linger, but considering his injuries, I would think no more than a day or two. I've given him some medication to help with the pain, but that's about all anyone can do at this point."

"I see." Aundy looked at the doctor with unshed tears in her eyes and unasked questions she was afraid to voice.

"I don't have the supplies with me to put a cast on your arm tonight, but we can splint it until I get back out here in the morning. I'll bring more medicine for Erik." Doc reached over and carefully examined Aundy's broken arm. The doctor knew from experience the pastor was practically useless when it came to medical situations and looked to Garrett. "I'm going to need some help setting this. Shall we do it in the kitchen?"

"Certainly," Nora said, getting to her feet and leading the way to the kitchen where she still had water boiling on the stove.

Garrett retrieved the doctor's bag from Erik's bedroom and set it down on the floor by the kitchen table. The doctor washed his hands at the sink while Nora handed the pastor a cup of coffee. The pastor sat at the far end of the table while the doctor motioned Aundy to take a seat on the opposite end. After pushing her sleeve high above her elbow, the doctor thoroughly probed her skin.

Gently pushing on her arm, he glanced at her. "As broken bones go, you have a clean break that will heal nicely, Mrs. Erikson."

"Please, call me Aundy," she requested, glancing at the doctor with eyes that held determination and fortitude.

"Aundy." Doc smiled kindly as he placed her arm on a stack of towels Nora set on the table. "This is going to hurt and if you need to scream, just go right ahead."

"That won't be necessary." Aundy sincerely hoped she wouldn't embarrass herself.

Garrett watched Aundy grasp the edge of the table with her good hand and brace her leg against the table before scooting back in her chair. He would help hold her shoulder while Doc set her arm. Nora had the splints and bandages at hand, ready for Doc to wrap her arm. Pastor Whitting hastily excused himself to sit with Erik.

"Ready?" Doc asked, waiting for Aundy's nod. "Okay. On the count of three. One, two…"

The doctor pulled on two and Garrett felt Aundy tense at the painful tugging. To her credit, she didn't scream or even cry. Garrett wanted to yell for her as he helped the doctor pull the broken bone back into place. She clamped her lips tightly together and gripped her right hand against the edge of the kitchen table so tightly her fingers turned white.

"Good lands, honey, I'd have been bawling and screaming so loud, people in town would hear the racket," Nora said with a smile. While the doctor wrapped the broken arm with the splints, Nora placed another steaming cup of fragrant tea in front of Aundy.

Aundy wasn't sure the tea would stay down and instead took a deep breath, followed by another. She wanted to scream and shout, maybe even throw something at how bad her arm hurt, but she'd learned long ago to quietly accept what had to be done without complaint.

"Will it hurt her more to cast the arm tomorrow?" Garrett asked, feeling pity for Aundy. She took having her arm set better than most men he knew could have handled the pain. He'd broken his arm once when he was a kid and he yelled like Lucifer himself touched the break when the doctor set it.

"No. The worst of it is over. I'd leave it like this, but something tells me Aundy isn't one to sit idly by for the next six weeks or so while it heals. A cast will protect it and give her more mobility. I think the best thing you can do is eat a little dinner and get some rest. I'll be back early in the morning." The doctor gathered his supplies and gulped down the cup of coffee Nora handed him. He walked to the front of the house, checked on Erik, then put on his hat and coat.

Garrett ran out to the barn to get the doctor's horse and buggy.

"Thank you for coming." Aundy stood at the door with Nora's arm around her waist. Although she'd only just met the woman, she appreciated the familiar and comforting gesture. "And for splinting my arm."

"You're welcome," Doc said. He looked compassionately at Erik's wife. Pastor Whitting told him she was fresh off the train when Erik brought her in so

43

they could wed. The farmer had talked of little else for weeks, since Aundy agreed to be his bride and travel to Pendleton. It was such a tragedy for their newly married life to end so harshly before it ever started. "Try and rest. There isn't a thing you can do to help Erik, so get some sleep."

"Yes, sir." Aundy couldn't sleep with Erik lying so injured, broken and alone, in another room. The least she could do was sit with him. No one else needed to know if she did that instead of slept.

"Aundy, I'm so sorry at the way things have gone this afternoon, but remember God has plans for our good, even when it might not seem like it at the time," Pastor Whitting said. He gave Aundy's back a gentle pat as he said his goodbyes. "Erik's a good man, a good Christian, so don't you worry about him."

"Thank you," Aundy whispered. Fear that the tears burning the backs of her eyes would escape and roll down her cheeks prevented her looking at the pastor. When she bit her tongue to keep a sob from escaping, Nora gently squeezed her waist, making it even harder to hold back her tears.

"I'll return tomorrow with the doctor," Pastor Whitting said, tipping his hat. "Rest well."

Aundy lifted her gaze long enough to watch him walk out the door then Nora led her to a chair by the fire.

"Why don't you sit and rest. I'll bring you a plate of food." Nora added another log to the fire. The warmth the sun added to the day dissipated when the evening settled in, leaving behind a cold, black night.

"I don't think I could eat." Aundy stared into the flames, trying to understand why a good man like Erik was lying in the other room near death. Beyond that, Aundy wondered what she would do. She absolutely wouldn't allow herself to think about returning to Chicago. There was no future there for her. None whatsoever.

"Yes, you can and you will. Anyone who's been through what you've been through today without breaking down into hysterics can manage a little supper." Nora placed her hands on her hips for emphasis before she bustled out of the room.

The front door opened. Aundy glanced at Garrett as he walked in, rubbing his hands to ward off the evening chill. "You might as well do as she says because she always gets her way." Garrett offered her a conspiratorial wink.

"I heard that," Nora called from the kitchen.

Garrett grinned, stepping closer to the fire and holding out his hands to the warmth. "I can stay and sit with Erik if you like or Ma will. You don't need to be here alone."

"I'll be fine." Aundy accepted the plate Nora held out to her. The woman set another cup of tea on the small table near her chair. At this rate, she might float away before Garrett and Nora went home for the evening. "I don't know how to thank either of you for all you've done today. You've both been so kind and..."

When Aundy's voice broke, Garrett felt an unfamiliar tug in the region of his heart. The girl had been so strong and stoic throughout the entire day's ordeal. He knew she had to be exhausted, frightened, and beleaguered by all that had happened on a day that should have been filled with love, happiness, and celebration.

"Don't give it another thought. That's what neighbors are for," he said, stepping away from the fire and Aundy as he picked up his mother's coat and held it for her.

"Pops will think we've abandoned him since we've been gone so long. We best get home. I sent Jim and Tom home earlier to oversee the chores, but it's getting late." Garrett picked up his mother's basket of medical supplies as well as the gloves he thought were in his coat pocket when he went outside earlier.

"I didn't even think to call your father and let him know what was happening." Nora glanced at her son then turned toward the kitchen. "If you need anything, Aundy, anything at all, you pick up the telephone and ask to be connected to the Nash family, our number is seventeen. The telephone is on the wall by the kitchen table. We'll be back to check on you in the morning."

"Thank you." Aundy started to get up from her chair, but Nora waved her back down. "Try to sleep, honey, and don't worry. We'll be praying for both you and Erik." Nora went out the door in a swish of her lavender skirts.

Aundy took a bite of the food Nora prepared and discovered that she was hungry, after all. She cleaned her plate and slowly drank her tea, lost in her sadness.

Her tired mind refused to register the thought that Erik might die after she travelled all the way across the country to marry him. The doctor had to be wrong. Maybe Erik just needed a good night's sleep. Maybe he'd wake up tomorrow and be fine. Maybe she'd wake up tomorrow and everything would just be a dream, and she'd find herself to be nineteen again, engaged to Gunther, and looking forward to a life with her beloved.

With a heavy sigh, Aundy placed her empty cup on her plate and carried both to the kitchen. It was awkward to wash the dishes one-handed, but she managed. She didn't take time to examine her new home. Instead, she walked back to Erik's room and nudged the chair she'd sat in earlier close to the side of the bed.

Gingerly taking Erik's hand in her own, she held it on her lap, rubbing the back of it with her right hand.

Her left arm ached and throbbed with a painful force and she was sure a multitude of bruises would show up tomorrow. She ignored the pain and her discomfort, swimming in sorrow for the man who had offered her a new home, a new life.

His breathing sounded shallow and raspy in his chest, but at least he continued taking one breath after another. His arm felt cool, so Aundy carefully slid it under the covers and reached up to smooth the hair back from his forehead.

A Bible on his nightstand caught her eye. Aundy turned up the wick in the lamp and pulled the leather-bound book to her lap. She opened it to one of her favorite Psalms and read aloud.

An hour later, she realized she should either go to bed or find a more comfortable chair. She turned down the lamp and she set the Bible where she found it.

Lest he should awaken and need her, she refused to leave Erik alone. Since they were technically married, she decided it would be acceptable for her to sleep on the other side of his bed. It had more than enough room for two people to rest comfortably and she was so tired.

After finding a quilt in a trunk in the corner of the room, she slowly stretched out on the bed, mindful of not disturbing Erik, and spread the quilt over the top of her. She rolled onto her right side, closed her eyes, and surrendered to her need for sleep.

❧

The sound of footsteps on the porch awakened Aundy. Slowly opening her eyes, she looked around an unfamiliar room, taking in a chest of drawers, a nightstand, and a small closet.

She rolled onto her back. Her arm felt heavy and she lifted it, surprised to see it bandaged with splints.

The nightmare that tormented her dreams failed to disappear with the morning light.

She sat up and studied Erik. He looked just as pale and still as he had when she'd fallen asleep.

Determined to face the day, she swung her legs over the edge of the bed, tossed the quilt onto the trunk where she'd found it, and walked into the front room. Noises from the kitchen drew her that direction and she wasn't surprised to find Nora taking food out of a basket and setting it on the table.

"Mornin', honey. You were sleeping so soundly when we came in, I told Garrett to keep the hands from banging on the door and waking you." Nora greeted Aundy with a motherly hug.

"Thank you." If possible, Aundy felt worse than she did the night before.

"Do you think you could eat a little something?" Nora took cups from the cupboard and began making tea.

Food was Nora's way of reaching out and helping, so Aundy nodded her head. If eating a bite or two would make the woman happy, Aundy wouldn't deny her that.

She sat at the table while Nora slid a plate with two muffins in front of her. A jar of jam and a bowl of butter appeared from the basket on the table and Nora cut open the muffins, slathering them with both.

After placing a cup of hot tea beside Aundy's plate, Nora waited while the girl bowed her head over her meal and gave thanks then quietly sipped a cup of tea.

Aundy ate both muffins, appreciative of the good food as it filled the empty hollows in her stomach.

"You'll no doubt have a lot of people trooping through here today. How about I iron a dress for you and we see about pinning your hair up?" Nora asked, rinsing the few dishes and putting them away.

"People?" Aundy rose to her feet. Her head felt fuzzy and she had trouble paying attention to what Nora said. Blinking her eyes, she regained control of her focus and looked at the older woman. "What people?"

"Doc and Pastor Whitting for starters," Nora said, setting an iron on the stove to heat. "The hands will all want to come meet you and see Erik. Pay their respects."

Aundy didn't feel up to dealing with anyone, but she would put on a fresh dress, ask for Nora's help with her hair, and accept whatever the day would bring.

She walked into the bedroom where Garrett and Jim left her things, chose a dress and left it on the bed, then gathered a few necessities and went to the bathroom. When she returned to the bedroom, the dress was gone, so she hurried to the kitchen. Nora pressed the last wrinkles from the gown.

"Your sister does such beautiful work," Nora said as she ironed the hem then held it out to admire.

"She is good at what she does." Aundy missed her sister and wished she could talk to her about what happened since she got off the train yesterday afternoon.

"Let's get this lovely thing on you and see what I can do with your hair." Nora walked toward the room Aundy thought of as hers. With her dress on and hair combed, she felt more like herself.

Critically studying her reflection in a big cheval mirror, Aundy decided she looked presentable and respectable. Her pale blue and cream gown was one of her best dresses. Nora managed to roll her hair on top of her head in the popular poufy style, leaving some soft tendrils to fall around her face and neck. Although they had to leave her sleeve unbuttoned to fit over her broken arm, Aundy hoped it wouldn't draw too much attention.

She truly didn't care about her appearance, but for Erik's sake, she would stand straight and tall, speak softly and pleasantly, and honor him in every way she could.

"Goodness, honey, you certainly look lovely. Blue is most definitely your color." Nora smiled at the vision Aundy made, even with her broken arm. The girl was modest when it came to her appearance. Whether she liked it or not, her height combined with her figure and the confident way she carried herself would turn a few heads. The crown of golden hair, sky-blue eyes, and creamy skin would definitely cause people to take notice of her.

Aundy turned a tear-filled gaze to Nora and offered her a small smile. If the woman kept being so nice, she knew she'd soon be in tears.

Timidly reaching out, she squeezed Nora's hand. "I don't know what to do or where to start today," she admitted as they returned to the kitchen.

Nora set a big pot of water on to boil and made more coffee. "Why don't you..." A sharp knock at the kitchen door interrupted their conversation. Nora opened it and welcomed Erik's foreman. "Dent, this is Erik's bride, Aundy." Nora motioned toward the tall girl standing by the table. "Aundy, this is Dent. He's worked here for years and years, back when Erik's folks were still with us."

"It's nice to meet you, Mr. Dent," Aundy said, mustering a smile for the foreman. The man was shorter than she was, but had kind brown eyes. Whiskers covered his weathered face, but he approached her respectfully. Aundy appreciated the way he took off his hat and tipped his head her direction.

"It's just Dent, ma'am. No mister is necessary. I'm right pleased to meet you. Erik has been so excited about you coming, he could hardly stand the wait until you got here." Dent ran a work-roughened hand through thick brown hair, sprinkled with liberal doses of gray. "We're all happy to have you here."

"Thank you." Aundy felt tears burn the backs of her eyes again.

"Garrett told us about the accident yesterday and what the doc said. I'm mighty sorry to hear about it. Mighty sorry." Dent nervously twirled his hat around in his hands. "If there's anything we can do to help you settle in, you let me know."

"I will." Aundy swallowed down the lump in her throat. She was not someone given to emotional displays and usually managed to keep her feelings on a tight rein, but today was going to be a challenge.

"May I see him?" Dent asked, looking from the kitchen in the direction of the front room.

"Certainly," Aundy said, smiling at Dent before he walked out of the room.

"He's a good man, honey. If you need anything, you just let Dent know. He'll take care of you," Nora said, adding pieces of stew meat and vegetables to the pot of boiling water. "I thought I'd make up a big batch of stew. No telling how many might be here to eat today and this will feed a good crowd."

The arrival of Doc and Pastor Whitting prevented Aundy from dwelling on the thought of the house filling with company.

After checking on Erik, the doctor brought his bag to the kitchen and set out the supplies for casting Aundy's arm. Nora volunteered to help while the pastor returned to sit with Dent in Erik's room, taking along a tray Nora prepared with coffee and muffins.

Once the cast was in place, Aundy sat with it resting on the table, waiting for the plaster to harden. She asked the doctor what she could and couldn't do with her arm. He was providing detailed instructions when Garrett walked inside the kitchen followed by a man he introduced as Erik's attorney, Mitchell Lawry.

"I asked Mitch to stop by and give you some papers," Doc said, leaning back in his chair and eating his second muffin.

The papers he referred to turned out to be Erik's will, leaving everything he owned to Aundy.

"He came in last week and had these drawn up. They're legal and binding, in the event of his death. Doc and Pastor Whitting thought you'd want to know sooner

51

rather than later that Erik provided for you," Mitch said, taking a drink of the coffee Nora handed him. "You'll see copies of his investments, holdings, bank statement. It's all there."

"Thank you for bringing this out." Aundy tapped the stack of papers with her fingers. "I appreciate it so much."

"My pleasure, Mrs. Erickson. Your husband is a smart businessman and a good friend," Mitch said. He finished his coffee and stood to his feet. "If there is anything I can do to help you, just let me know."

❧

Grateful for the presence of Nora on one side of her and Garrett on the other, Aundy stared at the rain-soaked grave swallowing Erik's coffin as two men slowly lowered it into the hole.

Unable to concentrate on the words Pastor Whitting said, Aundy fought back her tears as she stood ramrod straight, heedless to the achingly cold wind and frigid rain falling on the large gathering at the cemetery.

Although Erik had no family, the number of people attending his service indicated he was rich in friends.

If his kindness to her through his letters and the things he had done in preparation for her arrival attested to his character, Erik would leave behind a legacy of a good, thoughtful man who put others ahead of himself.

Erik lingered for three long days. The doctor kept him medicated so he didn't feel pain, but it also prevented him from being lucid.

Aundy sat next to his bed, holding his hand in hers. As she read aloud passages he'd underlined in his Bible, she felt pressure on her fingers. She was surprised to see Erik's pain-glazed eyes staring at her when she looked at his face.

"Aundy," he whispered in a raspy breath. "I'm sorry."

"Erik, don't be sorry. Don't worry. Everything will be fine." She smiled reassuringly although she couldn't stop the tears rolling down her cheeks.

"You're a good wife." Erik's voice was weak as he squeezed her hand. "Thank you for coming."

"You're a wonderful husband, Erik. Thank you for marrying me, for providing for me. I can't thank you enough for all you've done."

"Glad to do it." Erik closed his eyes and drifted off. He drew his last breath a few hours later.

Mourning a life cut short and the loss of her dreams, Aundy grieved for the life she and Erik would have built together as she stood at her husband's graveside.

Thoughts of other funerals, other lives that ended too soon, caused a sob to wrack across her shoulders. She compressed her lips to keep it from escaping.

Nora, who stood to her right, found her hand and squeezed her fingers, trying to infuse a touch of comfort.

However, Aundy was beyond comforting. She was tired of death, tired of mourning, tired of life taking such unexpected and unpleasant turns.

Two years earlier, her father and fiancé, her beloved Gunther, died when the trench they were digging for a new water line collapsed and buried them, along with three other men. By the time the company they worked for dug them out, only one of the men survived. After their funerals, Aundy's mother took to her bed and died a month later.

Financially struggling to keep their family together, Aundy's younger siblings looked to her for strength and guidance. Ilsa was only fifteen at the time and Lars was eighteen. He ran away a few weeks later, leaving a note saying he was off to make his way in the world and not to worry about him.

To deal with so much loss in such a short time, Aundy threw herself into looking for a job, applying for secretarial and teaching positions, but found it impossible to secure anything due to her lack of experience. Desperate for work, she took the job as a seamstress at the factory. She managed to keep their apartment for a while before she had to let it go.

Ilsa agreed to work for their aunt in her dress shop. Aunt Louisa would provide room and board, promising to pay Ilsa a dollar a week for her work and allow her access to all her scrap fabrics to use as she wished. Although both girls thought Louisa was harsh and mean-spirited, it was a better alternative for Ilsa than factory work.

The girls packed up the belongings they absolutely couldn't bear to lose. Ilsa took most of them with her to Aunt Louisa's home. Aundy kept a few heirlooms and moved into a boarding house near the factory. She helped cook and clean in the mornings and evenings in trade for her room and board, saving every penny she could, hoping someday life would improve.

Bone-tired and dispirited after a miserable day at work, the discovery of Erik's ad had been like a ray of light illuminating a pitch-black night.

Convinced she had found a way to not only better her future but also Ilsa's, Aundy's hopes and dreams were once again in tatters, along with her heart.

She swiped at the tears she could no longer hold back as they mingled with raindrops on her cheeks. Aundy nodded at Pastor Whitting as he finished the service and looked her direction.

"Come on, honey, let's get you out of this rain," Nora said, steering Aundy in the direction of their canopy-topped surrey. Numbly, she followed Nora and accepted Garrett's help into the back seat.

His father, J.B., sat on the front seat, unable to walk in the mud to the graveside service, but wanting to pay his respects to his neighbor and friend.

Thrown by his horse the previous year, the injuries to J.B.'s back and leg had been so severe, he'd spent months in bed, unable to move. Recently, he'd shown improvement, getting up and walking short distances with the help of a cane.

Garrett, who moved to Portland after graduating from college, wanted to experience life in a bigger city while working for an agriculture export company. When he learned of his father's accident, he hurried home to take over management of the ranch and decided to stay.

After helping Nora into the surrey next to Aundy, Garrett sat beside his father and picked up the reins to the team. He read worry and sorrow on the young widow's face.

She'd proven repeatedly in the last few days that she was tough and resilient. Aundy barely left Erik's side as he hung between life and death after the accident, holding his hand and reading aloud to him for hours until her voice grew hoarse.

Garrett and Nora, along with Dent, took turns staying in the house, wanting to be available if Aundy should need them. There seemed to be a steady stream of visitors, coming to pay their respects as news of the accident traveled throughout the community.

Although he admired his newly widowed neighbor for her inner fortitude and bravery, Garrett wished he could do or say something to make her feel better. It would take time for her to get used to living in a new place, for her heart and arm to heal, and for life to move forward.

His heart ached as he watched her brush at her cheeks with a handkerchief already soggy from both the rain and her tears. He removed a snowy-white square from his pocket, reached behind him, and handed it to her.

"Thank you," Aundy said between sniffles.

Nora patted her shoulder and wiped at her own tears. "The ladies from church fixed a nice lunch," Nora said, as

Garrett stopped the horses in front of the church. "We'll eat and let everyone express their condolences then take you home."

Aundy nodded her head, knowing whether she wanted to or not, she needed to draw on every reserve of strength she possessed to get through the next few hours.

Losing Gunther had shattered her heart, watching Erik die had pierced her spirit. As she followed Nora into the church, she knew love or marriage would never be a part of her future.

She couldn't bear the thought of going through this sort of pain and anguish again.

Chapter Four

Aundy released a deep sigh as she sat at the kitchen table, drinking a cup of tea and staring out the window.

A week ago, she smiled graciously, accepting condolences from Erik's neighbors and friends as they laid him to rest. Nora or Garrett, along with Dent, checked on her daily to make sure she was fine and Doc had been by once to look at her arm. Pastor Whitting had also been out to check on her a few times.

She rose from the table and wandered through the house, stopping to admire the gleaming china in the cupboard in the dining room. Nora told her it belonged to Erik's mother. She loved the dainty blue flowers on the creamy porcelain background and wondered if she'd ever feel like it was truly hers to use.

In the front room, she looked around at the comfortable furnishings, purchased new by Erik when she agreed to marry him. Nora said he hired someone in town to make the curtains and throw pillows that finished the room.

All the effort Erik went to on her behalf, all the money he spent to make sure she felt comfortable and welcome, was almost more than she could comprehend. He had been a generous and caring man.

Aundy glanced at the closed door of what had been his room. She couldn't bring herself to venture inside. Not when losing him was still so fresh. Quickly turning back toward the kitchen, she walked down the hall to her bedroom.

From the information Nora shared with her, Erik and Garrett finished the room just a few weeks before her arrival. Erik wanted to make things as nice as possible for his bride, and added a large bedroom next to the newly constructed bathroom. Although he hadn't moved his belongings into the room, it was clear he intended it to be the bedroom they shared.

Aundy studied the big bed with a soft mattress, the rich, cherry wood furniture, and a large closet designed for two.

A padded rocking chair sat by the window and Aundy noticed sunlight streaming through the lace curtains covering the glass. A small table next to the chair held an oil lamp and a stack of books, making it a cozy place to sit and read.

With Nora's help, her trunks had been unpacked, her belongings put away, and Garrett hauled the empty trunks out to the attic of a storage shed near the barn.

Thoughts of Garrett made Aundy's stomach flutter with a nervous feeling that left her unsettled, so she pushed them aside.

She left the big bedroom, and wandered into the third bedroom that had obviously belonged to Erik's parents. A photo of a handsome couple sat on the dresser and their clothes still hung in the closet.

Wishing she knew more about Erik's family, Aundy returned to the kitchen where additional evidence of her husband's thoughtfulness and care was evident in the shiny new cook stove, a refrigerator, and the silverware he purchased just for her. Out on the back porch she'd found a new washing machine that would be a huge help for doing laundry once she could use both hands.

After rinsing out her teacup, Aundy wiped the already clean counter. Tired of sitting around the house, wondering what to do, she was ready to move forward as the owner of Erik's farm. It had taken her a week to get used to the idea of owning it and the fact that Erik was truly gone.

Grief still weighed heavy on her heart. Although she didn't know Erik intimately, she knew enough about him to realize she had lost a friend. Someone who would have cherished her, cared for her, and supported her even if love never filled either of their hearts.

It was no secret people wondered what she planned to do with the farm. Returning to Chicago was out of the question. What she really wanted was to stay and pick up where Erik left off. She might even succeed, because she was just stubborn enough to try and determined enough not to quit.

Aundy did not intend to sell Erik's farm. As soon as she figured out what she was doing, she planned to send for Ilsa.

Between the two of them, Aundy knew they could make a go of things. At least they would when she got the cast off her arm and regained full use of both hands. Limited as she was, she could barely comb her hair and dress herself each day.

Nora asked her to stay with them until her arm healed, but Aundy felt like she'd already taken so much from the Nash family. Erik said they were good people and he'd been correct in that statement.

Aundy didn't know what she would have done without Garrett and Nora's support and guidance since she arrived in Pendleton. J.B. had been a comfort as well, although he was unable to do much more than offer encouragement and words of wisdom.

In the past few days, Aundy read all the documents Erik's attorney gave her multiple times. Erik had truly left her everything he owned.

Relieved the farm was doing well and there was money in the bank, Aundy knew that even if she never made another penny in income, she'd survive.

Erik had worked so hard to make his farm prosperous. Aundy wasn't content to sit by and do nothing. She wanted to finish what Erik and his parents started, as a way of honoring him, thanking him, for offering her hope and a future.

Tears stung her eyes at thoughts of Erik, she hastily wiped them away when a knock sounded at the kitchen door. She pulled it open and smiled at Dent. He stood on the back step, hat in his hand.

"Morning, Missy." He started calling her Missy somewhere between the first day they met and Erik's funeral service. Since he was old enough to be her grandfather and had been nothing but kind, Aundy didn't mind.

"Good morning, Dent. How are you today?"

"Fair to middlin', but I can't complain." He stepped inside when Aundy motioned for him to come in.

"May I make you a cup of coffee?" Aundy asked, knowing Dent preferred it to the tea she liked to drink.

"No, thank you. I… um…" Dent hesitated, waiting for Aundy to sit at the kitchen table before taking a seat. "The fellas are wondering what your plans are for the place."

"Plans? For the farm?" Aundy wanted to make sure she understood what Dent was asking.

"Yes, ma'am. They want to know if you're gonna sell it or keep it. We're all a little curious as to what exactly you're gonna do. It's almost calving time and Erik usually hired on more help as we headed into spring. We're shorthanded without him as it is and we really need to hire some help if you're of a mind to keep the farm going."

Dent worked for Erik's parents for years, then for Erik when his folks passed away. He could run the farm with his eyes closed, but there were some young bucks on the payroll who didn't like the notion of a woman being in charge.

After getting to know Erik's bride, Dent thought the girl had spirit and sense, a combination he greatly admired.

"I see," Aundy said. She took a breath and looked Dent in the eye. There was no time like the present to put her thoughts into action. "I have no intention of selling the farm, Dent. My plans are to continue where Erik left off. Obviously, I have a wealth of information to learn, but I'm willing and able. At least I will be as soon as my arm heals. I was hoping you could teach me what I need to know about the livestock, crops, and such."

"That's a lot to learn in a short time, Missy." Dent studied Aundy. He was glad she was staying, even if it was going to annoy some of the men in the area to have a woman running the place. "I'm happy to help you, but I've also got to be out there supervising the rest of the men. Maybe Garrett and J.B. could be of assistance with some of that learning. Between the three of us, we can teach you what you need to know."

"Oh, well, I don't want to be a bother to anyone." Aundy had already monopolized enough of Garrett's time. Besides, she found it hard to concentrate when he was near. Her thoughts tangled in his silvery gaze, engaging smile, and dark hair.

"It won't be a bother." Dent got to his feet and walked to the door. "Come out to the barn after lunch and you can have a lesson in getting to know the horses."

"Okay. I will." Aundy smiled at the foreman who was quickly becoming a friend. Dent was hardworking and loyal, and right now that was more than she dared hope to have.

"Use that telephone thing and call Mrs. Nash. She'll let you know if Garrett has time to help with your lessons or not. And tell her you need to learn to shoot while you're at it. There are plenty of varmints, both two and four-legged, you need to learn to take out if they pose any danger."

Aundy looked at him with wide blue eyes as he tipped his head, slapped on his hat, and hurried out the door.

She'd never before held a gun in her hand, but she supposed if she wanted to become a true Westerner, she'd have to put aside her fears and embrace her new lifestyle.

At the desk in the front room, Aundy wrote a long letter to her sister. She described what had transpired in the last week and asked Ilsa to come to Pendleton as soon as possible. With spring balls and parties keeping her aunt's creations in high demand, she assumed Ilsa probably wouldn't be able to get away anytime in the near future.

When she finished the letter, Aundy picked up a book on animal husbandry she began reading days ago. The information in the book made her take stock of how much she really needed to learn. Absorbing one chapter at a time, she felt a little more confident in her abilities to be a help on the farm.

Aundy made herself a simple lunch of bread and jam with a slice of cheese. She tried to eat slowly, taking time to savor another cup of tea.

With her thoughts on visiting the barn, she washed her plate and cup and wiped the table. A quick glance at the clock let her know it was time to head out the door but the telephone jangled.

The sound still startled her even though she should be used to it by now. It seemed at least one person called every day, whether it was Nora, the doctor, one of the women she'd met at church, or Pastor Whitting.

"Hello?" Aundy spoke into the phone on the kitchen wall.

"Aundy, dear, how are you today?" Nora asked in her usual cheery voice.

"I'm fine, Nora. How are things at the ranch?"

"Wonderful. Our first two calves dropped last night. You should come over and see them." Nora quickly realized Aundy probably wouldn't know what she meant. "That means two of our cows had their babies."

"Thank you for clarifying." The smile on her face was evident in her voice. "I didn't think you'd really drop the calves."

Nora giggled and chatted a few minutes, then invited Aundy to come for supper.

"I've more than worn out my welcome with you all." Aundy was reluctant to impose further on the Nash family. "You've done so much for me already."

"Oh, that's a bunch of flapdoodle," Nora said, exasperated by the girl's independent nature. "I'm going to have someone bring you over for supper and you can spend the evening before we take you back home. You know you're welcome to spend the night."

"No, Nora. I just couldn't." Aundy glanced out the kitchen window and noticed Dent walking toward the house. "Thank you for the invitation, though."

"You just be ready about four this afternoon and I'll send one of the boys to get you. Bye, honey."

"Bye." Aundy hung up the phone and opened the kitchen door before Dent had a chance to knock.

"Ready for your lesson, Missy?" Dent touched the brim of his hat as she walked outside and down the back porch steps.

"Yes, sir." Aundy hoped he wouldn't notice how afraid she was of the big animals. As she followed the foreman to the barn, she listened as he discussed the different types of horses used on the farm and the purpose each served. He showed her the draft horses, Hans and Henry, that ran away with the wagon, as well as another big team he called Nut and Bolt.

"Nut is a little on the wild side, so be sure you give him plenty of room," Dent cautioned, watching as Aundy

SHANNA HATFIELD

stepped further away from the horse when he snorted her direction. He pointed out several of the stock horses in the pasture behind the barn. Dent explained Erik kept the horses for his men to ride. When she asked questions about the different breeds and coloring, Dent was impressed with her ability to understand the information he shared.

When they stood at the stall of a pretty mare, Dent dug a piece of dried apple from his pocket and held it out to the horse. She took it from his hand and looked at him with big, sad eyes.

"This is Bell. She belonged to Erik's mother. Although she's getting on in years, Bell is a good, solid mustang who'll take you where you need to go." Dent scratched the horse on her neck and behind her ears. "When you get that cast off your arm, I'll teach you how to ride her."

"I will do my best to look forward to that experience." Aundy held a cautious hand out to the horse. Bell turned liquid eyes to Aundy and offered a soft whicker.

"I think she likes you." Dent motioned for Aundy to touch the horse. "Go on and pet her, she won't bite you." He refrained from mentioning that she not only bit but also refused to let any of the men ride her, preferring females.

Aundy rubbed Bell on her nose and patted her neck. The horse moved forward in her stall and leaned her head against her before releasing a sigh.

"Well, I'll be. It looks like she decided you're friends," Dent said, breaking into a broad grin. "She hasn't taken to any of the fellas. Guess she just missed having a woman around."

"As soon as I'm able, we'll have to rectify that situation." Aundy scratched Bell's neck before she and Dent moved through the rest of the barn.

64

By the time Dent finished giving her a grand tour of the barnyard, Aundy discovered she owned milk cows, several pigs, and a coop full of chickens.

"Thank you for that introduction to the livestock, Dent. I very much appreciate it," Aundy said as they walked toward the house. "I think I could gather the eggs from now on. I feel like I've been such a burden since I arrived instead of a help."

"You haven't been a burden to anyone, Missy. If you're sure you want to gather the eggs, just go in there each morning, toss out their feed, then snatch the eggs before the chickens are any the wiser. Watch out for the rooster. If he gives you any trouble, let me know. He's got a big attitude for such a little chicken."

Aundy laughed, making Dent smile. "I'll keep my eye on him. I'm going over to the Nash's for dinner, so don't worry if you don't see me around for an hour or two this evening."

"Yes, ma'am." Dent tipped his hat and returned to the barn.

Aundy hurried up the back porch steps and inside the house, deciding she smelled like the barn. Quickly filling the bathtub, she took a bath and washed her hair, finding it a challenge to accomplish with only one arm.

When she finished, she climbed out of the tub, towel-dried her hair and shook it with her good hand, trying to get out most of the water before working her way into her clothes. Everything took twice as long with only one usable arm.

Unable to put up her hair, she had become adept at pulling it back in combs and letting it hang loose. It always seemed to be in her way, but she didn't know what else to do. Incapable of braiding it one handed or pinning it up, she managed the best she could. She was adjusting the second comb in her hair when she heard a knock on the front door. She rushed from her bedroom, grabbed her coat from a peg by the kitchen door, and hastened to the front room.

Surprise filled her features as she opened the door and stared at Garrett, standing on the porch with his hat in his hand.

"Mrs. Erickson." He smiled, flashing white teeth against his tan face, as he took in Aundy's fresh scent and glowing cheeks. Despite being highly improper to think it, he wanted to pull the combs out of her hair and bury his hands in the waving golden mass. Although he shouldn't have been, he was glad the cast on her arm kept her from putting up all that glorious hair.

He gazed at her and felt drawn into the depths of her sky-blue eyes.

Desperate to divert his attention away from her face and hair, he looked down and admired the fancy stitching on her skirt.

Astounded by the beautiful clothes she wore, he wouldn't have expected someone who worked in a factory and traveled out west as a mail-order bride to be so well dressed. His mother mentioned something about Aundy's sister being a talented seamstress. Maybe she'd added the elaborate embellishments to the woman's wardrobe.

"Ma said you were coming for dinner and asked me to fetch you."

"I'm fairly certain you have better things to do than escort me, Mr. Nash," Aundy said, aware that Garrett spent a lot of time helping her since Erik's accident. She knew he had his own ranch to run.

Garrett's silvery gaze met hers with a playful grin. "I reckon I might, but when Ma barks an order, we all jump to carry it out."

He refused to admit he would have volunteered for the job if his mother had asked someone else to fetch Aundy.

For reasons he didn't want to examine, he looked forward to time spent with the plucky widow. Garrett could listen to her soft voice for hours on end and never grow tired of the sound, although she wasn't one given to idle chatter.

"So it would seem." Her neighbor's light-hearted comment made her lips turn up in a smile.

"You ready to go?" Garrett took Aundy's coat from her hand and held it for her.

"I believe so." Aundy slipped on her coat then stepped outside while Garrett pulled the front door closed. Not seeing a wagon or buggy waiting, just Garrett's saddle horse, she looked around, wondering how he planned to take her to the ranch.

Garrett tried not to grin at Aundy's confused look. "Before you get too excited, I thought I'd show you how to hitch a horse to the buggy and take it to the ranch then I'll bring you home after supper and reclaim Jester."

She followed Garrett as he took Jester's reins and led the animal to the barn.

Aundy watched, taking mental notes, as Garrett described each step in the process of hitching the horse to the buggy. The animal stood quietly during the entire procedure.

"Erik's horses are well trained. You always need to be watchful of any animal, but Erik's won't intentionally try to harm you. Even ol' Nut will behave as long as Bolt is close by."

"I appreciate that information," Aundy said, standing so close to Garrett, she could smell his unique, manly scent. Combined with the warmth radiating from him and the way he kept looking at her with those silvery eyes, she found it impossible to pay attention to his detailed instruction. She took a sudden step back, and would have tripped over a feed bucket if Garrett hadn't grabbed her good arm and pulled her forward against his chest.

Overwhelmed with strange emotions and sensations, Aundy kept her gaze down when he dropped his hand and stepped away.

"Thank you," she said, embarrassed and flustered. "I wasn't paying attention."

"It's quite all right." Garrett attempted to gather his thoughts. They'd scattered every direction the moment he touched Aundy. Sparks worked their way from his fingers all the way up his arm. "Shall we head over to Nash's Folly?"

"Nash's Folly?" She gave him a quizzical look as he assisted her onto the buggy seat.

"That's the official name of our ranch." Garrett guided the horse out of the barnyard and down the lane toward the road. "You mean Ma hasn't told you that story?"

"No, she hasn't." Garrett's statement piqued her curiosity. "Why don't you tell me?"

"When Ma and Pops arrived in Pendleton, they came out here and saw this land. Ma was humming the hymn *My Jesus, I love Thee*. Do you know it?"

When Aundy shook her head, Garrett began singing the hymn in a deep baritone. She blinked in surprise as his rich voice filled the afternoon air with perfectly pitched notes.

My Jesus, I love Thee
I know Thou art mine;
For Thee all the follies of sin I resign...

"She and Pops thought God's grace led them here to Pendleton and they wanted to make the best of it. They declared they were 'resigning their follies' and starting a new life. Pops named the ranch Nash's Folly so none of us would forget their promise. We're still human and make mistakes, but that story helps keep us on the straight and narrow." Garrett turned to look at Aundy with a devilish grin. "That, and the threat of Ma taking a switch to us."

"I can't imagine Nora taking a switch to anyone." Aundy smiled at him. "But I do like that story and the name Nash's Folly."

They rode along in silence for a few minutes before Aundy gave Garrett a thoughtful look. "Did Erik have a name for his farm?"

"No. Everyone round these parts refers to it as the Erickson Farm. His folks settled there a long time ago. Guess no one felt the need to give it any other name." Garrett wondered what Aundy was thinking. Her eyes had narrowed and she pressed her lips together. He noticed she did that anytime she was in pain or contemplating something.

When she continued to appear lost in her thoughts, Garrett talked about some of the neighboring ranches, who owned them, and if any of them had names. He cautioned her to stay away from Marvin Tooley, much in the same way as Erik.

"Why does everyone tell me to stay away from Mr. Tooley? Is he really that mean?" Aundy asked as Garrett stopped the buggy at the end of the front walk and waved at Nora when she stepped out onto the porch.

"Even more so," Garrett said solemnly, although she detected the slightest hint of a grin working at the corners of his mouth.

"Hello!" Nora called, hurrying down the walk, barely waiting for Garrett to help Aundy out of the buggy before pulling her into a welcoming hug. "Don't you look pretty today? My goodness, but you have some beautiful clothes. And your hair is so thick and long and lovely."

"I…" Aundy spluttered, not accustomed to being paid compliments. She knew she wasn't beautiful like her younger sister and had long ago resigned herself to just being who she was - sturdy, strong, and hardworking.

"Doesn't she Garrett?" Nora prodded, staring at her son. "Isn't she one of the most striking girls you've ever seen?"

At Nora's hasty nod and glare, Garrett was quick to agree. "Yes, Ma," he said, tipping his hat to the women before hurrying toward the barn with the horse and buggy. He glanced over his shoulder and watched Nora herd Aundy up the steps and inside the house. Her fancy-stitched skirt swished around her long legs while her golden hair rippled down her back.

He wasn't just paying lip service because his mother wanted him to. Erik's widow had turned more than a few heads since her arrival in Pendleton.

She wasn't beautiful by society's stilted standards, but she was very attractive. His mother summed it up well when she said the girl was striking. With that golden hair, blue eyes, creamy skin, and tall height, she was hard to miss.

Since her arrival on their doorstep covered in mud, he discovered she was a caring and gentle, yet determined person. Although Garrett thought inner beauty was much more important than outward, it was hard not to admire how she carried herself, or the way her city clothes accented her becoming curves.

Irritated by his wayward thoughts, Garrett unhooked the horse and gave him a portion of feed before starting on the evening chores. An hour later, he walked inside the house, after reminding himself a dozen times it was inappropriate to think about Erik's widow. Even if the marriage had been in name only and Erik spent nearly all of the few days he and Aundy were together unconscious, Garrett's thoughts were still out of line.

Sincerely missing his friend, Garrett let grief and guilt chase away any lingering interest he had in the girl as he washed up for supper.

Waiting until she and his mother took their seats at the dining table, he pulled out the chair across from Aundy and sat down, bowing his head. His father asked the blessing on the meal then his mother started a lively discussion about upcoming events at church and things happening in town.

After dinner, Aundy helped with the dishes then Nora insisted everyone gather in the parlor for a while before Garrett took Aundy home.

"Have you decided what you want to do with the farm yet?" J.B. asked. He knew Aundy had been weighing all of her options.

"I've decided to stay and make it a success as a way of honoring Erik." Aundy sipped the tea Nora served as the two of them sat together on the sofa.

"That's wonderful, honey." Nora patted her leg, offering an encouraging smile. "What are your plans?"

"I want to learn all I can about managing a farm. I need to learn about animals, crops, everything. Dent said he'd help, but suggested Garrett might be able to provide assistance with some of my lessons, like shooting."

Garrett, who'd been drinking a cup of coffee, choked in his efforts not to spew the drink all over his mother's prized set of furniture. J.B. reached over and slapped his back a few times.

"Sounds like a grand idea to me." J.B. winked at Nora as Aundy watched Garrett with concern.

"I don't want to be any more of a burden to anyone. I'm sure I can figure things out." Aundy glanced down at the teacup she held in her hand.

"Nonsense." J.B. settled back in his chair, pinning his gaze on his son. "Garrett would be happy to teach you how to shoot and whatever other lessons you need help with. I might not be much use outdoors yet, but I can teach you about cattle and crops if you're of a mind to come here for a little schooling. We've got a few books that might be a help to you."

"Thank you, Mr. Nash." Aundy offered him a shy smile. "I've been reading a book I found on Erik's desk, but I still have some questions about what I've read. I hate to bother Dent because he's so busy and he informed me today we need to hire more hands."

"Well, you probably could use a few more. Erik always hired some seasonal help once the farm work began." J.B. continued to wait for Garrett to recover from his choking fit and join the conversation. "Do the men know you're planning to keep the farm and run it yourself?"

"Dent said he'd tell them after supper tonight." Aundy watched out of the corner of her eye as Garrett took a cautious sip of his coffee. "I realize I've got a lot to learn, but I'm willing to work hard."

"We know you are, honey," Nora said, patting Aundy's leg again. "Don't you worry about a thing. We'll help you learn about farm life. You can count on us. All of us." Nora gave Garrett a pointed look and he numbly nodded his head, trying not to look at Aundy.

The firelight in the room made her hair glimmer and shine while the look on her face, filled with animation and excitement as she talked about learning to farm, made him want to promise to do everything in his power to help her succeed.

After visiting for another hour, Garrett finally went to hitch the horse to the buggy while J.B. and Aundy worked out a schedule for her to learn what he could teach her from the kitchen table about crops, livestock, and rural life.

Nora gave her another hug as she walked out the door and waved enthusiastically as Garrett helped her in the buggy and started down the lane back toward the road.

"Thank you," Aundy said quietly, taking in the beautiful colors filling the sky as the sun set. She would never tire of the smell of clean air and the wide-open spaces she'd found in Pendleton. Unlike anything she'd ever experienced, she felt such peace here in the country.

"For what?" Garrett kept his gaze fastened on the horse instead of his companion.

"For being so kind and encouraging," Aundy said, releasing a sigh. "Most people would have told me to sell the farm, get on a train, and return to the city life I know. Your family hasn't offered any opinions on what I should do and have been supportive of my decisions. Not everyone would encourage a woman from Chicago to stick it out and learn about farming."

"We're not everyone," Garrett said with a smile that made her stomach flutter. "Everyone should have the opportunity to learn and grow regardless of their age, color, or gender. If you want to learn about farming, who are we to tell you no? You should know, though, that learning from Pops means you'll be learning from one of the best."

"I assumed as much." Aundy watched Garrett as he stopped the buggy and hurried around to offer her his hand. "It's easy to see you've got a prosperous well-run ranch and that doesn't happen by chance. I do know enough to realize that only happens because of skill and hard work."

Garrett grinned, pleased at Aundy's compliment. He walked her up the steps to the front door and tipped his hat. "After you finish your lesson with Pops, I can give you a shooting lesson. You should be able to get in some practice one-handed with a revolver until that arm of yours heals."

"Thank you." Aundy opened the door and stepped inside before turning to smile at Garrett. Her stomach fluttered as her eyes connected with his silvery gaze and he offered her another broad grin.

Garrett backed up and almost fell off the porch step with his attention centered on the intriguing golden-haired woman instead of where he was going.

He thought he heard her giggle, but when he looked up, all he saw was a closing door.

Chapter Five

Aundy swung open the kitchen door as the sun began to chase away the early morning darkness and walked toward the chicken coop with a determined step.

After her tour around the farm with Dent the previous afternoon, she was confident she could at least feed the chickens and gather eggs. She located the feed bucket Dent indicated she should give the chickens and carefully opened the door to the enclosed pen then shut it behind her. The chickens were still inside the coop, sitting on their nests.

Aundy used her good hand to shake the bucket, making a racket she hoped rousted the chickens. Quickly switching the bucket to her other hand, she held it against her waist and tossed out handfuls of the feed, calling to the chickens. "Here chick, chick. Here chick."

Soon, chickens were all around her, pecking at the feed. Aundy emptied the bucket then entered the coop, sticking her hand in the nests like Dent showed her. As she gathered the eggs, she felt a growing satisfaction in having accomplished something worthwhile. Although a little frightened by the chickens, she decided they were only harmless birds, after all.

As she reached the last nest, a sharp stinging on her leg drew her gaze down. A little rooster pecked at her. He stared up at her with angry eyes. Aundy started backing toward the door. The sound he emitted made Aundy's eyes widen with fear and she hurried out of the coop and through the chickens as they ate their feed. Frantic, she worked to lift the latch on the gate. The rooster flew up with his spurs set to dig into her.

Anticipating the attack, Aundy raised her arm and the rooster's head connected with her cast, thumping loudly. He fell to the ground and she escaped the pen, closing the gate behind her. A quick glance into the bucket revealed she hadn't broken a single egg in her haste to get away from the rooster.

When she turned away from the coop, she discovered several sets of eyes looked her direction. Dent and the hands all stared at her, most with smirks on their faces.

"I see you met Napoleon," Dent said, trying not to laugh. He and the boys heard a commotion in the coop and hurried over in time to see the little rooster chase Aundy to the gate. It was hard to keep from breaking out in chuckles when she held up her cast and knocked the bird senseless.

"What a fitting name." Aundy stared at the rooster that had yet to move. "I didn't kill him, did I?"

"Probably just stunned him is all." Dent watched as the bird shook his head and staggered to his feet.

Aundy decided she and Napoleon needed to reach a compromise or one of them was going to have to leave the farm, and it wouldn't be her. "Too bad. I'll have to try harder next time. Chicken stew would have tasted good for supper."

The hands broke out in laughter and watched as Aundy walked up the steps to the kitchen door, disappearing inside.

"Chores won't do themselves," Dent said, pointing toward the barn when the men continued to stare at the house. He didn't get a chance to talk to them about Aundy keeping the farm the previous evening, but if he were a betting man, he'd wager after breakfast they'd be short a few more hands. He supposed he ought to get it over with and quit putting off the inevitable.

He removed his hat, ran his hand through his hair, and released a sigh. "You might as well all know, I spoke with Mrs. Erikson yesterday and she intends to not only keep the farm but be in control of it."

"You mean that citified woman thinks she's gonna run this place?" one of the men asked, glaring at Dent in disgust.

"That's what the lady said." Dent glared back at the hand, daring him to say anything more.

"Then I quit." The man stalked off toward the bunkhouse.

"Any of the rest of you agree with Harry?" Dent asked, looking at each face and anticipating a few more would follow. At the nod of three more heads, Dent shook his and pointed toward the bunkhouse.

"Pack your gear and I'll get your wages ready for you. You can light out after breakfast." Dent was disappointed but not surprised. With the four men leaving, that left him with just four other bodies besides his own to do all the work. Aundy was going to have to hire more men if they hoped to make it through spring calving and farm work.

He hated to start the day with bad news, but he needed to let her know what was going on as well as discuss paying the men. Erik always took care of paying wages and the men received theirs at the end of each month.

"Come in," Aundy called as Dent raised a hand to knock on the door. He didn't know how she knew he was out there, but he opened the door, took off his hat, and stepped inside. She smiled at him over her shoulder. "If nothing else, I guess I'm good for providing the morning entertainment."

Dent grinned in spite of himself. "You did just fine for your first time in the chicken coop. That lil' rooster is full of attitude, but I have a feeling he'll leave you alone for now."

"If he doesn't, you'll have to teach me how to kill a chicken. I've plucked and cooked them, but never had to execute one before." Aundy glanced at Dent as she continued wiping off the eggs and placing them in a basket on the counter. "Napoleon may make me anxious to learn that particular skill."

"Missy, you are something else," Dent said, leaning against the door. He watched Aundy carefully hold an egg in her hand then use a soft cloth to wipe it clean. "I've got some news you aren't gonna like, but need to hear."

"Oh?" Aundy set down the egg and gave him her full attention.

"I told the men you're planning to run the farm and four of them quit this morning." Dent hoped Aundy didn't take it personally. The hands would have quit if any woman had taken over the farm. It wasn't that they disliked her, just the idea of having a woman as their employer.

"I suppose I should have anticipated the possibility of that happening." Aundy took a seat at the table and stared down at her lap. She was quiet so long, Dent didn't know what to make of it. He finally pulled out a chair and straddled it.

"We need to pay them for wages due. Erik always paid everyone on the last day of the month, so we need to talk about pay for all of the hands."

"I recall seeing the monthly withdrawal in the ledger book, but it slipped my mind that you all will want your wages soon." Aundy lifted her gaze to look at Dent. "If I forget going forward, please just remind me. It won't be intentional. I'm just not used to taking care of paying wages. Do I need to go to the bank to collect the funds?"

"Yep. Erik usually went in and got the money, picked up supplies, and made a day of it."

"I see. Do you know how much is owed the men who are leaving?" Aundy vaguely recalled a list of payroll in Erik's ledger.

Dent listed the men's names and the amount of wages they were owed. Aundy told him she would have the funds ready for him by the time the men were finished with breakfast.

"That would be good, Missy." Dent decided they might as well get all the problems out on the table. "We can't operate five men short, which is what we'll be now. We've got to hire more help."

"Do you feel comfortable hiring more men?" Aundy could judge character, but wasn't sure she'd know what to look for in a hired hand.

"I can do that." Dent sat quietly for a moment, lost in his thoughts, before looking at her across the table. "If I help you write an advertisement, can you make sure it gets in the paper? We could post it around town, too."

"That would be satisfactory. Perhaps after you pay the men and see them on their way, we can come up with something I can take to town. I'll need to go to the bank to collect wages for the rest of the men. If anyone needs supplies, please let me know and I can pick them up when I go.

"How are you going to get to town?" Dent asked. She couldn't drive the buggy and she didn't know how to ride a horse.

"I'm not entirely certain, but I'll figure something out," Aundy said, getting up from the table. Dent stood, shook his head, and walked outside.

Aundy sat back down at the table and raised her gaze heavenward, praying for strength and wisdom. She was going to need an extra helping of both to get through the day.

She went to Erik's desk, took out his ledger, and noted a final payment made to the four men who quit along with the date. She took out a scrap of paper and wrote down the amount of wages from the previous month and placed it in her pocket then began opening drawers, hoping to find some cash Erik might have on hand. After searching through the desk, she came up with enough to pay one of the men.

Since there was no help for it, she walked to Erik's bedroom and stood with her forehead resting against his door. Slowly turning the knob, she looked around the room for a moment before stepping inside.

Nora made sure the room had a good airing and clean linens covered the bed, but everything else was just as Erik left it.

The nightstand drew her attention, so she looked there first for any money he might have left behind. Grateful when she found his wallet, she emptied it then searched the dresser. A box shoved in the back of one drawer contained more than enough money to cover the wages of the men leaving.

Relief flowed over her. Aundy took out what she needed, put the rest of the money back in the box and returned it to Erik's drawer. She needed to clean out his things, but she'd worry about it another day.

Hurriedly exiting the room, she shut the door behind her and walked back to his desk in the front room. She placed money in four envelopes, addressing each to the appropriate farm hand. After setting the envelopes on the kitchen table, she finished cleaning the eggs, made herself a simple breakfast, and waited for her foreman to return.

Dent knocked softly and opened the door, sticking his head inside. Aundy handed him the envelopes without a word and he hurried back toward the bunkhouse.

She mulled over her options for getting herself to town when a knock at the kitchen door brought her out of her musings. She steeled herself for whatever waited and opened the door.

"Mrs. Erikson?" The men stared down at their scuffed boots instead of looking her direction.

"Yes?" Aundy opened the door wider and studied the four hands that quit. All but one of them looked uncomfortable to be there. The fourth boldly lifted his gaze to hers with a gleam in his eye she found unsettling.

"We just wanted to thank you for paying us for a full month and for treating us good since you've been here. Us leaving ain't about you specifically." The designated speaker looked to his comrades for agreement. At their nods, he continued. "We just don't cotton to working for no woman, no matter how nice she might be."

"Thank you for providing me with that information." Aundy wanted to give them a piece of her mind. Instead, she bit her tongue and forced herself to smile. "I appreciate the work you've done here on the farm and wish you all much success in your future endeavors."

"Thank you, ma'am," the speaker said, tipping his head as they all backed off the steps and walked around to where their horses waited.

Once they were out of sight, Aundy gave in to the urge to stamp her foot. "Bunch of club-dragging cavedwellers," Aundy muttered to herself, marching into her bedroom and getting out one of her best day gowns. Quickly deciding she couldn't possibly get into her corset without assistance, she gave up and placed a call to Nora.

"Nash's Folly," a deep voice resonated in her ear, making tingles race down her spine.

"Garrett?"

"Yep, the one and only." His light-hearted tone caused a smile to break out on Aundy's face while her heartbeat skipped into a faster tempo.

"This is Mrs. Erickson. May I please speak with your mother?"

"Nope."

"Oh… I… well… I…"

Laughter filled the earpiece of the phone and Aundy held it away from her head, staring at it, perplexed, before returning it to her ear.

"I'm teasing you, Mrs. Erickson. Just a moment, I'll get her for you."

"Thank you." Aundy breathed a sigh of relief. She could hear rumbling sounds in the background then Nora's cheery voice greeted her.

"What can I do for you today, honey?"

"Nora, I hate to ask, but I sorely need your assistance with a matter here at my home. Would there possibly be any way you could come over this morning?"

"Certainly. I can be there in an hour. Anything I need to bring?"

"No, ma'am, and thank you," Aundy said, remembering that many people listened in on the phone lines so anything she said could be fodder for community gossip.

"I'll be there as soon as I can, honey."

"Thank you, Nora. I appreciate it."

She hung up from her call with Nora as Dent knocked once before stepping inside the kitchen. Aundy retrieved a pencil and a pad of paper from Erik's desk, poured Dent a cup of coffee, and sat with him at the table writing an advertisement for hired help. They worked to finish the wording when the front door shut and footsteps echoed down the hall. The two of them looked up as Nora bustled into the kitchen.

"What are you working on?" Nora asked, peering over Aundy's shoulder.

"Four of the men quit this morning when Dent told them I was keeping the farm. We're in dire need of more help," Aundy said. She looked at Dent as he stood and edged toward the door.

"With Erik gone, you're running five short? Is that right?" Nora asked, looking to Dent for confirmation. At his nod, Nora shook her head. "We can send over some help until you hire more men."

"Absolutely not, Nora. You've done so much already." Aundy rose and looked at Dent for support. Inconspicuously, he nodded his head at Nora.

"Looks like you're outvoted, Missy." Dent grinned then hurried out the door before Aundy could reply.

"Nora, I..." Aundy turned to the woman who had been mother, friend, and mentor to her since she'd stood dripping mud all over her clean porch.

"Not another word, Aundy. It's what neighbors and friends do." Nora set a basket on the table and pulled out a few jars of jam, a napkin filled with cookies, and a loaf of bread that smelled delicious, filling the kitchen with a wonderful yeasty scent.

Aundy couldn't do much cooking with one hand and tried to get by as best she could. Dent invited her to join the men in the bunkhouse for meals, but she didn't feel right about that either.

Nora removed her hat and set it on the table. "Now, what requires my assistance?"

"I need to go into town and get the men's wages from the bank, pick up supplies, and place an advertisement in the newspaper. I should be dressed in something more presentable than the clothes I've been wearing and for that, I need someone to help me put on that blasted corset. I hate to bother you, but I don't know what else to do. I would also be forever grateful if you can help me get my hair put up proper before I head into town." Aundy walked to her bedroom with Nora following close behind her.

"And just how, precisely, do you plan to get into town to run all these errands?" Nora helped Aundy remove her shirtwaist and skirt then settled the corset into place.

"I hadn't exactly gotten that far in my plans. I watched Garrett with the buggy and horse yesterday. I think I could handle it."

Nora laughed. "No doubt you'd try, but you better wait until that arm of yours has healed. My buggy is right outside and I'd be happy to run into Pendleton with you. I'll call J.B. and let him know you and I are eating lunch in town today. He and Garrett can fend for themselves."

"No, Nora. I can't disrupt your day like that."

"Yes, you can. I insist," Nora said. She expertly pulled Aundy's long hair up and fastened it in a loose pompadour before pinning a stylish hat in place.

"My gracious, but you sure have such lovely clothes." Nora admired Aundy's outfit. A skirt and short jacket, in the same striking shade of light blue as Aundy's eyes, topped a crisp white shirtwaist with thick lace around the collar and along the front. The hat, adorned with white roses, featured loops of blue ribbon that matched her stylish ensemble.

Aundy looked down and smoothed the front of her skirt with her good hand. She felt blessed to have a very nice wardrobe. Most people in a working class family like hers wouldn't have been able to afford the clothing she, her mother, and sister wore. Their wardrobes were a benefit of having sewing in their blood and access to quality materials.

She pulled on her gloves as they walked back to the kitchen. Nora plucked her empty basket off the table while Aundy folded the advertisement she and Dent had worked on into her reticule.

"My mother's parents worked very hard before they moved to America. My grandfather was a tailor, serving only the most affluent clients. My grandmother was a seamstress and milliner. She rented a small space in a shop not far from my grandfather's. One day, he happened to be walking by the shop on his way back to his store after lunch and saw my grandmother in the window. He decided to be bold, walked right in, and asked her if she would make a hat for his mother. She agreed. It didn't take long for them to fall in love and wed."

"What a romantic story," Nora said, as she and Aundy climbed into the buggy and started down the lane. "So how did they end up in Chicago?"

"My grandfather decided there were fortunes to be made in America so he and my grandmother shipped what they could, sold the rest, and made arrangements to begin a new life in Chicago. One of my grandfather's friends started a bakery there and helped them settle in with their two young daughters. They had a large shop that offered tailored men's clothing on one side and everything a fashionably dressed woman could want on the other. My mother and aunt grew up knowing how to sew, design gowns, create hats, alter clothes flawlessly, and get the most out of a piece of yardage. They also learned how to do the fancy stitching that set their creations apart from other dress shops."

Aundy looked around, observing hints of spring as the rolling fields and pastures began turning green. The breath she drew in carried a new, earthy aroma.

"And?" Nora asked, anxious to hear the rest of the story as they made their way to Pendleton.

"A French man came to have a suit made by my grandfather. My aunt decided right then she was going to marry the man and she did. With her new last name and the loss of her Norwegian ties, she opened her own dress shop that catered to the elite in Chicago's social circles. Unlike my aunt, Mother fell in love with a common laborer. Despite my grandparents' protests she married beneath her, she didn't care. My parents were so happy and so in love. My father's charm quickly won over my grandparents, but he wouldn't take a dime of their money while they were alive," Aundy said, letting memories flood through her.

"My mother worked for my grandparents and then my aunt. Because of the skills she taught us, my sister and I both worked for Aunt Louisa, too. Ilsa does such beautiful work, she truly is talented. I don't have the patience for all the intricate stitching. When both our parents died, I took the job in the factory because I was good at basic sewing and needed the work. The factory owners thought their employees should dress in the clothes we made, so people could see the items out and about town. A clothing allotment was part of our wages."

Nora gave Aundy a dubious look, convinced the lovely outfit she wore did not come from a factory. The attention to detail hinted that it was handmade by someone who definitely knew her way around a needle.

Aundy smiled at Nora's raised brow. "When my grandparents passed away, my aunt didn't want the inventory from their store. She said it wasn't good enough for her clientele, so we had more bolts of fabric, trims, laces, ribbons, hat forms, and sewing supplies than you could imagine. I did the basic stitching for our clothes and Ilsa made them beautiful."

"Why didn't your mother open her own dress shop, instead of working for your aunt?" Nora asked with open curiosity.

"Mother didn't have a head for business and she didn't want to deal with the clients, so she kept the arrangement with my aunt. My father agreed to use the money we inherited from my grandparents to move to a nicer apartment and to put us in better schools. Thanks to what my grandparents left us, we were well-dressed and well-educated," Aundy said, smiling at Nora. "My mother always said a well-dressed lady who walked with confidence and spoke intelligently could go far in life. I sure hope she's right because I've got a long way to go and not a lot to take me there but a few nice clothes and a determination to succeed."

Nora laughed and teasingly bumped Aundy's side. "If that's what it takes, you'll go far, honey. You'll go far."

When they arrived in town, Nora went straight to the bank and sat outside in the buggy. Aundy could take care of herself without her interference. The girl soon returned looking relieved.

"That went better than I anticipated. Unlike some men around here, the banker doesn't seem to mind dealing with a woman."

"Grant Hill is a nice boy. He was raised by good parents, back in Philadelphia, I think," Nora said, guiding the buggy to her favorite store. "Why don't we do our shopping? While someone carries our purchases out to the buggy, we can run over to the newspaper office with your advertisement."

"That sounds like a fine plan." A look of anticipation filled Aundy's face as Nora parked the buggy outside a large store with interesting window displays. They stopped to admire a spring scene with seed packets, baskets, and garden tools. "When do you plant a garden?"

"Not for another month or two. We have to wait until the threat of frost is past. By then, you'll have your cast off."

"I wonder if they have any books on gardening." Aundy commented as they walked inside the store. A handful of women from church stood at the counter paying for their purchases and offered them a friendly greeting.

After visiting for a few moments, Nora led Aundy toward the garden supplies. "Why do you need a gardening book?"

"I've never planted one before and have no idea how to go about it," Aundy said, picking up a garden trowel and trying to decide what purpose it served.

"Well, silly girl, I'll be teaching you all about gardens, then." Nora took the trowel out of Aundy's hand and shook her head. "Erik always planted a garden, although none of the men liked taking care of it. He has all the tools you need, I'm sure of it. If not, you can always purchase them later. We'll have to make a list of seeds you want to order. I have some extras, but you might want some different vegetables than what I plan to plant. Erik also has some lovely fruit trees."

"Fruit trees? What kind of trees?" Aundy was excited at the prospect of growing her own fruit. She had a sweet tooth and being able to make pies and crisps, as well as put up preserves for winter sounded wonderful.

"A couple of cherry, some apple, and pear," Nora said, sorting through a stack of gloves, looking for a new pair. "And peach. He brought me the loveliest peaches last summer."

Busy dreaming about the first bite of a ripe, juicy peach, Aundy forgot where she was until someone bumped into her back, nearly knocking her into a display of baskets.

"Begging your pardon, miss," a good-looking man said as he stepped back from her. Aundy noticed he was about her height and quite handsome with an aristocratic appeal. He probably had women whispering about him behind their hands for miles around.

"Ashton Monroe, I didn't know you were back in town," Nora said, looking at the man as he stared at Aundy. "You were gone when poor Erik had his accident so you probably haven't had a chance to meet his wife."

"Wife? So it's true. Erik really did send for a mail-order bride?" Ashton tipped his head at Aundy and offered her an engaging smile. "I can't believe someone as lovely as you, Mrs. Erickson, would have been unattached."

The man was either full of poppycock, as her father used to say, or had impaired vision. A glance at the thick fringe of lashes around his intense, dark eyes, made her doubt he had any problems seeing.

"Thank you, Mr. Monroe," Aundy said, tipping her head demurely. Her mother instilled impeccable manners in both her daughters, despite the fact their father thought it was a bunch of unnecessary nonsense.

"My condolences on your loss, Mrs. Erickson, particularly so soon after your arrival in our little town." Ashton took Aundy's gloved hand in his and pressed a light kiss to her knuckles.

"Again, thank you, Mr. Monroe."

He released her hand and gazed into her eyes. "I insist you call me Ashton. All my friends do, and I certainly hope you'll allow me to be your friend."

Aundy gave her head a barely perceptible nod, watching Nora roll her eyes. "Very well, Ashton."

"That's better." Ashton beamed a brilliant smile Aundy's direction. "Now, what brings you ladies to town today?"

"We had a few things we needed to do." The smile Nora turned to Ashton lacked any real warmth or sincerity. "What about you?"

"Just a few business matters that sorely needed my attention," Ashton said, glancing from Aundy to Nora. "Perhaps you ladies would join me for tea at Dogwood Corners one afternoon?"

"Perhaps." Nora placed a hand on Aundy's arm to keep her from saying anything. "We need to get through calving season first."

"Oh, yes. How is the illustrious cattle business at Nash's Folly?" Ashton asked.

The disdain in his voice shocked Aundy.

"As good as ever," Nora said. She looped her arm through Aundy's and gave it a gentle tug. "Now, if you'll excuse us, we need to finish our shopping."

"Of course, Nora. It was a pleasure to meet you, Mrs. Erickson." Ashton tipped his hat solicitously. "I look forward to seeing you again."

After watching him walk toward a group of men gathered at the back of the store, Aundy glanced down. Nora's narrowed gaze followed him.

She gave Aundy a look of warning. "Don't let his nice manners and fancy talk turn your head, honey. He's not one to dally with. As handsome as he is, not to mention smooth talking, Ashton has broken more hearts than you can imagine. He's nothing but trouble when it comes to pretty women."

"Yes, ma'am," Aundy said, following Nora to the store's counter. "I don't believe he'd be interested in someone like me anyway."

"What do you mean?" Nora stopped to study Aundy's face.

"You know, someone plain and simple, without wealth or station or beauty," Aundy said, stating what she felt was a fact. "Besides, I have no interest in becoming involved with a man. None at all. I've only been a widow for less than two weeks."

Nora laughed and wrapped an arm around Aundy's waist. "You may not have grown up wealthy or in high society, but there is nothing plain or simple about you, honey. We all know you and Eric weren't in love, didn't really know each other. I wouldn't worry too much about being the grieving widow. After all, we did talk you out of wearing black. When the right man comes along, the one who makes your stomach fill with butterflies and your breath catch in your throat and all sense fly right out of your head, you'll be ready to rethink that notion about staying away from the male species."

Aundy looked at her friend in surprise and felt a grin tugging up the corners of her mouth as Nora smiled back at her. She'd never admit it, but Nora had accurately described what happened to her whenever she was near Garrett.

The women finished their shopping, placed Aundy's ad in the paper, and left word with a few of the businesses in town they were hiring out at the Erickson farm.

At a charming little restaurant, they enjoyed a leisurely lunch. Nora introduced Aundy to several people she hadn't yet met.

Aundy insisted on buying lunch then the two women climbed into the buggy and headed out of town.

"When Ashton invited us to Dogwood Corners, where is that?" Aundy asked. Curiosity about the strange yet handsome man nearly got the best of her.

"That direction," Nora said, pointing down a road as they passed it. "If you follow that for a mile or so, you'll see a big house up on a hill. He had dogwoods sent out here and hires a gardener to try to keep them alive. So far, he's been successful, although with our cold winters, I don't know how."

"I'm sure the trees are lovely." Aundy tried to envision an imposing house surrounded by dogwoods. She didn't think she'd ever find out what it looked like, and that was probably for the best.

Chapter Six

"Site down the barrel and hold it steady." Garrett found it increasingly difficult to instruct Aundy in how to shoot his revolver with her floral scent tantalizing his nose and a wayward wisp of hair engaged in a teasing dance by his cheek.

His mother returned from town with Aundy in tow, insisting J.B. begin her lessons in agriculture that afternoon. Aundy spent a couple of hours at the kitchen table taking notes as J.B. shared information about farming.

Garrett interrupted the lessons when he stopped by the house to ask his father a question.

Aundy appeared to share his stunned feelings when Nora insisted he give the girl a shooting lesson right then.

"Ma, I just needed to ask Pops a question," Garrett said, backing toward the door, hoping to escape. It wasn't that he didn't want to be around Aundy. The problem was that he wanted it too much. He'd like nothing better than to spend the afternoon sitting somewhere quiet listening to her lilting voice and getting lost in her sky blue eyes. He'd promised himself to stay away from the widow, and he had more than enough work to keep him busy.

"I'm sure Garrett has much more pressing matters this afternoon," Aundy protested, rising to her feet from her place at the table. "I really should be getting home anyway."

"Nonsense. Garrett could use a break from his work, couldn't you?" The silvery stare she sent his direction let him know she wouldn't tolerate any argument from him.

"Sure, Ma, but Mrs. Erikson isn't exactly dressed for a shooting lesson." Garrett tried not to stare at Aundy's pretty outfit, from the frill of lace around her long neck to the elaborate stitching on the hem of a skirt that was the exact same shade of blue as her sky-colored eyes.

"She can leave off her jacket and put on one of my aprons. She'll be fine." Nora hustled to pluck a clean apron off a peg on the wall and tied it around Aundy before she could generate an excuse for immediately returning home. Quickly placing a handful of cookies in Garrett's hand, Nora pushed him and Aundy toward the door. "Have fun."

Garrett stared at his mother with a narrowed gaze. He bit back a smart comment and held the door for Aundy. He led the way behind the barn where he set some old cans they saved for target practice on top of a few fence posts.

Although he planned to have Aundy shoot his revolver once or twice and send her back to the house, she held the gun in her hand, looking at it then him expectantly. Resigned to giving her a real lesson, he took the gun from her. He described in detail how it worked, how she should hold it, gun safety, and everything a beginner needed to know about the weapon.

When he finished, she smiled at him, causing him to forget what it was he was going to say. He pointed toward a post and told her to try to shoot one of the cans.

Aundy had a hard time holding the gun steady using only one hand and her first shot went wild.

"Here, let me help you."

She started to hand him the gun, but he stepped close behind her and put his arms around her. Garrett placed his big hands over her smaller one, helped her raise the gun, his cheek pressed against her temple.

That was his first mistake.

His second was taking a deep breath. Nearly undone by her soft rose fragrance, her warmth seeped into him, making him feel slightly overheated.

"Normally, you'd learn to shoot using both hands to steady your weapon. Since that isn't an option, you'll just learn to do it one-handed from the start." Garrett desperately wanted to kiss Aundy. He could almost taste the sweetness of her lips. "You hold it like this, see?"

Aundy nodded her head, unable to see or think. Not with Garrett so close to her. He smelled of horses and sunshine, and some musky scent she found to be both alluring and inviting.

When he stepped behind her, pressing close, her knees wobbled and she fought the desire to lean back into his strength. Her stomach fluttered as his breath stirred the hair by her ear then she felt his cheek against her temple. His deep voice filled the air and her soul.

She blinked her eyes, trying to keep from collapsing at his feet. Intentionally blocking out just how wonderful it felt to have Garrett's arms around her, she focused on the can on top of the fencepost.

"When you feel ready, gently squeeze the trigger. Don't pull or tug it, just let it come easy." Garrett drew on what was left of his restraint as he kept his arms around Aundy, helping steady the gun in her hand.

She pulled the trigger and hit the can, knocking it off the post.

"That's great, Aundy!" Garrett shared an enthusiastic hug with his arms around her waist, pulling her close. Mindful of what he'd done, he dropped his hands and stepped back. "You seem to be a fast learner. Try the next one."

Aundy wasn't sure she could concentrate enough to hit the side of the barn, but tried to regain her focus. She missed a few, but the more she shot the more she hit, gaining confidence. Garrett reloaded the gun for her several times. The last round, she hit five out of six cans.

"I'm very proud of you." Garrett was amazed at how quickly she picked up shooting, especially since she was learning one-handed.

"Thanks." Aundy beamed a smile at Garrett, rather pleased with her efforts considering she'd never before held a gun. "I can see why Dent said you should teach me to shoot. You've been so patient and informative."

"Glad you think so." He took the gun from her and reloaded it. "Want to try again?"

"I've killed enough cans today. However, I'd like to see you shoot." She wondered if he would hit all the cans he lined up on the posts.

"Are you sure?" Garrett asked, returning to stand beside her, holstering the gun.

"I'm absolutely certain." Aundy nodded her head for emphasis.

Garrett whipped out the gun, knocked all the cans off the posts, and returned it to his holster so rapidly Aundy had barely seen anything. She wasn't sure she'd even had time to blink.

She laughed, thrilled at the opportunity to watch Garrett in action. "No wonder Dent said you should teach me. Were you a gun slinger in a past lifetime?"

"No, ma'am." Garrett grinned. He didn't usually show off, but he was in the mood to do so today, wanting to impress his neighbor. "I practiced a lot growing up. I guess I read one too many western adventures as a kid."

"I can't believe your mother would allow you to read dime novels." The look she gave him made him wonder what kind of retribution he'd face if he kissed her. She looked so lively and pretty with her cheeks flushed and errant strands of silky golden hair twirling in the afternoon breeze.

"No one said she knew I was reading them." Garrett offered her a devilish smile. "She'd have boxed my ears if she knew I was reading those instead of the books she deemed acceptable."

"Now I've got something to hold over your head." Aundy teased as they walked together.

"Just try."

"I'll save it for a day when I really need it."

As they strolled around the side of the barn toward the house, Garrett breathed deeply of Aundy's fragrance that put him in mind of summer roses. He tried not to stare at her tall figure and trim waist. "I'll come over soon and we can set up some targets so you can use Erik's guns. They're yours now, so you should practice shooting them, get familiar with how they feel in your hand."

Elated at the idea of being with Garrett, Aundy knew she shouldn't be. A wave of guilt swept over her for enjoying the time she spent with her handsome neighbor as much as she did. Her husband had only been gone a few weeks and she told Nora earlier that morning she refused to get involved with another man.

Her last two relationships ended with the men she cared for dying and she couldn't go through the pain of losing someone else again.

She stopped on the front walk and turned to Garrett. "Thank you for teaching me to shoot. I hope I never need to do it, but I appreciate you helping me learn."

"You're welcome, Aundy. Most welcome." He marveled at the way the sun played in her golden hair. His mother must have been the one to pin it up in the poufy style because he knew Aundy couldn't manage it with her arm in the cast. Although it looked stylish, he much preferred it rippling in golden waves down her back.

Dreams of burying his hands in all that hair made his temperature climb. He cleared his throat, trying to chase his thoughts in a less amorous direction.

"Are you staying for supper?" he asked, motioning Aundy to precede him down the walk.

"I've been enough of a burden to all of you today. If someone wouldn't mind taking me home, I need to see to some things there." She waited as Garrett opened the kitchen door for her.

"If you're certain," Garrett said, hoping she'd stay. He enjoyed hearing the cadence of her voice and the conversations around the dinner table were much livelier with her there.

"I'm certain." Aundy stepped into Nora's kitchen where the woman bustled around with dinner preparations.

"Certain of what?" Nora asked, sliding a pan of rolls into the oven.

"That I need to go home. Dent will be wondering if things went well in town today." Aundy removed Nora's apron, returning it to the peg on the wall. She slipped her arms in her jacket sleeves and picked up her hat. After setting it on her head, she attempted to jab a hatpin in one handed and struggled to get it into place without the ability to hold her hat steady with her other hand.

Garrett wondered what she'd do if he helped her. He quickly shoved his hands into his pockets before he found out. "Dent? What did he need in town?" He tried not to grin when Aundy's tongue came out of the corner of her mouth as she fussed with her hat.

"Aundy lost four hands this morning. Up and quit when they found out she's keeping the farm and staying. I neglected to mention it earlier," Nora said. She asked Garrett to send over some extra help and gave him the names of the men who'd quit.

He wasn't surprised by the news.

"That leaves you really short-handed." Garrett studied Aundy, wondering if she'd accept their assistance. "I'll send over a couple of men in the morning. Did you put an advertisement in the paper? Let people around town know?"

"Yes, we did." Aundy gave up on her hat and pulled on her gloves. "That was one of the reasons we went to town. I hope someone responds to the advertisement."

"I'm sure you'll have plenty of people answer the ad, honey." Nora took Aundy's hatpin and jabbed it into the hat then put her arm around the girl's waist as she walked her to the door. "You're more than welcome to stay for dinner, but if you're of a mind to go home, Garrett can take you."

"Thank you, Nora. I appreciate all your help today." Aundy hugged the woman before walking down the porch steps. Garrett quickly hitched the horse to the buggy and in no time, they were on the road to her house.

"Do you think Dent can interview and hire the men?" Aundy asked as Garrett easily held the reins in one hand.

He turned his silvery gaze to her and observed her for a moment before answering. "He's more than capable. Why?"

"I don't think it would be in anyone's best interest for me to conduct the interviews. With my lack of agricultural knowledge and the obvious problem of having a woman in charge, I thought it might be best to have Dent do the hiring."

"Maybe, but whoever you hire will have to come to terms with the fact they are working for a woman at some point. Why don't you and Dent interview them together?"

Aundy nodded her head, giving it some thought. She'd talk to Dent and see what he wanted to do. All of it depended on someone being interested in working for them. If they couldn't get anyone willing to work for her, she didn't know what they'd do. Running cattle and farming was extremely hard work and required many hands to make it successful.

"If you have trouble finding some help, you could always sell the cattle. That would lessen the load and the men you have could handle the farming part of the operation." Garrett tried to think of ways to make things easier on Aundy and her crew.

A few of the men at Aundy's place would rather work with cattle than the land, but the ones who stayed on were good hands who'd do what needed to be done. "You could also think about renting out some of the ground to someone else. On the other hand, you could run more cattle and put the wheat ground into pasture or plant seed to cut for hay. If you run more cattle, you'd have to have a way to feed them."

"What would you do, if you were in this situation?" Aundy asked, looking at Garrett with her beautiful blue eyes moist and intent.

He turned his gaze to the road and had to swallow twice before he answered her. His thoughts lingered on her inviting lips. "I'd see what kind of response comes from the advertisement. If that doesn't go well, I'd probably sell the cattle. The price is good this year and then you wouldn't have to worry about their feed and care."

Garrett took in the determined look on her face. While his gaze rested on her, he couldn't help but notice the freckles dotting her nose, or the pink hue the pleasant afternoon brought to her cheeks.

Lovely. She was absolutely lovely. Although he greatly appreciated her outward appearance, he also respected her intelligence, fortitude, and gentle spirit.

"I'll take that into consideration." She smiled at him with such tenderness, he leaned toward her, wanting to kiss those rosy lips of hers in the worst way. Her eyes widened and he caught himself before he did something he'd later regret.

"If you decide you do want to sell the cattle, I'd be happy to help you find a buyer that will give you a good price. There's a man in Umatilla who raises Shorthorns. He might be interested in expanding his herd."

"Thank you. If I decide to sell the cattle, I'll be sure to let you know." Aundy was relieved they were nearly to the house. She didn't know how much more time she could spend in Garrett's presence without losing all her common sense.

For some reason, she got the distinct idea he almost kissed her a moment ago, but that was impossible. Someone as handsome, generous, and fun as Garrett Nash wouldn't want anything to do with her. He needed a beautiful, charming wife content to sit in the house and be domestic.

Aundy had never been fond of the domestic arts, as her mother called them. She was a good cook, could maintain order in a home and perform all the duties flawlessly, but now that she had a farm of her own, she'd much rather be outside than in the house. Her spirit felt free out in the warm sunshine and clean air.

Maybe too free, she thought as she glanced at Garrett out of the corner of her eye. Reminding herself she was a new widow with no plans to commit to another man, she straightened her spine along with her resolve and lifted her head. She would not allow her imagination or her longings to get the best of her.

"Here we are." Garrett stopped the buggy at the end of her walk. Before she could get out, he was at her side, placing his hands to her waist and swinging her to the ground. His hand engulfed hers and she felt a charge of something powerful work its way from her fingers up her arm at his touch.

While she still possessed the ability to do so, she pulled her hand free. She hurried up the porch steps and opened the door. Garrett followed behind her, carrying her purchases from town. He set them on the kitchen table, tipped his hat to her, and walked out the door without another word.

Aundy sank onto a kitchen chair, wondering what she was going to do about her farm, her lack of employees, and her feelings for Garrett Nash.

Chapter Seven

"I don't care what you think, I ain't leaving til I talk to her," a raspy voice yelled from outside the front of the house.

Aundy dropped the book J.B. had given her to read about farming practices and hurried to open the door. Dent blocked the steps to a grizzled man dressed in overalls so dirty it looked like he'd rolled around in a pigpen. When she drew in a breath, Aundy decided he smelled like it, too.

"You her?" the man asked. He raised a narrowed gaze to her and spit a stream of tobacco on the grass next to the front walk.

"I'm Mrs. Erickson," Aundy said, pulling the door shut behind her. There was no way on earth she wanted the dirty, smelly man in her clean house. She took a step forward and Dent backed up a step so he stood directly in front of her.

"Mrs. Erickson," the man mimicked, waving a grime-encrusted hand in the air. "Ain't she all prissy and proper?"

"Marvin, if you think you need to speak to her, fine. Speak. But you'll keep a civil tongue in your head," Dent warned, trying to keep between the man and Aundy.

"I'll be fine, Dent," Aundy whispered, stepping beside him, trying to act much braver than she felt. "I'm sorry, sir. I've not yet had the pleasure of making your acquaintance."

"I'm certain it ain't gonna be a pleasure to either one of us, gal. My name's Marvin Tooley. Live over yonder." The man stabbed his finger in the direction of the farm both Garrett and Erik had mentioned. No wonder they'd warned her to stay away from the crotchety neighbor. "I come to see if you and I could strike a deal."

"What sort of deal?" Aundy asked. It had been three weeks since her hands quit and she and Dent hadn't been able to find anyone willing to work for a woman. Even though Dent would be doing the supervising, word had gotten around town she was running the Erikson place. She'd been reading the book J.B. gave her trying to decide the best course of action. She was strongly considering selling her cattle to try to relieve some of Dent's burden.

"I think it would be a right smart idea for us to get hitched," Marvin said, spitting another stream of tobacco.

Aundy had to fight to keep from wrinkling her nose in disgust. She was certain she'd misheard the man. "My apologies. I don't believe I heard you correctly. Could you please repeat your statement?"

"I said I want us to get hitched." Marvin took a step forward while Aundy backed up behind Dent. Maybe she should have let him run the man off without speaking to him. If Marvin Tooley was the last man on the planet and the only way to keep from falling into a black abyss was to marry him, Aundy would gather her skirts and jump into the dark void without looking back.

"No." Aundy glared at him. "No, Mr. Tooley. I won't marry you. The only reason you ask is that you want my farm. The answer is no."

"Figured you'd see it that way." Marvin scratched his rotund belly. "Then I'll make you an offer. I'll buy your place, fair and square. Everything on it, and I'll even let Dent and the boys keep working here, just to prove my generous nature."

Marvin threw out a figure that made Aundy laugh.

Dent and Marvin both stared at her in surprise.

"I can assure you, Mr. Tooley, I may be a woman, but my father didn't raise me to be a stupid one. The house is worth more than that by itself. If you're trying to insult me, you have more than accomplished the job." No longer afraid of the man, she stepped forward. "I'll say this once and you can tell it to whomever you like, but my farm isn't for sale. Not today, not tomorrow, not next month, not ever. I'm not interested in your deal or proposal and I won't be, so please don't offer again. Furthermore, my hands are not property. They are trusted friends so don't speak of them in such a manner. I'm sure you can find your way off my land. Good day."

Aundy turned and marched back inside the house, shutting the door firmly behind her before going to the kitchen and making herself a bracing cup of tea. She sat at the table sipping it when a knock sounded on the kitchen door. Dent stuck his head inside, grinning broadly.

"Well, Missy. You sure set ol' Marvin on his ear. He lit out of here so mad, I'm fairly certain a layer or two of dirt may have steamed right off him," Dent said, letting out a chuckle as he sat down at the table and took the plate of cookies Aundy held out to him. She got up and poured him a glass of milk before resuming her seat.

"I didn't intend to make an enemy, but I'd die before I married someone like Marvin Tooley. I refuse to let the likes of him get his grimy hands on Erik's farm." Aundy's anger stirred again at the thought of what Marvin Tooley suggested. Insulted, she couldn't fathom how he would think she'd be interested in tying herself to a filthy old man like him.

"Truth to tell, Marvin doesn't have any friends and he likes it that way. I heard he had a nice little family a long time ago, but something happened to them and he wasn't ever the same after it."

"That's terrible." Aundy helped herself to a cookie from the plate near Dent and dipped it in her tea before taking a bite. "I should have been kinder, but he caught me off guard."

"As fair warning, you ought to know he won't be the last. I heard some talk last time I was in town that there's a young widow out here and some fellers think they could take advantage of you."

"I'd like to see them try." Aundy was glad Garrett continued to provide shooting lessons. She was proficient with Erik's revolver and as soon as she got the cast off her arm, she planned to become equally as skilled at handling his rifle. A little gun that would fit in her reticule caught her eye at one of the stores the last time she and Nora went to town. With the information Dent just shared, she didn't think it would be a bad idea to look at purchasing it or something similar.

"Just be careful, Missy. Some of the men around here aren't what they seem." Dent cautioned before finishing his milk and taking another cookie.

Recently, Aundy had been able to use her arm enough to do a few things, like baking. The sweets she made endeared her to the hands who hadn't abandoned her and the farm. Fresh-baked pastries also went a long way in soothing any ruffled feathers about a woman taking over the place. She'd also made an effort to get to know her employees. She liked the men who stayed behind to work for her.

"Dent, what would you think if I decided to sell the cattle? Do you think it's the best decision?" Aundy wanted his opinion about the matter that weighed so heavily on her mind.

Instead of answering immediately, Dent brushed the crumbs from his cookies off the table into his hand and carried them to the sink. He leaned against it for a moment before answering her question. "As much as I hate to say it, there is no way we're going to make it with so few hands and so much work to do. If you sold the cattle, it would definitely ease the burden or you could think about renting out one of the sections of ground. Garrett would rent the one that borders their farm. If you did that, we might be able to make things work. A few more hands would sure make a big difference, but if we didn't have the cattle to look after, we could get along okay."

"That's what I thought." Aundy sighed, resigned to selling Erik's Shorthorns. She knew from his letters how proud he was of his herd, but she needed to save the farm and if selling the cattle would accomplish it, then so be it. "I'll speak with Garrett about finding a buyer. He said he knew someone in Umatilla who might be interested."

"That's a sound plan, Missy. Don't worry about it overmuch. Erik would be proud of how hard you're trying to keep things going." Dent smiled at her as he picked up his hat then walked out the back door.

She certainly hoped what she was planning wouldn't have Erik turning over in his grave. From the information she'd read and from what J.B. told her, she had more in mind than just selling the cattle.

Due to her gender, she'd gotten the farm into an unexpected bind. Creative thinking might be the only way out of the mess she unknowingly created. They were far behind on the farm work because the hands had been taking care of the cows as they calved. Now that the calving was mostly finished, Dent split the work between the cattle and fields.

Garrett had been good to send over extra help, but he had his own place to run. Aundy told him he had to stop sending over his men because he needed them at Nash's Folly. He'd argued with her, but she refused to discuss the matter further.

Since their disagreement, she hadn't talked to Garrett. She missed his friendly smile and deep voice. Steadfastly refusing to examine the reasons why his absence made her sad and lonesome, she needed to clear her head.

Aundy rushed out to the barn and caught one of the hands coming out the door. She asked him to saddle Bell. Although she'd ridden the horse several times, Dent worried she'd fall off and hurt her arm. He'd only allowed her to ride under close supervision.

The voice in her head warned her to be cautious, but Aundy chose to ignore it. She wanted to feel the warm spring breeze on her face and think about what she needed to do. Quickly setting her full skirt over the back of Bell, she rode off toward one of the pastures.

Dent would have a fit if he found out she'd gone off by herself, but she loved riding. She'd never envisioned herself on a horse, let alone riding it astride, but found it both exhilarating and calming. Bell seemed to like being out in the fresh air as well, tossing her head and taking a few dancing steps.

"It's a beautiful day, isn't it, Bell?"

The horse appeared to nod her head and Aundy smiled. She loved the farm, the rolling fields that would soon be bursting with wheat, the green pastures, and the open sky. The animals brought her much joy, except for the chickens. She disliked the chickens and had a deep-seated fear of them flogging her, but she tamped it down and dutifully gathered the eggs every day.

The little rooster, Napoleon, had given her a wide berth since she knocked him senseless with her cast. Nonetheless, she didn't trust him. Convinced he plotted his next evil move, she kept an eye on him the entire time she gathered eggs. As soon as she brought her sister to the farm, Aundy decided gathering eggs would become Ilsa's responsibility.

A smile crossed her face at the thought of her lovely, feminine sister carefully plucking an egg from a nest.

Aundy couldn't stop the laughter that bubbled inside her from spilling over her lips.

"What's so funny?"

Aundy gasped and spun around in the saddle, yanking Bell to a stop. The horse sidestepped and jerked her head, but obeyed Aundy's command. She looked across the fence at Garrett. A smile lingered on his handsome face as he leaned on the saddle horn with his hat tipped back and his eyes glowing like liquid metal.

"You startled me," Aundy said, her voice a little breathless from being caught off guard and seeing Garrett again.

Erik's closest neighbor had to be one of the most attractive men she'd ever seen, with an easy-going personality and engaging smile. It would be so much easier to deal with one who was short, homely and cranky. One like Marvin Tooley.

"Sorry." Garrett rubbed his hand along Jester's neck. He'd been out riding, checking the fence line, and was surprised to see Aundy on Bell. He knew Dent was teaching her to ride, but didn't realize she'd taken to it so quickly. Then again, the widow from Chicago seemed to be a farmer at heart. He observed that she'd rapidly picked up whatever knowledge anyone shared with her concerning ranching and farming.

When he saw the smile on her sweet lips break into a laugh, the sound penetrated his heart so deeply, he felt the need to rub his hand across his chest to release the ache. "Something must have made you laugh."

"It did." She turned Bell around so she headed the same direction as Garrett. They rode together on either side of the fence. "I'm not particularly fond of the chickens and one little rooster has declared me a sworn enemy. What made me laugh was picturing my sister gathering the eggs."

"She doesn't like chickens?"

Aundy grinned. "She's never seen a chicken. At least before it was ready to be fried or baked." The man who married Ilsa would have to be wealthy enough to hire a cook. While her sister received the same training from their mother that Aundy did, she abhorred cooking, especially anything that had once been alive. The girl much preferred to sew than anything else. With her dislike of noise, dust and smells, life on the farm was going to be an even bigger adjustment for Ilsa than it was for Aundy. "Ilsa is not fond of the outdoors."

"Really? I assumed sisters would be alike. Is she tall like you?" Garrett pictured a younger version of Aundy - a tall girl with freckles on her nose and blonde hair in braids.

Aundy laughed again. "Goodness, no. My sister looks like a girl should. Petite, ladylike, delicate. She's perfect."

"She can't be perfect," Garrett teased. "You just said she isn't like you."

His words made her cheeks throb with heat and flush a becoming shade of pink.

"What people view as perfect back in the big city might not be as perfect out here in the country. A woman not afraid to learn something new, to get her hands dirty, to do what needs done without complaint, I'd call that close to perfect." Garrett cast an approving glance toward his spirited neighbor.

She never complained about anything and made great strides the last few weeks learning about farming. His dad thought she was smart and clever. He tried to block what else his father said from his mind because the comments about "hanging on to a gal like that" echoed his own sentiments on the subject.

There was very little about Aundy he didn't admire. Except maybe the way she could clamp her lips together, lift her chin, and be so stubborn even he backed down. Just like she forced him to do when she told him to quit sending over his hands. He knew Dent and the men were struggling, but he wouldn't go behind her back and send some of his men over after she'd asked him to refrain. It was hard not to get involved, but he was trying to mind his own business.

Determined to see her home, Garrett stopped Jester and opened a gate in the fence, leading the horse through before closing the gate.

"I'll ride home with you," Garrett said, trying to think of some excuse to escort her home. "I've been meaning to ask Dent something, so if you don't mind, I'll do it now before I forget."

Pleased to ride alongside Garrett, Aundy nodded her head as they continued toward the house.

"I'm ready to sell the cattle," Aundy blurted, taking him by surprise.

Unsure he heard her correctly, he turned his gaze from the path ahead to look at her. "Are you certain?"

"Yes." Aundy released a soft sigh Garrett would have missed if he hadn't been watching her face so attentively. "Dent and I discussed it earlier this afternoon and we agree it's what needs to happen if we're going to keep the farm. Apparently, working for a woman is something akin to selling your soul to Beelzebub, so we're just going to have to figure out how to run this place with a smaller crew."

Garrett couldn't help the chuckle that escaped at her comment, causing her to glance at him with a raised brow, although she smiled.

"I'd sign on to work for you without thinking twice."

"Thank you, Garrett. I appreciate that." From their vantage point on top of the hill behind the barn, Aundy looked over the farm with pride. She loved this land with a possessive fierceness she'd never imagined she could feel. "However, since you're in charge of Nash's Folly and a very busy man, I'll have to make the best of things. I do have a favor to ask, though."

"Anything," he said, meaning it. He'd do anything for the woman riding beside him. Although he'd known her for only a short while, he felt like she'd been part of his life for a long time, like a cherished friend.

"Would you contact the man you said might be interested in buying the herd? It would make me feel better to keep them together. I know it's silly, but... I..."

"I'll get in touch with him as soon as possible." Garrett reached out a hand and placed it on Aundy's arm. She could feel the heat of his fingers searing her skin even through his glove and her sleeve. "And it isn't silly. I'm certain he'll want them all. If not, I'll see if I can find another buyer."

"I appreciate your help with the matter. Perhaps you or your father could advise me as to a fair asking price." She had no idea what three hundred head of cattle would be worth, along with their newborn calves.

Garrett stated a number that made Aundy shoot him a wide-eyed look, indicating her shock at the amount.

"I think I mentioned cattle are bringing a good price right now in the local market, so it really is a good time to take advantage of it. Don't worry about the negotiations. I'd be happy to make the arrangements."

"Would the buyer object to working with a woman?" She had to jump in and learn at some point. Aundy couldn't always depend on the Nash family, particularly Garrett, to come to her rescue.

"I don't know, but I guess we'll find out, won't we?" Garrett grinned at her.

"I guess we will."

"Thank you, Mrs. Erickson. We'll be out tomorrow to move the cattle," Hiram Anderson said as he shook Aundy's hand and walked out of the bank.

After Garrett contacted Hiram about buying Aundy's cattle, the man agreed to meet with her over lunch to discuss the purchase.

Although he trusted Hiram, Garrett still felt the need to escort her to not only make the introductions, but also ensure the deal was fair.

As he introduced Hiram to his neighbor, he watched the man size her up and could see she earned his approval. When he stuck out a beefy hand to her in greeting, Garrett was pleased Hiram conducted business with Aundy as he would have any man, minus the usual questionable language and a trip to the saloon to seal the deal.

Aundy seemed to like Hiram as well, offering him a genuine smile and speaking to him confidently. When they agreed upon a price and terms, Garrett suggested they run by the attorney's office to have paperwork completed then to the bank where Hiram left payment for the herd he planned to take into his possession the following day.

Garrett watched Hiram shake Aundy's hand a second time as warmth invaded his heart. He was proud of the woman who had come so far from the mud-covered girl standing on his mother's front porch.

"I'll look forward to seeing you at the farm tomorrow, Mr. Anderson. Thank you, again." Aundy turned and caught Garrett staring at her. She put a hand up to her hat but it felt like it was on straight, so she glanced at her shirtwaist and didn't see anything amiss. Nervously smoothing her skirt and tugging on the hem of her jacket, she shifted her gaze down the street and began walking in the direction of the doctor's office.

"Before we leave town, do you mind if we stop by Doc's office?" Aundy asked as Garrett fell into step beside her. He tried to ignore the admiring glances men shot Aundy's direction. If he paid too close attention to them, he might give in to the temptation to punch someone in the nose.

Garrett was the last person who would lose his temper or pick a fight, but something about Aundy made him feel protective and slightly unreasonable. "That's fine. Are you not feeling well?" Visually checking her over from head to toe, he didn't see anything amiss. Pink roses blossomed on each cheek and she looked like a picture of health with her freckled nose, bright eyes, and rosy lips tipped up in a grin.

"I'm fine." The look in her eye, along with an impish smile said she kept secrets. "I just want to ask Doc a question."

"I see," Garrett said, although he didn't. He had no idea what kind of question Aundy would ask the doctor. Worry niggled in the back of his mind. He'd never been a worrier before meeting the intriguing woman, either.

About as easy-going and laid-back as they came, Garrett didn't like the feeling of unease that settled over him as he thought about all the possible reasons why Aundy would need to see the doctor.

"I'll just be a moment." Aundy stepped inside the doctor's office. Garrett followed on her heels, taking a seat in the waiting room while Aundy spoke with a woman seated at a desk, trying to maintain order in the doctor's chaotic office.

The woman smiled and nodded her head at Aundy's inquiry, then motioned for her to take a seat. She sat down beside Garrett and he fought the urge to take her hand in his. Instead, he leaned forward with his elbows on his knees and jiggled one foot impatiently, one more thing he'd never done until he met Aundy.

"If you'd rather wait outside or have any errands you'd like to run, I can meet you back at the buggy." Aundy tried to hide her amusement at Garrett's restlessness, but couldn't help the grin that tipped the corners of her mouth upward.

"I'm fine right here."

"Of course you are. How silly of me." The hint of sarcasm in her tone made Garrett stop jiggling his foot and sit back in the chair. Aundy asked him questions about his herd of cattle, if he was through with spring planting, and if he thought he would have time to give her another shooting lesson the following week.

"You can practice without me there," Garrett said, encouraging Aundy to use the guns that had been Erik's and were now hers. "You're good enough you don't need anyone watching over you."

"Thank you." A pleased smile blossomed on her face at his words of praise. "I wanted..."

Interrupted by the doctor's assistant, the woman escorted Aundy to an examination room where the doctor greeted her.

"Aundy, what a pleasure to see you." Doc smiled as he motioned for her to sit on the examination table. "You look too healthy to be ailing with anything, so I guess you'd probably like to see about getting that cast off your arm. Has it been six weeks already?"

"Yes, sir." Aundy removed her jacket and held out her arm while the doctor pushed up her sleeve. "Six weeks and five days, to be exact."

"In that case, let's see if we can take this off today," Doc said, examining Aundy's arm. He stepped out of the room, returning with his assistant. In no time at all, Aundy's arm was free of the cast. The skin looked a little pale and shriveled, but other than that, it felt wonderful to have the cast off.

The doctor made her move her arm in a range of motions then gave her a list of exercises to build back the strength.

"I know this is going to be challenging for you, but you really do need to gradually put your arm back into use and not over do it. If you do, you'll be sorry down the road. If you follow my orders, you'll be back to one hundred percent in no time at all," Doc instructed as Aundy fastened the buttons on her sleeve and slipped on her jacket.

"Thank you so much, Doc. I promise to behave." Aundy grinned at the man, then hurried back to the waiting area and paid for her visit. Garrett got to his feet, still wondering what ailed Aundy.

"Are you okay?" he asked as they walked down the boardwalk in the direction of the buggy.

"Better than okay. Great, actually." Aundy felt so much lighter with the cast gone. She swung her arm as they walked and Garrett suddenly grabbed her other arm, pulling them to a stop beside his buggy.

"I completely forgot about your cast. Did Doc take it off?" Garrett placed his hand on Aundy's arm through her jacket, unconcerned if it was appropriate or not. Warmth seeped into his palm from the light touch and he grinned. "Why didn't you tell me you were getting the cast off?"

"I wasn't sure Doc would take it off and besides, I thoroughly enjoyed your inability to figure out why I wanted to visit Doc. Honestly, Garrett, what did you think was wrong with me? I'm as fit as a fiddle, with a stubborn streak a mile-wide. You won't find a woman in much better health than me." Aundy smiled tauntingly at Garrett as he helped her into the buggy.

"How did you...? Never mind." Garrett felt silly and a little stupid.

He agreed with Aundy, though. He'd be hard-pressed to find a female more robust and vibrant than the one sitting beside him.

Chapter Eight

"There they go," Dent said, watching as Hiram Anderson and his men drove the cattle up the road. Once they hit open range to the north, they'd drive the cattle west to Hiram's ranch. Dent sent their hands along to help until they got past the neighboring farms.

"Indeed." Aundy sat on Bell as she watched the mass of cattle plod along, churning the road to dust.

"Are you doing okay, Missy?" Dent looked at Aundy in concern. He knew how hard it was for her to make the decision to sell the cattle.

"I'm fine, Dent. I just feel like I've somehow let Erik down." Her normally straight spine bent forward and her shoulders drooped.

"Erik would be proud that you made a good decision and are doing what you can to keep the farm going. Don't worry about the cattle. Maybe we'll have another herd on the place someday." Dent turned his horse toward the house.

Aundy followed behind, glad a broken piece of equipment that required immediate repairs kept Garrett away. She didn't want him to see her fight back the tears that threatened to spill over or the defeat that weighed heavy on her shoulders.

She wished she could think of some way to generate more income without increasing the workload. Her crew was stretched way too thin as it was. The payment from the cattle was a boon, but Aundy felt driven to make the farm prosperous, like it would have been under Erik's direction.

Keeping her thoughts to herself, she unsaddled Bell and brushed her down at the barn before returning to the house. In need of a distraction, she made a batch of butter cookies then decided to prepare a dinner for her men. She pulled a pan of rolls out of the oven when the hands rode up to the barn.

Aundy rushed out the kitchen door and down the steps, waving a dishtowel at them to get their attention. She needed to have someone make her a triangle like Nora had at her house. It would sure come in handy.

"Something wrong, Mrs. Erickson?" The hand who did most of the cooking at the bunkhouse hurried her direction when he saw her approach.

"No, George. I just wanted to invite you boys for supper. You've had a long day and I thought you might like a hot meal."

"That's right nice of you, Mrs. Erickson. We'll wash up and be in directly." George looked toward the other hands, busy storing their tack and brushing down their horses.

"Wonderful." Aundy hurried back to the house and set the big kitchen table. She didn't think the men would appreciate eating in the dining room surrounded by gleaming china and starched linen.

A knock sounded on the kitchen door and Dent stuck his head inside as she placed a bowl of mashed potatoes on the table. "Please, come in."

"You sure you want all of us in here?" Dent stepped inside followed by the other four hands. George, Bill, Glen, and Fred all had freshly scrubbed hands and faces. George and Glen had gone to the effort of changing their shirts and combing their hair.

"Please, have a seat. Feeding you dinner is the least I can do after all your hard work rounding up the cattle today," Aundy said, taking a seat at the table so the men would stop feeling the need to be formal and stand. They all sat and Aundy looked at Dent, asking him to say grace. Although the words he said were brief, they were heartfelt.

The men dug into the food with enthusiasm, offering praise for Aundy's cooking. When she brought out a chocolate cake for dessert, more than one of them appeared excited at the prospect of enjoying a slice.

"You didn't make that just for us, did you?" Fred asked, trying not to appear overly enthusiastic for a piece of cake.

"I did." Aundy smiled as she cut generous slices and placed them on plates along with a dollop of freshly whipped cream.

Thanks to the milk cows, she never lacked for fresh milk, cream, or butter. Although the men brought her a pail of milk every morning, not one of them said a word about her learning to milk the cows. As soon as she regained the strength in her arm, she knew the chore was one she should eventually take over.

Dent kept a few cows for milking and beef. He mentioned they'd need to get a new bull or borrow one from a neighbor.

Garrett would give her good advice on whether to buy or borrow one. Since she depended more and more on his input, Aundy needed to stop leaning on him and stand on her own two feet.

"Mrs. Erickson, I think this is the best thing I've ever tasted," Glen said, closing his eyes as he savored the last bite.

"Would you like more? There's plenty."

"Yes, ma'am!" Five eager faces looked at her, waiting for a second piece.

When they finished their cake and sat drinking cups of hot coffee, Aundy asked them for ideas on bringing in more income. They discussed several options, including everything from planting experimental crops to renting out one or two sections of land.

"Maybe we could get us a herd of sheep," Bill said, grinning at Fred before glancing at Aundy. "They don't take much care and some people are making a small fortune from the wool."

"There ain't no way on God's green earth I'm gonna wrangle woolies for a living," Fred said, shooting Bill a dark glare.

Bill gave Fred a good-natured shove. "I was only joshing ya. We all know how much you hate sheep."

"They stink, they're stupid, and I can't abide them," Fred said hotly as he finished his coffee. Aundy refilled his cup then returned to her seat.

"Are they really easy to care for?" Aundy asked, curious. She hadn't seen any sheep on nearby farms and tried to remember what she read about them in the books J.B. had given her.

"All you need to raise sheep is pasture, a good dog, and a shepherd. From what I've seen, you can run five to eight head of sheep on what it takes to feed one cow. You don't have to ride herd over them like you do cattle. Just turn 'em loose and let 'em grow," Bill said, ignoring the venomous looks Fred directed his way.

"Do they really stink?" Aundy asked, turning her attention to Fred.

He nodded his head. "To high heaven and back again."

After a few more teasing comments, the men drained their coffee cups, thanked Aundy again for the meal, and sauntered out the door.

When she finished washing the dishes, Aundy sauntered to the front room and flipped through the books she borrowed from J.B. One of them had to contain information about sheep.

Aundy stood with Nora after the Sunday church service listening to a group of women talk about getting together for a quilting bee. She absently agreed when one of the women asked if she would join them.

Her attention centered on the discussion of a group of men off to her left. Frustrated she couldn't march right up to them and be a part of it, the words sheep and wool pricked her ears. Aundy tried to listen to the conversation over the chatter of the women.

Inconspicuously taking a few steps their direction, she finally heard enough to figure out the men talked about the price of wool and who raised the best sheep in the area. She caught a few details and wished she had something to write on, desperately wanting to take notes. For just a moment, she considered the simplicity of being a man.

An idea she thought would bring in a good profit for the farm with a minimal amount of additional work was simmering in her head, but finding someone who would do business with a woman was proving difficult. It would have been a simple thing to ask Garrett to help her, but she wanted to do this on her own, without his help or that of J.B.

After asking at the general store, the post office, the newspaper office, and a few other businesses around town, she was told repeatedly to go back to taking care of her house and leave the discussion of farming to men.

"Eavesdropping?" a deep, familiar voice asked, stirring the hair by her ear. She turned her head and looked into the broad smile and silvery eyes of Garrett. "What are you doing?"

"Trying to listen, but the chatter of the magpies is drowning out the conversation." Aundy tipped her head toward the group of elderly women gathered around Nora.

Garrett threw back his head and laughed, causing more than a few glances their direction. He ignored his mother's scowl as he ushered Aundy out to the surrey where J.B. waited.

"You want to come over for more lessons this week?" J.B. asked as Garrett helped her into the back of the surrey.

"If you have time, I'd like that very much. I have some questions I wanted to ask you," Aundy said, adjusting her skirts as she settled back against the plush seat. Nora had taken Aundy to town several times in a small buggy, but on Sunday, the family drove the canopy-topped surrey to church.

Garrett ignored her protests she could get herself to town. He always made sure he had plenty of time to pick her up and stop back by Nash's Folly for his folks. Dent and two of her four hands often rode their horses into church. She knew if she asked, Dent would hitch up the buggy or wagon for her and take her himself.

"Why don't you come over tomorrow morning once you get done scaring your chickens," J.B. looked over his shoulder at Aundy. She suddenly realized where Garrett got his teasing grin. It came straight from his father.

"You boys be nice to our girl," Nora warned, stepping up to the surrey just in time to hear J.B.'s teasing remark that made Aundy's cheeks turn bright red.

"Yes, ma'am," J.B. and Garrett said in unison. Garrett shot Aundy a wink before he picked up the reins and guided the horse out of town.

Later that week, Aundy saddled Bell and rode her to Nash's Folly, taking along a basket of fresh cinnamon muffins she'd made. Nora would no doubt have already served breakfast, but the men often liked a mid-morning snack.

After leaving Bell at the barn, she walked to the kitchen door and knocked. The clomp of boots let her know Garrett remained in the house. He pulled the door open and gave her a smile that weakened her knees.

"Good morning." Garrett welcomed her into the kitchen. "Pops will be right out. He was helping Ma get something off a shelf in their room. Who knows what she's got planned today."

Smiling, Aundy set the basket on the table and removed her hat and gloves, leaving them by the door.

"Do I smell cinnamon?" Garrett asked, pushing aside the napkin covering the basket. "Did you make these?"

"No, I plucked them from the muffin tree on my way here." Aundy kept a serious expression on her face as she spoke.

Garrett glanced at her in surprise then broke into a broad grin.

"Mrs. Erickson, I do believe you're sassy this morning." Garrett snatched a warm muffin from the basket and bit into it. "This is really good. Maybe you can give Ma your recipe, or just make me some more. I'm quite partial to cinnamon treats."

"I'll keep that in mind." Aundy tucked away that bit of information for later use.

Nora breezed into the kitchen, followed by J.B., and gave Aundy a big hug. "What did you bring, honey?"

"Cinnamon muffins. Apparently they grow on trees over at the Erickson place," Garrett said, taking another one from the basket as he grabbed his hat and work gloves and went out the door with a teasing grin.

"I think that boy is working too hard. He's talking crazy." Nora made Aundy a cup of tea and poured a cup of coffee for J.B. "I'm going to work on cutting out some quilt pieces in the parlor, but if you need anything, just let me know."

"Thanks, Nora." Aundy sat down at the table with a notebook and pencil she'd brought along.

"What would you like to talk about today?" J.B. asked, leaning back in his chair and taking a drink of hot coffee.

"Animals." Aundy proceeded to ask J.B. about every type of farm animal she could think of, including sheep.

"What's the interest in animals?" J.B. helped himself to a muffin while Aundy poured him another cup of coffee. She spent so much time in the Nash's kitchen, she felt as at home there as she did anywhere.

"Just curious." She toyed with her teacup. "If you knew someone who wanted to find out more about a certain type of enterprise, where would you recommend they go to glean the information they would need to further pursue their interests?"

J.B. chuckled. "If it was a man, I'd tell him to go Underground on a Friday night. You can hear more gossip and truth in an hour there than you can anywhere else the rest of the week combined."

"The underground? Like in a hole?" Aundy asked.

"Land sakes, girl. You haven't heard about the Underground?"

When Aundy shook her head, J.B. leaned toward her conspiratorially. "Nora'd have my head if she knew I told you, but there are tunnels under part of the town connecting several businesses, a few of questionable nature. They started out as service tunnels to legitimate businesses then they added a card room and saloons, Chinese laundries, that sort of thing. A lot of men spend their free time down there and you can hear just about any news you want."

"Really?" Aundy was shocked by this revelation. "Where are the tunnels?"

"You ever notice the grates set in the boardwalks in town?" J.B. asked.

"Yes, I commented on them to Nora one day. All she said was to never stand on top of one and they were nothing I wanted to be concerned with."

J.B. laughed and shook his head. "That sounds about like my Nora. Any number of businesses near those grates has an entry to the tunnels."

"Oh, my." Aundy digested the tidbit of information.

"I hope you keep in mind that the tunnels aren't a fit place for a lady, especially a young lady who's already been getting more attention than she wants."

Aundy nodded in agreement. Since the weather warmed and the roads dried out, a steady stream of callers had arrived at her door, with both propositions and proposals. Young, old, poor, rich, handsome, and filthy - she'd seen just about every type of man come calling in an effort to gain access to Erik's farm.

Garrett had taken to coming around in the evenings, when the men seemed most inclined to call, after their daily work was finished. When he couldn't make it over, he somehow made sure Dent or one of the hands was conveniently working near the house to keep an eye on things.

Sincerely hoping the novelty of her being unwed and available would soon wear off, Aundy was thoroughly tired of the callers. She never thought she'd live to see the day she was popular with the male population, but then again, they weren't interested in her. All they could see were acres of farmland ready for the taking. Or so they thought.

The only visitor who arrived not spouting proposals was Ashton Monroe. Garrett and Dent didn't get worked up when he came to visit, although neither one of them seemed very fond of the man.

Ashton was funny, charming, and almost pretty in his features. He told entertaining stories, made Aundy feel smart and witty, and seemed to enjoy being friends.

Although Nora disliked him, Aundy couldn't help but enjoy his company. She hadn't seen him for a while and wondered if he was out of town again. She wasn't exactly sure what it was Ashton did for a living, since he was frequently gone on business trips, other than travel around and check on his investments.

"I better get home," Aundy said, gathering her things before slipping on her hat and gloves.

"Remember what I said," J.B. cautioned, helping himself to another muffin. "No ladies Underground, especially not on a busy Friday night."

"I remember." Aundy walked into the parlor where Nora sat in a side chair cutting fabric into quilt pieces.

"Leaving so soon, honey?" Nora set down down her scissors and rose to her feet to give Aundy a hug. Aundy would have thought it comical since she was so tall and Nora so petite, but she wouldn't trade the motherly hugs for anything.

"I need to get home. I have some things I should take care of today." Aundy brushed at her skirt. She loved to ride, but her clothes weren't designed for straddling a horse. She planned to make a few riding skirts, but hadn't found time to sew. She might stay up late and make one just to be able to ride more comfortably. With her sewing knowledge, she could make her own pattern, but it would save her time if Nora had one she could borrow. "You don't happen to have any patterns for riding skirts, do you?"

"I don't, but Erik's mother had several. She loved to ride Bell, you know. Didn't you say Erik never bothered to clean out their room? Her clothes might be a little short for you, but if they have a wide hem, you could let it out and they should work just fine."

"I'll have to see what I can find." Aundy needed to clean out the two empty bedrooms in the house, at least go through Mrs. Erickson's clothes. If Erik's mother had dresses more suited to a farm wife than the city clothes she'd been wearing, she would alter them as well. She had already ruined one of her favorite skirts working outside. The fine fabric wasn't made for farm work.

"Sure you don't want to stay for lunch?" Nora asked, walking Aundy to the door.

"Not today, but thanks for asking." Aundy kissed Nora's cheek then hurried down the steps and out to the barn. Bell greeted her with a happy whinny and they soon raced down the road toward home.

After brushing the horse and returning to the house, Aundy sat at the kitchen table reviewing her notes from J.B. and reading through a few pages of Erik's animal husbandry book.

With her mind made up of what she wanted to do, she decided to clean out the two vacant bedrooms after lunch.

She started with Mr. and Mrs. Erickson's room. Slowly opening the door, she studied the colorful quilt on the bed. After stripping off all the linens, she set them in a pile by the washing machine on the back porch to take care of later.

Upon returning to the room, she discovered Erik left everything as his parents had, since the drawers in the dresser were full of personal belongings. Aundy looked around the room at the items that once belonged to Mr. and Mrs. Erickson and felt like a trespasser or thief. She wanted to shut the drawers, slam the door, and not ever enter the room again.

Instead, her practical nature ruled over her emotions as she went to the storage shed where Dent kept things they might need and found several old fruit crates. She carried them to the back porch and wiped them down with a rag before taking them inside the house to the bedroom.

One drawer at a time, she sorted the Erickson's belongings into piles. Some things needed to be thrown away. Worn clothes would become rags. The packets of letters from Norway she would set aside to decide what to do with later. Books she placed on the bookshelf in the front room. Photographs went into the box with the letters.

A trunk in the closet revealed three heavy sweaters in Nordic patterns, a beautiful white shawl made of the finest wool, extra linens and another colorful quilt, along with pieces of Rosemaling painted china.

The detailed work and warm colors on the china drew her interest. Aundy decided the dishes should be displayed in the dining room instead of hidden away in the closet. After finding places for the pieces in the china cupboard, she finished digging in the trunk and discovered a few more books printed in Norwegian. She added those to the bookshelf in the front room.

A smaller trunk on a shelf featured a vibrant Rosemaling design of blue with green and gold accents. Aundy loved it and decided she'd like to have it in her room. The lid creaked when she opened it and a hint of lavender tickled her nose. She removed what must have been Mrs. Erickson's wedding gown. Gently shaking out the folds, Aundy appreciated the skillful stitching and care that had gone into the garment. Carefully folding it, she set it in the trunk with the sweaters, linens and quilt, keeping out the white shawl to wear.

She took the small trunk to her room and set it on a chest of drawers. The trunk matched the blue and yellow colors in the quilt on her bed to perfection.

Again returning to the other bedroom, she sorted through Mrs. Erickson's clothing, finding several calico dresses that would be much better suited to wearing on the farm than her current wardrobe. Although somewhat dated and out of style, Aundy didn't think the chickens or the vegetable garden would care.

She found three riding skirts in good condition and tried them on, glancing in the mirror. The reflection showed the skirts were short, but otherwise fit her well.

Relieved to discover wide hems, she could lengthen the skirts enough to wear without causing any scandal over a short hemline.

More digging resulted in the discovery of a pair of cowboy boots and two pairs of shoes. Thrilled with her find, she removed her shoes and tried on Mrs. Erickson's. The shoes fit her well, if not somewhat loose. A little padding in the toe would fix the problem.

Aundy fingered the soft leather of the boots, observing the scuffed toes and worn-down heels. Unlike any boots she'd seen a woman wear, they must have been made for Erik's mother. They definitely looked like men's western boots, only smaller. She tried them and wiggled her toes, concluding a pair of thicker socks would remedy the problem of the boots being slightly too big.

An idea began to blossom in her head when she stood and clomped around the room. As the blossom reached full bloom, Aundy upended the box of men's clothes she'd just carefully packed onto the bed and searched through the items. Swiftly pulling out pants, a shirt, vest and tie, she reached into the closet to grab a coat. She tried on the clothes and decided to put her plan into action that very night.

Giddy with excitement, she dug around on the closet shelf, finding a broad-brimmed hat. She set it on her head and stared into the dresser mirror. Pleased at her appearance, she adjusted the strap beneath her chin to hold the hat in place and pulled down the brim until it shadowed her eyes. With some soot on her cheeks and jaw to look like a man's stubbly whiskers, she might just get away with her little deception.

Changing back to her clothes, she took the men's clothes to her room. She finished packing up the bedroom, leaving the boxes stacked by the door then went to Erik's room, looking for some cologne or aftershave. She sniffed a bottle of Bay Rum then took it to the bathroom and left it sitting on a shelf by the mirror.

When Dent stopped by after supper to see if she needed anything, it was difficult for her not to share her plans. Instead, she told him she was fine, but thought she might like to go for a ride before it got dark. Dent said he'd have someone saddle Bell and leave her tied to the fence out front.

"Thanks so much, Dent," Aundy said, giving him a handful of the butter cookies he seemed to enjoy as he made his way out the door.

When he'd disappeared from sight, she opened the stove door and gathered a cup of ashes, carrying it to the bathroom. After washing her hands, she returned to her room where her disguise, as she had decided to call it, awaited.

Although she recalled what J.B. said about the Underground not being a place for a lady, Aundy also remembered what he said about it being the best place to gather information.

And information is what she wanted.

No one took her seriously as a woman, so if she had to pretend to be a man to accomplish what she wanted to do, then so be it.

Tightly wrapping her chest, so it looked as flat as possible, Aundy pulled on a thick, coarse man's undershirt. Over her bloomers, she tugged on a pair of pants that belonged to Erik's father. Erik must have gotten his height from his mother's side of the family, because his father's pants were just a little too short for Aundy.

A thick pair of socks went on her feet, followed by the boots. She tugged the pant legs down over the tops of the boots.

Slipping her arms in a cotton work shirt, she buttoned it then stuffed the hem into the waistband of the pants. The blue and white striped shirt reminded her of hundreds just like it she'd sewn at the factory. When she fastened the suspenders, she gave them a playful snap, grinning to herself as she settled them in place. After putting on a dark blue vest, she buttoned it then glanced in the mirror.

The transformation took shape, but she'd have to do something about her hair. Hastily unpinning it, she combed it back from her forehead and wove it into a tight braid. She caught the end and stuffed it back up under itself then pinned it into place.

She tied a black cloth over her head, secured the ends in back, and tucked them into the neck of the shirt. No one would notice it once she had the hat in place.

Aundy stepped into the bathroom, looked in the small mirror above the sink, and carefully rubbed ashes into the skin along her jaw and chin, turning it a shade of gray. From a distance, in muted light, it might pass for a day's growth of beard.

A little flour made her rosy lips look pale and dry. She reminded herself not to lick them.

Back in her room, she put money into her vest pocket and a piece of paper with a pencil stub in her coat pocket. After shrugging into the coat, she pulled the hat down on her head and stood in front of the mirror, eyeing herself critically.

With her tall height and build, she might just get away with pretending to be a man. Aundy practiced a swaggering walk a few times, giggling before she calmed down and took a deep breath.

She could do this and she would.

At the front door, she stopped and turned back to unlock the desk drawer where she kept Erik's revolver. She removed it from the drawer, retrieved the holster and gun belt from his room, and fastened it around her hips like she'd seen men wear them.

The first steps she took felt lopsided until she adjusted her gait to the extra weight on her hip. As she walked a few circles around the front room, she remembered the Bay Rum in the bathroom. She splashed a little of the scent onto her hands, rubbed it on her neck, and wiped her still damp fingers down the front of her coat and pants.

A quick detour to the kitchen unearthed a pair of worn gloves she'd used outside. She jammed her hands inside and decided she had to leave before she came to her senses and changed her mind.

Aundy felt wondrously free and unhampered without her petticoats and skirts as she ran out the front door and down the porch steps. Able to mount Bell with ease, she could quickly become accustomed to wearing pants.

Before someone caught sight of her, she urged Bell into a fast canter down the lane and headed toward town.

Uncertain which saloon would grant the fastest access to the Underground, she decided on one she'd heard the hands talk about when they thought she wasn't listening.

Quickly tying Bell to a hitching post around the corner, she swaggered down the boardwalk and through the swinging doors of a busy saloon. The stench of booze and cigar smoke made her want to cough while she fought to keep her eyes from watering. Discreetly pulling the brim of her hat down and turning up the collar of her coat, she walked up to the bar and leaned one elbow on it.

"Help you, mister?" The middle-aged man who stared at her from behind the bar seemed rather bookish for a bartender.

"Maybe," Aundy spoke in a voice as deep and raspy as she could make it. "Have some business to do in the Underground."

"Is that so?" The bartender continued to polish a glass, appearing disinterested.

Aundy nodded her head.

"What makes you think we know anything about the Underground?" The bartender set the shiny glass on the counter and picked up another to polish.

"Heard you were the best place in town. Figured you'd have other enterprises, beyond the saloon." Aundy kept her head down, pretending to study the worn finger of her glove.

The bartender laughed. "Right you are. Go through that door and down the hall. Last door on the left will take you where you want to go."

"Much obliged." Aundy took a coin from her vest pocket and placed it on the bar.

The bartender grinned and tipped his head toward a door off to his right.

Aundy went through the doorway he indicated and found herself in a hall, flanked by doors on either side. The muffled sounds she could hear made her want to cover her ears, so she hurried to the end of the hall, turning the knob on the door to her left. It opened to reveal a dark staircase.

Cautiously easing her way down the stairs, Aundy came to another door and opened it into a narrow corridor. As she followed it, strange scents assaulted her nose and the rumble of a crowd floated around her. At the end of the hallway, she straightened her vest, tightened the string under her chin holding the hat firmly in place, and opened the door.

Aundy stepped into what appeared to be a small underground city. From her position, she could see a saloon, a sign for a bathhouse, and a Chinese laundry. Stunned to see so many people wandering around below the city, she ambled along, joining the crowd. Businessmen and even a few men from church were among the faces she passed.

Mindful of blending in, she listened to several conversations, but didn't pick up any good leads that would help satisfy her mission.

Covertly following a group of men into a saloon, she found an empty spot at the end of a long bar and ordered a sarsaparilla. The bartender gave her an odd look, but didn't ask any questions when she handed him a coin and nodded her head in thanks. She didn't intend to drink anything, but people would pay less attention to her if she looked like she was nursing a drink.

Without raising her head, she cast a glance around the room and took in a group of men sitting at a nearby table. Dusty and a little disheveled, they seemed to be having a good time. Leisurely turning their direction, she listened to their conversation as they played cards. Caught up in the tales of ranching and life on the trail, she didn't notice a saloon girl sidle up next to her until someone squeezed her arm.

"Hey, sugar, ain't seen you round here afore," the girl said, leaning to press herself against Aundy's side. "You're a little shy, aren't you?"

Aundy thought she might die of embarrassment. She raised her head just enough to take in the girl's face and was surprised to see someone extremely young. If she scrubbed off the makeup and dressed in respectable clothes, the girl would probably be quite pretty. Although she guessed her to be around sixteen, the girl's eyes held a haunted look - the gaze of one who had lost all innocence.

Tawdry and gauche, the girl seemed excessively friendly for Aundy's liking.

"Not interested." Aundy stared down at her feet. "Please move along, miss."

"Everyone's interested, at least all men are." The girl took a step back and studied Aundy speculatively. The way she grinned, Aundy wondered if she'd figured out she wasn't a man.

"My name's Marnie. And you are?"

"Looking for information," Aundy said quietly, working to keep her voice low and rough.

"What kind of information?" Marnie leaned against the bar and twirled a gaudy fan by a silk cord wrapped around her wrist.

"Buying sheep." Nervous, she barely remembered not to lick her lips or press them together.

"Sheep, is it? Well, you probably ought to talk to Mr. O'Connell over there in the corner. He has a bunch he's been trying to sell so he can move on to greener pastures. Says he wants to head to California where they don't get snow and cold winters like we have here." Marnie pointed to a man sitting at a table in the corner by himself. "He's a nice man, even when he's drunk, and always gentle around women, at least to those who dress the part."

Astounded by Marnie's comment, Aundy tried not to let it show on her face. She tipped her head to Marnie and touched the brim of her hat in thanks, like she'd watched men do all her life, then walked across the room.

"Mr. O'Connell?" she asked, standing beside his table. He looked up at her with a glazed expression. Aundy noticed an empty whiskey bottle on the table. Repressing the sigh that inched up from her chest, she sat down when he motioned to a chair across from him.

"Heard you have sheep for sale. I might know someone who'd be interested in buying."

"Oh, might ya now?" Mr. O'Connell said with an Irish lilt that made his words seem musical. "Faith, I've been a' tryin' to get rid of me woolies for months long past and had no takers. I was sittin' here tonight, ready to drown me sorrows and there ya' be. Giving me hope, at last."

Aundy asked questions about the type of sheep, the size of the herd, how much he wanted for the animals, and if he was willing to deliver them to her farm. When she was satisfied with the information, she took out her pencil and piece of paper and wrote down her name, instructing Mr. O'Connell to give Mrs. Erickson a call Monday morning or to stop by her farm to discuss the details. In turn, Aundy wrote down his last name and the approximate location of his farm, in case the half-drunk man lost the piece of paper before he got in touch with her.

"Thank you for your time." Aundy stood up from the table, more than ready to make an escape.

"Ya' can't up and leave yet. A drink must be shared at the prospect of selling me flock of sheep." Mr. O'Connell held up his empty shot glass. "Marnie, me love, bring another bottle."

Aware the situation could go quite badly from there, Aundy knew a man would stay and take a drink to seal the deal.

Marnie brought over a bottle and another glass, setting it in front of Aundy. With a flirty wink, Marnie poured whiskey into each glass, then stood back, eyeing Aundy. Certain the girl saw through her disguise, Aundy hoped she wouldn't give her away.

"To a future without woolies," Mr. O'Connell toasted, holding up his glass before downing the contents in one quick swallow.

"To the future," Aundy said, holding her glass and pretending to take a drink. There was no way that devil's poison, as she'd heard her mother call it, was touching her lips let alone sliding down her throat. She could almost feel the fire burning in her stomach from the smell alone.

"Ya hardly took a sip," Mr. O'Connell pointed out.

"Trying to cut back." Aundy reached out her gloved hand to the man across the table and gave him a firm handshake. "Thank you."

"You're most welcome, boyo. Thank you for giving me Mrs. Erickson's name."

In what she hoped was a masculine gesture, Aundy tipped her head, turned to leave, and ran right into Ashton Monroe.

"Watch where you're going," Ashton grumbled giving Aundy a hard shove that sent her stumbling into an empty table. She kept herself from falling by sheer determination and mumbled an apology without lifting her gaze.

Shocked to see Ashton, Aundy wasn't sure what to make of his grumpy, rumpled presence. Always dressed immaculately with impeccable manners, he appeared quite disheveled. His suit was wrinkled and flecked with dark stains. He wore no hat, and it looked as though he'd run his hands through his hair numerous times since it stood on end.

She started to walk past him, but he grabbed her shoulder and held on.

"If you'd learn to walk with your head up instead of shuffling along looking at your feet, you might not go around bumping into people." Viciously, Ashton squeezed her shoulder before turning her loose.

Anger boiled inside her. Aundy wanted, more than anything, to kick Ashton in the shin and slap his pretty face. What a pompous brute! Instead, she kept her head down, holding on to her temper with both hands.

"Yes, sir," she said quietly, once again attempting to leave.

"Say, haven't I seen you around somewhere?" Ashton reached out to grab the hat from her head. Aundy ducked out of reach at the same moment Marnie latched onto Ashton's arm, pulling his attention her direction.

"Ashton, honey, you come on over here and tell me where you've been the last week. I haven't seen you for days and days, and it looks like you rode into town on a twister." Marnie sent Aundy another wink as Ashton followed her to the bar.

Hastily mouthing "thank you" to the girl, Aundy hurried into the throng of people milling about and tried to figure out a way back up to street level. Since she probably wasn't going to be able to leave the same way she came in, she followed a couple of men who appeared to be going somewhere.

When they turned and entered an establishment Aundy refused to acknowledge even existed, she kept walking. The din of the crowd faded behind her. She followed a tunnel around a corner and was thrilled to notice a doorway up ahead.

Cautiously turning the knob, she let out the breath she'd held. Her eyes adjusted to the dim light and she saw a staircase. On her race upward, she tripped over something on the top step and crashed into a solid door.

"Gracious," she whispered, convinced she'd have a bruise on her shoulder. If Ashton's vice-like grip hadn't done it, her fall into the door would.

When she glanced down at the object she tripped over, her jaw dropped to discover it was a man. Unable to see more than an outline of shape in the darkness, she prayed the door would open outside somewhere and gave the knob a twist.

Fresh air blew across her face. She looked around, realizing the door opened into a narrow alley.

The man at her feet moaned and Aundy bent over, trying to decide if he was drunk or injured. Light spilling from the upstairs windows coupled with the last of fading daylight provided enough illumination for her to see the man was Chinese and his face was covered in blood.

"Mister, can you hear me?" Aundy knelt by him. Incapable of going off and leaving someone hurting, she felt compelled to offer her assistance.

A moan answered her question.

"We need to get you out of this place," Aundy said, not bothering to disguise her voice. She placed her hands beneath the man's shoulders and lifted, hoping he'd be able to get to his feet. He opened the one eye that wasn't swollen shut and looked at her in surprise. She could tell he was in pain, but he managed to stand. He let her help him as she shut the door and quietly tread down the alley.

"Is there somewhere I can take you?" Aundy asked, wondering where the man lived.

He shook his head, and then gasped in pain, leaning more heavily on her. Several inches taller than he was, she easily bore his weight as she kept an arm around him.

"Then I guess you're going to have to let me take you to Doc's place or go home with me."

"You," the man whispered.

"You're going to have to ride my horse with me, then." The alley opened onto a street she thought she recognized. Walking as fast as she dared, Aundy kept hidden in the shadows. She turned another corner and breathed a sigh of relief. Bell stood tied to the hitching post down the street.

"Almost there."

When they reached the horse, Aundy glanced around while Bell rubbed her head on her arm. She studied the man at her side, trying to decide how she would get him to her home not to mention what she'd do with him once she got him there.

"You have to help me, mister. I can't get you up on Bell without you putting in a little effort." Aundy bent down and made a step by intertwining her fingers. The man swayed and began to fall to the ground, but strong arms caught him, keeping him upright.

"Thunderation, Aundy! That better not be you."

Chapter Nine

"What in blazes are you doing, woman?" Garrett fumed, clearly angry although his voice was barely more than a whisper.

Swallowing hard, Aundy found it impossible to make her brain and mouth function simultaneously.

Garrett glared at her, irritation oozing from him in booming waves that threatened to overtake her.

"Dressed like a man, dragging around half-dead Chinese immigrants. Are you wearing a gun? What in the h…" Garrett snapped his mouth shut before he said something he'd regret and expelled a sigh. "What exactly is going through that head of yours?" Garrett demanded. He carried the Chinese man to his wagon parked across the street then gently placed him on a pile of sacks filled with feed.

Aundy followed him, grateful the injured man still breathed. "He indicated he didn't want to go to Doc's. I was going to take him home and see if I could help him."

"Just like that, you'd open your home to any stranger? You don't know a thing about him. For all you know, he could be a thief or a murderer. Ever consider that maybe he did something to get beat up like this?" Garrett's anger caused his shoulders to bunch and his jaw to clench.

"I…" Garrett held up his hand, cutting off whatever excuse Aundy planned to offer.

"Don't, Aundy. Just don't. You get on that horse and go home and we'll talk about why you're dressed like that later. I'll see if Ma can help your friend here. If he isn't better in the morning, I'll send for Doc." Garrett walked around the wagon and climbed onto the seat. He watched as Aundy mounted and started down the street before guiding the wagon behind her.

After driving into town for a load of supplies at the feed store earlier in the afternoon, he ran into his friend, Kade Rawlings, one of the sheriff's deputies. They enjoyed dinner at their favorite restaurant, taking time to catch up on news.

Garrett started home when he noticed Bell tied to a hitching post around the corner from a saloon. Genuinely hoping he was mistaken, he parked the wagon and walked over to the horse, confirming it was, in fact, Bell.

Since the only person the persnickety horse would let ride her was Aundy, he began searching for his neighbor. Curious as to what brought her to town on a Friday night, he was surprised she rode the horse instead of using the buggy.

Garrett went into every respectable business that was still open then ventured to the saloon, wondering where Aundy could have disappeared.

Relieved he didn't find her in the drinking establishment, he went back outside and made another trip on foot through downtown, trying to think of anywhere she might be. Concerned, he hoped she was at the church. He started back to the wagon to head that direction when he noticed a cowhand help a drunken Chinese worker down the street. He didn't think anything of it until they neared Bell.

The horse, who didn't tolerate any strangers and refused to let a man ride her, rubbed her head on the man's arm while the two stopped by her side.

With each step that drew him closer to the duo, Garrett felt something in his gut twist tighter and tighter, concluding the cowpuncher had to be his spirited neighbor. Convinced his suspicion was accurate, terror washed over him at what could have happened to her if anyone discovered her disguise. The terror quickly gave way to anger at her putting herself in danger whether she realized it or not.

Garrett knew it was Aundy when the cowboy bent down and laced fingers together to make a step for the Chinese man. Men just didn't have curvy backsides like that or look so graceful in their movements. When she glanced at him with those beautiful blue eyes, he knew he was right.

He felt like turning her over his knee and paddling her attractive posterior. Instead, he caught the Chinese man before he could fall to the ground, carried him to the wagon, and somehow heard himself say he was taking him home to Ma instead of to Doc or the sheriff's office.

As he watched Aundy ride Bell with a straight spine and her head uplifted, he had no idea what she'd been thinking.

Why in the world was she dressed like a man and how on earth did she come to have a beaten Chinese man in her care?

He supposed he'd get the answers to his questions soon enough.

As they neared the lane that led to Nash's Folly, Aundy dropped back to ride beside him.

"Garrett, I'm sorry, but I'd rather not go to your house looking like this. I don't want to upset Nora." Some little part of her had died the moment Garrett figured out who she was. It was one thing to be dressed like a man when no one knew she was really a woman. It was an entirely different matter for Garrett to see her dressed that way, knowing the truth.

As much as she tried to deny it, she wanted to look nice when he was around. She knew she wasn't beautiful, but something about seeing him smile at her with his silvery eyes glowing like liquid metal made her feel feminine and attractive. The very last person she'd want to see her dressed like a man was Garrett Nash.

He'd not only seen her, but also seen right through her guise. She'd have to ask him sometime how he so easily figured out who she was. Right after he started speaking to her again.

"Fine," he said, pointing a hand down the road toward the Erickson farm. "Get yourself home and be prepared to tell me all about your little adventure later. And don't you ever try something like this again. You hear me?"

Since he was already fuming, she let her temper rise, too. She didn't appreciate the way he bossed her around, especially since her trip to town resulted in finding a herd of sheep to purchase. That was the whole point of her adventure and she was inordinately pleased with her successful efforts.

"I appreciate your assistance, Mr. Nash, truly I do. However, I'm perfectly capable of taking care of myself. I'm a woman grown with a mind of her own, a strong constitution, and no man to answer to. Don't feel the need to give yourself the job because I'm not looking to fill the vacancy!"

Aundy gave Bell her head and took off down the road.

Stunned by Aundy's outburst, Garrett watched her ride away, unable to formulate a reply even if the infuriating woman had stayed to argue with him.

A chuckle worked its way up his chest and out his mouth as he turned the wagon toward home. "She is something else," Garrett muttered to himself. He would probably never again meet anyone quite like Aundy Erickson in his lifetime.

Reluctantly admitting he may have been a little high-handed with her, he couldn't help it. Anytime he was around her, he felt an unreasonable need to protect her, to keep her safe and sheltered. Only Aundy wasn't the type of person to want protection. She was strong and resilient and, as he discovered, a bit of a free spirit.

Although he didn't approve of her dressing like a cowhand out for a night on the town, he had to acknowledge she did do a good job of posing as a man. If he hadn't been so curious about the horse's reaction to her, he wouldn't have thought twice about how she looked. Bell's friendly greeting made him realize there was only one person the persnickety mare would allow that close.

Garrett stopped the wagon at the end of the front walk. He set the brake, jumped down, and ran inside the house to let his parents know they were about to have unexpected company.

Nora hastened to prepare a bed and J.B. hobbled to the door, holding it open as Garrett carried the Chinese man inside.

An hour later, Nora declared the man badly beaten, but thought he would be fine with some rest and care. He had a few cracked ribs, numerous cuts on his face, and he'd have a doozy of a black eye. Other than looking like someone used him for a punching bag, he'd make a full recovery.

The man stirred and looked around with the one eye that would open. Nora assured him he was safe and offered him a drink of water. After taking a sip, he settled back down and went to sleep.

"I'll sit with him for a while." J.B. took a seat on the chair near the bed. "Nora, honey, go on to bed and rest. You'll no doubt have a full day of doctoring our guest tomorrow. I can take the night watch."

"I can sit up with him, Pops," Garrett said, watching as his dad leaned back in the chair and stretched out his leg.

"So can I," J.B. said with a smile. "Go on and put up the wagon. I can take care of things here. You say you found this fellow on the street outside the saloon?"

"Yep." Garrett left out the part that he was on the street outside the saloon with Aundy. That portion of the story he'd take to his grave.

"Wonder who worked him over and why?" J.B. asked, not expecting an answer.

Garrett shrugged his shoulders then went outside to unload the feed and put away the wagon. Tom was still in the barn, so he helped put away the load and offered to brush down the horses when Garrett said he had something he needed to do. Quickly saddling Jester, he rode off at a fast clip. He'd never be able to sleep if he didn't talk to Aundy.

Although he was mad at her for behaving so recklessly, he still wanted to make sure she arrived home in one piece. He wondered how she'd explain her outfit to Dent or one of the hands if they still happened to be out working when she arrived home.

He hurried up her lane then slowed the horse to a walk, stopping outside the front of the house. Looping Jester's reins around a post near the fence enclosing the yard, he took the porch steps in two long strides and knocked on the door.

A light was on in the front room, indicating Aundy remained awake.

When no sound was forthcoming, he knocked again. He debated between going home or walking around back to the kitchen when the door suddenly swung open. Lamp light surrounded Aundy as she greeted him wearing a blue robe that matched her eyes.

"Garrett? Is everything okay?" She stepped back so he could walk inside.

Without responding, he wrapped his arms around her and drew her close while toeing the door closed. Her hair fell in a golden tumble to her waist and smelled faintly of roses.

She held herself stiffly until he rubbed his hands up and down her back. He felt her soften against him.

Before he let sense overrule desire, he yanked off his gloves and tossed them on the nearest chair then took her face in his hands. Slowly, he brushed his work-roughened thumbs over her cheekbones, gazing into her eyes and getting lost in the warm blue depths.

He lowered his head to hers, intending to give her a swift, chaste kiss. Heat exploded between them at the touch of their lips. His ability to think vanished as he repeatedly pressed his mouth, hard and hungry, to hers. When her arms slid around his neck, he drew her even closer and deepened the kiss.

Garrett felt lost to everything except the woman in his arms, the woman who fit there so perfectly. He admired her spirit, appreciated her fine figure, enjoyed her laughter, and liked her caring heart. What he felt now, though, was so much more.

He felt passion and, if he cared to admit it, soul-deep love for the girl who kissed him with every bit as much yearning as he kissed her.

Aundy finally pulled back with a ragged breath, eyes wide in delighted wonder. She'd promised herself she would never get involved with another man, but her feelings for Garrett were more than just involved.

Involved meant there was care and concern, maybe friendship and fun.

The wild currents of longing swirling inside her were so strong they made her bones ache. The emotions Garrett stirred in her were much, much more than she ever imagined feeling for anyone and most definitely beyond being merely involved.

"Garrett, I… you…" she said, unable to think with the sensational tingle of his kisses still riding her lips. She couldn't believe he'd kissed her. Or that she'd kissed him in return.

Never, not once, had any kiss ever made her feel like her heart would pound right out of her chest. Her stomach felt light and her knees weak while she scrambled to regain the ability to have a coherent thought. How could one kiss, one magnificent kiss, affect her so?

She glanced at Garrett and noticed his hard breathing while his eyes filled with an intense light. He looked ready to reach for her again.

He couldn't possibly be interested in her. Someone as handsome and charming as Garrett Nash could have his pick of women. There was no chance he'd set his affections on a plain, sturdy girl who was too stubborn and independent for her own good.

Irritated as she snatched her thoughts back together, she reminded herself that she did not intend to join her life with another man. Not even one as attractive, strong, and amazing as the one who'd just kissed her so ardently.

Drawn to him by something beyond her ability to resist, Aundy unknowingly focused her bright gaze on his lips, leaning enticingly closer.

Garrett groaned and buried his hands in her hair, taking her lips with his again.

"I'm sorry. I shouldn't have done that," Garrett said when he finally lifted his mouth from hers. He tossed his hat onto the chair where his gloves had landed and raked a hand through his hair. Boldly staring at Aundy, he wanted to wind her silky tresses around his hands and feel her body close to his again. If he did, though, he couldn't promise to let her go. No matter how madly he wanted to, he wouldn't hold her that close again, at least at that moment. "I wanted to make sure you made it home, that you were fine."

"I'm perfectly fine, as you can see." Aundy took another step back from Garrett. She needed to put some space between them before she succumbed to the desire to be in his arms again. "You shouldn't be here this late. It's not proper."

Garrett laughed and gave her a pointed look. "Says the woman who dressed as a man and went places no lady should."

Aundy had the grace to blush although she kept her back straight and held his gaze.

"How about I drink a cup of your tea and you tell me what adventure led you to finding our Chinese friend?"

Aundy led the way to the kitchen where she turned up the lamps, made tea, and took a plate out of the refrigerator. Generously sprinkling cinnamon and sugar on what looked like flat pancakes, she rolled each one into a tidy bundle then handed the plate to Garrett.

"What's this?" he asked, studying the unfamiliar dish.

"Lefse. It's Norwegian," Aundy said, sitting at the table with a cup of tea. "Try it, you'll enjoy it."

Garrett took a bite and his eyes lit with pleasure.

"What did you call it?" he asked, devouring his first piece and starting on a second.

"Lefse. It's made with potatoes and flour, mostly. My grandmother made the best lefse." A wistful look passed over her face and, for a moment, she drifted in her memories.

Garrett cleaned his plate then took a drink of tea, waiting for Aundy to explain her evening's actions.

When she quietly sat sipping her tea, he decided she wasn't going to volunteer any information.

"Why did you dress like a man?"

"Because no one will give me the information I want when I ask them dressed as a woman." A spark of defiance flashed across her face and settled in her eyes.

"Fair enough. Where did you go?"

"I went to the saloon around the corner from where I tied Bell."

"You went to the saloon." Garrett digested that information and found it gave him heartburn. "What did you do at the saloon?"

"I walked up to the bar and asked the bartender how to get to the Underground." Aundy took a sip of her tea. She nearly choked when Garrett smacked the top of the table with the flat of his hand.

"You what!"

She cleared her throat and sat a little taller in her chair then leveled her gaze to his. "I asked how to get to the Underground."

"Why in blazes would you want to go there? It's no place for a lady like you, Aundy. Not at all." Garrett stared at her as if she'd taken leave of her senses.

"So I discovered," Aundy said, remembering the things she'd seen and heard, wishing she could block the memories from her mind.

Garrett attempted to calm down so she'd keep talking. He drew in a few deep breaths before he continued. "You asked the bartender and he gave you directions."

"I suppose you could call what he said directions, although I wasn't sure at first I'd ever find the end of the corridor and come out anywhere. It cost me two bits to get that piece of information," Aundy said with obvious disgust. "I had no idea there was a city beneath the city, so to speak. I think I even saw a candy shop down there."

"Yeah, you did." Garrett sincerely hoped that was all Aundy saw. "You found your way there, then what?"

"I got close enough to several groups of men to listen to their conversations, but didn't have any luck in finding what I was looking for, so I went into a saloon and ordered a sarsaparilla. I was standing at the bar when one of the women who worked at the establishment began conversing with me."

A smile tugged at the corners of his mouth as he imagined the look on Aundy's face when one of the saloon girls sidled up next to her, thinking she was a man. "You mean one of the working girls propositioned you?"

The amusement on Garrett's face fanned the flames of her temper. "I didn't see anything amusing about the situation then or now. It was quite unsettling and disturbing."

"I'm sure it was." Garrett buried his grin behind his cup.

"I suggested she move along and she asked me what I was doing in the saloon. When I told her I was looking for information, she pointed out a patron who turned out to be most helpful. I concluded my business and tried to work my way back up to the street, but by then I found myself completely turned around. I kept walking and ended up in a corridor that took me to a set of stairs. I tripped over the injured man on the top step," Aundy said, absently rubbing her shoulder.

When she bathed after removing her disguise, she couldn't help but notice the bruise already forming on her shoulder. It ached and throbbed. The door probably wouldn't have done much damage, but the fact that wretched Ashton Monroe squeezed it like a piece of dough compounded the problem.

Garrett stood from his chair and walked around the table, pulling down the edge of Aundy's robe and gown until it revealed a large bruise. She slapped at his hands and voiced her disapproval of his actions, yanking her clothing back in place.

Although he forced himself to step back, he really wanted to pull her clothing down and cover the discolored skin with soft kisses. What he'd seen of Aundy's creamy neck and shoulder, beyond the bruise, made his temperature spike and muddled his thoughts.

He regained his seat and raised an eyebrow at her in question.

"I hit the door pretty hard." Aundy glared at him, miffed he bared her bruise and made her skin tingle at his touch. With no idea what he was trying to do to her, she sincerely wished he'd stop. She could barely keep her thoughts together with him sitting across the table, let alone when he put his hands on her bare skin. A part of her wished he'd do it again.

"Then...?" Garrett prompted.

"I couldn't just leave him there. What if whoever beat him came back? What if he was truly about to die? Although, I suppose if he was, he wouldn't have been able to get up and walk with my help," Aundy speculated as she spoke. "When I said I could either take him to Doc or home with me, he chose me and you know the rest of the story."

"What, may I ask, was so important it required you to don men's clothes, go places no respectable woman should go, and endanger yourself in the process?" Garrett asked, clearly upset with her behavior.

"I wasn't in any danger. You said yourself I'm a pretty good shot and I wore my gun. It seemed to me if you didn't cause trouble, you could stay out of trouble." Convinced she handled herself well, she didn't know why Garrett was so vexed.

"So you agree that Mr. Chinaman, who is right now sleeping in a room in my parent's home, is trouble. That he did something terrible resulting in him being beaten so badly it will take weeks to fully recover."

The calculating stare from his steely gray eyes was completely unsettling.

Determined not to squirm in her seat, Aundy shook her head. "No, I don't think he did anything to get in trouble, but I don't know that for a fact. You know what I meant, though."

"Dang it, Aundy. What if one of them decided to pull a gun on you? Were you prepared for a gunfight? Or a fistfight? Even worse, what if one of those men down there found out you're a woman? There's no telling what would've happened to you. You have no idea what some of them are capable of." Fear tightened his chest again as thoughts of what might have happened filled his head.

He reached across the table and grasped Aundy's soft fingers in his rough calloused hands. "Please promise me you'll never do that again."

Aundy didn't want to promise anything. She didn't think she'd ever again have a need to dress as a man or venture beneath the city, but she didn't like the way the promise conceded some of her freedom.

However, at the look on Garrett's face, a look that made her heart quicken and her stomach flutter, she released a sigh. "I promise."

"Thank you." Garrett squeezed her hands before letting them go. "Now, what information was so important you couldn't just ask me or Pops?"

"I could have asked you, but I needed to do this on my own, Garrett. You and your family have been so good to me, taken such good care of me. I need to stand on my own two feet. I can't depend on you for everything. If I'm going to run this farm, I need to learn to be self-sufficient."

"You are one of the most stubborn, hard-headed women I've ever met, Aundy Erickson." Garrett ran a hand through his hair, sending the dark locks into a state of complete disarray. His movements made Aundy want to run her fingers through it as well. "Your ability to be self-sufficient would never come into question. If you need help, ask for it. We're more than happy to give it. You've been through so much since you've arrived here and handled it all in stride. After growing up in the city without any rural background, you're going to need some help. Never hesitate to ask."

"I know, but I've imposed on all of you too much as it is." Aundy felt tears prick the backs of her eyes. She would not cry. As jumbled as they were, surrendering to her emotions wouldn't help prove she could care for herself and Erik's farm. Her farm.

"You've never imposed on us. Ever." Aundy was so obstinate. He couldn't recall ever meeting such a stubborn, headstrong woman. She made him want to... Thoughts of what he really wanted to do made his blood zing through his veins. He refocused his attention on why she went to the Underground. "Regardless of all that, what information were you hoping to find?"

"I wanted to buy something and no one would talk to me about it. Dressed as a man, I didn't have a bit of trouble making the deal."

"What did you buy?" Garrett tried to think of anything Aundy would have purchased in the Underground that could possibly be beneficial to the farm.

"I don't think you're going to like my answer." Aundy didn't want to tell Garrett about her sheep. He'd been quite vocal when she and J.B. were discussing the pros and cons of raising sheep the other day, about how much he disliked the "stinky little boogers," as he referred to them.

"What did you do?" Garrett pinned her with his silver gaze.

"I made arrangements with a man to buy something he wanted to sell."

Garrett's patience was nearly exhausted. "Which was?"

She hesitated, taking a deep breath before answering. "Sheep."

He let out a whoosh of air and sat back in his chair. Blinking his eyes twice, he was sure Aundy couldn't have said what he thought she did.

"Did you say sheep?"

"Yes," Aundy whispered, staring down at the cloth covering the table.

"Smelly, nasty, bleating little sheep?"

"Well, I don't know about the smelly, nasty, or bleating part, but yes, I did agree to purchase sheep."

"Woman! What are you thinking? Did you sign papers, make payment? Is the deal final?"

"Not yet. Mr. O'Connell was under the impression I was helping a new widow. I asked him to call Mrs. Erickson Monday morning to make arrangements for the sale."

"O'Connell? The whiskey drinking Irishman?" Garrett yelled as his eyes flashed fire. "Why he'll…"

Aundy reached across the table and clapped a hand across his mouth. "Shh. You'll have Dent and the boys in here if you don't quiet down. Not only should you not be here, especially with me dressed like this, but I'm not quite ready to impart the knowledge to them that we'll soon be raising sheep."

"Fred will quit." Garrett stated a fact Aundy already knew. He'd made it perfectly clear that he had no interest in tending sheep, so it was a gamble she had to make.

"I've taken that possibility into consideration."

"Did you also take into consideration that a lot of the neighbors around here hate sheep? Not just dislike them, but hate them. I know many people in the area raise sheep, but our neighbors are all wheat growers and cattlemen. If you think about it, there isn't one little lamb to be found from here all the way to Pendleton. You could be asking for a lot of trouble." Aware of the stubborn set to Aundy's chin, he knew she had no intention of listening to reason or changing her mind.

SHANNA HATFIELD

"I'll handle any problems should they arise."

"Did you at least talk to Dent about your plans?" Garrett asked. Aundy had lost her mind. Sheep. Of all the things she could have done, decided to raise or grow, she had to pick sheep.

This was going to be disastrous.

"Not exactly." Aundy knew it would have been a good idea to involve Dent in her decision, but she was sure he, like Garrett, would do his best to dissuade her from buying the sheep and she'd already made up her mind.

"Look, Aundy, I think you..."

Aundy placed her hand over Garrett's mouth again and fought the tremor that shot from her fingers up her arm then spiraled down to her toes. The feel of his lips beneath her fingers made her wish he'd take her in his arms and kiss her again in the very worst way. She didn't want to think about why she wanted, needed, him to hold her. She just knew that she did.

"I'm buying the sheep, Garrett. It's my decision to make and mine alone. If it's a mistake, I'll face the consequences." Aundy yanked back her hand like she'd singed her fingers and jumped to her feet. "I do appreciate your concern and you riding over here to make sure I arrived home without incident. I'd be happy to take care of the Chinese man if you think he could be moved."

"Leave him be. It gives Ma someone to fuss over." Garrett wondered how Aundy's fingers could spark a fire that burned from his lips all the way to the tips of his toes. He could hardly function with his thoughts so centered on her lips and his desire to kiss them until neither of them could think.

He needed to leave before he got any more out of line. He walked to the front room, slipped on his gloves, and grabbed his hat.

154

"Will you at least let me go with you to sign the paperwork with O'Connell?" Garrett asked as he stood with one hand on the doorknob.

"Perhaps," Aundy said with a teasing smile. Despite her best intentions to stay away from Garrett, she couldn't stop her fingers from brushing softly over the little cleft in his chin that had intrigued her from the first time she'd noticed it. "If you promise to let me make the deal and behave yourself."

"I always behave." Garrett surrendered to the temptation to wrap his arms around Aundy's waist. He pulled her against him and breathed of her scent again, getting a tiny whiff of Bay Rum. That cooled his desire as he reminded himself of the heap of trouble she could have gotten herself into with her shenanigans. He kissed her cheek, placed his hat on his head, and opened the door. "You didn't say if I had to behave well or like a wild ruffian. I'll assume either will do."

Aundy laughed as Garrett hurried down the steps and across the yard to where his horse waited. She watched him mount Jester in the gathering darkness, waving at him before closing the door. As she blew out the flame in the lamp, she hoped her decision would turn out to be sound.

If not, she'd soon know.

Chapter Ten

Tired of pacing the kitchen floor, waiting for the phone to ring Monday morning, Aundy finally sat down at the table with one of the books J.B. let her borrow and read the chapter on sheep again. She hoped Mr. O'Connell would call and prayed she hadn't made a bad decision.

Absorbed in the information she read, she jumped when the telephone rang. After rushing to answer it, the lyrical Irish voice of Mr. O'Connell on the line brought out her smile.

"Mrs. Erickson?"

"Yes, this is Mrs. Erickson." Aundy wanted to dance a jig. The man had called just like he said he would. "May I help you?"

"I'd like to think so," Mr. O'Connell said. Aundy could hear the smile in his voice. "I met a boyo Friday night who indicated the fair and lovely Mrs. Erickson might take a shine to the critters I have for sale. If that's correct, would ya have time to meet me in town today to discuss the details? If they are satisfactory to both parties, we could sign the paperwork and I could bring the animals to ya tomorrow. It's with haste and hurry I am to be on me way to the sunny warmth of California."

"That would be satisfactory, Mr. O'Connell," Aundy said, grinning from ear to ear. She asked him to meet her at her attorney's office and thanked him for the call. She hung up the phone then placed a call to Nash's Folly. Relief flooded over her when Garrett answered.

"Mr. Nash, this is Mrs. Erickson." Aundy was all too aware of the many ears listening to their conversation since the phone lines were far from private. The buzzing static in her ear hinted that several people listened in on the party line. "I have a business matter to conduct today and was hoping you might offer your insight into the matter. Would you be able to provide your assistance?"

"I'd be happy to, Mrs. Erickson." Garrett maintained a formal tone. "What time shall I expect to meet with you?"

"I could stop by around ten on my way into town, if that wouldn't be in imposition." Aundy wanted to ask how the Chinese man was doing, if Garrett was still mad at her, and if he'd experienced as much difficulty sleeping as she had after sharing such heat-filled kisses the other night. Instead, she squeezed her lips together to keep from blurting out something she shouldn't.

Now that she'd set the wheels in motion for buying the sheep, she was frightened of what she'd done. What if she invested the money in the flock and they ended up being worthless, or causing all her hands to quit?

"I'll see you then," Garrett said, then hung up.

Aundy was sure that meant he was still upset over her escapade Friday evening.

She packed a basket with cookies she'd made earlier that morning and finished a few things around the house. Aundy took a bath and dressed in one of her nicest suits with a frothy ruffle of lace at the throat of the shirtwaist. She picked up her reticule, gathered a pair of creamy gloves to go with her buttery-yellow and cream striped outfit, and pinned a hat on her head.

Suddenly realizing she should have hitched the horse to the buggy before she dressed in her finery, she hoped one of the men would be nearby. Fortunately, she discovered Glen mending tack at the barn. It took him just a few minutes to hitch a horse to the buggy and have Aundy on her way to Nash's Folly.

She parked at the end of the walk and hurried up the steps. With a perfunctory knock at the front door, she stuck her head inside and greeted Nora as the woman approached the front entry.

"Aundy, don't you look like a picture of spring today. That soft yellow color is a perfect complement for your hair." Nora hugged Aundy warmly then pulled her inside the house, accepting the basket of cookies the girl held out to her.

"Thank you."

"You won't believe what Garrett dragged home the other night." Nora took Aundy's hand, once she'd set down her reticule and removed her gloves, leading her to a bedroom near the kitchen.

"A puppy?" Aundy asked, giving Nora a silly grin.

"No, you goose. A man from China."

Aundy followed Nora into the room. The man looked even worse in the morning light than he had Friday in the evening shadows. His face was a swollen mess and he slept on one side with his knees slightly bent. Aundy felt pity for him and the pain he had to be feeling. Maybe they should have the doctor examine him. "Will he be okay?"

"I think so. Other than a few cracked ribs and his poor face, he didn't seem to have any other injuries. He doesn't speak very good English, but we think he said his name is Li Hong."

"Li Hong," Aundy repeated, testing out the foreign name. She hoped Li Hong wouldn't remember her part in his coming to be at Nash's Folly.

He opened one eye and glanced first at Nora then at Aundy. His eyes widened when he saw her, but he held her gaze. When he didn't appear to plan to say anything, Aundy released the breath she held.

"Mr. Hong, this is our neighbor, Aundy Erickson. She lives on the next farm over," Nora said, making introductions.

Aundy took a step closer to the bed and inclined her head toward him. "It's a pleasure to meet you Mr. Hong." Uncertain if she should extend her hand, nod her head, or bow, Aundy decided to stick with a friendly smile. "I hope you aren't in too much pain."

"No," Li said, working up something that could have been a smile had one side of his mouth not been badly swollen. "Li fine."

Aundy smiled again and backed toward the door. She was glad he could talk and seemed coherent. It must have been frightening for him to wake up in a strange place, beaten and in pain.

"I'll get you a fresh glass of water, Mr. Hong," Nora said, following Aundy out the door to the kitchen where J.B. sat reading a newspaper and drinking coffee.

"Well, look at you, Aundy. Don't you look like summer sunshine?" J.B. offered her a smile that reminded her of Garrett as he helped himself to a handful of cookies from the basket Nora set on the table.

"Thank you, J.B. I need to pay a visit to my attorney and then possibly the bank, so I decided I better be dressed for the part."

"She has a talent for dressing the part," Garrett said, giving her a wicked smile as he strolled into the room. Dressed in pressed pants with a crisp shirt, light coat and vest, Aundy thought he looked too handsome for words. The burgundy vest and dark gray coat accented the liquid silver of his eyes and the rich color of his dark brown hair.

"Lands sakes, honey, what's got you all fancied up?" Nora asked, knowing Garrett much preferred to wear the denims the cowhands all favored with a soft cotton shirt than his "fancy duds" as he and J.B. called their town clothes.

"I promised Aundy I'd go with her to meet a man about some business she wants to conduct this morning. If you want more detail than that, you'll have to pry it out of her." Garrett kissed his mother's cheek and grabbed his hat off a peg by the back door.

"Shall we?" Garrett asked, holding out his arm to Aundy.

Gingerly, she placed her hand on his offered arm then turned to Nora. The woman looked at her expectantly. "I'll give you all the details when we return. May I bring anything back for Mr. Hong?"

"I can't think of a thing." Nora waved them out the door. "Remember, I want all the news when you get back. We didn't get to visit at all yesterday and I'm feeling neglected."

Aundy insisted on driving herself to church and left immediately after the service. She and Nora didn't have a chance to visit about the unexpected houseguest at Nash's Folly. Garrett was sure Aundy's avoidance of them had been intentional. He wondered if his disapproval of the sheep or his ardent kisses kept her away.

"Yes, Ma," Garrett called, settling his hat on his head once they were outside the door.

Aundy studied him from the top of his dark cattleman's hat to the tips of his freshly polished boots and thought Garrett looked far more handsome than Ashton Monroe ever would.

She was still irritated at Ashton for treating her so roughly in the saloon, even if he didn't know who she was. He shouldn't be that brusque with anyone.

While Ashton was what she'd call aristocratic in appearance, Garrett was all muscle and rugged man with a little rogue thrown in to further discombobulate her senses.

The strong arm that helped her into the buggy made her knees feel wobbly and the friendly grin that promised more teasing drew a smile from her own lips. She breathed in his spicy scent and longed to have his mouth pressed against hers again.

His fervent kisses Friday night were so mesmerizing, she'd completely lost herself in the experience despite her vow to stay far, far away from men and romance.

Aundy settled her skirts on the buggy seat and noticed Garrett staring at her. Apparently, he waited for a response to a question she hadn't heard him ask while she was lost in thoughts of his kisses.

"My apologies, Garrett. I didn't hear what you said." Flustered under his intense gaze, she fussed with her hat, and tugged at her gloves. She smoothed down each finger just to have something to do to keep her hands busy.

Garrett snapped the reins and the horse ambled down the lane at a moderate pace. It was a beautiful day.

He sat elbow to elbow with a girl who sent his heart skittering into a rapid beat at thoughts of her kisses while her soft rose scent made him think things he knew were highly inappropriate, but didn't really care.

"I asked how your shoulder is today. You don't seem to be favoring it, but you're sure to have a bruise."

"It's fine." Aundy appreciated his concern, but wasn't worried about something as trivial as a bruise when she had much more important matters on her mind. "Did you find out anything about Mr. Hong, other than his name?"

"Not much. He said he works for different people, doing odd jobs. He refuses to discuss what happened. I got the idea that someone asked him to do something he wasn't willing to do, so they beat him up and tossed him in the doorway. He fell down the stairs and crawled up to the top, where you found him."

He glanced at her, swallowing hard.

Aundy made such a beautiful picture in her yellow striped dress with her golden hair piled on her head. A few errant tendrils worked their way loose, swirling temptingly along her neck and thoroughly distracting Garrett.

It took every ounce of willpower he possessed to keep from hauling her into his arms and kissing her until they both forgot where they were going or what they were doing.

Instead, he turned his attention to the horse and looked out at the rolling fields of green against the bright blue sky. Eastern Oregon was a spectacular place to be in the spring, before the heat of the summer turned things brown and dry.

"That's terrible." Aundy was thankful she had found Mr. Hong and was able to help him. She wondered what he refused to do that resulted in the beating. They'd probably never know. "Are you sure he's fine at your house? I could take care of him."

"I don't think so." With his dad in the house, Garrett wasn't concerned their guest would try anything. If Li Hong were at Aundy's, Garrett wouldn't get a wink of sleep, worrying about her well-being. "He's just fine at Nash's Folly."

Determined to get to the reason they headed into town, Garrett broached the subject of sheep. He wasn't happy that Aundy had agreed to buy the flock and knew her hands would like the idea even less than he did. However, as she pointed out Friday night, it was her decision to make.

"Did you talk to Dent and the others about your sheep?"

"No." Aundy made a point of looking at the green fields they drove by rather than the very good-looking man beside her. She wanted to avoid his question along with the disapproving look he'd turned on her.

"Don't you think you should? You can't exactly hide the sheep from them."

"I wasn't intending to," Aundy said defensively, leaning away from Garrett. She needed to focus on how annoying she found his persistent questioning instead of how handsome he looked or how good he smelled. His warmth at her side made her stomach flutter in a most disconcerting way.

If she wanted to be in any condition to negotiate with Mr. O'Connell, she needed to tear her thoughts away from how much she enjoyed being around Garrett and how well he filled out his coat and pants.

Flushed with heat from her forbidden musings, she wished she'd brought along a parasol or at least a fan. Instead, she fanned her gloved hand in front of her face.

Garrett raised an eyebrow her direction and gave her a mocking grin. "A little warm out for you?"

"No!" Aundy wondered why he insisted on goading her. "And to answer your question, I plan to tell Dent and the boys tomorrow. I wanted to make sure the deal was final before I said anything and jeopardized losing Fred. I'd really like to find a way to keep them all working for me."

"Could you hire someone to tend the sheep and tell the rest of them they won't have to worry about the woolies?" Garrett suggested. As fiercely as Fred hated sheep, he wasn't sure that would be enough to keep him from quitting.

"Perhaps." If she could find someone willing to work for her, she'd hire him in a heartbeat.

"I take it you spoke with Owen this morning."

"Owen?" Aundy asked, confused.

"O'Connell. His name is Owen O'Connell." Garrett scowled. "Didn't you get the full name of the man you're doing business with? Might be good to know, don't you think?"

Quickly realizing her mistake, Aundy felt like a chastised child. The feeling irked her considerably. "Yes. Of course."

"What did you discuss?" Garrett asked, wondering if she'd offered a price, made a verbal agreement.

Aundy repeated the brief conversation she had with Mr. O'Connell. Garrett nodded, pleased that she hadn't made any promises.

When she pulled up in front of the attorney's office, Garrett noticed Owen O'Connell sat on a bench near the door, waiting.

He hurried around the buggy to give Aundy his hand and then turned to the Irishman.

"O'Connell. Good to see you again," Garrett said in his typical friendly fashion, shaking hands with the man as he stood from the bench. "Hear you're getting ready to head south and leave our lovely Eastern Oregon weather behind."

"It's lovely now, boyo, but when the snow blows and the ice freezes everything, I'll be sunnin' meself in the warm, balmy California weather."

"So you will." Garrett reached a hand over to place on the small of Aundy's back and gently pushed her forward. "May I introduce Mrs. Erickson? Aundy Erickson. She married Erik the day of his injury."

"I'm so sorry for your loss, Miz Erickson. Terrible thing that happened to Erik," O'Connell said, doffing his hat and tipping his head to Aundy.

"Thank you, Mr. O'Connell. I appreciate your condolences." Aundy smiled at the man, noting his eyes looked bloodshot and tired. "Shall we go in?"

"Certainly." O'Connell held the door for Aundy and Garrett to precede him.

An hour and a half later, they left the bank together and O'Connell shook both their hands. Once he delivered the sheep, he would receive payment in full. For now, Aundy paid him half of the agreed upon price, after drawing up papers at the attorney's office.

"We'll be at the farm tomorrow afternoon with your woolies, Mrs. Erickson. See you then." O'Connell touched the brim of his hat then walked away in the direction of a saloon.

"While we're in town, I'd like to go by the sheriff's office," Garrett said as he helped Aundy into the buggy and started down the street. "I want to ask about Li Hong and see if any of them have heard anything."

"Do you think he's wanted by the law?" Aundy asked, hoping the man wasn't. For some reason, she felt a little protective of the poor immigrant who'd been beaten so badly.

"Probably not, but never hurts to ask." Garrett stopped the buggy when he noticed his friend Kade walking toward them. He set the brake and turned to Aundy. "Mind waiting just a moment?"

"Not at all," Aundy assured him. She watched as he ran across the street and enthusiastically shook the hand of a man who looked like an officer of the law with a shiny star pinned to his vest. The tall, brawny man looked familiar then she realized he was the handsome cowboy she'd seen at the train station the day she arrived in town. He'd also been at church several times although he usually left before the service ended.

Garrett visited with the officer a few minutes then both of them looked her direction. Far enough away she couldn't hear what they said, she smiled when Garrett walked back across the street with the man.

"Aundy, this is my very good friend, Kade Rawlings. He's a sheriff's deputy," Garrett said, making the introduction.

"It's a pleasure to make your acquaintance, Mrs. Erickson." Kade doffed his hat and nodded to her. "I've known Garrett since we chased tadpoles in the creek and terrorized the little girls at school."

"It's very nice to meet you," Aundy said, shaking the man's hand and offering him a smile. It was hard not to notice his handsome face, brawny frame, or towering height. Garrett was quite tall and his friend Kade stood an inch or so over him.

"Garrett tells me he made a new friend Friday night. I might ride out later and ask him a few questions," Kade said, watching the way Aundy and Garrett snuck glances at each other. So that was the way the wind blew. He'd have to torment Garrett about his obvious interest in the winsome widow later. "He also said you purchased a few head of sheep. Good for you. My uncle raises sheep south of here and does well with them."

"Thank you, Deputy Rawlings. I hope the sheep will be a good addition to our farm." Aundy caught Garrett rolling his eyes. "Although Garrett has made it clear he much prefers cattle."

Kade chuckled as he slapped Garrett on the back. "You'll have to ask him sometime where he got his dislike of sheep."

Aundy smiled and looked over at Garrett. He narrowed his gaze and shook his head at the deputy. She laughed and offered Kade an approving nod. "I will do that."

"I better be on my way." Kade tipped his hat to Aundy with an engaging smile. "It was truly a pleasure to meet you, ma'am. If you ever need anything, please don't hesitate to contact me."

"Thank you, sir," Aundy said, liking Garrett's friend. He was fun and seemed kind.

Garrett sat on the buggy seat and picked up the reins. "Since we're here, want to have some lunch?"

"That would be agreeable," Aundy said, pleased at the idea of spending more time with Garrett.

He parked the buggy a few blocks from a busy restaurant and they strolled along, her hand on his arm. Anyone looking at them saw an attractive couple, one fair, the other dark, enjoying a beautiful spring day.

After lunch, Aundy requested a few moments to purchase supplies at the store. Garrett left her there while he attended to some errands of his own and caught up with her just in time to carry a box packed full of supplies to the buggy.

"You buy out the store?" Garrett teased, easily carrying the loaded box.

"Of course not," Aundy said, waiting for Garrett to assist her in the buggy, not because she needed the help, but because it was the proper thing to do. At least that's what she tried to tell herself. It couldn't have anything to do with the proximity of Garrett, or the feel of her hand in his, or the opportunity to inhale his masculine scent.

Once the busyness of town was behind them, Aundy let out a deep breath.

"Do you really think Fred will quit?" She looked at him with such concern in her moist eyes, he felt his chest constrict with pain.

"Fred is the only one who can answer that question, but it's certainly a possibility." Garrett wasn't convinced Aundy going into the sheep business was a good idea, but it was too late to worry about it now. She'd signed on the dotted line and made a partial payment to O'Connell.

Garrett sat in the meeting with the attorney and then the banker, but he kept quiet. Fully expecting to help Aundy negotiate the price and terms, he was surprised she did so well without any assistance. She even bartered down the price on the sheep and got O'Connell to agree to deliver them.

O'Connell blustered and fumed, putting on a good show. Aundy appeared calm and collected, refusing to budge from her offer. Everyone in the room, including O'Connell, knew he would agree to her terms.

"Do you plan on telling Dent about the sheep before they show up?" Garrett thought Aundy had already waited longer than she should have to share her plans with the foreman. He might have a thing or two to say about a flock of sheep descending on the farm.

Due to the reaction she anticipated receiving from the men in her life, she kept her plans a secret. Regardless, she still should have been more forthcoming about what she wanted to do.

Then again, it was her farm and she could do whatever she wanted, whether Garrett, or any of the men, liked it.

"Of course. I plan to make a nice breakfast and tell the men after they're full of good food and strong coffee. I figure I need all the help I can get and they always seem to appreciate a hot meal." Aundy's impish grin made Garrett chuckle.

"You are something else." Garrett placed his hand on her knee and squeezed before realizing the gesture was far too intimate for two people who were just friends. Jerking his hand back, he grabbed the reins with both hands and glanced at Aundy. "If a home-cooked meal changes Fred's mind, your pancakes must be a lot lighter and fluffier than Ma's."

"Maybe." Aundy shot him a sassy grin. "Why don't you tell me why you don't like sheep? Either you do, or I'll have to pay a visit to Deputy Rawlings."

Chapter Eleven

Unable to rest most of the night due to a dreadful case of nerves, Aundy finally gave up on sleep and found things to do to keep her hands busy. Long before the sun began sending streaks of golden light across the horizon, she had baked a sheet cake and cookies, washed a load of laundry and strung it on the clothesline to dry, and dusted the front room.

By the time she heard the men clomping their way down the bunkhouse steps, she'd already gathered the eggs and made her morning threat to Napoleon to turn him into chicken dumplings if he didn't refrain from pecking at her or flogging her head.

She hurried back to the house, whipped up a batch of biscuits, set bread to rise and put a big pot of beef stew on to cook for lunch. Strips of crispy bacon scented the morning air while she scrambled a big pan of eggs. Potatoes fried in another pan as she made a pot of coffee then called to Dent through the open window when she saw him walk toward the barn.

Although he didn't appear to increase the speed of his steps, his stride quickly covered the distance to the house. He stuck his head inside the kitchen where Aundy stood at the stove making sure the eggs didn't burn.

"Morning, Missy. Need something?" he asked, taking in the smells of breakfast. His stomach rumbled in anticipation.

"I'd like you and the boys to join me for breakfast if you haven't eaten. It will be ready in just a few minutes." Aundy smiled over her shoulder at her foreman. If she could get the hands in a good mood, maybe they'd be more receptive to her plans. Despite Garrett's skepticism, a hearty breakfast had to be a good start.

"I'm sure they'll appreciate a hot meal none of us had to prepare. I'll round them up." Dent hustled down the steps and across the yard toward the bunkhouse.

He soon returned with the other men, their hands and faces bearing traces of a thorough scrubbing.

"Good morning," Aundy said, setting a bowl of fried potatoes on the table next to the eggs.

"Mornin', Miz Erickson," Bill said, stepping behind a chair at the table. "We're mighty grateful for the invite to breakfast."

"I'm glad you all could join me." Aundy poured five cups of coffee and made herself a cup of tea. She sat in the chair Dent held out for her. The hands took their seats and Dent asked a blessing on the meal.

Aundy encouraged small talk, asking the men about things they'd done or seen in the past few days, their growing up years, anything she could think of besides the topic of sheep.

George consumed the last piece of bacon while Aundy refilled coffee cups and took a deep breath.

"You're probably wondering why I asked you to join me for breakfast." Aundy looked around the table. At Dent's nod, she continued. "I purchased something that I think will add to the value of the farm and provide additional income without increasing the work load."

"Did you buy one of those new-fangled gas-engine tractors?" George asked with a hopeful look on his face.

"I did not," Aundy said, glancing at the man who was usually quiet. "However, if you all agree it would be a sound investment that will pay for itself in saved labor and increased production, we can discuss it at a later date."

"What'd you buy?" Glen asked, swirling the last dregs of his coffee around in his cup.

"A surprise." Aundy couldn't force the word sheep past her lips. If the hands reacted even half as badly as Garrett did, she wasn't up to facing all five of them at once.

"What kind of surprise?" Dent asked, giving Aundy a long, inquisitive look.

"One I hope you all will give a chance before you form opinions," Aundy answered cryptically.

"We can do that, Miz Erickson." Bill looked around at the other fellows. Dent was the only one who appeared to disagree.

"Wonderful. In that case, I'll hope you'll join me for lunch today. The surprise should arrive early this afternoon." Aundy smiled and started to rise from her chair.

"In order to be prepared for this surprise, why don't you just tell us what it is," Dent said, his voice taking on an unfamiliar, hard tone. She quickly surmised Dent didn't like surprises of any kind, unless they involved food.

Aundy sat down, put some starch in her spine, and looked directly at Dent. "Yesterday, I bought some sheep."

Fred, who had been leaning on the back legs of his chair, let it thump forward. "Goldurn it! How many of those filthy, stinkin' monsters did you buy?"

"Roughly five hundred," Aundy said, not letting Fred's annoyance cause her to back down. She gave each man a cool glare before continuing. "I intend to raise them for their wool. The man I purchased them from will deliver them this afternoon. He assured me they should take far less care and feed than cattle."

"Five hundred woolies! Five hundred!" Fred ranted and started to jump to his feet. A restraining hand on his arm from Dent kept him in his seat.

"That's a lot of sheep, Missy." Dent gave her a look that said she had lost her mind. "Don't you think we should have discussed this before you bought them?"

"Perhaps, but I assumed you men would belittle my idea, think I'd gone crazy, and do your best to talk me out of it." Aundy was fast losing the tenuous hold she had on her temper. She needed the men and appreciated their hard work, but she sorely wished they'd quit treating her as if she had rocks in her head. "I researched the options extensively and came to the conclusion that sheep would provide additional income, could be pastured on less acreage than the cattle, and should require far less care."

"But I done told ya…" Fred started to say, but closed his mouth at a glare from Aundy.

Hastily rising to her feet and stretching to her full height, she gave her temper free rein. Angry blue sparks shot from her eyes, burning into those seated at her table, rendering them speechless.

"I quite clearly heard what you told me, Fred. I did consider your opinion. More than you can possibly know. I need all of you here on the farm. The thought of any of you leaving, for any reason, saddens me greatly." Aundy's gaze moved over each man sitting at the table. "You work harder than I expect and are far more dedicated than I deserve. I appreciate each one of you, which is why I don't want any of you to have to spend time working with the sheep. Mr. O'Connell said his shepherd would be happy to keep his job regardless of who employs him."

Aundy inhaled a calming breath and sat down again. "Perhaps at some point, once we get our feet back under us, we can look at running cattle again. For now, though, we are short on people willing to work for a woman. If you'll stick with me, I will do my very best to make it worth your while."

"You really aren't going to make us work with the sheep?" Bill asked, glancing at Fred who appeared mad enough to chew nails.

"No, I'm not. You certainly may if you choose, but I won't demand any of you work with the sheep on a daily basis. If they get out or we need to move them to another pasture, I may ask for your assistance, but other than that, you won't have to work with the sheep. When it's time to cut their wool, I plan to hire a crew to see that done."

The men sat quietly for a few minutes, considering their options. Aundy treated them fairly, paid them well, and often made them special treats. They all knew finding somewhere to work where they earned similar wages with comparable working conditions wouldn't be easy.

"I apologize for springing this on you, but I didn't know what else to do." Aundy looked pointedly at Dent.

Resigned, he stared at her for a minute before nodding his head.

She could have mustered some tears and turned the men in her favor. She'd seen countless women do just that, but she didn't operate that way. If she wanted the men to treat her like the owner of a farm, then she'd swallow back her emotions and act like one. "Please, give me and the sheep a chance."

The men glanced at one another and finally Dent gave her a tight smile. "We'll give it a chance, but if it looks like it isn't going to work, will you agree to sell them?"

"Absolutely." Aundy was glad the conversation went as well as it had. "If you'll come back just before noon, I'll feed you lunch and then the sheep should be here."

"Yes, ma'am." Dent stood and opened the door while the other men filed out. He studied Aundy for a moment, appearing thoughtful. "I sure hope you know what you're doing."

"Me, too," Aundy said, with a bravado she was far from feeling as Dent went out the door.

After washing the breakfast dishes, she checked on the stew, and finished what lunch preparations she could. She carried in the clean laundry from the line, ironed and then put away the pieces.

A glance at the clock confirmed she had a couple of hours before the men would return to eat. She took a pile of dresses that belonged to Erik's mother to her bedroom and began trying them on to see if she could wear any of the clothes.

She buttoned a navy calico dress sprigged with dainty pink flowers and ran her hand down the front of the skirt. Although out of style, the dress still had plenty of wear left in it. It billowed around her, but she decided with an apron over the top, it would serve well to wear on the farm. The dark color would help hide dirt or stains and the loose gown would be welcome on hot summer days.

Aundy glanced in the mirror and noticed her petticoat hanging out of the bottom of the dress. She pulled up the hem to see if she could let it out. As she studied it, she heard a commotion outside and the sound of a dog barking. Without taking time to change, she ran to the front of the house and yanked open the door.

Wooly animals milled around as far as she could see, filling the barnyard and trailing down the lane.

Owen O'Connell rode his horse to the end of her walk and waved his hat at her. "Mrs. Erickson! Top o' the morning to ya."

She hurried down the steps and across the front walk, grateful for the fence around the yard that kept the sheep away from the flowerbeds she'd carefully weeded. "Mr. O'Connell, I wasn't expecting you until this afternoon."

"I know, lassie, but these woolies whispered bright and early they were ready to head to their new home, and moved right along," O'Connell said with a beaming smile.

174

At Dent's approach, Aundy started to make introductions, but her foreman greeted the Irishman by name and shook his hand.

"If you'll bring the sheep this way, we'll pasture them in the north section over there." Dent waved to an area behind the house.

"Sure and certain, Dent," O'Connell said, herding the sheep in the direction the foreman indicated.

When all the sheep grazed in the pasture, O'Connell returned to the house with a dog and a boy. The dog, a Border collie, wagged his tail in friendly greeting. Aundy had heard that particular breed was excellent at herding sheep.

The boy, who looked to be about fourteen or so, was all skinny arms and legs, with dusty, worn clothes, a happy-go-lucky grin, and a mop of shiny brown hair topped by a bedraggled cap. He carried a small lamb in his arms, giving it a tender glance as he rubbed its head.

Aundy knew right away that the youth had a soft heart and a gentle hand.

"Mrs. Erickson, I'd like ya to meet yer new shepherd. He'll do a good job for ya, or answer to me." O'Connell thumped the boy on his shoulder. "Tell her yer name, boyo."

The boy set the lamb down. It bleated once then nuzzled the grass of Aundy's yard.

As he swept the cap from his head, the boy bowed and raised big, brown, soulful eyes to Aundy. "I am Nikola Zorian Gandiaga, your humble shepherd."

Aundy fought down a smile and politely tipped her head to him.

"It's a pleasure to meet you, Nikola Zorian Gandiaga." Her tongue worked to pronounce the strange name properly. "Is this your dog?"

"Yes, ma'am." The boy rubbed his hand on the canine's head. The dog leaned against his leg and looked up affectionately. "This is Bob. He's a good helper."

"And how about this little one?" Aundy bent down and petted the lamb. The wool was softer than anything she could have imagined.

"This is a poor orphan baby," Nikola said, offering Aundy a smile that would someday make women swoon. "Just like me and Bob."

"An orphan? What happened to his mother?" Aundy turned her gaze to O'Connell.

"When we were passing by a farm this morning, a huge dog ran out and killed one of the ewes before we could stop him. Beast looked more like a wolf than a dog. Came out of nowhere, it did. It's a bottle for this baby, unless ya can convince one of the mammas to adopt him."

"I'll make sure he's cared for." Nikola took a protective step toward the lamb.

"Any other mishaps?" Aundy asked, glancing at the Irishman. O'Connell shook his head.

"No, ma'am. That was it. Ye are now the proud owner of four hundred and ninety-eight head of sheep, counting the babies."

She gave O'Connell a jaunty smile. "I suppose you'd like the rest of your money, then."

"If yer of a mind to give it to me, I'd surely like to get the funds and be on me way. Me fondest hope is to begin the journey to sunny California by sunrise the day after tomorrow."

"Then by all means, let's get you on your way." Aundy turned toward the house. When she looked back over her shoulder, she studied the shepherd boy. "Nikola, if you wait right here, I'll be back and we can talk about your wages and getting you settled in the bunkhouse."

O'Connell soon rode down her lane with his hands following behind. Two of them approached Dent about working there and he discussed his thoughts with Aundy. She agreed to give them a chance and they promised to return the following evening.

Aundy waved one last time at O'Connell then stared at the lamb, asleep in her yard. The dog rested his head on his master's lap, as the boy sat by the lamb.

What a picture it made. One she never thought to see, but dearly loved all the same.

"Young man, the first order of business will be to get you settled. You go on over to the bunkhouse and pick out an empty bed for your own." Aundy studied the slender boy. He looked like he needed good food and some motherly attention. Since he mentioned being an orphan, she wondered how long he'd been taking care of himself.

"Yes, ma'am," he said, getting to his feet. "I appreciate you giving me a job and letting me stay with the sheep. When Mr. O'Connell said he was leaving, I didn't know what I'd do. Thank you for giving me a home and a place to work. I usually sleep out with the sheep, though, so I don't need a bunk."

"You pick a bunk, anyway. I'm not sure I like the idea of you sleeping outside when the nights are still cold. You're most welcome about the job. My men almost revolted until I told them the sheep came with their own shepherd."

Nikola grinned at her and she smiled.

"I'm very glad you decided to come along with the sheep and bring Bob." Aundy placed a gentle hand on the boy's shoulder. Although he was painfully thin, she had an idea he was stronger than he appeared. "Do you prefer to be called Nikola?"

"I answer to Nik. It's what my mother always called me and what my friends call me. I hope to have friends here."

"Nik it is." Aundy's throat tightened at the sad look on Nik's face when he mentioned his mother. She wondered where he came from, where his family lived. From what she'd observed since he set foot in her yard, he'd been raised with good manners and someone who had been kind.

"You go settle in. I'll keep an eye on Bob and…" Aundy looked from the lamb to Nik. "Does the lamb have a name?"

"He doesn't, yet." Nik grinned as he lifted a knapsack and walked out of the yard. "You could give him one, if you like."

Aundy watched Nik saunter toward the bunkhouse, whistling a happy tune. Her attention returned to the dog and the lamb. She dropped to her knees and patted both on the head. Softly murmuring to them, warmth penetrated her back and she looked up into Garrett's silvery eyes.

"Couldn't help but see the parade go by," Garrett said with a grin, hunkering down and holding out his hand toward the dog. Bob sniffed it and licked Garrett's fingers. He rubbed the dog's ears and scratched his back, making a new friend for life.

When the dog rolled over onto his back, Garrett gave his stomach a thorough rub, watching Aundy stroke the lamb's little head.

"I already see disaster looming." He inclined his head toward the lamb.

"What?" Aundy asked, turning her gaze from the lamb to the man squatting so close to her she could feel his warmth through the sleeve of her dress.

"You're going to make a pet of that one, aren't you?" Garrett studied the lamb. It did look kind of helpless and cute, for a stinky wooly monster.

"Quite possibly." Aundy grinned as she continued stroking the lamb along his back. "Feel his coat. It's so soft, like touching butter."

"No thanks." Garrett continued to pet the dog.

"Oh, don't be so obstinate." Aundy grabbed Garrett's hand and placed it on the lamb's back. The contact of their skin sent wild sparks shooting throughout her entire being. She quickly released his fingers.

Garrett hesitantly rubbed the lamb before petting the dog.

Aundy stood and looked down at Garrett. He gazed up at her with those silvery eyes drawing her to him like magnets.

He slowly rose to his feet and fastened his full attention on her, taking her in from the golden braid wound around her head like a crown to the toes of her shoes. As he gave her a second glance, he stepped back and raised an eyebrow.

"Where did you get that dress, Mrs. Erickson? I know for a fact it isn't one of your creations or one your sister made." Garrett was unsuccessful in his efforts to hide his smirk. The dress was several inches too short, revealing Aundy's petticoats and giving him a view of slender ankles encased in light stockings. The billowing gown looked wide enough to fit two of her inside, but the color suited her well, especially now that her cheeks had blushed pink.

"Oh, I..." Aundy glanced down at the dress and realized she still had on the gown that was too short and far too wide. "My goodness."

Embarrassed, she started to race up the steps into the house, but Garrett caught her around the waist before she made it to the door. He pulled her back to his chest and bent his head so his breath caressed her ear. "Don't change on my account. I don't mind seeing your pretty ankles."

Aundy should have slapped his face or at least rushed into the house and slammed the door. Unfortunately, her limbs turned languid when her back touched his chest while his breath churned up new, disquieting sensations as it danced tantalizingly around her ear.

"You're intractable." Aundy huffed, trying to regain the ability to move her arms and legs. All she wanted was to fall back against Garrett's solid chest and stay there forever, wrapped in his arms.

"So I've been told." Garrett made no effort to move his hands from her waist or his lips from their place so close to her cheek.

"Garrett..." Aundy's voice came out in a whisper. She turned her head and he fell into her liquid blue eyes. "I think..."

"Me, too." His voice was deep and husky as he slowly turned her in his arms.

The kiss he would have surely given her failed to materialize when Nik's whistling interrupted them from a few steps away.

"Thought I better come get Bob and the lamb," Nik said, grinning at both Aundy and Garrett.

"I'm Garrett Nash." Garrett stepped away from Aundy and held his hand out to the young man. "Our place is the next one over, Nash's Folly. If you ever need anything, you just let me know."

"Thank you, sir. I'm Nikola Zorian Gandiaga, shepherd of the sheep," the boy said, once again executing a bow with his cap held to his chest. "But my friends call me Nik."

"A pleasure to meet you, Nik. I hope you enjoy working here with Mrs. Erickson. If she beats you too hard, refuses to feed you, or threatens you in any way, just tell me or Dent. We'll set her straight."

Nik's eyes grew wide, but then he grinned, seeing the appalled look on Aundy's face and the teasing smile on Garrett's.

"Yes, she looks like a cruel woman," Nik said, joining in the joking. "I'll have to be on guard at all times."

"For sure." Garrett reached out and grabbed Aundy's hand, squeezing it without even realizing what he did.

Annoyed by their teasing, all thoughts of kissing Garrett fled right out of her head. Aundy marched to the door and glared at Garrett then Nik.

"If you both think you can behave, you can wash up and tell the rest of the men to get ready for lunch. Nik, you may bring Bob and Butter to the back porch."

"Butter?" Nik asked looking at the lamb. "Guess you named him."

"Yes, I did." Aundy stepped inside the house, quietly closing the door behind her.

She raced through the house, pulled off the dress in her bedroom and slipped on one of her own. Aundy dashed to the kitchen where she donned a large apron, slipped a pan of rolls into the oven, and hurried to set the table.

By the time the men filed inside the kitchen, she had everything ready and greeted them all with a smile.

"Don't know why you think they are smelly, evil beasts, Fred. Even young Nikola can see they're harmless. Too bad a big fella like you is scared of a few little wooly sheep," Glen teased as they sauntered inside.

The daggers Fred shot at Glen with his eyes would have bled him out on the kitchen floor if they'd been able to pierce him. Glen laughed and slapped Fred's back as they all stood at the table, waiting for Aundy to be seated.

"Garrett, not surprised to see you here," Dent said, winking at Aundy. "Couldn't keep from coming over to check things out, could you?"

"You know it." Garrett held Aundy's chair for her while she took her seat. Dent gave thanks and the men all dug into the food. Nik filled his bowl twice with stew and looked around the table, sizing up the men.

"So, Nik, where do you come from?" Dent asked, wanting to know more about their young shepherd.

"Mr. O'Connell's place," he answered with a cheeky grin.

"Before that, if you please." Aundy smiled at the fun-loving boy.

"I grew up near Jordan Valley, about as south from here as you can get and still be in Oregon." Nik buttered another roll and took a bite before continuing. "My family came from the Pyrenees Mountains in Spain before my brother and I were born. There are many sheep farms around Jordan Valley and most hire Basque shepherds to care for the sheep."

"So you're Basque?" Aundy asked, realizing with Nik's name, his heritage should have been evident.

"Yes, ma'am."

"Are your parents and brother still in Jordan Valley?"

"No, ma'am. They died in a blizzard when I was ten. They went to town to get supplies and never came back. I was sick, so they left me home, planning to return before it got dark. It was early spring and no one thought it would snow. Just came up suddenly." Nik's happy smile slipped from his face as he remembered the blizzard and the days he spent trapped in the small cabin, alone and frightened. "A neighbor found the wagon just a few miles from our cabin."

"I'm so sorry for your loss, Nik." Aundy reached over to pat the boy on the arm. He was so young to bear such heartache.

"Thank you."

"What did you do... after..." Glen asked, voicing the question they all were thinking.

"My father's friend took me in for a while, but he had his own children to look after. I went to work as a shepherd that summer and have been doing it since. When the man I worked for sold part of his flock to Mr. O'Connell, I decided to go along with the sheep." Nik looked around the table at the friendly faces. He thought it would be easy to get used to living here with Mrs. Erickson and her hands. They all seemed like good people. "And here I am."

"I, for one, am mighty glad you're here." Fred grinned at Aundy then Nik. "Mrs. Erickson has assured me you will take care of the sheep so I don't have to get close to them."

Nik laughed. "Caring for the sheep is my pleasure."

"It would be my nightmare," Fred said, making everyone laugh.

After Aundy served slices of cake with coffee, and a big glass of milk for Nik, she gave each man a handful of cookies as he went out the door and thanked them all for their hard work.

Garrett leaned against the kitchen counter, watching her as she started to clean off the table.

"Don't you have work you need to see to?" Aundy asked, unsettled by his concentrated gaze.

"I sure do." Garrett made no effort to leave. However, he did walk over to the table and help carry dishes to the sink. Silence settled around them as they cleared the table.

"What are you about, Garrett Nash?" Aundy asked, glancing at him speculatively as she began washing the dishes.

"Not a thing, Mrs. Erickson." Garrett tried to force himself to walk out the door, but something about Aundy held him captive.

She'd traded the dress he'd teased her about earlier for a soft pink gown that put rosy blossoms in each cheek and made her lips look ripe for the picking. Studying her bottom lip, he recalled how delicious her kisses had tasted when he'd sampled them previously.

Suddenly, he could think of nothing else beyond kissing Aundy, melding his lips to hers. When he gazed into her eyes, he saw something flicker there, something that looked like wanting, mixed with a little fear.

Unable to bear the thought she might be afraid of him, he took a step closer and leaned down until his lips were near her ear.

"I won't hurt you, Aundy. I promise." Garrett's voice was deep and husky as his breath stirred the tendrils floating around her ear. His lips seared her skin when he pressed a hot kiss to the tender flesh of her neck.

"Garrett," she moaned, grabbing onto the front of his shirt to hold herself steady. Her knees weakened as soon he put his arms around her. His kiss nearly made her collapse.

If he let go of her, she'd surely sink to the floor. Deprived of the ability to do anything but cling to the man who held her so lovingly in his arms, Aundy raised her lips to his. Eagerly, Garrett claimed them, kissing her until she felt lightheaded.

"I think I better leave." His lips hovered agonizingly close to Aundy's.

"I think that is a very good idea." Aundy leaned against him with her eyes closed. Finally drawing back, she opened one eye, then the other. The broad grin on Garrett's handsome face left her feeling self-conscious.

"What?" She asked as she gathered the loose threads of her composure together. Aundy patted her hair with still damp hands then looked down to see if she had something on her dress or apron. Garrett continued to grin at her. "I insist you tell me what you're staring at."

"You." Garrett grabbed his hat and walked to the door, wet handprints on the front of his shirt providing evidence she'd held onto him. "Beautiful, sassy, spirited you."

Her cheeks felt hot as Garrett tipped his head and went out the door. How in the world was she going to keep her heart locked away from Garrett Nash when she knew, without a doubt, she'd fallen in love with him?

Chapter Twelve

Aundy released a sigh as she looked up from the weeds she pulled from her flowerbed on the front side of the house. Marvin Tooley jerked his horse to a stop at the end of the walk.

Quickly rising to her feet, she brushed off the knees of her skirt and met the grumpy man halfway across the yard.

"Mr. Tooley, to what do I owe the pleasure of your visit today?" Aundy asked, forcing herself to greet him with a smile.

"Ya dad-burned fool woman! Did ya really go and buy a herd of sheep?" Marvin spewed a disgusting stream of tobacco just inches from Aundy's feet.

"My goodness, news travels fast around here, doesn't it?" Aundy struggled to be pleasant although she'd rather yell at her nasty neighbor. "As a matter of fact, I did buy some sheep. Would you like to see them?"

"No, I don't want to see 'em." Marvin glowered at her. "What I want is 'em gone. They stink, they'll bring diseases to our farms, and they ain't nothin' but a nuisance. You get rid of 'em, or I'll do it for you."

"Now, see here, Mr. Tooley. You have no right to tell me what to do on my own land. Unless you'd like me to return the favor, I suggest you get on your horse and ride back down the road." Aundy's rising temper made her fight to hold on to her ability to be civil.

"Why, I ought to…"

"Bid the lady good day," Ashton Monroe said, as he dismounted his horse and walked briskly to Aundy's side. "If I'm not mistaken, she asked you to leave."

"Should've known ya'd be in cahoots with the troublemaker," Marvin said. He glared at Ashton as he mounted his horse then turned his attention back to Aundy. He spit another stream of tobacco her direction. "Ya ain't heard the last of this, Miz Erickson. Far from it."

Marvin smacked the end of his reins to the rump of the horse and raced down the lane in a cloud of dust.

Aundy watched him go, wondering how she'd missed Ashton's arrival. She'd been too distracted by her conversation with Marvin.

Her attention shifted to the man standing next to her with his seeming impeccable manners. She gave him a long look. Dressed in an expensive tailored suit, Ashton wore a brocade vest, silk tie, and crisp white shirt. His boots were polished to a high shine and the hat he held in his hand looked like it had recently been brushed or was new.

Ashton Monroe gave the appearance of a southern gentleman, but Aundy's bruised shoulder reminded her that he didn't always behave like one, at least when he wasn't in the presence of ladies.

"Thank you, Ashton, for your assistance with Mr. Tooley." Annoyed another man had come to her rescue, Aundy wished he had waited to see if she could handle the situation before getting involved.

Was there something about her that screamed helpless female? She was quite certain the men she'd met since moving to Pendleton would be hard pressed to find a woman more capable than she was at taking care of herself. With her fierce determination to be independent, there was no reason she couldn't face whatever came her way.

"I'm just glad I was here. No telling what could have happened if I hadn't run him off when I did." Ashton puffed out his chest as he spoke.

Aundy would have laughed aloud if she could have gotten away with it. Ashton would have demanded to know what was funny and she didn't want to explain to him he looked like her pompous rooster, Napoleon.

"Yes, wasn't I fortunate that you happened to come by this morning?" The tone of her voice dripped with sarcasm and she turned away so she could roll her eyes without her unexpected visitor noticing. "I suppose you heard about my sheep and are here to tell me I've lost my sense and need to sell them."

"Not at all, fair lady." Ashton took her elbow in his hand and walked her up the porch steps so they could sit on two chairs by the door. "I did hear you'd purchased sheep and thought I'd stop by to make sure everything was going well. Your hands aren't fond of the animals, or so I've heard."

"That is a fact," Aundy said with a smile.

Ashton laughed and launched into a conversation about interesting things he'd seen on his last trip out of town. For a few minutes, Aundy forgot her work and troubles as she listened to Ashton's tales.

When Nik strolled around the corner of the house carrying Butter, she rose to her feet. Aundy hurried down the steps and took the lamb from the boy. "Nik, this is one of our neighbors, Mr. Ashton Monroe. Ashton, this is Nikola, my shepherd."

"Nikola. Sounds like a foreign name. Are you not from around here?" Ashton asked, turning a probing gaze to Nik.

"No, sir." Nik looked at the man before him with a disinterested glance before returning his attention to the lamb Aundy held.

"Well, Mrs. Erickson, I won't detain you from your duties any longer this morning," Ashton said, setting his hat on his head and stepping away from Aundy and the lamb. "Enjoy your day."

"Thank you, Mr. Monroe. I plan to." Aundy largely ignored her departing company as she scratched Butter behind his ears. The lamb leaned his little head against her chest and Aundy thought she heard him release a contented sigh.

"Time to feed this one?" she asked Nik. He'd tried to get several of the ewes to take the orphaned lamb, but none of them seemed interested in feeding the hungry baby. Nik suggested they bottle-feed him. Dent found a baby bottle Erik had used with a runt piglet the previous year and they were able to keep Butter fed with it.

"Yes, ma'am. He let me know he was nearly starving." Nik pointed to slobbers on his pant leg. "He's hungry enough to eat anything that doesn't run away from him."

Laughing, Aundy set down the lamb. She and Nik fed him then the boy started to pick up Butter to take him back to the flock.

"You can leave him here, if you like." Aundy waved her hand toward a grassy spot in the shade of a tree in the yard. We'll close the gate on the yard and he should be fine, don't you think?"

"He might make a mess of your flower beds," Nik said, shaking his head. "I think I should take him back."

"Oh, he'll be fine. If he causes too much trouble, I'll bring him out to you," Aundy said, realizing it was almost noon. "Would you like to eat lunch with me before you go back out?"

"Are you sure, ma'am? I don't want to leave Bob in charge for too long." Nik glanced nervously toward the pasture where his dog kept watch over the sheep.

"It will just take a moment to make sandwiches." Aundy motioned to the lamb. "Why don't you wash up and I'll bring the food out here. We can eat on the porch and keep an eye on Butter."

"Yes, ma'am." Nik smiled then headed around to the pump on the side of the house.

Aundy returned carrying a tray laden with sandwiches, glasses of milk, and cookies. She asked a blessing on the food then she and Nik talked while they ate.

She asked his thoughts on the hands who wanted to work for her. Nik said he liked them and they always worked hard for Mr. O'Connell. They were used to working around the sheep, so they could help as needed.

Appreciative of his honesty, Aundy was grateful the men would arrive that evening. Her hands were doing more than their share as it was and she knew she needed to hire someone to cook for them. She didn't want to be tied to the kitchen and it was going to be impossible to learn to manage the farm if she was the one who prepared two big meals a day for the men.

Since her other advertisement was for farm hands, she decided to place an ad for a cook in the newspaper. She hoped someone would respond to it. If not, she was going to have to resign herself to cooking for hands.

"Thank you for the meal, Mrs. Erickson." Nik helped himself to one more cookie and gulped down the last of his milk. He carried the tray inside the house then followed her outside. Nik picked up Butter and took him back to the flock for the afternoon.

Aundy waved at Nik as he whistled his way back to the sheep. She counted her blessings over his arrival. Although he'd spent the last four years without any parental guidance, he was a sweet boy with a positive outlook on life. It was hard not to smile when you heard his happy whistle floating out on the breeze.

After washing the lunch dishes, Aundy changed into a riding skirt and shirtwaist with a light jacket. She took down her hair and braided it then tied a ribbon on the end. She pulled on her boots and ran out the kitchen door to the barn, carrying a basket of cookies.

Quickly saddling Bell, she headed toward the road and waved at George as he worked on a fence near pasture across from the house. In no time, she turned up the lane to Nash's Folly, rode past the house, and dismounted.

Aundy walked Bell to the barn. One of the hands greeted her and took the horse's reins, encouraging her to go on to the house. She raised her hand to knock on the kitchen door but it swung open and Nora greeted her with a cheery smile.

"How is the shepherdess?" Nora teased, pulling her inside with a hug.

"Fine." Aundy set her basket on the table and removed her jacket, leaving it on a peg by the back door. "How's Mr. Hong?"

"Much better." Nora peeked into the basket and took out a cookie. "He insists we call him Li, or at the very least Hong, but no mister."

"Oh. That's interesting." Aundy glanced around Nora's tidy kitchen. The smells of a roast cooking filled the air with a rich, beefy scent. Belatedly, she realized she should have put something in the oven for supper.

"What's that look for?" Nora asked, catching the frown that passed across Aundy's face.

"I need to hire a cook for the men. They've been taking turns, but they are so busy I've started cooking two meals for them. I can't learn what I need to about farming and cook for them all, too. I don't know what to do."

"Why don't you put another advertisement in the newspaper and leave a notice at the post office?" Nora asked, walking with Aundy toward the bedroom where Li Hong stayed.

"I can, but it didn't work very well the last time."

"I know, honey, but maybe someone new is in town who'd like to cook for you, or maybe someone's situation has changed and they need a job," Nora said as they sauntered down the hall. Li sat up in bed, looking much improved, when they stepped into the room. Although his eye was still swollen and bruised, he had it open a slit.

"Hello, Mr. Hong." Aundy stood at the foot of the bed. "I wanted to see how you're doing today."

"Better." Li nodded his head at Aundy. "Call me Li."

"Okay, Li, but only if you call me Aundy."

The man grinned and tried to say her name, which sounded like Audee.

Aundy smiled at him encouragingly.

"You need cook?" Li asked, having heard most of the conversation between the two women on their way to his room. He understood far more English than he could verbalize.

"Yes, I do need a cook. Do you know one?" Aundy cast a hopeful gaze his direction.

"Me."

"You? Oh, well, I…"

"I can cook. Good cook. Make good things." Li nodded his head so enthusiastically, Aundy was afraid he'd make his injuries worse.

"What can you cook?" Aundy asked. Her men would not be excited at the prospect of eating Chinese food on a regular basis.

"Anything. Everything. Li good cook." The man stared hopefully at the women. "Need job, you need cook." He pointed at Aundy.

"Can you make meat and potatoes? Biscuits? Bacon and eggs?"

"Yes. Cook American food." Li waved his hands to emphasize his words. "I cook anything."

Aundy looked at Nora and shrugged her shoulders.

"You get well and we'll see about trying you out as a cook. If the men don't complain, you can stay. Does that sound fair?"

"Yes." Li grinned broadly, at least as broadly as he could with his wounded face.

"You work on healing, then, because we are in dire need of a cook." Aundy smiled kindly at the man. She had a good feeling about him, even if he hadn't exposed who beat him or what happened.

"Thank you."

"You're welcome, although you might not thank me after you meet the hungry men at my place."

Aundy and Nora returned to the kitchen, visiting for a while. When Aundy announced it was time for her to go home, Nora took the cookies out of the basket and set them on a plate. She placed a wrapped loaf of fresh bread in Aundy's basket and held her jacket while she slipped it on.

"You should come see the sheep, Nora. We have one baby we're bottle-feeding and he's adorable. I named him Butter," Aundy said as she prepared to go out the door.

"I'll be over soon, honey. If you need anything, though, you let us know," Nora said as she walked Aundy down the back steps.

"I will. Thank you." Aundy hugged her friend before hurrying out to the barn. No one was around when she walked in, so she located Bell and led the horse outside to mount when Garrett came around the corner, almost bumping into her.

"Well, hello." Garrett shoved his hands into his pockets to keep from wrapping his arms around Aundy and kissing her. "What brings you by today?"

"I wanted to check on Li and I brought over some cookies for Nora to try. I was experimenting with a recipe and wanted her opinion."

"Cookies?" Garrett perked up at the thought of baked goods. Aundy made the best cookies. He'd have to find an excuse to run inside the house and grab some before his dad ate them all.

"You're worse than a child." Aundy's laugh resonated from Garrett's ears all the way down to the bottom of his heart, drawing out a warm smile.

"Maybe." He walked with her across the barnyard toward the lane leading back to the road. "How are things going today? The sheep settled in? Nik doing fine?"

"Yes. Nik is such a sweet boy and the sheep seem so docile. Fred has decided to stay, for now, and the two new hands should arrive this evening. Other than some unexpected visitors this morning, everything is fine."

"Unexpected visitors?"

"Nothing to be concerned about." Marvin Tooley's threats had her worried and a little nervous. Would he really do something to her sheep? "I better get home, though."

"I'm sorry I didn't realize you were here sooner. I'd have come in while you were visiting Ma." Garrett easily lifted her to the saddle. Aundy would have expressed her ability to get herself on the back of Bell without his assistance, but she liked the feel of his hands on her waist too much to protest.

"Then I wouldn't have gotten to visit with Nora and she wouldn't have been able to tell me what a naughty little boy you were," Aundy teased.

"Were? I thought the two of you decided weeks ago I'm still a naughty boy." The devilish grin on his face made heat climb up her neck and fill her cheeks.

"You're impossible." She shook her head and laughed again.

"That I am." Garrett admired the way her riding skirt fit her tall figure as well as the way she sat on the horse as she started down the lane. "I'll see you later."

Aundy waved and urged Bell into a canter.

She raced the horse home as fast as she dared. After brushing down Bell and giving her a portion of her evening feed, Aundy hurried inside the house. Hastily changing back into her dress and tying on a clean apron, she set about preparing dinner for the men. Dent and the hands were out doing fieldwork and would arrive for dinner bone-tired. Aundy told Dent that morning to bring in everyone for the evening meal.

Aundy rushed to dish up the food as the sound of boots outside the kitchen door let her know the men were on time for supper.

Although they weren't rowdy, they walked in laughing and teasing each other. She smiled at their good-natured ribbing as she scooped the last of the mashed potatoes into a bowl.

A loud knock sounded from the front door.

"Should I get that, Missy?" Dent asked. At Aundy's nod, he disappeared toward the front of the house.

Aundy heard low voices then footsteps approaching the kitchen. Her new hands arrived in time to eat. It was a good thing she'd prepared plenty of food.

"Bill, would you place two more plates on the table, please?" Aundy asked, then set out more silverware and coffee mugs for the new arrivals. She turned to the newly hired men and offered them a warm smile. "Welcome, gentlemen. Please join us for supper."

"We didn't mean to intrude, ma'am," the taller of the two said. They looked with both hunger and uncertainty at the loaded table as they stood holding their hats in their hands.

"No intrusion." Aundy motioned them toward the table. "Glen, if you and George could carry in a couple of chairs from the dining room, we should be able to squeeze everyone in."

Carefully wiping her hands on her apron, Aundy approached her newest employees. "Please, tell me your names again. I apologize, but in all the excitement yesterday, I seem to have forgotten."

"That's okay, ma'am," the shorter one said, his brown eyes filled with humor. "It was kind of hard to hear yourself think with all of the hubbub going on. I'm Lem Perkins and this is Hank Lawson."

"Nice to meet you both." Aundy politely nodded to each of them. "Why don't you wash at the sink and then have a seat? You can get settled in the bunkhouse after we eat."

"Yes, ma'am." They didn't need to be asked twice to sit down to a hot meal.

Conversation was lively as they ate. When the meal was finished, Aundy asked Dent to stay for a few minutes. He helped her clear the table, discussing what work needed to be completed the following day, and how he thought the sheep and Nik were doing.

"Do you think Nik would be receptive to being tutored?" Aundy asked, up to her elbows in dishwater.

"Tutored? What for?" Dent wiped off the kitchen table with a rag.

"He's such a bright boy, but it's obvious his education is severely lacking. I assume he probably hasn't had any schooling since his parents died. With a sharp mind like his, he could do better for himself than being a shepherd all his life."

"He does seem like a good kid and he is smart, at least from what I've seen." Dent carried the two extra chairs back to the dining room then returned to lean against the counter. "But he spends all his time out with the sheep. Even insists on sleeping out there with them. How do you propose to teach him? You can't sit out there in the sheep pasture with him."

Aundy refrained from saying she could if she wanted to and offered another solution. "Could one of the men watch the sheep for an hour or two each evening? Nik could stay after supper and work on his book learning while I do dishes and get things ready for the following day."

"Don't see anything wrong with that, but you won't get Fred out there," Dent said with a grin.

"Thank you for pointing out the obvious." Aundy smiled at her foreman. "Do you think we need to hire another shepherd?"

"No. I think Nik can handle the sheep just fine. We don't have too much problem with coyotes around here. Once he and the sheep settle in, I think he'll realize he doesn't have to watch over them day and night." Dent walked to the door, then turned back to look at her. "I'll have Lem and Hank take turns with the sheep in the evenings for now, provided you can talk Nik into being your student."

"Thank you, Dent. I'll speak with Nik tomorrow."

Aundy listened to Nik recite his multiplication tables while she washed the dishes one evening.

Although reluctant to leave his sheep, the boy proved to be an eager student and jumped into his studies with enthusiasm. Aundy had been tutoring him in the evenings for the last week and the arrangement worked well. The hands took turns keeping an eye on the sheep while Nik stayed in the house after supper. Even Fred had taken a turn without much complaint.

Dent claimed he caught Nik conjugating verbs that afternoon when he rode by to check on him. The other men had mentioned that Nik talked constantly about something new he'd learned.

Grateful for her mother's inheritance that had paid for her, Ilsa, and Lars to receive a good education, Aundy dug through her things and found one of her old school books. A raid of Erik's bookshelves provided more material for Nik to study. As soon as she went to town, Aundy planned to order more educational supplies for the boy.

And buy him some new clothes.

His pants were too short, his shirtsleeves hit inches away from his wrists, and his shoes were worn completely through. She wondered that Mr. O'Connell didn't provide better for the boy. When she asked Nik about it, he shrugged his shoulders and said he was just the shepherd. Since he spent most of his time with the sheep, they didn't care about his appearance.

"Let's work on your spelling," Aundy said as she began drying the clean dishes and putting them away. She would say a word and Nik would spell it. He got about half of them correct. The ones he did not, she made him write on a sheet of paper. With the dictionary she found in Erik's things, Nik was supposed to look up the definition of each word and learn it, along with the proper spelling.

"Very good, Nik," Aundy said, when he spelled the last three words correctly. "I think that's enough learning tonight."

"Please, may I study a little while longer?" Nik picked up a copy of *Gulliver's Travels* by Jonathan Swift.

"Yes, you may." Aundy smiled indulgently as Nik lost himself in the adventure. She had no idea he would be so excited for the opportunity to further his education. It was like pouring water into a bottomless pitcher. He never seemed to tire of learning. She wondered, with the right opportunities, what career Nik would choose. A mind as sharp as his shouldn't be wasted sitting in a pasture watching sheep. "Why don't you read aloud and I'll enjoy the story, too."

Nik grinned at her and returned to the beginning of the chapter he read. She listened to Nik's voice and mixed up a batch of molasses cookies. The rich, spicy dough filled the kitchen with a delicious scent. Aundy made a cup of tea and sat at the table, enjoying the story while the cookies baked.

After removing the cookies from the oven, Aundy let them cool slightly before putting three on a plate. She poured a tall glass of milk, setting the snack by Nik. Although still thin, he seemed to be filling out a little with plenty of good food. She ruffled his hair as she stood by his chair. He grinned at her again then continued the story, stopping only to take a bite of cookie or a drink of milk.

They were both lost in the adventure when Aundy heard a loud thump on the front porch. She and Nik hurried to the door, opening it to find a small bundle of wool blazing with flame.

Aundy bit back a scream and glared at a rider clad all in black on a dark horse. In the shadows of late evening, she couldn't distinguish any features.

"Git rid a them stinking sheep, woman, or ya'll be sorry," the man's voice yelled before he thundered down her lane.

Nik kicked the burning ball of wool off the porch into the grass and Aundy ran to the kitchen to get a pitcher of water. Nik tried stomping the flames, but the kerosene-soaked wool was nearly impossible to extinguish. In the damp grass, it wouldn't spread, so he watched it smolder, pulling the collar of his shirt over his nose to try to filter the stench of the burning fiber.

"Aundy? What is this? Would someone hurt you or our sheep?" Nik stood beside her when she returned with the water. She grasped his hand in hers, hoping it would comfort them both.

"I don't know, Nik," she said, distressed by the threat. She turned to go back inside the house when Dent and Bill ran into the yard.

"Thought we heard something." Dent tried to catch his breath as he took in Aundy and Nik's frightened faces and the scorched smell of wool. "What happened?"

"Some man threw that wool on fire at the door then yelled at Aundy to get rid of the sheep or she'd be sorry. They won't really hurt her or the sheep, will they?" Nik looked at Dent for reassurance.

"Of course not, Nik. We won't let anything happen." Dent stepped onto the porch and patted the boy on the back. "Why don't you gather your things and call it a night."

"Yes, sir." Nik cast one more glance at Aundy before he went into the house.

"Who do you think it was, Missy?" Dent waited to see if Aundy would fall apart. She had a strong backbone and not much rattled her, but most women would have been in hysterics by now.

"I don't know, Dent. He was dressed all in black, his horse was dark in coloring and with it being almost dark out, I just couldn't tell. I didn't recognize his voice either. It was higher-pitched than Marvin Tooley's, because he made a similar threat the other day."

"He did?" Dent wondered why Aundy hadn't imparted that information sooner. He heard some of the neighbors grumbling about Aundy bringing sheep into the area, but most of them would get over it and forget they were there in a few weeks. Honestly, he thought Aundy had a good idea with the sheep. So far, they'd been easy to care for, especially with Nik's constant watch over them. "Why didn't you tell me?"

"I didn't want to worry anyone. Besides, I don't think he'd actually do anything."

"You never know with him, Missy. He's a little unpredictable." Dent recalled any number of odd things that had happened over the years since Marvin lost his family and changed into a different man. He thought they should at least give Marvin's threat some consideration. "If he comes around again, you let one of us know right away."

"Giving orders now, are you?" A smile tugged up the corners of Aundy's mouth. She and Dent both knew he was essentially in charge. At least until she learned what she needed to know to successfully manage the farm. Even then, Dent would still be the one giving orders and laying down the law to the men.

"Durn right I am," Dent said, still unsettled by what had happened. If someone truly had it out for Aundy and the sheep, he worried about what they would do next.

Chapter Thirteen

Aundy gave Dent a look that let him know she wanted to talk as the hands made their way out the door after breakfast the next morning. He poured himself another cup of coffee, sat back down at the table, and waited.

When they were the only two left in the kitchen, Aundy sank onto a chair with a cup of tea. "I have a favor to ask."

"I'm in trouble now," Dent teased, smiling at her as he sipped the hot liquid in his cup. "What do you need, Missy?"

"Can you spare someone to watch the sheep for a few hours today or at least check on them? I want to take Nik into town with me. He absolutely needs some new clothes and I honestly wouldn't mind the company." Aundy knew her request would leave Dent shorthanded while she and Nik were gone. Lem and Hank fit right in with the other hands and they all worked well together, but none of them particularly liked working with the sheep.

"I'll have Lem keep an eye on the sheep, but are you sure it's a good idea to go to town. What if…"

"Don't start that." Aundy silenced him when she held up her hand. "I won't allow anyone to scare me into getting rid of the sheep. The men around here need to realize a little burning wool isn't going to change my mind on the matter."

Dent hid his grin behind his coffee cup. He had an idea if someone backed Aundy into a corner, she'd come out swinging and probably win.

"Okay, then. Want me to tell Nik he's about to go on an adventure?" Dent got to his feet and placed his cup in the sink.

"Yes, please, and have him take a bath, too. I don't want people wrinkling their noses at him when we go shopping today." Aundy grinned, thinking of the protests Nik would no doubt utter at taking a bath in the middle of the week. "I'll be ready to go at nine. Tell Nik to meet me at the barn then."

"If you say so." Dent snitched a cookie on his way out the door.

After finishing the dishes and writing out a shopping list, Aundy donned her yellow and cream walking suit Garrett had admired. She styled her hair on top of her head with a few loose tendrils trailing down her neck and pinned her hat in place. She picked up a pair of gloves and her reticule, stuffed the grocery list inside, checked to make sure the house was set to rights then hurried down the kitchen steps toward the barn.

Nik sat on the buggy seat, freshly scrubbed and ready for an adventure.

"Ready?" Aundy asked, climbing in beside him and giving him a thorough observation. He'd carefully combed his shiny brown hair and left off his tattered old cap. Although his attire wasn't new by any means, the outfit he had on fit a little better than the clothes he normally wore. He'd attempted to polish his shoes, but they were so far gone it only served to highlight their sorry state.

"Dent said I'm to accompany you to town today," Nik said, doing his best to sound formal and educated.

"That is correct, kind sir." Aundy offered him a playful wink. "I think I'll sit back and enjoy this beautiful day while you drive the buggy."

"Really?" With an animated grin, Nik picked up the reins.

"Really. Just be careful, though. No wild racing or terrifying tomfoolery," Aundy cautioned, trying to look and sound serious.

"No, ma'am." Nik gave the reins a gentle flick that started the horse moving forward.

On the way to town, Aundy listened to Nik talk about his family, his heritage, and things he enjoyed doing when he was a small boy.

As they drove down a busy street in Pendleton, Nik turned his attention to handling the horse in the traffic.

He stopped near Aundy's favorite store and they went inside. She gave her shopping list to the clerk to fill while she took Nik over to the ready-made clothing section. Aundy helped him pick out two pairs of denim overalls, a pair of pants and a vest to wear to church, and four shirts, along with a sturdy pair of boots and a new hat.

"Aundy, this is too much." Nik's eyes shined with gratitude and awe. "I haven't earned this much pay. I can't take this."

"You can and you will." She patted Nik on the back with motherly affection. "Anyone in my employ will be properly fed and clothed, and that's all there is to it."

Nik looked at her and saw her grin, smiling in return. "Yes, ma'am." He brushed his hands over his new shirts. Aundy quietly asked the clerk to add socks and underclothes for the boy to her growing pile.

As the clerk boxed up her purchases, he snapped his fingers suddenly. "Those seeds you ordered just arrived, Mrs. Erickson. Let me get them for you."

"Seeds?" Nik asked as he stood next to Aundy. It took a great effort on his part not to jump off one foot to the other in his excitement at having brand new clothes. He couldn't remember the last time he'd owned something new that wasn't someone else's used castoff.

"For the garden. We need to get it planted soon." She lifted the lid on a jar of lemon drops and motioned for Nik to take one. His eyes twinkled as he fished out two pieces, and held one out to her. She was going to refuse then decided she wasn't quite grown up enough that she'd turn down candy. The two of them popped the lemon drops in their mouths, enjoying the sweet treat.

"Please add two lemon drops to the bill, Mr. Johnson."

"No need, Mrs. Erickson. You've purchased more than enough to earn a few pieces of candy." The man tucked Aundy's seeds into one of the boxes while she handed Nik his new cap. He settled it on his head with a wide smile.

Aundy paid her bill while Nik carried their purchases out to the buggy. She asked Mr. Johnson to have someone call when her order for Nik's school supplies arrived.

"Have a wonderful day, Mrs. Erickson." Mr. Johnson waved as she followed Nik out the door. Aundy stared at a plow on display outside the store when a bump to her side nearly knocked her into the street. She would have fallen, had she not caught herself on a post.

"Might want to watch yourself, Miz Erickson." Marvin Tooley sneered at her. His hand flexed into a fist. He took a menacing step toward her, reaching out and grabbing her upper arm in a vise-like grip. "No telling what might happen if you let your guard down."

She yanked her arm out of his grasp and narrowed her gaze. Nik hurried to her side with a frightened look on his face, trying to figure out what happened. He watched as Marvin growled and stalked into the store.

"Who is that man?"

"No one to worry about." Aundy took Nik's arm and directed him down the boardwalk. Although she'd been considering the purchase of a small gun, Marvin had just helped make up her mind.

After entering a store that sold both new and used merchandise, Aundy left Nik browsing through a section of musical instruments while she went straight to the proprietor behind the counter.

"I'd like to purchase the gun in the window," she said, pointing to a display in a glass case by the front door.

"A gun?" the man asked, shocked that a woman marched into his store and wanted to buy a weapon.

"Yes, that small one in the case by the door," Aundy said, walking to the case and pointing to the one she wanted.

Reluctantly the man took out the one she indicated and handed it to her.

"That's a Baby Hammerless pocket revolver," the proprietor explained, pointing out the gun's lack of a visible hammer.

Aundy liked the light feel of it in her hand as well as the lovely pearl grips. It would fit perfectly in her reticule or a pocket. She warmed to the idea of having a gun on hand if she needed some protection without having to carry a bigger weapon.

From her lessons with Garrett, she knew to open the chamber and check to make sure there weren't any bullets inside. She pointed the gun at a display of traps across the store and asked the storeowner to give her details about how it worked. He answered her questions and told her the gun was only a few years old, having had one previous owner.

"What happened to the owner?" She balanced the gun on her palm.

"Got shot."

That bit of information, unsettling as it was, didn't deter Aundy's determination to purchase the weapon. The proprietor started to ring up the sale, but Aundy asked him for several boxes of cartridges. While he retrieved them from the back room, she walked over to where Nik gazed fondly at a display of harmonicas.

"Do you play?"

"No," Nik said quietly.

Aundy wondered who in his past had played. From the wistful expression on his face, it must have been someone he cared about deeply. The boy seemed to whistle and hum all the time, so she wondered if he'd appreciate his own instrument.

"What harmonica would you recommend to a new student?" Aundy asked the storeowner when he returned with her cartridges. He pointed out what he thought was the best model and Aundy added it to her purchases.

"You can't buy me the harmonica, too," Nik whispered as they walked toward the counter.

"Yes, I can." Aundy patted Nik on the back, much like she would a small child. "Just promise you'll play it for me some winter evening when I'm bored out of my mind and tired of the snow. I've heard the winters out here are dreadful."

"They can be bad." Nik's eyes fastened on the shiny new harmonica in his hands. "I promise to play for you any time you want."

"Very well, then," Aundy said, putting the gun in her reticule and picking up the boxes of cartridges. She turned to the proprietor, gave him a polite smile, and tipped her head. "Thank you, sir. Have a lovely day."

After talking Nik into eating lunch with her at a restaurant, they headed out of town toward home. Aundy drove while Nik played the harmonica. With a natural musical talent, he was already starting to play a tune instead of just making random noise.

"You'll be an expert at playing in no time." Aundy parked the buggy by the side gate of the yard so it would be easier to carry her purchases to the kitchen door.

Nik shoved the harmonica into his pocket and began lugging in the loaded boxes. Aundy held the door for Nik to carry in the last box when she heard the distinctive jingle of a harness. She walked around the side of the house as Nora stopped her buggy at the end of the front walk with Li Hong beside her.

"Nora! What a surprise!" Aundy hurried over to give the woman a hug as she got out of the buggy. Li Hong stepped down and bowed to her then watched Nik approach.

"Nora, Li Hong, this is my shepherd, Nikola Zorian Gandiaga. We call him Nik." Aundy placed a hand on Nik's shoulder, drawing him forward as she made introductions.

"Hello," Nik said, doffing his hat to Nora and reaching out to shake Li Hong's hand. When the man bowed at him, Nik grinned and mimicked his motions. "I better get back to the sheep. Lem will be tired of watching them." Nik climbed into Aundy's buggy and drove it to the barn.

"What brings you two out today?" Aundy asked, looping her arm around Nora's and motioning Li to follow them up the porch steps.

"I wanted to see your sheep and Li thinks he is ready to begin his duties as cook. I brought him over to see your place and make sure that's what he really wants to do." Nora looked over her shoulder at Li with a smile.

"I ready to cook. Make good food." Li grinned at both women while nodding his head enthusiastically.

"Why don't we plan on you starting in the morning, then?" Aundy led the way into her house. "Please, have a seat and I'll be back with some tea."

Nora and Aundy visited with Li making occasional comments to their chatter while they drank tea and ate cookies.

Dent marched to the house, set to ask Aundy what she thought she was doing buying a gun after Nik told him what she'd purchased, when he noticed the Nash's buggy parked out front. He entered through the back door and held his hat in his hand as he walked into the front room.

Not surprised to see a Chinese man drinking tea with Aundy and Mrs. Nash, he smiled in greeting.

"Afternoon," Dent said, tipping his head toward Nora.

"Hello, Dent," Nora said, giving him a friendly smile. "How does this day find you?"

"Well enough. I can't complain about a thing." Dent grinned at Nora. "How's J.B.?"

"He improves every day. By the end of summer, Doc thinks he'll be back in the saddle and up to his old tricks." Nora's face gave away her relief that her husband was finally getting better.

"That's wonderful news." Dent was happy to hear his friend would make a full recovery. For a while, no one knew if J.B. would ever walk again. "Tell him I said hello."

"I'll do that, but you should come visit him one of these days. He'd love to play a game of checkers with you." Nora knew how much J.B. and Dent enjoyed their checker rivalry.

"If my slave-driving employer ever gives me a day off, I might just do that." Dent winked at Aundy.

Not bothered in the least by his teasing, Aundy turned to Li. "Dent, this is Li Hong. He's been staying with the Nash's while he recuperated from an unfortunate accident. Since we are in need of a cook, he volunteered for the job, on a trial basis. He says he feels well enough to get started. I thought he could begin by making breakfast tomorrow."

After the sheep incident, Aundy made sure she discussed hiring Li as a cook with Dent. He agreed to have the man fill the position temporarily, until the hands were assured Li could cook food they would all eat.

"Works for me." Dent nodded his head in approval. After studying the Chinese man, with his long braid and odd manner of dress, Dent decided the man didn't look dangerous, just wary. "I can take you out and show you the bunkhouse and where you'll be doing the cooking."

"Okay, Mr. Dent," Li said, getting to his feet. He turned to Aundy, bowed and thanked her for the tea. He thanked Nora for her care while he was injured then followed Dent to the door.

"Just call me Dent, no mister," the foreman said as he opened the front door and walked out with Li.

Aundy heard Li tell Dent to call him Li or Hong, no mister.

"I think they'll get along fine," Nora whispered as they watched the older cowboy and the younger Chinese man walk across the front yard and toward the bunkhouse.

"I hope Li works out." Aundy sat back in her chair and sipped her tea. Cooking for the men while trying to keep up with everything else reminded her of the frantic days she put in before moving to Pendleton. They left her weary and exhausted, which wasn't all bad. That way she didn't stay awake at night worrying about who wanted to harm her sheep or dreaming about Garrett.

With his mother sitting across from her chatting about a new quilt pattern she saw in a magazine, Aundy's cheeks blushed as she thought about Garrett and his kisses.

"Are you feeling well, honey? You look a little flushed." Nora leaned over and put a hand on Aundy's forehead.

"I'm fine, just a little warm." Aundy sipped her tea, attempting to hide her embarrassment. A knock on the door saved her from having to explain her flushed cheeks.

She opened the door to Ashton Monroe. He stood on her front step smiling broadly and dressed impeccably.

"Ashton," Aundy said, opening the door wider to allow him entry. "I didn't expect a visit from you today. I thought you were out of town."

"I just returned and thought I'd stop to say hello on my way home." Ashton didn't smile quite as broadly when he saw Nora in the room. "Mrs. Nash, you're looking lovely as always." Ashton took her hand in his, exhibiting manners befitting a fine gentleman.

"Thank you, Ashton. Been out of town again?" Nora kept her voice even although her eyes had lost the warmth they held earlier when she and Aundy chatted.

"Yes, ma'am. Business, you know." Ashton sat down and accepted the cup of tea Aundy poured for him along with a cookie. Aundy's stylish outfit caught his attention and he watched her for a moment before he felt Nora's glare.

"My, but you are a busy man," Nora said dryly although Ashton didn't notice.

He soaked up the comment like praise and puffed out his chest. Aundy thought he looked a little like the peacocks she'd seen in Chicago.

"A busy man is a successful man." Ashton set down his cup of tea and cleared his throat. "It is serendipitous to find you here, Mrs. Nash." Ashton spoke to Nora while his gaze lingered on Aundy.

Although he would never consider her beautiful, she was attractive. He hated seeing the plain dresses she tended to wear around the farm. The smart ensemble she currently wore meant she'd either been calling or to town. "I would like to invite all of you, along with Mrs. Erickson, to be my dinner guests Friday evening. I haven't entertained company at Dogwood Corners for far too long. Won't you please join me?"

The last thing Nora wanted to do was force J.B. and Garrett to eat dinner with the pompous Ashton Monroe, but if he was trying to be neighborly, she didn't feel she could refuse. "That's a lovely invitation, Ashton. We'd be happy to join you, if Mrs. Erickson is of a mind to go, of course."

"Of course," Aundy echoed, wondering what thoughts tumbled through Nora's head. Busy with an abundance of work on the farm, Aundy didn't really want to make time to go to Ashton's, especially when he did behave somewhat arrogantly if he had an audience. However, she did like the thought of finally seeing his home. "May we bring something?"

"No. Just your lovely faces." Ashton stood and picked up his hat. "I might turn it into a regular dinner party. Let's plan on six that evening to dine."

"We'll be there." Nora frowned as she watched him kiss Aundy's hand on his way out the door.

Unless she was completely mistaken, Garrett was in love with Aundy. It might prove interesting for him to watch Ashton slobber all over her hand a few times Friday evening. Interesting, indeed.

"I better get back to J.B. and think about putting supper on the table." Nora rose from her chair and walked toward the door. "Let me know how things go with Li Hong. Garrett has tried to get him to talk about who beat him, but he won't say a thing. I don't know whom he's protecting, but I certainly wish he'd tell us. No one should be allowed to treat another human that way and get away with it."

"I agree," Aundy said, walking Nora out to her buggy. "Maybe he'll talk to someone here once he settles in. I just hope he's as good a cook as he claims. I'm more than ready to let him take over."

Laughing, Nora flicked the reins and turned her buggy around in the barnyard. As she was leaving, she called over her shoulder. "We'll pick you up Friday to go to Ashton's."

SHANNA HATFIELD

Chapter Fourteen

"Do like this, Missy," Li said, as he bent over a row of freshly tilled earth and showed Aundy how to drop carrot seeds into the ground then cover them with the rich soil.

Aundy hid her smile. She found it amusing Li decided to call her Missy, just like Dent. Li was as good a cook as he claimed and fixed tasty, filling food the men ate without complaint.

It was the pledge of a special treat that resulted in a freshly plowed garden that morning. After Li promised to make Glen fritters for supper in trade for preparing the garden ground, he swiftly plowed a space near the house.

Li volunteered to help plant the seeds. Since he had experience and she didn't, Aundy was more than happy to follow his direction.

"Yes, sir." Aundy walked next to him, planting a row of carrots. She ordered a wide variety of vegetable seeds for their garden and was excited to discover Erik's mother had long ago planted blackberries and strawberries. With the trees in the orchard, they'd have plenty of fresh produce to eat as well as preserve for the winter months.

They worked most of the morning planting the garden then Aundy made sandwiches and took lunch out to Nik. Since she was supposed to accompany the Nash family to Ashton's for dinner that night, she didn't want the boy to miss his lessons.

As she walked out to the far pasture where Nik had the flock, she breathed deeply of the fresh air and soaked up the warm sunshine while listening to her shepherd play a cheerful tune on his harmonica.

When she arrived in Pendleton, she had no idea at the time she'd find herself truly thinking of the place as home.

Aundy loved the clean air, the quiet peacefulness of the country, and the freedom she felt on the farm. Guilt stabbed at her over Erik's absence and the reason she was so free to do as she wished. She offered up a prayer of gratitude for all her many blessings.

Nik noticed her approach and ran over with Bob and Butter at his heels. "Hello, Aundy. What are you doing out here?" Nik took the basket she carried and walked with her toward a spot under a shady tree.

"I brought some lunch and thought we could have your lesson now. I'll be gone this evening and didn't want you to miss out on your studies." Aundy spread a cloth beneath the tree before sitting down. Butter rubbed against her side and Bob flopped near her feet, his tongue lolling out of his mouth while his tail wagged in a happy rhythm.

"I don't have any of my books or papers with me." Nik sat by Aundy and waited while she handed him a thick ham sandwich and a jar of milk that was still cold.

"Today can be a nature lesson."

A lively discussion of the clouds overhead, geological facts, and what made the grass green took place as they ate their sandwiches. Nik munched on the cookies she brought along while Aundy asked him how he thought the sheep liked their new home.

"Your soil is much richer than Mr. O'Connell's," Nik said, gazing around the green hills with pride. "The sheep have such good pasture, they stay fat and content."

"I'm glad to hear that." Aundy studied the flock. Watching them was so restful. They were quiet and calm as they nibbled at the pasture grass, presenting such as serene picture. Aundy's mind wandered to a sermon the pastor shared recently about the Good Shepherd and his sheep.

"…it was really good," Nik said, brushing crumbs off his hands and setting his empty milk jar inside Aundy's basket.

"I'm sorry, Nik. I didn't hear what you said," Aundy admitted.

Nik grinned at her with a knowing smile. "Gathering wool or chasing dreams?"

"Both. Neither." Aundy laughed, shaking her head.

"You were thinking about Mr. Nash," Nik teased, leaning back on his elbows.

"I was not thinking about J.B. or Nora, for that matter," Aundy answered with a saucy grin.

"I didn't mean them. I meant Garrett and you know it." Nik helped Aundy pack the remnants of lunch.

"I know no such thing." Aundy was surprised Nik noticed her interest in Garrett, although he had caught them almost kissing a time or two. "Tell me what you said and I'll pay attention this time."

"I said Li made Chinese food for dinner the other night and it was really good. None of us thought we'd be able to eat it, but even though it tasted different, I liked it. I think everyone else did, too. There wasn't any left."

"I'm glad you all enjoyed it." Aundy wished she'd had a bite or two. With Li taking over the cooking, she was able to spend more time learning about farming and taking care of some chores around the house that needed attention, but she missed the lively conversations that took place during breakfast and supper.

Now, the meals seemed so quiet and somewhat lonely with all the men eating at the bunkhouse. Occasionally, Nik would eat with her before they launched into his lessons. The boy had already figured out to ask what was on the menu at her house and the bunkhouse before he made up his mind where he'd eat.

"You should come next time he makes it. Everyone would be glad to have you there," Nik said, walking with Aundy as she started back toward the house.

"Maybe." Aundy smiled at Nik and rubbed her hand across his shoulders. Although he remained thin, he was starting to fill out his frame.

Butter bleated and ran around her legs. She knelt and gave the lamb a thorough petting before doing the same for Bob. The dog rolled onto his back and held still, in perfect bliss, while Aundy scratched his belly.

"Okay, you three, I really do need to get back." Aundy rose to her feet again.

"Where did you say you're going?" Nik asked.

"Ashton Monroe's place. The Nash family will be going as well, for dinner."

"Oh." Nik studied the toe of his boot.

"Why? Something wrong?" Aundy wondered what caused his sudden pensive mood.

"Nothing. It's just… I think Mr. Monroe likes you." Nik let out a sigh as he looked at Aundy, trying to judge her reaction to his words. "I like Garrett much better, though."

"Thank you for sharing your thoughts on the subject, although I'm here to tell you right now, I'll be staying single."

Nik looked at her with his happy-go-lucky smile back in place. "That's good, Aundy. You stay single and when I'm old enough, you'll marry me."

"You are a tease, Nikola Zorian Gandiaga!" Aundy laughed again, walking away with a wave. "A real tease."

Back at the house, she washed the few dishes she'd dirtied to make lunch and decided to clean the chicken coop. She hated the job even more than she did gathering eggs, but she had time to take care of it before she had to get ready for dinner.

Almost finished with the unwelcome chore, she noticed a horse stirring a cloud of dust as it raced up her lane.

She expelled a heavy sigh as she watched Marvin Tooley pull his horse to a stop at the end of her walk. He weaved his way through the front gate, down the walk, and up the porch steps, pounding on the front door.

Aundy wished she had her gun with her. Instead, she rushed out of the coop, grabbed a shovel on her way to the house, and ran around to the front yard. Fearful Marvin's wild thumping would break the frosted glass panel out of the door, she raised her voice to be heard above the racket he made.

"Mr. Tooley, cease your pounding!"

He stared at her with bleary eyes. "Told ya to sell them durn sheep, woman. Done told ya to," he slurred.

Aundy hadn't seen many drunk people in her life but it was obvious Marvin imbibed in something either quite potent or quite a lot of it.

Marvin sneered at her. "Now ya'll pay the piper."

"What's that supposed to mean?" Aundy asked, standing her ground. "Is that another of your threats?"

"Nope. Not a threat. It's a fact." He cackled loudly. The sound made the hair on the back of Aundy's neck prickle. Marvin Tooley sounded like a lunatic.

"Be that as it may, would you please take yourself and your facts off my property this instant?" Aundy pointed her hand in the direction of Marvin's lathered horse.

"I warned ya, woman. Done told ya. But ya jes won't listen." Marvin weaved down the steps.

Aundy wasn't sure the crazy drunk would be able to get back on his horse much less take himself home.

He glanced back at her as he fumbled to put a foot into his stirrup. "Stubborn, fool woman. It'll teach her to listen to me."

Unbothered by his comments, she offered him an insincere smile. "Thank you for sharing your thoughts, Mr. Tooley. Have a lovely afternoon. If you come back making more threats, I'll pay a visit to the sheriff about you."

"Don't threaten me!" Marvin yelled, somehow managing to get on his horse. He rode a few yards down the lane before falling off.

Aundy tossed aside the shovel and marched to where Marvin sprawled in the dirt.

"You are completely pathetic," Aundy muttered as she grabbed his horse's reins and led it to the barn. The last thing, the very last thing, she wanted to do was take Marvin Tooley home, but she couldn't very well leave him in the road and there was no way she was letting the man in her house, the barn, or the bunkhouse. She wanted him off her property, posthaste.

Swiftly hitching a horse to the buggy, she tied Marvin's horse to the back then pulled up beside the drunken man. Without any of the hands around, she was on her own if she planned to take Marvin home.

"Mr. Tooley, I can't and won't lift you up. You've got to get to your feet without my assistance. Now up!" Aundy prodded him with the toe of her boot.

Although he grumbled at her, Marvin did manage to stagger to his feet long enough to collapse into the back of the buggy with his legs dangling off the end.

"If you fall out, so help me, I'll leave you there," Aundy warned then set the horse down the lane at a good clip. She'd never been to Mr. Tooley's farm, but had an idea where to find it from everyone warning her to stay away.

Not daring to think about what she did, she drove north until she came to a crossroad and turned left. She followed it for a mile or so until she reached another cross road and turned left again. A short distance down the road, she looked to her right, spotting a derelict house and barn off the side of the road. Since it was most likely her destination, she turned the buggy that direction.

When Marvin's horse whinnied from behind the buggy, Aundy was sure she'd found the right place.

She stopped the buggy close to the door of a house that may have at one time been nice. Quickly stepping out of the buggy, she untied Marvin's horse and led him to the barn. After removing his saddle and bridle, she turned him into the pasture.

When she returned to the buggy, Marvin was nowhere in sight. Grateful she wouldn't have to smell or speak to him again, Aundy climbed into the buggy and headed home.

What a wretched, detestable man!

Thanks to the time she spent taking Marvin home, she would be hard-pressed to be ready in time to go to Ashton's for dinner. While she'd dearly love to stay home, her curiosity drove her to visit his place. From what she heard, it was quite something to see.

At the barn, Aundy unhitched the horse and started brushing him down when George walked in.

"Howdy, Aundy," he said with a friendly smile, taking in her windblown hair and sun-reddened cheeks. "Can I help you with something?"

"George, you're timing is providential. Would you mind finishing this for me? I've got to get up to the house." Aundy dropped the currycomb in his hand. On her way out the door, she called "thank you" before lifting her skirts and breaking into a very unladylike run across the yard and up the steps to the kitchen.

While water filled the bathtub, she laid out the clothes she planned to wear, glad she'd pressed the dress the previous evening after Nik finished his lessons.

After taking a bath and washing her hair, she stood in front of the kitchen stove combing out her long tresses, hoping to dry them faster.

As quickly as possible, she tugged on her dress and slipped her feet into a pair of dressy shoes that originally belonged to Mrs. Erickson. She rushed to style her hair in a loose upsweep with a few wispy tendrils falling along her neck and by her ears. Hastily fastening a rose made out of ribbon in her hair, she gave herself one more perusal in the mirror before deciding she looked as good as she could.

Aundy yanked on her gloves and picked up her reticule then decided she might need a shawl on the way home. She chose the soft white covering that belonged to Erik's mother then rushed into the front room as the jingle of harness let her know the Nash family arrived.

Garrett offered her a startled glance with his hand still poised to knock when she suddenly swung open the door.

"Hi," she said, breathless from her frenzied preparations to be ready on time.

"Hi." Garrett stared at her, mesmerized. He had no idea about women's fashions, but the pale blue gown Aundy wore with touches of lace made her eyes sparkle and accented her fine figure. The blue rose in her hair just made him want to take it out and unpin all her glorious wavy locks.

Quickly pulling the door shut behind her, Aundy smiled at Garrett, wondering why he looked at her so strangely.

"Shall we?" Aundy motioned toward the surrey where his parents waited. "We don't want to be late."

"No, not late," Garrett mumbled, holding out his arm to her. Instead of acting the part of a gentleman, he really wanted to pull her to his chest and kiss her repeatedly. "You look beautiful, Mrs. Erickson."

"Thank you, Mr. Nash." Aundy felt warmth fill her cheeks at Garrett's intense study from the flower on top of her head to the toes of her ivory shoes. Brazenly returning his gaze, she nearly stumbled on the walk as she took in how utterly appealing he appeared. "You look quite handsome this evening."

"You think so?" Garrett glanced down at his pressed pants, fancy vest, and suit coat. Nora insisted he dress up instead of going to Ashton's in his denims and a cotton work shirt.

"Yes, I do." Aundy turned her attention to J.B. and Nora in the front of the surrey. This was the first time she'd seen J.B. take the reins. It must mean he felt better.

"Good evening." Aundy squeezed Nora's hand in hers before Garrett helped her into the back seat of the surrey.

"I don't know how you manage it, honey, but you get prettier every time I see you," Nora said, turning around in her seat to smile at Aundy. "Blue is definitely your color."

"Thank you." Aundy blushed again at Nora's compliment.

"Don't you think she looks lovely, Garrett?" Nora asked, aware of her son's gaze lingering on Aundy's face. When he didn't answer, she stretched her arm behind the seat and swatted his leg. "Isn't that right, son?"

"Yes, Ma," Garrett said, not paying any attention to what Nora said. He was too absorbed in watching the way evening light played in Aundy's hair and highlighted the freckles across her nose. She was breathtaking. At least he felt like she'd stolen his breath away. When he tried to inhale a calming breath, her soft rose fragrance floated around him, drawing him into an invisible web he had no desire to escape.

Nora turned around and squeezed J.B.'s arm, leaning close to him. "I think our boy is a goner," she whispered.

J.B. grinned and nodded his head. "That he is, but who could blame him. She's quite a girl."

"Did you have a good day at the ranch?" Aundy asked Garrett, eager to divert his attention elsewhere. The way his silvery eyes flickered with heat made her completely unsettled.

"Nothing out of the ordinary." Garrett finally regained his ability to both think and speak, although he continued to be distracted. It was hard to concentrate on anything with Aundy at his side, looking and smelling so lovely. "How about your day? What did you do?"

"Li helped me plant the garden this morning," Aundy said, then gave Garrett a saucy grin. "Perhaps it would be more truthful to state I helped Li plant the garden this morning. He knew what he was doing and told me what to drop where and how much dirt to put over it."

Garrett chuckled and took Aundy's gloved hand in his. Sparks shot from their fingers up both their arms. "Then what did you do?"

"I took lunch out to Nik and we had a nature lesson." Aundy's eyes shone with excitement as she looked at him. "He's such a bright boy, and so sweet. I want him to learn all he can. Maybe he'll go to college someday."

"Maybe he will. Anything is possible." Garrett studied the way Aundy's lips moved. Her mouth tempted him when she smiled. "How's he doing with that harmonica you bought him?"

"Wonderful. I heard him playing *Daisy Bell* today and recognized it right away."

"If you aren't careful, you'll spoil that boy," Garrett teased. Love and care couldn't spoil a boy with a heart like Nik's. "Maybe you should lavish some of that attention on me."

Aundy released Garrett's hand to smack him on the leg. He used the opportunity to put his arm around her and draw her closer to his side. When she didn't protest, he let out the breath he held and relaxed.

"The sheep are so peaceful to watch, Garrett. I'm ever so glad I bought them, even if most of the neighbors disapprove."

"Who's been jabbering about the woolies now?" Garrett might have been quite vocal in his displeasure with Aundy purchasing sheep, but he didn't like the way so many of the neighbors had given her a piece of their mind about them. He had to admit, they hadn't been any trouble so far, except for providing fodder for the neighborhood gripers.

"I think most everyone has been by at least once to let me know their thoughts on my flock, although Marvin Tooley seems the most concerned. He came by a little inebriated this afternoon." When a look of fury and concern settled on Garrett's face, Aundy wished she hadn't said anything. He frowned and she felt his arm tense behind her.

"He showed up at the farm drunk?" Garrett asked, angry with Tooley for his inappropriate behavior.

"I think that is what you'd call it. He couldn't stand up straight and slurred his words. He fell off his horse when he tried to leave and seemed quite incoherent. I hitched up the buggy and took him home. My goodness, but his place could use some attention. Does he have any hands to help out?"

"You what? Back up, honey. You took Tooley home? While he was drunk? What were you thinking? What if he'd done something to harm you?" Garrett pelted her with questions so fast, she didn't have a chance to answer. He scowled at her, waiting for a response.

"He was too drunk to do anything and I couldn't just leave him passed out in front of the house. Taking him home seemed the logical thing to do, so I did. No harm done."

Garrett was coming to realize Aundy's matter-of-fact tone coincided with the stubborn set of her chin.

With the hand that wasn't already wrapped around her shoulders, he reached our and took her fingers in his, gently rubbing his thumb along her glove-covered palm. Unsettled by the sensations it stirred inside him, Garrett assumed Aundy felt something similar. She melted against his side and released a soft sigh. "I'm very glad no harm was done, Aundy. Very glad. Next time, call and I'll come over."

"You're a busy man with your own place to run, Garrett. I could have had one of the hands take care of it, but they were all out working. I'm capable of handling things." Aundy wondered how many times she would have variations of the same conversation with Garrett. She wished he'd realize she was no weak little female who depended on a man to take care of her and protect her. She could and would take care of herself.

Occasionally, though, it was nice to feel cared for and sheltered. Like now, with Garrett's spicy scent tickling her nose as she sat against his side, letting her know she was safe and secure in his arms.

J.B. turned the surrey off the road onto a lane lined with dogwoods that were full of beautiful blooms.

"Oh, my," Aundy whispered, impressed with the beauty of the trees and the setting of the house up on a hill.

"I forget how pretty it is out here in the spring," Nora said, gazing at the trees. "I don't know how Ashton keeps these trees alive as cold as it gets in the winter."

"Must be his special fertilizer," Garrett commented. J.B. laughed and Nora looked at her son with a glare that would have chastised him had she not been fighting to contain her own smile.

The surrey rolled around a circular drive. J.B. stopped in front of a three-story house that could rival any picture Aundy had seen of a stately plantation home.

"Something, isn't it?" Nora asked as J.B. helped her out of the surrey while Garrett gave Aundy his arm.

"That it is," Aundy agreed, tipping back her head to take in the grand white columns and balconies. They walked up the steps together. J.B. raised his hand to knock on the door as a buggy travelled down the drive, followed by a lone rider on horseback.

Garrett grinned as Kade climbed off his horse. Politely offering his arm to one of the town's schoolteachers, Almira Raines, her spinster sister wrapped her bony hand around his other bicep and they started up the steps. Their brother, owner of a barbershop in Pendleton, followed behind. The two Raines sisters could talk a dead man into his grave and they were each doing their best to capture Kade's attention, chatting up a storm with every step they took.

Swallowing down the chuckle that began to erupt from his mouth, Garrett tipped his head at Kade.

"Evening, Deputy. Here for dinner?" Garrett kept a firm grip on Aundy's elbow as they stood at the door.

"Yep. Ashton invited the sheriff, but he had to cancel at the last moment. He asked me to come in his place." Kade tried not to roll his eyes at the two women who had him caught like a mouse between two sparring cats.

"Lucky you," Garrett teased.

Kade would have replied, but the door opened and Ashton's butler welcomed them into the entry hall.

"Ladies, I'd be happy to take your outerwear." The butler gathered wraps and shawls while the men removed their hats and handed them to the stoic man. With a nod, the butler inclined his head toward a large gathering room. "Please be seated. Mr. Monroe will be down shortly."

The group moved into a room with an enormous fireplace, expensive furnishings, and fine art. They chatted for a few minutes until Ashton appeared in the door. He greeted them with his usual charm and did his best to put his guests at ease.

The butler announced dinner was ready. Ashton maintained a lively conversation as he ushered his guests into the dining room. Aundy found herself seated between Ashton at the head of the table and Garrett to her right.

The undercurrents flowing between the two men were enough to make her feel battered from both directions. She didn't know what was going on with Garrett and Ashton, but she wished it would stop.

When Ashton reached out and clasped her hand in his, Garrett dropped his arm around the back of her chair and leaned closer to her. Ashton kept bumping her leg beneath the table and Garrett made sure his hand brushed against her arm any number of times.

By the end of the meal, the two of them had her so jumpy and irritated, she couldn't wait to go home.

Ashton had other plans, though, as he invited them to stay and play parlor games. After dividing into teams, they played a few games of charades before Kade and Garrett had their fill of listening to the Raines sisters' chatter.

Deliberately executing a yawn that should have cracked the joint in his jaw, Kade begged pardon and said he had to get back to town since he had the night shift.

"We should be going, too." Garrett nudged his dad's foot with his own as he rose from his seat.

"So soon?" Ashton asked. "But the fun is just beginning."

"It was a lovely evening, Ashton. We appreciate your hospitality, but we really should go," Nora said. She'd noticed Garrett's desire to leave sooner rather than later. Aundy looked like she'd swallowed something bitter halfway through dinner and the frown that puckered her brow hadn't gone away.

"Yes, Ashton, thank you so much for inviting us. Your home is very impressive." For all the beauty of the architecture, Aundy thought Dogwood Corners was missing some vital welcoming element. She couldn't pinpoint what, exactly, but something seemed off.

"I hope, now that you know where to find me, you'll come back to visit again." Ashton draped Aundy's shawl around her shoulders with much more lingering care than was necessary.

Garrett picked up her gloves and reticule, handing them to her before grabbing his hat.

"I'd be happy to bring her back anytime she's of a mind to visit." Garrett hustled Aundy out the door. He shook Ashton's hand, thanked him for the meal, and urged Aundy down the broad steps to where the surrey waited.

"That was a little rude, don't you think?" She asked as he helped her in the back of the surrey.

"Not at all." Garrett's tone sounded clipped as he draped his arm along the seat behind her, glad to be out of Ashton's oppressive house and presence.

Quiet on the ride home, Garrett seemed more like himself as they neared her place. He wrapped his arm around her shoulders and pulling her against his side.

"Don't want you to catch a chill." His voice was warm and husky by her ear.

An involuntarily shiver raced from her head to her toes. Garrett's proximity, combined with his voice, made Aundy think of sweet, thick molasses. She could picture it pouring over her heart right down to her soul.

If she had a brain in her head, she'd move away from him. Unfortunately, she seemed to have left her sense at home. It appeared to have fled the moment she opened the door earlier that evening and gazed into Garrett's silvery eyes.

Nestled against his side, breathing in his unique masculine scent, she savored every moment until J.B. stopped the surrey at the end of her walk. Garrett walked her to the door and that's when they noticed a note nailed to the house.

Aundy jerked it free and gasped at the writing that appeared to be in blood. She sincerely hoped her imagination ran away with her and it was only paint.

Garrett took the note from her hand and read it in the fading light. He folded Aundy into his arms. Whoever wrote the note was clearly lacking in basic spelling skills.

"Git rid a 'em sheep or git of the farm, ya dum wuman!"

"I'm sorry, honey. Do you think Marvin Tooley wrote this?" Garrett asked as Aundy stood with her head pressed to his chest. Although he appreciated the opportunity to wrap his arms around her, he was outraged that anyone would threaten her. She had every right to raise whatever she wanted on the farm and if he had anything to say about it, she'd never leave.

"I don't know. He was quite drunk earlier. I don't know if he would have come back this soon." Aundy breathed deeply and stepped away from Garrett. Taking back the note, she stared at it a moment before opening her door.

"Thank you for seeing me home, Garrett. I appreciate it," she said and walked inside the house.

Garrett stood in the doorframe, peering into the empty house. "Want me to come inside and make sure everything is fine?"

"That won't be necessary." Aundy was determined not to let fear override her need for independence. "Thanks again."

"Are you certain…?" Garrett started to ask, but she quietly closed the door, shutting him out.

Aundy trembled with fear. She wanted Garrett to hold her hand, light all the lamps, and promise her everything would be fine.

Since that wasn't going to happen, she pulled the gun out of her reticule and walked through the house, prepared to shoot if anything moved.

In her bedroom, she lit a lamp and heaved a sigh. Why did the neighbors have such a hard time accepting her sheep? They weren't hurting anyone. Nik kept them contained. She didn't go around commenting on the state of her neighbors' livestock, which included a herd of scrawny cattle, some horses that looked abused, and a pair of mean dogs that had to be part wolf for as vicious as they seemed.

Maybe it wasn't so much about the sheep but about her, a woman, taking over the farm. Although she had a lot to learn, she was willing to try and gave her best each day to make the place a success.

Not a thing could be done right then, so Aundy changed into her nightgown, blew out the lamp, and slid between her cool sheets.

Chapter Fifteen

Aundy didn't mention the note she found on the door to anyone the next morning. Nora called right after breakfast to see how she was and she told her everything was fine.

It was fine.

Or it would be when whoever was trying to frighten her figured out she wasn't leaving, wasn't selling, and wasn't giving up.

With renewed determination to ignore whoever was taunting her, especially if it was Marvin Tooley, Aundy did laundry all morning and hung the last sheet up to dry when Li suddenly appeared next to her clothesbasket.

"Missy, come eat with us?" Li asked, smiling at her imploringly. She'd eaten a few meals he prepared and the food was always delicious. The thought of not having to make herself dinner was too appealing to tell him no. That, and the fact he looked at her nodding his head, trying his best to make her agree.

"I'd love to, Li. Thank you for the invitation." Aundy smiled gratefully at her cook. "May I bring something?"

"No. Li cook." He continued smiling and nodding his head.

"Okay, I'll see you later then."

"Yep, Missy." Li started to go back to the bunkhouse then stopped and gave her an inquisitive look. "Missy, why wear britches, big hat, day you help Li?"

Aundy almost swallowed the clothespin she held in her mouth. Quickly snatching it from between her lips and hooking it on the sheet, she looked at Li with raised eyebrows.

In the weeks since she'd met the man, he hadn't once mentioned her being the person who found him. She'd hoped, in his pain-induced state, he wouldn't remember. It looked like he wasn't quite as incoherent as she thought when she'd dragged him out of the stairwell to her horse.

"I didn't think you knew that was me," Aundy said quietly, looking around to see if anyone else was close enough to hear the conversation. It appeared they were alone. "I was trying to buy sheep and no one would talk to me as a woman, so I dressed like a man. I don't plan on making a habit of it."

"That good." Li grinned at his boss. "You pretty lady, not man."

Aundy laughed. "Thank you, I think."

"Pretty boss lady," Li said in a singsong voice, making Aundy grin. "Pretty lady. Pretty lady."

"Can you keep that under your hat?"

"What under hat?" Li looked confused.

"That means please don't tell anyone I was dressed like a man. The men wouldn't take that news favorably."

"Not tell nobody." Li bowed at Aundy then hurried back to the bunkhouse.

Aundy finished hanging her laundry before retreating to Erik's desk for the afternoon.

After completing bookwork she'd put off, she rolled her shoulders and looked at the clock on the mantle across the room. If she didn't hurry, she'd be late for dinner and she didn't want to keep hungry men waiting. She washed her hands and face then tidied her hair before rushing out the kitchen door and down the steps. Green sprouts poked up from the dirt in the garden and she added weeding to her ever-growing list of chores. Li made sure she knew what plants were weeds and what ones were supposed to be growing.

Boisterously knocking on the bunkhouse door, she smiled at Dent when he opened it, motioning her inside.

"Welcome, Missy. Heard you were joining us for supper." Dent pointed to the big table, lined with benches on both sides and chairs on each end. He escorted her to a chair and held it while she sat down.

"Li was quite persuasive in his argument that I share supper with you," Aundy said, winking at the cook as he set a bowl of rice on the table.

"We liked his Chinese food so well the other day, we asked him to make some more," Bill said, looking a little sheepish. No doubt, he and Fred were the loudest protestors at eating something new. "Nik said you wanted to try it."

"I do." Aundy bowed her head while Dent gave thanks. When he finished, she looked around the table. "I have eaten Chinese food before, though."

"You have?" Nik shot Aundy a questioning glance as he passed a bowl to her.

"Yes, I have. In fact, there was a special event in Chicago I attended that provided the opportunity to sample food from all over the world." Aundy let her thoughts drift back to an adventure she experienced with her parents, brother, and sister.

"Where was that?" George asked, helping himself to a mixture of meat and vegetables in a savory sauce.

"At the World's Columbian Exposition of 1893." Aundy took a bite of the food and enjoyed the flavors that exploded on her tongue.

"Really? You were there?" Fred asked, his eyes lighting with curiosity. "I heard it was something to see."

"It was. There were all kinds of food booths, and people from every walk of life as well as games and exhibits and rides," Aundy said, thoughtful as the memories resurfaced. "I think my favorite thing of all was the Ferris wheel."

"What's a Ferris Wheel?" Nik asked, waiting for her to explain.

"It was a ride that could hold more than two thousand people. It was literally a huge wheel standing more than two-hundred and sixty-feet tall. It sat on a monstrous axle and had thirty-six passenger cars attached to the rim of the wheel. People sat, or stood, in the cars and the wheel would take them up in the air and bring them back down to platforms." Aundy used her index finger to show how the wheel moved. "At the very top, you could see not only the fairgrounds and the city of Chicago, but also for miles and miles around. It was amazing."

"I want to ride a Ferris wheel," Nik said, imagining how wonderful it would be to see so far in the distance.

"Perhaps, someday you will." Aundy offered the boy an encouraging smile.

The men asked more questions about Chicago, the fair, and things she'd experienced. They talked about some of the more interesting things they'd seen in some of their travels and before they realized the lateness of the hour, it was well past time for the last of the evening chores to be completed.

"Goodness, I didn't mean to distract you boys for so long." Aundy rose to her feet, ready to help Li clear the table. He shooed her away, so she started to walk out with the men.

"We enjoyed your stories, Missy," Dent said, patting her on the shoulder as he settled his hat on his head then opened the door.

A dead lamb hanging from a limb in the cottonwood tree between the bunkhouse and the barn captured their attention as they stepped outside. A wicked looking knife, covered in blood, pinned a note to the tree by.

Aundy screamed and Dent pulled her around, shielding her from the gruesome sight.

"Bill, cut that thing down. Fred, bring that letter over here, and the knife," Dent ordered as his gaze took in the quiet barnyard. Nothing seemed unusual or out of place, other than the disturbing sight in the tree.

Nik ran over to the tree with Bill and bravely held back his tears as he cradled the dead animal. At least it wasn't Butter. After gently laying the lamb on a mound of grass, Nik scrambled to his feet and sprinted toward the pasture where the flock grazed. George, Lem, and Hank raced behind him.

"I'm okay, Dent." Aundy took a deep breath and stepped back from her foreman. She couldn't believe anyone would be so cruel as to kill a helpless lamb and string it up from a tree, but evidently, someone was desperate to make his point.

Aundy read the note and dropped it as if something poisonous had bitten her. She rubbed her hands on her skirt, as if she tried to wipe off something filthy. How had she and the men missed someone lurking around right outside the door while they enjoyed dinner?

Dent picked up the note. Rage pounded through him as he read the words.

"I dun tol' ya but yer two stupid to pay me mind. I'm dun talkin. Say gudbuy to yer stinkin sheep."

"Glen, run up to the house and call the sheriff," Dent said, taking Aundy's arm and walking her toward the house. He'd make sure it was safe and one of them would stay with her until the sheriff arrived.

They were almost to the back porch when Aundy came out of the trance she seemed to be in and realized

Dent escorted her inside. She stopped walking and pulled her arm away from his hand where it had held her elbow, guiding her along.

"No, Dent." She took another step back. "I need to go check on the rest of the sheep and Nik."

"The guys will take care of Nik and watch out for the sheep. We'll put someone on night watch from now on until this thing settles down. Don't you worry, Missy." Dent was sure his reassurances fell on deaf ears.

Aundy would have run off to the pasture except Glen hurried down the back steps. "The sheriff is sending someone out right away. He asked if Aundy would wait in the house. He said something about looking at the note from yesterday."

"What note?" Dent gave Aundy a probing glare.

"That tattletale Nash." Aundy stormed up the steps with Dent and Glen right behind her.

"What note?" Dent asked again, wanting to grab Aundy by the arm and give her a shake to bring her to her senses. Sometimes the woman was too independent for her own good.

"When I arrived home last night, there was a note on the door. Garrett was the only one who saw it. He must have said something to Deputy Rawlings." Aundy marched to the front room where she plucked the note from a galvanized pail she used to hold discarded papers to burn in the stove and fireplace.

Carefully unfolding the wadded piece of paper, she turned up the lamp on the desk and handed the letter to Dent.

He read it and compared the handwriting to the note they'd just found. The same hand wrote both notes.

"Glen, check the house, would ya?" Dent asked. While Glen looked in each room to make sure the house was secure, Dent and Aundy returned to the kitchen. The foreman set the warning letters on a corner of the table.

"No one wants to hurt me, just my poor little sheep." Aundy banged the coffee pot as she filled it with water and slammed it on the stove. She stoked the fire and set a kettle of water on to heat, assuming it would be a long evening.

Taken aback by her anger, Dent expected her to be frightened or tearful, but not fuming. He was plenty mad for everyone.

"I hope Nik is okay," Aundy muttered more to herself than Dent.

When Glen returned to kitchen and nodded his head, Dent asked him to keep an eye on Aundy while he went out to check on the sheep and Nik.

"Keep her in the house," Dent whispered to Glen as he opened the kitchen door.

Aundy watched him leave and frowned at her hired hand. "You don't have to stay here and keep me company. I'd much rather be out there, so I'm sure you would, too."

Glen watched Aundy pace around the kitchen. His nerves twisted tighter with each step she took. He had to do something to calm them both down. "That's okay. I don't mind. Anything I can do to help around the house? Maybe we could find something to work on until the deputy comes. You need shelves hung or anything repaired?"

Aundy was right. He would rather have been just about anywhere other than in the house with her at that moment, but he was grateful she was mad and slamming things around instead of crying hysterically. He assumed that was what most women would do after seeing the lamb in the tree. Just thinking about it made a cold shiver slither down his spine. Anyone who could do that was capable of just about anything.

"Want me to call Garrett and have him come over?"

"Absolutely not," Aundy said hotly, glaring at Glen as she stirred something in a bowl. He'd noticed she liked to bake when she was upset. It worked out well for the men, since it meant cookies, cake, or pie for them.

"How about I…" Glen didn't know who pounded at the front door, but as he hurried to answer it, he didn't care. Any interruption was welcome.

Almost any.

Glen could have done without seeing the pretty-faced Ashton Monroe standing on the doorstep, dressed in an expensive tailored suit with brocade vest and fancy tie in place. Glen was gratified to see, for once, Ashton's boots weren't polished to a shine that reflected his face.

"Where's Mrs. Erickson?" Ashton barged his way inside. "I just heard the terrible news and rushed right over."

"How could you hear the news? We barely discovered it ourselves," Glen asked with a narrowed gaze.

"You know how the phone line buzzes with all the latest gossip." Ashton looked around the room, expecting Aundy to materialize. When she didn't, Glen sighed and walked Ashton to the kitchen.

Aundy dropped cookie dough onto a baking sheet before sliding it into the oven. "Ashton? Now isn't a good time for a social call." Her tone was flat with a hint of irritation as she rinsed her hands and dried them on a dishtowel.

"I realize that, my dearest Mrs. Erickson." Ashton sidled next to her and took her hand in his. He led her to the table and held out a chair for her. When she reluctantly sat down, he gallantly dropped to one knee, looking at her with tender eyes. "I heard about the tragedy that befell one of your sheep and rushed right over, knowing how distraught you'd be."

"I appreciate your thoughtfulness, but as you can see, I'm fine." Annoyed to have Ashton fawning over her, Aundy wished he'd leave. He wasn't normally quite so… attentive. It irritated her that the men all seemed to expect her to fall to the floor in a faint, or sob until she lost the ability to function coherently.

As the owner of the farm and the sheep, she wouldn't allow herself the luxury of giving in to the urge to cry until she drained the well dry.

"My dear, you look anything but fine. You seem quite distressed." Ashton pulled a chair so close to hers their knees brushed. Aundy drew back her legs and frowned at Ashton.

"Truly, I'll be fine, Ashton. Please don't worry yourself on my behalf. Someone from the sheriff's office will be here soon, so it's probably best if you leave now." Aundy rose from her chair and removed the cookies from the oven, glad to have something to keep her busy. If she had to sit with Ashton patting her hand and consoling her one more minute, she might give in to the urge to slap him.

"If you're certain." Ashton sounded hurt as he got to his feet and started toward the front door.

"I'm certain, but thank you again for thinking of me." Aundy tipped her head toward Glen, indicating he should walk Ashton to the door.

With the last of the cookies in the oven to bake, Aundy washed the dishes she dirtied to make cookies as Glen returned to the kitchen.

"Do you like Ashton?" Glen asked, picking up a hot cookie then juggling it from one hand to the other until it was cool enough to eat.

"Of course I like him, just like I do all the neighbors." Aundy dried a bowl and put it away.

"No, I mean like him... you know?" Glen wondered why he brought up the subject in the first place. It was clear Ashton's presence annoyed Aundy and she wanted him out of the house as quickly as possible.

"If you mean would I consider giving my heart to a man like him, then the answer is no." Aundy observed Glen as he snitched another cookie. She poured a cup of coffee and handed it to him as the kitchen door opened and Dent entered with Kade.

The deputy took the two notes and asked Aundy questions about any threats she received. She told him about Marvin Tooley, including taking him home when he showed up drunk the previous afternoon.

"Why in tarnation didn't you find one of us?" Dent asked, trying to keep from yelling. He couldn't believe Aundy hauled the filthy drunk home all by herself. She might be the boss, but she was still an innocent woman who shouldn't be dealing with some of the things she'd resigned herself to managing as the owner of the place.

"You were busy, I handled the situation and that was that." Aundy offered Kade a cup of coffee and a plate of cookies. Appreciative, he accepted both.

"That isn't that. That is asking for a whole lot of trouble, Missy. You can't be going around hauling home drunks. You just can't." Dent slapped the hat he'd been twisting around in his hands on his leg, stirring up a cloud of dust.

"We'll discuss your thoughts on that subject later," Aundy said, turning her attention back to Kade. He asked her a few more questions, took another handful of cookies, and left. Dent gave him the bloody knife to take with him.

Lem decided to stay with Nik out by the sheep. Other than the dead lamb, they didn't find any missing or wounded animals when they checked the pasture.

"Missy, you and I are going to have a long conversation about what is acceptable for you to do and what is not." Dent waggled his finger at her.

She prepared to let him have an earful about doing whatever she deemed necessary when the back door opened and Garrett stepped inside.

"Aundy, are you okay?" His silvery gaze locked on hers. He opened his arms as he walked toward her. She rushed into the warmth and comfort he offered.

Despite her attempts to keep her emotions from showing, to keep her fear and hurt from overwhelming her, the sight of Garrett opened the floodgates and she couldn't hold back any longer. Although she'd kept her back straight and chin up throughout the evening, as soon as Garrett touched her, all the starch went out of her spine and she melted against him.

As the first sob wracked her shoulders, Garrett sat on a chair at the table and pulled her onto his lap, cradling her head to his chest.

Stroking her back, he murmured softly to her. "It's okay, honey. It's okay." Garrett handed her the dishtowel Dent held out to dry her tears.

"It's not okay," she said between sobs. "They killed my lamb, Garrett. They killed my poor little lamb."

"I know, honey. I'm sorry." Garrett noticed Glen sitting at the table, grinning at him as if he knew some big secret.

"We'll just um… Come on, Glen," Dent said, hurrying out the door with Glen right behind him.

"I'll leave them alone for a minute or two before I go make sure he ain't doing nothing he shouldn't be," Dent said as they walked toward the bunkhouse.

"Ol' Garrett better be sure he wants the boss lady because she's plumb sold on him. She would barely give Ashton Monroe the time of day and fairly ran him out of the house, but she sure don't seem to mind Garrett being there." Glen concluded Aundy had better taste in men than most of the female population around town. Garrett Nash could have his choice of women, but Ashton had the looks, money, and suave manners that made the ladies practically fall at his feet.

"When was Ashton here?" Dent stopped outside the bunkhouse.

"Just before you and Kade came in. Aundy didn't seem none too pleased he showed up. She told him she was fine and to go home. He finally got the idea she wasn't of a mind to visit and left."

"Did he know something had happened or was it a social call?"

"He knew all about it. Said news travels fast. Suppose that's true enough. I heard some busybodies round here can't get any of their housework done cause they spend all day listening in on the telephone line."

"That so?" Dent asked distractedly, looking toward the house and deciding to give Aundy a few more minutes alone with Garrett.

Half an hour later, Dent knocked on the kitchen door and stepped inside. Garrett drank coffee and ate cookies while Aundy sipped a cup of tea. She no longer cried and seemed calm.

"Everything okay?" Dent poured himself a cup of coffee.

"For now," Aundy said, looking at Dent and mustering a small smile.

"Lem's gonna stay with Nik and the sheep for a while. Hank's gonna catch a few winks then head out to pick up the second shift. Fred and Bill will keep an eye out around here tonight," Dent said, letting Aundy know someone would watch to make sure she was safe.

"Why don't you come back with me to Nash's Folly, Aundy? No one will know you're there and you can rest easy," Garrett said, reaching across the table to take her hand in his.

Once she stopped crying, he'd attempted to convince her to stay at his place. Nora could mother her and he could keep an eye on her until they caught whoever made the threats.

Adamant that she wasn't going to abandon the farm, the sheep, or her men, Aundy refused. Like she did now.

Grateful, she smiled and squeezed his fingers, but shook her head.

"That's exactly what someone wants me to do, isn't it? Run off scared. I think someone wants me off this place and they're trying to frighten me into leaving by harming my sheep." Aundy glanced from Garrett to Dent. The two men passed some unspoken message through lifted brows and nearly imperceptible nods of their heads.

"You two agree, don't you?" Aundy rose and began pacing around the kitchen again. "Why? What did I do? Who did I offend?"

"No one, Missy." Dent took a drink of his coffee. "Some folks, men, just don't cotton to the idea of a woman running her own place and doing it quite well."

Garrett agreed. "Their way of thinking may be outdated, but you aren't going to change their minds." His parents raised him to believe everyone should have equal opportunities regardless of gender or race. "Are you sure I can't convince you to stay at our house tonight?"

"No, Garrett. I thank you for your concern, but I'll be fine." Aundy rinsed out the cups in the sink. Dent mumbled something about seeing them later and ambled out the door. Garrett leaned against the counter, watching Aundy wipe off the table and store the leftover cookies in a tin.

As she walked by, he pulled her against him.

"Don't, Garrett. Please." Tears filled her eyes as she looked into his silvery depths. He'd been so good to her, letting her cry, making her feel safe in his strong arms. If he offered more gentle assurances, she would break down sobbing again and that wouldn't help anyone. "I'll be fine. I promise."

"I know you will be. You're one of the strongest women I know," Garrett said, offering a loving smile. When he lowered his head to hers, their lips connected in a fiery kiss.

Aundy wrapped her arms around his neck, clinging to him, to her dreams, to her desires for a future with Garrett.

241

Pressed against him with his lips moving insistently against hers, she could easily forget about the farm, the sheep, and everything else.

Unfortunately, she didn't have the luxury of forgetting and abruptly pulled back, pulled herself down to earth and reality.

"Thank you, Garrett. You can't know how much I appreciate you being here when I needed you most," Aundy said, meaning every word. Although she refused to let Glen call him, Aundy hadn't realized how desperately she needed Garrett until he walked in the door. She wanted to go with him to Nash's Folly where Nora would make her tea, J.B. would offer sage wisdom, and Garrett would keep her safe. Instead, she had to stay, take a stand, and let it be known that nothing was going to run her off Erik's land.

"Anytime you need me, I'll be here." He settled his hat on his head and disappeared into the evening darkness.

Chapter Sixteen

Endless inquiries following church services about what happened at the farm left Aundy exhausted. She declined Nora's invitation to stay for lunch and instead went home to spend the afternoon in the peace and quiet of her own house.

Unable to sleep the previous night due to being both frightened and angry, Aundy wanted nothing more than to curl up on her bed and take a nap.

She removed her church dress and shoes and pulled on one of the old calico dresses she'd altered to fit her taller, thinner frame. Plucking the pins out of her hair, she braided it and fastened the end with a ribbon.

Drained, she flopped down on the bed, tugged a quilt over her legs, and was soon asleep.

Loud, insistent rapping woke her from her dreams of Garrett. Disoriented and half-awake, she scrambled to her feet and hurried to the door.

"My gracious, Aundy, are you unwell?" Ashton asked, pushing his way inside the front room.

"I'm well." Aundy knew she probably looked like a rumpled mess but didn't care if she did.

Ashton had been fun to visit with on numerous occasions, it was interesting to see his huge, stately home, but he'd never be a close friend, someone Aundy counted on.

Something about him seemed secretive. Even she could tell Ashton wasn't always telling her the truth. With no idea what he wanted or why he'd dropped by unannounced, she really wasn't in the mood to visit with him. "May I help you with something?"

"No, my dear." Ashton motioned for Aundy to have a seat. Instead of sitting on the sofa Ashton indicated, Aundy chose the rocking chair. A sense of foreboding settled over her and she studied Ashton as he settled into the armchair across the room.

He fidgeted with his pocket watch, taking it out of his vest then shoving it back without ever looking at the time. One of his polished boots tapped out an erratic rhythm and he looked like he'd buttoned his collar too tight.

"Are you well?" Aundy thought he looked quite unlike himself.

"Quite, my dear." Ashton leaned back in the chair. "I realize you've had a time of it the last few days and I wanted to offer my assistance. If there is anything I can do to help you, please let me know."

"That's very kind, Ashton. Thank you." Aundy offered a smile that didn't quite reach her eyes.

"It isn't kindness, Aundy," Ashton said, looking at her with a probing gaze. "It's quite selfish on my part. You see, I've been meaning to ask you something and well, with things like they are, it seems like the most favorable time."

Confused by Ashton's words, she was startled when he strode across the room to her chair and dropped to one knee.

"Let me care for you. Let me keep you safe from harm. Let me love and cherish you. Become my bride." Ashton brought Aundy's hand to his mouth and kissed the back of it fervently.

Barely resisting the urge to jerk her hand away and wipe it on her skirt, Aundy worked up a smile. She had no idea why Ashton would propose to her. He needed some dainty beauty for a wife, one whose only concern was making him comfortable. Aundy was most definitely not the woman best suited for the position.

"Ashton, your proposal is quite flattering, but I know it's just this situation that has driven you to ask." Aundy rose to her feet, forcing Ashton to do the same. She stepped behind a chair to keep space between them. In an effort to appear sincere, she held a hand to her chest. "You are a dear, sweet man, Ashton. I appreciate your friendship and your proposal, but you deserve more than I can give you."

Ashton looked crushed as he picked up his hat and gloves from where he'd tossed them when he arrived.

"I'm sorry. I just assumed you felt the same way I do." Ashton mumbled something she couldn't hear.

"Begging your pardon?" Aundy asked as Ashton walked toward the door.

"Please, forgive me for attempting to thrust my attentions on you." He offered her a remorseful look then rushed out the door.

Aundy released the breath she didn't even realize she held. She sank into a chair and replayed the conversation with Ashton in her head. His proposal made no sense to her.

He was the type of man who preferred beauty to brains, submissive to independent, feeble to strong.

Sincerely hoping she hadn't hurt his feelings, Aundy decided to go for a ride to clear her head. Quickly changing into a riding skirt and boots, she left her hair in a braid, but added a wide-brimmed hat and hurried out to the barn.

Bell greeted her with a friendly whinny.

"You want to go for a run, girl?" Aundy asked as she saddled the horse and led her out of the barn. After mounting Bell, she decided to check on Nik.

George and Bill helped move the sheep to a pasture closer to the house, where it would be easier to keep an eye on them.

All was calm as Aundy approached. Nik sat beneath a tree playing a mournful tune on his harmonica while Bob and Butter rested at his side.

"That's a sad song you're playing," Aundy said, as she swung out of the saddle.

"I know, but I feel sad today." Nik stuffed his harmonica into his pocket and stood. He'd grown in the weeks since he came to the farm. His new overalls, which Aundy bought to give him growing room, fit him well. It wouldn't be long before he'd outgrow them and they'd be too short. She expected Nik to be a tall, big man when he reached his full weight and height.

For now, she was glad to have the gangly boy with her on the farm. Affectionately throwing an arm around his shoulders, Aundy gave him a quick squeeze before kneeling down and petting both Butter and Bob.

"Why does someone want to hurt our sheep?" Nik couldn't understand what his sheep had done to incur someone's wrath. "They're harmless."

"I know, Nik." Aundy reached out a hand to the boy. He took it and sat beside her. She rubbed his back and sighed as she looked over the flock of sheep. The herd grazed peacefully on the green pasture with the blue sky above them. "I'm having a hard time understanding it myself. Let's just pray whoever it is decides to leave us alone."

"But what if they hurt you?"

"Oh, Nik." Aundy gave the boy a one-armed hug. "I'll be fine. Don't you worry."

She tried to talk him into going to the bunkhouse to rest, but he refused to leave the sheep.

"Don't wear yourself out, Nik. You need your rest. If you don't take care of yourself, you won't be any good to the sheep." Aundy gave Bob and Butter a little more attention before she mounted Bell.

"Yes, ma'am. I'll get some rest later." Nik waved as she rode off along the fence line.

Aundy let Bell have her head, riding with no direction in mind. She enjoyed the feel of the breeze on her face, the sun on her back, and the quiet of the afternoon.

Feeling much better than she had when she left the house, she stopped at the creek that ran through a section of the farm and let Bell get a drink.

She thought she saw a fish dart into the shadows and smiled. Light reflected off the water in shimmering beams, making the place seem almost magical.

As she sat on the bank, she studied the bugs landing on the surface of the water. A crawdad hid beneath a broken tree limb. Rocks of all types, shapes and sizes that made up the creek bed glistened in the sunlight.

She trailed her hand in the cool water and picked up a handful of rocks. Carefully sorting through them, she kept a few that caught her eye and stuffed them in her pocket.

Easily mounting Bell, she turned the horse toward home, in no hurry to get there. When she topped the rise behind the barn, she stopped to take in the sight of the farm.

If someone had told her a year, or even six months ago, she'd be riding a horse, sitting on a hill in the sunshine admiring a neat red barn, planted fields, and a pasture full of sheep, she would have thought they'd lost their ability to think rationally. Chicago, and the life she'd had there, seemed like a lifetime ago. It was a place where she'd been marking time instead of truly living before her arrival in Pendleton.

Aundy felt fully alive in her new home. She had good friends, something exciting that drove her out of bed each day and, if she'd let herself admit it, a man she loved who stirred feelings in her she'd never known existed.

Her love for Gunther had been real, even though it was the first love of a young girl. This passion, this demanding current that flowed between Garrett and her, was something entirely different. It had depth and breadth, lightness and darkness, gentleness and wildness all rolled into one.

It scared her. Unsettled her with its intensity. It also made her feel beautiful, wanted, and loved.

Determined not to become involved with another man, her heart whispered it was already far too late.

If she didn't know Garrett, didn't know how he made her feel, she wondered if she would have turned down Ashton. Despite his pretty face and southern charm, she would never marry Ashton.

Thanks to Erik and his belief in her, she no longer had to depend on a husband to be successful. She could do that on her own.

Grateful again for her many blessings, Aundy rode Bell home and gave her a good brushing before stopping by the bunkhouse. She asked Li to have Dent make sure Nik came in for the night. She knew he'd have someone else keep an eye on the sheep. The boy would collapse if he didn't soon get some rest.

After spending a quiet evening reading, a big yawn nearly cracked her jaw, reminding her it was time for bed. She turned out the lights in the front room and kitchen then walked down the hallway to the bathroom when a thump resonated outside on the front porch.

Fearful of what she might find, she rushed into her room, grabbed the revolver from her reticule, and slipped out the kitchen door.

The smart thing to do would have been to run to the bunkhouse and get reinforcements, but Aundy didn't want to take a chance her tormentor would get away.

Cautiously edging around the corner of the house, she peeked up on the porch and saw no one. Glad the moon illuminated the night, she stayed in the shadows and moved along the front of the house.

Quiet surrounded her so she decided to go back to make sure someone didn't sneak in the kitchen door. She turned to retrace her steps and bumped into a solid wall of man.

"What are you doing?" Garrett's voice sounded husky in her ear as his hands gripped her arms.

"Are you insane? I almost shot you," Aundy hissed, dropping her arm away from Garrett. If she hadn't been careful like he taught her, he'd be lying on the ground with a bullet in his chest. The thought of that made her lightheaded and woozy.

When she swayed on her feet, Garrett put his arm around her waist and pulled her against his side, hurrying up the steps and inside the kitchen.

Seating her at the table, he lit a lamp and studied her pale face.

"What do you mean almost shot me?" he asked, looking for evidence of Erik's pistol.

Aundy held out her hand, showing him the small pocket revolver resting on her palm.

"Where did you get that?" Garrett picked up the gun and looked it over.

"I bought it. It makes me feel safer when I go to town." Stubbornly, Aundy set her chin, daring him to tell her she shouldn't carry it.

"Okay." Carefully, Garrett placed the gun on the table, pointed away from them both, before removing his hat. "That's a sound reason."

"What are you doing here?" Aundy stared at Garrett as he sank down beside her and ran a hand through his hair. She clasped her hands tightly in her lap to keep her own fingers from following the trails his made. It was just wrong for a man to have such thick, lush hair and not even know what a temptation it was to women.

"I wanted to make sure you were well, that nothing else had happened." Garrett leaned back in the chair and drummed his fingers on the table. "I stepped onto the front porch when the lights went off in the front room and then the kitchen lights. I worried someone might be in here with you and was going to run around to the kitchen door when I tripped over that pot of flowers you have by the chairs out front. Your posies might not look too good in the morning."

Aundy took his nervous hand in hers and squeezed his fingers. "As you can see, I'm fine. Nothing happened today. I went for a ride this afternoon and visited with Nik then rode out to the creek. It was so peaceful."

"It is peaceful there, and such a nice day for a ride." He wanted to get away earlier to check on her, but one thing or another had delayed him all afternoon. Garrett hoped she'd stay at Nash's Folly after church, but wasn't surprised when she insisted on going home.

Still dressed in her riding skirt, Aundy patted her pocket, recalling the rocks she plucked from the creek bed. She fished them out and placed them in Garrett's hand.

For a moment, he studied the rocks then dropped them back in her hand, closing her fingers around them. "Those are interesting rocks. You find those in the creek?"

"Yes." Aundy took a small glass bowl from a shelf and put the rocks inside before setting it on the table. "I thought they were pretty."

"That they are." Garrett pulled Aundy onto his lap and into his arms. "Not near as pretty as you, though."

Laughing, Aundy pushed back just enough from Garrett she could see his face. "You clearly have a problem with your vision, Mr. Nash."

"I don't think so." Garrett lowered his head to hers. The demanding clash of their lips caused heat to swirl in his belly. He wanted Aundy. Wanted to spend his life with her, more than he'd wanted anything before.

Consumed.

He was utterly consumed with the woman, and he didn't care if everyone knew it. He loved her with an intensity he'd never imagined feeling.

She was his Viking queen. Strong, independent, and confident with that head of golden hair she so often wore braided into a crown, sky blue eyes, and striking appearance. She had roamed into his life and conquered him completely. It took no time at all for her to pillage his heart, plunder his soul, and lay siege to his mind so his thoughts continually turned to her.

The whisper of his name, as she opened herself to him, made Garrett fight to keep his control.

Moaning, he grasped her face in his hands and deepened the kiss. Aundy held tight to him, her hands clinging to his shoulders. This was the reason he'd been born - to hold this woman in his arms and love her with everything he had.

Suddenly, she trembled and jerked back.

"What's wrong?" he asked quietly. Moving his hand, he grasped her chin and lifted it, forcing her to meet his gaze.

"I can't... I promised... I..." Aundy would have turned her face from him, but Garrett held her chin firmly, but gently, keeping her from moving away. She loved him so much an ache beyond any pain she'd ever experienced tightened her chest. It was because she loved him she had to stop what was between them.

"What did you promise?"

"I promised myself I wouldn't get involved with another man. It ends so badly when I do and I care for you far too much to hurt you," Aundy admitted, although it aggrieved her to do so.

Why couldn't Garrett just leave her alone? Why did he have to look at her until her heart thundered in her chest? Why did he have to tease her and protect her and make her feel beautiful?

Garrett had become an integral part of her life and captured her heart, although she couldn't name the specific moment it had happened. Now, she had to push him away. It was the only way to keep him safe, especially with someone after her sheep and out to get her.

"You're not making sense. How could you possibly hurt me?" Garrett asked, confused. He drew back, but didn't let go. "You don't honestly blame yourself for what happened to Erik, do you?"

Instead of answering, Aundy stood and walked to the kitchen window, watching moonlight illuminate the yard. Garrett stepped behind her and placed his hands on her waist, drawing her against him, into his strength. She was coming to depend on it all too much.

"Aundy, you had nothing to do with Erik's death. Not a thing. Maybe the horses would have bolted another day or something else would have happened. It wasn't anything you did."

"Just being with me seems to be enough to drive men to their deaths." Aundy wrapped her arms around herself. She needed to muster her defenses and keep away from Garrett. It was the only way for her to protect him.

"That's ridiculous. One freak accident doesn't mean anything."

"It happened to my fiancé and my father, too." She brushed at the tears threatening to roll down her cheeks. "Gunther and I had plans to wed and he died alongside my father in a terrible accident that should never have happened."

"For a smart girl with a lot of common sense, you aren't making any." Garrett ran a hand through his hair in frustration. When he considered the fact just moments earlier she'd been every bit as involved in whatever it was that sizzled between them, he didn't know how she could try to push him away now. "Aundy, what are you afraid of?"

"That something will happen to you, too." Aundy spoke so quietly, Garrett had to strain to hear.

"Nothing is going to happen to me, unless God decides it's my time to be called home to glory. You have no control over that, Aundy." He turned her around so she could see his face. "I'm pleased to know you care about me enough to want to protect me, but I think you're worried for no reason."

"I mean it, Garrett. I just can't get involved with you. I can't. I…"

"You what?"

Aundy shook her head and swiped at the tears that spilled from her eyes. Garrett tried to hug her, but she pushed at his chest until he let her go.

"Please, Garrett, I think it's best you leave now."

"Fine, but let me give you one thing to mull over while I'm leaving you alone." Garrett caught her roughly to him, kissing her like he'd never have the opportunity to do it again. Her arms wound around his neck as he held her close. She returned every ounce of the yearning and hunger he poured out to her.

Abruptly letting her go, he grabbed his hat and gave her one last, longing look. "I meant what I said last night. Anytime you need me, I'll be here."

When he slammed the door on his way out, Aundy was sure Dent and the boys could hear it at the bunkhouse.

Aundy leaned against the counter, uncertain her legs could hold her without support. Not when she watched every dream she'd ever had for a happy ever after walk out the door.

Forcing herself to stay away from Garrett was going to be the hardest thing she'd ever done, especially when her heart kept whispering he was the one she would love for a lifetime.

Chapter Seventeen

"It says, 'Titus gave the city of Jerusalem over to his soldiers with orders for them to sack, burn, and raze. More than a million people died in the siege with those kept alive turned into slaves. Many were sent to be fodder for the gladiators and beasts in the Roman arenas.'" Nik stopped reading the history book in his hand and looked at Aundy as she mixed cake batter from a recipe handed down in her family for many generations. "What do you suppose it was like, being in one of those arenas?"

After pouring the batter into a pan and placing it in the oven, Aundy sat down across from Nik and thought about his question.

"I suppose it would have been loud. Think of all the people there, not to mention the noise from beneath the arena where they kept the slaves and beasts. From what I understand, there were vendors selling all sorts of things, so they were probably calling out to people, trying to get them to buy their wares. It probably smelled bad with all the blood and animals, and the sheer number of people watching. It was most likely hot, standing on the sand they used in the arena." Aundy tried to recall her ancient history lessons. "What do you think it would have been like to be a gladiator? What if you were in your own country, minding your own business, when one day the Roman army arrives and declares war against you. You fight, but despite your best efforts, you're captured. Resistance is futile and you're forced to comply. After days, maybe weeks of travelling, you find yourself at a ludus where you're told you'll train to fight in the arena or you'll be killed."

"What's a ludus?" Nik asked. Enraptured with Aundy's perspective of ancient history, he appreciated the interesting way she shared it with him.

"It was a training school for gladiators. They would break the men down and then build them back up as fighting machines." She'd always liked history lessons. When they finished studying Roman history, she'd move Nik on to the Vikings. Tales of her ancestors' battles often stirred her blood.

Thoughts of her blood stirring made images of Garrett come to mind, so she slammed the door on those mental pictures, much like he'd slammed the door on her several nights ago.

"How do you know so much about history, and everything?" Nik swept his hand over the table to emphasize his point. Piles of books and papers covered the surface.

Aundy smiled, straightening a stack of the boy's homework. "I enjoyed school and learning. Books were a way to travel to faraway places I knew I'd never see in my lifetime."

Nik looked at her, balancing what she said against what some of the men told him about book learning being a waste of time for a poor shepherd boy.

Mindful of his hesitation, Aundy grabbed his hand and pulled him to his feet. "Come with me," she said, tugging him to the front room.

Quickly perusing the bookshelf, Aundy pulled several titles from their places and set them on the table in front of the sofa. She pushed Nik down on the seat and grinned at him.

Picking up the first book on the pile, she handed it to Nik then grabbed a parasol from the hall tree by the front door. She held it like a sword, prepared for an imaginary battle. "Dumas' *The Three Musketeers* lets you engage in sword fights and great battles for honor and truth," Aundy said, jumping around the room, lunging at Nik with her makeshift sword, making him laugh.

After selecting the next book, she tossed it to him.

He caught it and read the title *From Pole to Pole.* "What's this one about?"

Aundy pulled a quilt off the arm of the sofa, draped it over her head so it fell down her back, and stuck her hands in front of her like claws. "You can read all about the adventures in the frigid zones of both poles. How else would you get up close and personal with a polar bear?"

When she leaped at him, pretending to be a wild animal intent on eating him, Nik jerked back against the sofa, surprised.

"What if you were stranded on a deserted island for years and years like Robinson Crusoe?" Aundy plopped on the chair across from him, looking forlorn, like she was lost and alone. "Just think of what it would be like. The things you'd see and smell and taste and hear."

Nik sat up, eager to discover what she'd do next. She handed him the last book from her stack and snatched the pail by the desk she used to collect discarded paper. Upending it, she beat on it like a drum and marched around the room, dragging a gimpy leg while humming *Yankee Doodle.*

"What if you could walk beside General George Washington as he defended our great country during the Revolutionary War? Imagine what those soldiers endured as they battled for our country's freedom."

Aundy set down the pail and picked up the scattered papers. She dumped them back inside. She collapsed on a chair and blew the tendrils of hair out of her eyes that escaped the braid around her head.

"Tell me, Nikola Zorian Gandiaga, don't you think books are a wonderful, magical thing?" Aundy thought she might have gone too far with her antics as the boy continued to stare at her, not saying a word.

When Nik finally jumped to his feet and clapped enthusiastically, she decided perhaps not.

"That was incredible!" Excitement filled his face. "Wait 'til I tell the guys about this."

"Hold on a minute." Aundy grabbed Nik's arm before he could rush out the front door. "There will be no telling of tales, young man. None at all. That performance was just for you, so you best keep it to yourself. I've got a dignified reputation to uphold, you know."

Aundy thrust her nose in the air with an exaggerated haughty demeanor until she smelled cake.

"Oh, gracious! I forgot the cake!" Aundy ran to the kitchen, pulled the pan from the oven, and released a sigh of relief it hadn't burned.

"The cake would have been a worthy sacrifice for all that." Nik offered Aundy a teasing smile.

"Oh, go on with you." Aundy helped Nik gather up his books and papers. He finished the glass of milk he'd been drinking and snatched a few cookies to take with him. "You can have a big piece of cake tomorrow, but only if you promise to be quiet about your lesson this evening."

"I promise." Nik wished the men in the bunkhouse could have seen Aundy in action. She would have made a great teacher, if she wasn't so busy trying to learn to be a farmer. "Night, Aundy."

"Good night, Nik. Be sure you get some sleep." On his way out the door, she hugged his shoulders.

As she watched him saunter to the bunkhouse with his gangly stride, Aundy smiled. He was such a bright boy with a good heart. She couldn't wait to see what kind of man he was going to grow up to be. She hoped one every bit as kind, gentle, and handsome as a certain neighbor whom she couldn't keep out of her thoughts.

Since she'd pushed Garrett out of her life, she forced herself to stay away from Nash's Folly. She picked up the telephone at least once a day to call and apologize. Those who listened in would have a heyday with the gossip if she did that.

Out riding the previous afternoon, she saw Garrett in one of the wheat fields across the fence and started to wave, then thought better of it.

If her traitorous heart had just listened to her head and not fallen for Garrett Nash, she wouldn't be feeling so heartbroken and desolate.

In the front room, she set the books back on the shelf and grinned, thinking of the fun she'd had with Nik. It reminded her of happy times she'd shared with her brother and sister when they were younger. Lars never liked school, always more interested in something that involved activity, so Aundy would act out some of his lessons in an effort to help him learn. Ilsa liked to join in, and the three of them had a high time studying and playing together.

A frown creased her forehead and turned her lips downward as she thought about the letter that arrived from her sister. Although Ilsa was more than ready to travel to Pendleton, their aunt kept finding reasons to keep her there. The girl thought she might have to steal away in the night to escape. Aundy certainly hoped it wouldn't come to that.

After folding the quilt and draping it back on the sofa, she checked the lock on the door and extinguished the lamp.

Exhausted, she fell into bed. Sleep was a long time coming as she thought about her farm, her family, her duties, and her love for Garrett.

Early the next morning, she heard several loud pops and dropped the glass she held, shattering it in the sink.

She raced out the kitchen door and was halfway to the barn when Dent and the hands poured out of the bunkhouse.

"What was that?" she asked, her eyes wide with fright. She thought she knew what made the sound, but hoped she was wrong.

"Gun shots." Dent ran in the direction of the sheep, yelling orders as he went. "Fred, Bill, saddle up and meet us in the pasture. George and Glen get out on patrol and see what you can find. Li, keep an eye on things here. Hank's with me, we'll check on Nik and Lem."

Aundy picked up her skirts and ran after Dent and Hank. Her side ached and her lungs burned, but she kept running.

As they topped the rise, they took in the sight of five dead sheep in a pool of blood that stained the grass crimson. Not far from them, they found a motionless dog, a bleating lamb, and the unmoving form of Nik.

"No, not Nik," Aundy whispered, willing her legs to carry her to the boy. Dent reached him first and carefully rolled him over. Blood poured from a wound in his upper chest.

Aundy dropped to her knees, held Nik's head on her lap, and brushed her hand along his forehead. "Oh, you poor baby. You'll be okay. We'll take care of you. Nik, please be okay." She turned her head to wipe her tear-stained cheek on her shoulder while Dent looked to Fred as he arrived on horseback.

"Call the doc and the sheriff. If they don't answer, ride for town." Dent yelled out the orders. Fred spun his horse around and took off to the house. Bill arrived, leading another horse that Dent mounted. He sent Bill to get the wagon so they could move Nik to the house.

"I need to find Lem, Missy. I'll stay here, but I'm gonna look around." Dent turned to Hank. He stood nearby, his face blanched white at the sight of all the blood. "Hank, walk over to that grove of trees and see if you find anything."

Dent rode off in the opposite direction, studying the ground.

Aundy fished her handkerchief out of her pocket and rubbed at Nik's dirty cheeks. His face had lost all color and the fact he hadn't stirred worried her. That reminded her too much of the day Erik was injured.

She should never have let Nik stay out with the sheep after she had the first threat. Regardless of what she said, he would have snuck out to be with the sheep.

Bumped from behind, Aundy lifted an arm and Butter wedged his little body next to her side, bleating pitifully.

"I know, Butter. I know." Aundy rubbed her arm over the lamb's head. He flopped down on the grass next to her and sniffed at Nik, bleating again.

She forced herself not to look back at Bob. The dog was beyond helping.

The pounding sound of hooves beating the ground drew her gaze as Bill and Fred topped the hill in the wagon, bouncing wildly as they urged the horses to go faster.

Dent dismounted behind a tree and she wondered if he found Lem. She prayed the cowboy was alive.

Hastily sending up prayers for Nik and all her men, Aundy held onto Butter as the wagon creaked to a stop beside them. Bill and Fred cushioned the bed of the wagon with a few saddle blankets. Aundy scrambled to climb into the back, sitting down so the men could place the boy with his head resting on her lap. Fred picked up Butter and set him beside her.

"Thank you." She glanced up at him with tear-filled eyes. She knew how much Fred disliked the sheep. To see him tenderly lift the lamb threatened to unravel the few threads keeping her from falling apart.

Dent waved frantically at them from the tree, so Bill and Fred guided the wagon that direction while Hank ran over.

"Help me get him loaded, boys." Dent motioned to Lem. Although unconscious, he was breathing. A bloody cut on his head appeared to be all the damage he'd suffered.

"Looks like someone knocked him out. Probably clubbed him with the butt end of a rifle," Dent said as they placed Lem in the wagon next to Nik. "Head back to the house. I'm gonna do a little sniffing around while we wait for the sheriff."

"He's out of town, but Kade and Doc both said they'd be here as quick as they could," Fred said as Bill turned the wagon toward the house.

When the wagon stopped at the end of the front walk, Aundy carefully moved and lowered Nik's head to the wagon bed before accepting Bill's hand and jumping down.

After running up the porch steps, she raced into Erik's former room, glad she'd aired it recently after sorting through his things. The room looked orderly, if impersonal.

She flung the quilt off the bed and ran to the kitchen for an oilcloth. As Bill and Fred carried the boy inside the door, she draped it over the bed.

"Bring him in here," Aundy said, watching as they gently placed Nik on the bed.

Aundy returned to the kitchen to start boiling water while Bill and Fred helped Lem into the house. Disoriented, he managed to walk into the front room with the support of the other two men.

Wracked with fear, Aundy hurried back to the bedroom with a pan of warm water and a stack of rags.

She held a cloth over Nik's wound, hoping to stop the flow of blood. Instructing Bill to hold the rag in place, she took another and wet it, wiping off Nik's face and hands.

"Nik, you're going to be just fine. You're back at the house and safe now," Aundy said as she rinsed the rag and washed his face again.

Bill peeled back the blood soaked rag and Aundy handed him a fresh one. She took a damp cloth to Lem and dabbed at the wound on his head that already formed a scab.

The thundering of hooves echoed up the drive and Fred ran outside to greet Kade.

"Doc's coming!" Kade yelled loud enough they could hear him in the house. Fred scooped up Butter from the front lawn before climbing into the wagon and driving it to the barn, following the deputy as he raced ahead.

"How's Nik?" Lem asked quietly, trying to look into the room where Bill bent over the boy.

"He's bleeding a lot," Aundy said, not knowing what else to do for Lem. She hurried to the kitchen and came back with a glass of water then handed it to him. He drank it down and leaned his head back against the chair, closing his eyes.

"Tried to stop him," Lem said, shaking his head then wincing at the pain.

"Stop who?" Aundy hoped Lem saw the man's face.

"Don't know. He wore a hood." Lem held his head in his hands. "Don't know who."

"Just rest for now, Lem." Aundy patted his arm. "You can tell us what happened later."

"Aundy?" Bill called. She hurried to the bedroom. Holding out his blood-slicked hands, he nodded to the basin on the nightstand. "I need more rags."

Terrified by the sight of the blood-soaked rags in the pan, Aundy took it to the kitchen and hurried back with another stack of cloths. Nik was going to bleed to death right there on the bed if they didn't do something soon. Uncertain if the bullet was still inside the boy, Aundy felt helpless.

She dropped to her knees next to the bed, took Nik's hand in hers, and prayed. When she lifted her head, Bill nodded and offered a tight smile. Before she could get to her feet, the doctor burst into the house through the front door.

He started toward Lem, but Bill caught his attention, motioning him into the bedroom.

"Nik's been shot," Bill said, pointing to the wound. "Lem's got a bump on his head. Reckon he can wait a spell before you tend him."

The doctor began barking orders and put both Bill and Aundy into service helping him. When he dug the bullet out of Nik, Aundy thought she would surely faint, but forced herself to breathe and continue following the doctor's directions.

"I can't promise anything, Aundy. That poor boy lost a lot of blood," Doc said, staring down at Nik's ashen face. "We'll just have to wait and see."

The doctor tended to Lem, declaring he had a concussion and a nasty cut. He gave him six stitches, told Lem to take it easy for a while, and stay away from any activities that might bump his head.

Lem decided to go back to the bunkhouse to rest and ambled off that direction, leaving Bill, Aundy and Doc in the house to watch over Nik.

The phone rang and Aundy answered it, not surprised to hear Nora's concerned voice on the line.

"Oh, honey, George told Jim what happened over the fence a little bit ago. I'll bring some food over and Garrett will help track down whoever did this. George mentioned someone was injured. Who was hurt?"

"Nik." Aundy's throat tightened with emotion. "Nik was shot."

She heard Nora's intake of breath. "Have mercy! Who would shoot that sweet boy?"

"I wish I knew." Anger began to overtake her other emotions. Who, indeed, would shoot an innocent boy? "Doc took out the bullet so we're just waiting."

Nora didn't have to ask what they were waiting for.

"I'll be over as soon as I can, honey. Just sit tight."

With Nora there, she'd be able to focus more on Nik and figuring out who had done such a horrid thing.

After making a fresh pot of coffee, Aundy walked back to the front room where Bill and Doc sat visiting quietly. They positioned their chairs so they could easily see into the bedroom where Nik fought for his life.

Uncertain what she should do, Aundy took a wet cloth and wiped Nik's face again, kissing his forehead as she pushed back his hair, whispering to him to fight to get well. She reminded him that he had many, many adventures to take and they'd barely got started on his schooling.

"Fight, Nik. You've got to fight." She brushed her fingers once more over his forehead before returning to the kitchen.

She poured two cups of coffee, carried the mugs to Doc and Bill, then went back to the kitchen to stir up a batch of sugar cookies. She needed something to keep her hands busy.

When the cookies were ready, she placed several on a plate, still warm from the oven. She carried it to the front room and set it on a table between the two men. Offering to refill their coffee cups, she took them back to the kitchen and returned to the front room, ready to climb the walls.

Not one who could sit and do nothing, Aundy knew she couldn't read, couldn't sew, couldn't do anything other than worry about and pray for Nik.

She rubbed her hand on her apron and looked down, noticing for the first time the blood that covered it.

Quickly excusing herself, she went to her room and changed into a clean dress. With her hair flying every direction, she took it down, combed it, and then braided it in a crown around her head, knowing that would help keep it contained. As she was leaving the room with her soiled clothes in hand, she thought about her little revolver. She slipped it into her pocket, deciding it might be a good idea to carry it with her.

She left her clothes soaking in a pan of water on the back porch by the washing machine, then tied on a clean apron and began thinking about making lunch. A quick look in the refrigerator confirmed she had enough leftover roast to make sandwiches. She started to lift out the platter then set it back inside when Nora bustled through the back door, followed by J.B., both carrying loaded baskets of food.

The couple set the baskets on the table and each gave her a hug. J.B. decided to walk out to the barn and see who was there while Nora removed her hat and hung it on a peg by the door.

"Let's go see that boy." Nora took Aundy's hand and walked to the bedroom. Aundy asked Bill if he'd walk with J.B. down to the barn, knowing he'd rather be outside than stuck in the house.

Nora and the doctor checked on Nik while Aundy stood at the foot of the bed. Tears threatened to spill as she patted Nik's sheet-covered foot. She turned away as a knock sounded at the front door.

Aundy opened it and bit back a sigh. Ashton stood on the front porch with his hat in hand.

"Aundy, I just heard the news. Is the boy going to live?"

"We're praying he will." She opened the door and stepped back so Ashton could walk inside. He gave a brief glance into the room where Doc and Nora stood over Nik's bed, then took Aundy's hand in his own, pulling her to the far side of the front room.

"When I find who has done this, I'll make sure he pays," Ashton said vehemently.

Aundy looked at Ashton, really looked at him. Something about him seemed different. Although dressed impeccably, his hair was a mess and a growth of stubble darkened his normally smooth cheeks. His eyes were what she noticed most. There was an odd light glinting in them that left her frightened.

"Missy, Dent say to…" Li rushed inside then came to a complete standstill a few feet away from where she stood with Ashton. The cook dropped his head and began backing toward the door. "Sorry, Missy. I come later."

"Please, come in." Aundy motioned for him to stay. "Have you met Mr. Monroe?"

"I leave now, Missy." Li hurried out the door.

"That wasn't like him," Aundy said absently, staring at the closed door, wondering what had gotten into her cook.

"What kind of help have you hired out here?" Ashton glared at her. "You've hired a Chinese laborer?"

"He's a wonderful cook and a good friend." Aundy didn't like Ashton's tone. "Speaking of good cooking, Nora brought food for lunch. I think I'll set it out. I'm sure everyone is hungry."

As she walked to the kitchen, Aundy wished Ashton would leave instead of following her. She opened one of the covered baskets Nora brought and set a platter of sandwiches on the table.

After retrieving plates from the cupboard, she turned around and watched Ashton grab the rocks she left in a bowl in the center of the table.

"Aren't those pretty?" Aundy set down the plates then pulled a cake from the second basket. "I found those down at the creek the other day."

"Down at the creek? On your property?" Ashton dumped the rocks into his hand, tossing all but three aside.

"What are you doing?" Aundy bent down to pick up the rocks Ashton threw on the floor. When she reached beneath the table, his fingers curled around her upper arm like an iron fist.

"Something I should have done weeks ago." Ashton yanked her upright and tugging her out the door behind him. Rushing around the corner of the house, he jerked Aundy along with him. So surprised by his behavior, she hadn't yet put up a fight, but when he neared the end of the front walk, Aundy pulled back.

"I'm not going anywhere. I need to be here, close to Nik," Aundy said, digging her feet into the yard.

"You're coming with me." Ashton held her arm in a painful grip, continuing toward his horse.

"I won't go with you." Panic began to overtake her and she struggled to pull away. If she screamed, would the men get there in time to help her? "You can't make me."

"Yes, I can." Ashton pulled a revolver from his holster and struck the handle against her head, knocking her unconscious.

Chapter Eighteen

Garrett couldn't get to Aundy's fast enough once he heard the news about Nik's wound and the dead sheep.

Since she still wasn't of a mind to speak to him, he rode out to where the sheep were pastured to see if he could do anything to help.

Dent and Kade were there, along with Fred, Hank, George, and Glen.

Garrett felt sick as he looked over the slaughtered animals. He had no idea why anyone would be so cruel. Forcing his thoughts from the wounded boy back at the house, he dismounted and walked over to where the men stood.

"Garrett, good to see you," Dent said, reaching out to shake his hand. "We picked up some shell casings by the tree where we found Lem. Looks like whoever did this took Lem by surprise, shot the dog, and then Nik. Probably killed the sheep first then did the shooting because we heard the shots go off early this morning and the sheep were already bleeding out when we found them."

Carefully surveying the area, Garrett wished the ground had been wet. Maybe then they'd be able to find a distinguishable boot or hoof mark.

As it was, all they had was some flattened grass.

They searched for clues when a yell drew their attention toward the barn. Garrett slapped his horse on the rump and mounted on the run with the rest of the men hurrying to follow.

He raced toward the home place, topped the rise, and nearly plowed over Aundy's cook.

Swiftly pulling back on the reins, he circled Li then bent down to look in the man's frightened face.

"Missy need help!" Li repeated over and over while Garrett stared at him, trying to make sense of his words.

"Help? Who needs help, Li?"

"Hurry! Bad man has Missy. Hurry fast!" Li waved his hands in the direction of the house while trying to catch his breath. "Bad man take Missy."

Garrett gave Li a hand, hauling him up behind him on the horse. They rode to the bunkhouse where Li jumped off and waved his hands toward the house. "Bad man, Ashton, take Missy with him."

"Ashton? Ashton Monroe?" Garrett asked, wishing Li could speak better English. As wound up as he was, it was nearly impossible to understand him. "How do you know Ashton?"

"He beat me, leave me to die when I not do something bad for him. Then Missy find me," Li said, pointing toward the road. "He hurt Missy. Hurry!"

"Who's gonna hurt Missy?" Dent asked as he and the rest of the men rode up while Bill and J.B. hurried out of the barn to see what created all the commotion.

"Ashton Monroe," Garrett said, looking at Kade. "Li said he took Aundy and rode off. We have to find her. If he's behind all this, there's no telling what he'll do."

"Why he want Missy?" Li asked, looking from Garrett to Dent.

"We're about to find out," Kade said. Hastily making plans, he asked J.B. to stay with Nora at the house, and Bill and Dent to keep an eye on the place while George and Glen went back out to watch over the sheep and clean up the dead carcasses. Garrett, Fred, and Hank would go with Kade to find Aundy. Li would watch over Lem at the bunkhouse.

"Any ideas on why Ashton would kidnap Aundy, kill her sheep, shoot the boy, and try to run her off the place?" Kade asked, wishing he'd paid more attention to Ashton at dinner the other night. Busy ignoring the Raines sisters, he hadn't noticed much else.

"Not really. There has to be something he wants real bad on the farm. Why else would he try to run her off?" Garrett asked, thinking aloud. Ashton's fawning over Aundy bothered him more than he cared to admit. Whenever the man got close to her, waves of jealousy washed over him until it was all he could do not to punch the sweet talking southerner in the face.

If he really did take Aundy and was behind all the terror at her place, he'd do a lot more than break Ashton's perfect, aristocratic nose.

Riddled with anger, Garrett should have told Aundy the truth the other night. She'd hurt him when she pushed him away. Instead of talking out the problem, making sure she knew how much he loved her and asking her to marry him, he'd kissed her with a ruthless intensity and stormed out the door.

If he planned to love Aundy for the rest of her life, he had to learn to let go of his pride and resign himself to the fact that she was anything but a typical woman.

Most women he knew were content keeping a home and raising children. Something in him knew Aundy would want more. Too bright and lively to stay in the house and be completely domestic, she wanted to be outside doing, learning, succeeding on the farm. Garrett would have to give her plenty of room to spread her wings if he didn't want to lose her altogether. He loved her too much to consider the possibility of a future without her in it.

Thoughts of telling her how he really felt spurred him on to Dogwood Corners.

"What if he isn't there? Then what?" Garrett asked Kade as they galloped down the road.

"Then we'll go to town and round up a posse and find him." Kade didn't want to drag more people into something that could quite likely end with gunfire, but he'd do whatever was needed to make sure Aundy returned home safe and sound.

At the point where the road met with the lane leading to Ashton's stately home, Kade stopped and looked around the group, hoping things went better than he was expecting. "Here's what we're gonna do…"

A sharp pounding behind her eyes roused Aundy. She struggled to remember what she'd done to hurt her head and recalled arguing with Ashton before everything went black.

Slowly opening her eyes, she was face down on a bed in an unfamiliar room. In case Ashton waited nearby, she cautiously looked around without moving.

Carefully listening, the only sound she heard was her own breathing and decided she was alone. She rolled onto her side to discover her hands tied together in front of her with what appeared to be Ashton's handkerchief.

She held the knot up to her mouth then yanked and tugged at it with her teeth. Aundy almost had it loose when the creak of a floorboard let her know someone was right outside the door. Quickly rolling onto her stomach, she made sure to tuck her hands beneath her then closed her eyes.

Footsteps thudded across the floor and stopped next to the bed. She smelled Ashton's cologne, a scent she now found nauseating. Everything in her wanted to jump up, kicking and screaming. Instead, she pretended to remain unconscious, carefully taking even breaths.

"Maybe I hit you a little harder than necessary, my dear," Ashton said, placing a hand to her head. When she didn't move, he withdrew his hand and paced the floor. It was like he'd opened the door to his thoughts and they all spilled out of his mouth. "You stupid bumpkins don't take a hint. I tried to buy you out, but you just don't listen. First, it was that idiot Nash family holding things up. Trying to get rid of J.B. didn't work. Who knew the old coot would recover? I thought when I spooked Erik's team and the wagon crashed, I'd be able to pick up his place for a song. Except he had to go and leave the land to you, the most stubborn, unreasonable female I've ever encountered. Now, I'm going to have to marry you and kill you all in the same day. Then I'll finally have my gold."

Stunned by Ashton's unwitting confession, Aundy had to bite her tongue until she tasted blood to keep from saying anything.

What gold?

Suddenly, the shiny rocks she pulled from the creek made sense. Ashton didn't want the land. He wanted the gold that was in the creek running through both the Erickson and Nash properties. She couldn't believe he'd been the reason J.B. was injured and that he'd essentially killed Erik.

What if he'd gone after Garrett? Maybe he had and she didn't know about it yet. The thought of anything happening to him made Aundy renew her determination to survive this ordeal just to tell Garrett how much she loved him.

"Rest while you can, dear Mrs. Erickson. As soon as the preacher arrives, you're marrying me, signing over the farm, then you're going to tragically fall down the stairs and break your lovely long neck." Ashton patted Aundy on the leg as he strode from the room.

The man had completely lost his mind.

Once the sound of his footsteps died away, Aundy sat up and tugged at the knot holding her hands captive. Frantically pulling it loose, she worked her hands free. She stood and a wave of dizziness almost dropped her to the floor. By holding onto the dresser, she balanced and waited until her vision cleared. Although her head felt like someone attempted to split it in two, she had to do something while Ashton worked on his scheme to kill her.

She strode over to the window and hoped the room was one that opened onto a balcony. Blue sky and a long drop to the ground dashed her plans to sneak outside.

If Ashton thought she'd obediently do whatever he said, he really didn't know her at all.

Aundy looked around the room and began devising a plan to escape.

Kade and Garrett were ready to ride up the lane to Ashton's house and execute their plan when Pastor Whitting waved and rode up beside them.

"Good afternoon, gentleman. Going to visit Ashton?" the pastor asked with a cheery smile.

"Something like that," Garrett muttered, trying to be civil. The pastor hadn't done anything to incur his wrath. "What brings you out here?"

"Ashton called and said he had a special matter that required my immediate attention." Pastor Whitting looked skeptical. "He wouldn't say what that matter was, just that I needed to hurry. Since I was going to come out anyway to check on Nik and Aundy, it was easy enough to stop by."

"Say, Kade, I have an idea." Garrett looked from Hank to the preacher.

A few minutes later, Hank was dressed in the pastor's clothes, his revolver hidden beneath the light coat, while the pastor wore Hank's denims, neckerchief, and western hat.

"I always wanted to be a cowboy," the pastor said, mounting Hank's horse and grinning broadly. "This is quite exciting."

"Just remember, you stay far back, out of the line of fire," Kade said to the pastor before falling in line behind Hank who rode Pastor Whitting's horse.

Halfway up the lane, Garret, Kade, Fred, and Pastor Whitting split up, urging their horses past the trees to flank the sides of the house where they could watch undetected from Ashton's thick rows of shrubbery and hedges. Hank continued up the lane to the front steps.

Since he couldn't recall ever meeting Ashton, they hoped Ashton had never seen Hank around town or at Aundy's place. He would pretend to be Pastor Whitting's nephew who stopped for a visit on his way through town.

As he adjusted the narrow brim of the wool crusher hat on his head, Hank decided this was probably as close to becoming a man of the cloth as he was ever going to get. He looped the reins of the horse around a hitching post at the bottom of a set of broad steps leading up to the front door. Hank straightened his coat, tucked Pastor Whitting's Bible in one hand, and took a deep breath.

Sedately strolling to the door, he knocked loudly and waited, praying their ruse would go undetected by Ashton.

The second time he knocked, Hank glanced over his shoulder, pretending to study the expansive yard while scouting to see if the men were in place. Out of the corner of his eye, he watched Kade signal him from the edge of the shrubbery and turned his attention back to the door.

Footsteps approached so he plastered a huge smile on his face.

"Yes? May I help you?" Ashton asked tersely as he opened the door and saw a stranger standing on his front steps.

"You sure can," Hank said, offering his friendliest smile. "My uncle said you called this morning and requested his services."

"Uncle? The only person I called was Pastor Whitting," Ashton said, clearly annoyed.

"Yes, that's right. Pastor Whitting is my uncle. I recently graduated from seminary and am on my way to minister my own little flock near The Dalles. I decided to stop and visit my dear auntie and uncle for a few days. He was just coming to see you when he was unavoidably detained with an emergency, so he asked me to offer my services and see if I may be of assistance."

"That's perfectly fine." Ashton didn't care who performed the ceremony as long as the result was a legal and binding marriage to Aundy.

With the exception of the cook, he gave all his help the day off so he'd have fewer witnesses around. Proud of his brilliant scheming, Ashton thought his plan came together quite nicely. If the bride would wake up from the little bump on her head, he could get on with his quest for the gold in her creek bed.

"May I come in?" Hank thought Ashton Monroe looked like a pretty-faced lunatic. Unsettled by the bizarre, feral gleam in the man's eyes, he wanted to turn around and run down the steps.

However, since Aundy was most likely somewhere in this monstrosity of a house, Hank swallowed back his fear and did his best to convince Ashton he was Pastor Whitting's nephew.

"Certainly." Ashton ushered Hank into a large gathering room overlooking the front yard. "I asked your uncle to come because today is going to be my wedding day and I wanted him to do the honors."

"Wedding, you say?" Hank asked, perplexed. If Ashton was getting married, then he probably wasn't plotting evil. "Surely you want to wait for my uncle, then. He should be available tomorrow."

"No, that won't be necessary. It must take place today. Right now." Ashton took Hank by the arm and pushed him down into an overstuffed chair. "The bride is somewhat reluctant. Young and scared of her matrimonial duties, I suppose. I'm afraid if I wait any longer, she won't be cooperative at all. You know how women can be."

"Yes, I do." Hank forced a broad grin, wishing he could black both of Ashton's deranged looking eyes. "I'll just wait here, then, while you bring in the bride."

"I'll see if she's ready." Ashton walked to the door. "I have a house servant who will stand as witness. I'll fetch her as soon as my bride comes downstairs."

Hank nodded his head. A trickle of sweat slid down his neck as Ashton closed the door. Quickly gaining his feet, he rushed to the window and looked outside. Slight movement from a tall hedge reminded him there were four men outside ready to rush in at his signal, although he sincerely hoped the pastor stayed hidden as Kade advised.

Ashton Monroe seemed completely unbalanced and dangerous. Hank had once watched a cat play with a mouse before devouring it. The cat swatted at the mouse, set it free, then caught it again and again before finally killing it.

He thought Ashton did an admirable job at being the cat.

Raucous thumping sounded overhead. Hank quickly stuffed the pastor's Bible into his coat pocket and opened the door as Ashton raced down the stairs, face distorted with fury.

"What's the matter?" Hank asked, wondering what caused Ashton to lose his calm facade.

"My bride seems to be playing games with me," Ashton said, quickly putting his pleasant lord of the manor face back in place. "It may take a moment or two for me to find her."

"What's your bride's name?" Hank asked.

Ashton glared at him.

"I can help look for her if you tell me what name to call out," Hank offered with an indifferent shrug.

"Aundy. Aundy Erickson," Ashton said. He turned and ran down the hall toward the back of the house.

Hank glanced upstairs and caught a glimpse of movement. Aundy peeked over the stair railing from the landing.

Quietly stepping into the foyer, he motioned for her to hurry and she raced down the stairs without making a sound.

"Get outside and run for the trees. Garrett and Kade are there," Hank whispered, opening the door and giving Aundy a push. "I'll try to keep him distracted."

Aundy picked up her skirts and ran down the steps. She started across the yard when she heard Ashton scream her name from inside the house. Running as fast as she could, she looked ahead as Garrett burst out of the shrubbery, racing her direction.

Ashton entered the foyer with a rifle in his hand, continuing to bellow Aundy's name.

"Oh, did I see her run down the hall?" Hank hurried toward Ashton, intentionally stumbling into him, dragging them both to the floor.

"You, fool, get out of the way!" Ashton yelled, shoving Hank and rising to his feet. Hank yanked the rifle from his hands before he ran out the door. Ashton pulled a revolver from a holster on his hip and aimed it at Aundy. "Stop or I'll kill you right now."

Aundy continued running. She was almost to Garrett when the pop of the gun drew her up short. Garrett dropped to his knees from the impact of the bullet ripping across the outside of his upper arm.

Terrified, Aundy sank down beside him and looked back at Ashton. He raced toward them in a weaving pattern and would soon be at her side. Although others hid behind the shrubs ready to jump into action, she didn't know what Ashton would do if someone else threatened him. Desperate to keep her friends safe, she resigned herself to doing Ashton's bidding.

"I give up, Ashton. I'll marry you." Aundy lurched to her feet, placing herself between Ashton and Garrett.

"Aundy, no." Garrett clenched his jaw as he regained his feet. "Don't do it."

"Be quiet or I'll put a bullet in your head." Ashton sneered at Garrett. "I win again. First I'll marry this troublesome piece of baggage then figure out a way to get Nash's Folly as well."

"Never. You won't get your filthy hands on our land and you certainly aren't putting them on Aundy." Garrett took a threatening step toward Ashton, whipping his gun from the holster on his hip. Ashton grabbed Aundy and pulled her against his chest, using her for a shield with one arm wrapped around her neck.

Slowly cocking his gun, Ashton held it to Aundy's head.

"One more step and she's dead. I'll kill her, Nash. You know I will." Ashton's tone was oddly even and calm. "I swear I'll pull the trigger if you move."

"What do you want, Ashton? What's this about?" Garrett held his gun in front of him with one hand. The other dangled uselessly at his side as blood from the gunshot wound dripped along his fingers, pooling on the grass of Ashton's neatly trimmed lawn.

"Property. I want hers," Ashton spoke as though they sat in a drawing room drinking tea. "I wanted it ever since I moved here and Erik refused to sell it to me. Yours was my first choice, but your father made it clear he wasn't willing to sell."

"What's wrong with the place you've got here?" Garrett asked, watching Aundy slowly move her hand beneath her apron. If he wasn't mistaken about what she had planned, he needed to keep Ashton distracted.

"Let's just say it's missing something." Ashton glared contemptuously at Garrett. "You've got something extremely valuable right under your nose but are too stupid to realize it."

"I'm not the only one with that affliction," Garrett mumbled. The real treasure, the rare irreplaceable treasure was the girl Ashton held in front of him. Garrett couldn't lose her. He wouldn't lose her, especially not to Ashton Monroe.

Aundy wanted to tell Garrett about Ashton thinking there was gold in the creek, but if she spoke up, it would draw Ashton's attention to her and that was something she couldn't do. Steadily moving her hand beneath her apron, she looked at Garrett and winked at him, hoping he understood her signal.

"What is it, exactly, you think we've got over there that you don't have here?" Garrett waited for Aundy to make her move. Hank edged up behind Ashton. Kade and the other men waited for a sign to come out with guns blazing.

"Gold, you illiterate cowpuncher," Ashton spat out. "You've got a creek full of gold and aren't even smart enough to know it."

"Is that all?" Garrett stared at Ashton with a scornful expression on his face. "You did all this because of those yellow rocks in the creek?"

"And they're going to be all mine." Ashton pointed his revolver at Garrett. "Can't have you carrying any tales, now, can we? That so-called preacher is going to marry us then I'll arrange it to look like Aundy's jealous beau came to stop the wedding too late, killing her before shooting himself. You just saved me the trouble of having to break her neck and shove her down the stairs later."

"You're despicable." Garrett took a step toward Ashton. "Go ahead. Shoot me if you're going to and be done with it."

"Fine, I will." Ashton pulled back the hammer on his revolver.

"No!" Aundy screamed, startling Ashton as she jerked away from him and fired her gun.

Hank hit Ashton from behind, knocking him to the ground as Kade, Fred, and Pastor Whitting hurried into the yard.

"My leg!" Ashton held his thigh where Aundy's bullet found its mark. She wasn't sure how much damage her little revolver could inflict, but from the look on Ashton's face, she must have been close enough to make the shot count.

"Stop whining," Kade ordered, handcuffing Ashton before Hank let go of him.

"Are you okay?" Aundy asked, gently touching Garrett's arm, the small revolver still held in her hand.

"Yes. Ashton's a terrible shot. I might be bleeding like a stuck pig, but it's just a little scratch." Garrett pulled Aundy against him with his good arm. "Will you forgive me for the other day?"

"Only if you'll forgive me," Aundy said. Tears pooled in her sky blue eyes. "I love you, Garrett Nash."

"I love you, too, Aundy." Mindful of the many pairs of eyes watching them, Garrett gave her a quick kiss. "But don't you ever scare me like that again. I thought for sure he was going to kill you."

"I thought that a time or two myself, especially when he kept repeating it." Now that she was safe, her knees trembled. Aundy glowered at Ashton as he stood between

Kade and Fred. "If there's a trial, I'd be more than happy to testify against him."

"I'm glad to hear that, Aundy. It most likely won't be necessary," Kade said, tipping his head to her. "He will, of course, pay the medical expenses for everyone as well as replace any lost sheep and damaged property."

"I'll do no such thing," Ashton spluttered before Fred popped him in the mouth, cutting his lip.

"Next word out of you and I'll break that pretty nose of yours," Fred warned, effectively silencing Ashton. "Although where you're going, there won't be any ladies to notice."

"Deputy Rawlings, I think you should know a few things." Aundy pointed to Ashton. "He said he tried to kill J.B. and that's why he had the accident. He also admitted to spooking Erik's horses the day the wagon flipped over."

At this news, Garrett wanted to beat Ashton to a pulp, but with Aundy leaning against him, he squelched his primal urges and instead stared at the conniving coward.

"You didn't write the notes or kill the sheep. Who did your dirty work for you?" Garrett asked, as Kade tightened the handcuffs around Ashton's wrists. When Ashton failed to answer Garrett's question, Kade thumped the butt of his gun against the man's wounded leg, making him gasp in pain.

"Some drifter wanted to earn a few dollars and was more than happy to terrorize a 'stupid woman' as he liked to call the fair Mrs. Erickson," Ashton said in a scornful tone. Fred popped him in the mouth again and Ashton spat out blood along with two of his teeth. "He got greedy and stupid, shooting the boy. I had to take care of him after that. Sloppy work, it was. I can't tolerate it. You won't find any evidence of him. I keep things neat and orderly."

Convinced Ashton had completely lost his mind, Garrett changed the subject. "Why do you think there's gold in the creek?"

"I met an old miner before I moved here who talked about striking gold north of Pendleton. He showed me some of the nuggets he found and made a crude map before he met a most unfortunate demise. His landmarks drew me to the creek that runs through the Erickson farm and Nash's Folly."

Garrett let out a derisive laugh and shook his head. "Just so you know, Ashton, that gold you were willing to murder for isn't real. Ever hear of pyrite?"

Ashton hung his head as Kade led him down the drive to the waiting horses.

"Pyrite?" Aundy asked, watching the men mount the horses. Kade threw Ashton across the back of his horse on his belly then tied him on. It would be a rough ride to town, especially with the wound to his thigh.

"Fool's gold. Looks like the real thing, but isn't," Garrett said. The description suited Ashton particularly well.

"That seems quite fitting," Aundy said, shaking her head.

"That it does."

She watched the other men ride away. "Do you suppose we'll ever know what devious enterprises and activities Ashton's undertaken?"

"Probably not. We're most likely better off not knowing. I'm just glad this is over and you're safe." Garrett walked toward his horse with an arm around Aundy's shoulders. "I think I'd better see you home."

"I think that's a very good idea." She stretched up to kiss Garrett's cheek. "I'm anxious to get back to Nik. I'm really worried about him."

"I am, too, but I have a feeling he's going to be fine." Garrett mounted Jester and held out a hand to help Aundy swing up behind him. "We've got a lot to discuss."

"We do?"

"Yep. We sure do, like what you'd think of sending Nik to school this fall and hiring someone else to watch the sheep. And of course, we need to talk about how soon you'll marry me and where you want the wedding and who all you plan to invite." Garrett turned to grin at Aundy. She stared at him, dumbfounded. "You will marry me, won't you?"

"Yes," Aundy whispered, wrapping her arms tightly around Garrett's waist and squeezing. "Oh, yes, Garrett."

SHANNA HATFIELD

Chapter Nineteen

"Ready, honey?" Nora asked as she poked her head around the door and smiled at Aundy.

"More than ready." Aundy gave one last glance in the mirror before lifting her veil to cover her face.

As she ventured out of the bedroom, Aundy grinned at her soon-to-be mother by marriage and strolled to the front door of Nora's house.

Dent waited to walk the bride down the aisle and gave Aundy an approving smile as she approached him.

"You're just beautiful, Missy." Dent kissed her cheek through the thin material of the veil.

"Thank you, Dent." Aundy noticed his suit and tie. "You clean up well."

Dent laughed and glanced down at his "fancy duds," looking uncomfortable in them as he escorted Aundy outside.

"Maybe, but I'll be glad enough when this shindig is over to get back into my regular clothes. I can't believe you invited that old goat Marvin Tooley to your wedding. I also can't believe he came and actually looks and smells like he took a bath."

Aundy was glad the man accepted her invitation. She thought part of Marvin Tooley's problem was that he had no one to care about him. She'd taken him muffins one morning and invited him to their wedding. He still grumbled at her, but not nearly as vehemently as he had in the past.

"Everyone deserves to have a friend," Aundy said, grinning at her foreman. "Even that old goat."

"If you say so," Dent chuckled. "At least he won't make the flowers wilt with his stench."

Since it was late spring and Nora's yard was full of beautiful flowers bursting with vibrant blooms, Aundy and Garrett decided to hold their wedding at Nash's Folly.

Although they both would have preferred a small ceremony, as Aundy peeked around the corner of the house, it looked like half of Umatilla County was there to watch them exchange vows.

The only dark spot in Aundy's day was the fact that her sister had not been able to come. As soon as she and Garrett set a date for the wedding, Aundy sent Ilsa a telegram.

She was thoroughly disappointed when the girl replied, saying their aunt wouldn't let her leave so close to the debut of her summer line of fashions.

Since there was nothing she could do beyond going to Chicago and stealing her sister away, Aundy resigned herself to not having any of her family at the wedding.

At least she wore her mother's wedding gown. Lightly brushing her hand along the beautiful silk of the skirt, Aundy hoped to one day have a daughter who would want to wear the gown at her own wedding. Although she and Ilsa had altered it to make the style more current and fit her tall figure, the gown was exquisite.

Aundy placed her hand on Dent's arm and nodded to him that she was ready.

When she walked around the corner of the house and down the aisle between the makeshift rows of benches, Aundy only had eyes for the tall, handsome man with the teasing smile waiting for her next to Pastor Whitting.

Garrett looked quite dashing in a new gray suit that highlighted the silver of his eyes.

Still in awe of the fact that he loved her completely and unconditionally, Aundy felt overwhelmed with blessings. She looked forward to building a future with the gentle, caring man who would give her the space she required to learn and grow while surrounding her with his love and security.

All the love she felt in her heart filled her eyes as she gazed at him. Her knees began to wobble, so she tightened her grip on Dent's arm.

Nora and J.B. stood with them. Aundy smiled at the couple then winked at Nik. He sat in the front row with her men. The boy made an almost miraculous recovery from his wound. Doc said it was because he was young, strong, and stubborn. Aundy thought it was because God watched closely over one very special shepherd boy.

As she glanced down, Aundy stifled a laugh, not surprised in the least to see Nik brought along Butter. The lamb wore a blue bow around his neck and rested contentedly at the boy's feet. Two Border collie puppies snuggled against the lamb, sleeping in the afternoon sunshine.

The day Nik was able to get out of bed, Garrett arrived with two puppies, giving one to Aundy and the other to the boy. Nik took his responsibilities of training the puppies to grow up to be good sheep tenders very seriously. For now, though, the pups, like the lamb, were well-loved pets.

Garrett winked at Aundy as he took her hand, trying to convince himself he wasn't dreaming. She looked lovely as she floated down the aisle in some fashionable white confection. He wondered when she'd had time to make the gown. Maybe it was something she'd brought along with her in one of her trunks crammed full of clothes.

Wherever it came from, the style accented her curves and made heat climb up his neck at the thought of helping her remove that dress later, back at their home.

The idea of having a home and a future with the lovely, lively, strong-willed girl filled him with contentment. He patted her hand where it rested on his arm, excited to begin their forever together as he breathed in her rosy fragrance.

The pastor smiled at them both as he began the ceremony. Although Aundy had gone through the experience once before with Erik, she realized how different, how much more meaningful it was to marry the person who already held your heart.

Through the lace of her veil, she drank in the sight and scent of Garrett. From the top of his dark hair to the tips of his polished boots, he was the embodiment of every single dream she'd ever had for a husband.

Solemnly reciting their vows, Aundy held out her hand as Garrett slid the ring on her finger through the slit in her glove.

When Pastor Whitting announced Garrett could kiss his bride, he folded back her veil then locked his silvery gaze to hers. It was hard for him to believe that just a few short weeks ago, he thought he'd lost her forever, and now she was his bride. His beloved, cherished bride.

Eagerly lowering his lips to hers, he kissed her more thoroughly than many would have deemed proper. Aundy blushed furiously and his mother smacked his arm.

With a wicked grin, he wrapped his hand around Aundy's waist as they turned to face those gathered to help them celebrate their nuptials.

Garrett leaned close to her ear. His breath on her neck stirred tendrils of her hair, making her shiver in anticipation of what was to come. "You ought to know, Mrs. Nash, that I'm just getting started with those kisses."

She shot him an inviting smile over her shoulder. The look in her eyes made Garrett's blood heat as it zinged through his veins. "I'm counting on it."

White Cake

Here is a simple sheet cake recipe that Aundy would have used to make a basic cake. She may have covered it in frosting, served it with freshly whipped cream, or topped it with fruit.

White Cake

3 eggs
2 cups sugar
3/4 cup butter
3 cups flour
1 cup milk
3 teaspoons baking powder
1 teaspoon salt
1 teaspoon vanilla extract

Preheat oven to 375 degrees. Grease a 9 x 13 baking pan and set aside.

Beat eggs until pale yellow and light. Cream butter and sugar, beat in eggs and milk. Sift together flour, salt, and baking powder. Add to egg mixture and beat until well blended. Add vanilla and mix well.

Pour in the baking pan and bake until light brown on top and springy in the middle, about 35 minutes.

Remove from oven and let cool before serving.

Butter Cookies

These cookies are simple and easy to make (especially with all our wonderful, modern conveniences). You can roll and slice them or drop them. The secret is to chill the dough so they hold their shape when they bake.

Butter Cookies

2 1/2 cups all-purpose flour
1 teaspoon baking powder
1 cup softened butter
1 cup sugar
1 teaspoon vanilla extract
2 eggs

In a small bowl, mix the flour and the baking powder, set aside.

Beat the sugar and softened butter separately in a large bowl until the mixture is pale and fluffy. Add in vanilla and eggs, one at a time. Add the flour and baking powder mixture until the entire mixture is evenly blended. Chill until firm.

Preheat your oven to 375 degrees. Grease the baking sheets lightly (or line with parchment). Keep your cookies about one-inch apart on the baking sheet. Bake for about 8 minutes or until cookies just start to turn brown. Remove from oven and cool on racks.

Author's Note

Writing historical fiction is such fun for me because I learn so much about the places, people, and experiences of the past.

I chose Pendleton, Oregon, for the setting of this series partly because my parents lived there in their early years of marriage and my dad has such great stories to tell about their time spent in Umatilla County.

After visiting the town myself, I knew it had a rich and intriguing past that would be exciting to capture in a western romance series set at the beginning of the 20th century.

Many people know Pendleton as the home of the world-famous Pendleton Round-Up and the Pendleton Woolen Mills. There is so much more to the city's story.

In fact, Pendleton was a happening place to be in the early 1900s.

Modern and progressive for its time, Pendleton was a unique blend of Wild West and culture. The town boasted an opera house and theater, a teashop, a French restaurant, and a wide variety of businesses in the early years of the new century. On any given day during that time, someone walking down the boardwalk could see well dressed ladies and gentlemen, as well as Chinese immigrants, Indians from the nearby reservation, miners, ranchers, and farmers.

Pendleton had an enviable railway facility with trains running east and west daily. Telephones as well as running water and sewer lines were available for those who could afford the services.

In the year 1900, it was the fourth largest city in Oregon. By 1902, the population grew to 6,000 and there were 32 saloons and 18 bordellos in the area.

If you're wondering why the town needed quite so much "entertainment," it was in part because of the sheer number of cowboys, wheat harvesters, sheepherders, railroad workers, and crews of men who descended on the town to work. In 1900 alone, an estimated 440,000 sheep produced more than two million pounds of wool.

The Pendleton Underground really did exist and you can visit it today through <u>Pendleton Underground Tours.</u> The tour provides a glimpse at everything from the card rooms and life of the Chinese below the city to the "working girls" who occupied many of the second story floors of business throughout that section of town.

For more details about Pendleton's past, I recommend Keith F. May's book *Pendleton: A Short History of a Real Western Town*.

Caterina *(Pendleton Petticoats Book 2)* – On the run from the Italian mafia in New York City, feisty Caterina Campanelli travels across the country to the small town of Pendleton, Oregon, trying to hide her past while she decides what to do about her uncertain future. Seeking comfort in her cooking, she battles her attraction to one of the town's most handsome men.

Kade Rawlings is dedicated to his work as a deputy in Pendleton. Determined to remain single and unfettered, he can't seem to stay away from the Italian spitfire who rolls into town keeping secrets and making the best food he's ever eaten. Using his charm, wit, and brawn to win her trust, he may just get more than he bargained for.

Turn the page for an exciting excerpt from *Caterina*…

Chapter One

1899 – New York City

"Mamma, stop fussing. I'll be fine."

Caterina Campanelli forced a smile as she stuffed the last of her dresses into a trunk and attempted to slam the lid. Flinging herself on top of the bulging chest, she bounced a few times, trying to hold the lid shut, while her mother quickly fastened the latches and hooked the buckles over the leather straps.

Angelina Campanelli muttered a string of complaints in Italian. Frustrated and fearful, she looked around her daughter's bedroom. Everything the girl decided she couldn't live without was hastily stuffed into trunks or bags. Even now, Caterina's five brothers loudly made their way up the stairs to carry the trunks outside to the waiting wagon.

"*La mia bambina,*" Angelina said. The woman sniffled, trying to hold back the tears stinging her eyes. "My poor baby girl. Isn't there another way?"

"No, Mamma." Caterina refused to cry as her mother held her close. Her mother's soft scent filled her nose. She wanted to memorize every detail about the woman in case she never saw her again.

The fragrance of lemon verbena and the smell of cinnamon would forever make her think of her mother. Tenderly rubbing her fingers along Angelina's cheek, she drew back with a brave smile, casting to memory the feel of velvety skin.

She never wanted to forget the look of complete love and acceptance in her mother's deep brown eyes. The youngest of six children, Caterina knew her mother spoiled and pampered her not only because she was the baby, but also because she was the only girl.

"I'll miss you, Mamma, so very much, but I'll be fine." Caterina stepped back from Angelina and gave the room one last glance. Assured she packed everything she might need, she threw her arm around her mother's slight shoulders and led her to the door.

The morning's first rays of sunlight filtered through the lace-covered window. Caterina inhaled the scent of roses from the sachets she'd made and stashed in her dresser drawers. She gathered her purse and gloves, picked up her traveling bag, draped a shawl over her arm, and said goodbye to the lovely room that had been hers since she was old enough to sleep in a bed instead of a cradle.

Without the time or energy to expend on thinking how painfully she would miss this house and her family, she strengthened her resolve to face her uncertain future bravely.

At the sound of men in the hall, Caterina pinned a smile in place and turned to look at her brothers as they entered the room.

"Mamma, must she take every single thing she owns?" Antonio grumbled as he hefted a trunk to his broad shoulder. "Can't the little wench make do with a bag or two?"

Angelina smacked her son's arm, shaking her head as she hid her smile. "No, Tony, she cannot. You boys haul whatever she wants down to the wagon and be quick about it. If she decides to take the piano, then be ready to pack it, too."

"Mamma!" Brando and Bruno, the twins of the family, protested while Alonzo and Carlo grinned. They each took a trunk or a bag and made a final trip down the stairs.

As jovial as the boys seemed, Caterina knew it would be easy to forget the danger that awaited them if things didn't go according to her father's hastily made plans.

"I'm so worried about you." Angelina clung to her daughter again, holding her so tightly Caterina thought her ribs might crack.

"Please, Mamma, don't make this harder." Caterina's throat tightened with emotion. "You know I must do this. I must go and never come back."

"I know, *bambina*, but you are taking a part of my heart with you." Angelina swiped at tears she couldn't contain as they rolled down her cheeks. "I love you, sweet Caterina."

Caterina shook her head. "Mamma, I've never been sweet. Sassy, spunky, most often in trouble, but not sweet."

Angelina smiled and kissed her daughter's cheek. "You've always been sweet to me. Sweet and beloved."

"Mamma." Tears pricked Caterina's eyes once again.

She blinked twice while her mother gave her a gentle nudge down the hall. "Hurry along to the kitchen. I'll be right there."

The Campanelli family owned a grocery store, catering to the Italian community by stocking their shelves with products hard to find in America. Caterina lived above the store with her parents and two of her brothers, Tony and Alonzo. Carlo, Brando, and Bruno were all married and lived in their own homes nearby.

As she entered the large, sunny kitchen, her three sisters-in-law were busy preparing breakfast and setting the long table for all eleven family members. Caterina swallowed back her tears. She would sorely miss being part of her loud, boisterous, loving family.

"Oh, Rina." Brando's wife, Natalia, reached out to pull her into a hug. The women soon surrounded Caterina as they hugged and cried and told her how much they'd miss her.

"I'll miss you all so much, but we must stop," Caterina said, grabbing a dishtowel to mop at her tears.

"But, Rina, what will we do without you around to keep things lively?" Bruno's wife, Elena, asked as she rubbed her protruding belly. The baby was due in another month and Caterina refused to think about not being there to see her first niece or nephew.

Unable to speak around the lump in her throat, Carlo's wife, Anna, squeezed her hand and offered an encouraging nod.

Caterina and Anna had been best friends for years, ever since the girl's family moved in across the street and opened a dry goods store. Although Anna's family came from England, they fit in well in the tight-knit community, or as tight as a community can be when it sat just beyond the edges of a slum where the mafia ruled.

Thanks to Anna and her family, Caterina had a glimmer of hope to escape the trouble the mafia would bring to the Campanelli's door if she spent one more day in New York.

When she drew in a deep breath, Caterina inhaled the scent of spices that filled the kitchen with a mouth-watering aroma. She would never be able to separate the smell from home and family. In her mind, the two would forever be inexplicably intertwined.

Angelina carefully packed a trunk with supplies, convinced Caterina wouldn't be able to find the specialty food carried in their store. It was her way of sending a taste of home with her daughter to savor when she was far, far away from those who loved her most.

The family's ability to create such wonderful tastes of Italy, combined with Caterina's temper, got them into this mess in the first place.

Although she wished she could go back and do things differently, Caterina realized that line of thinking wasn't going to help her now.

She looked up as her mother hurried into the kitchen and noticed something clutched tightly in the woman's hand.

"You must take this, Caterina," Angelina said as she fastened a pietra dura pendant around her daughter's neck. "Take care of it for me."

"But, Mamma, this belonged to your grandmother. I can't take it." Caterina held the cool metal in her hand as she looked at the large piece of jewelry. The mosaic, cut from hardstones, featured a pink rose and leaves on a black background. Caterina always thought the piece was lovely, even if it seemed a little heavy.

Gently closing her fingers around Caterina's, Angelina shook her head. "And now I pass it on to you. Someday you will have a wild, headstrong daughter who means the world to you and you will give it into her keeping."

"Oh, Mamma," Caterina cried, throwing her arms around her mother, convinced she'd never again embrace the woman in her lifetime. "I love you so much."

"I love you, too, *bambina*," Angelina said, frowning at her husband as he entered the room. Hunched shoulders gave away his feelings every bit as much as the tension riding every angle and plane of his face. "Franco, isn't there any other way?"

"No. It must be done. Soon, before we raise any suspicion." Caterina's father gave her a long, sad look before he washed his hands and stood at the table. When Caterina's brothers came in, they all took seats and shared the morning meal together as a family.

While Natalia and Elena did the dishes, Angelina took Anna to her room to help her change her appearance. She was going to pretend to be Caterina, since she was close to the same height and shape. Although her dark hair didn't hold the same midnight luster as Caterina's, beneath a broad-brimmed hat, no one would notice.

Franco took his sons to his office and they returned grim-faced and quiet. Tony tucked a revolver into a holster. Although he was the closest in age to Caterina and her favorite brother, he was also the biggest and strongest of the Campanelli men. There was no question of his ability to protect his sister, perhaps better than anyone.

At Caterina's frightened look, Franco drew her to his chest. "Our beautiful *bambina*, if there was a way to keep you here and safe, I would not do this thing. We must get you out of town this morning and I'll do whatever it takes to make that happen."

Caterina hugged him tightly as memories of all the wonderful times she'd spent with him flooded through her mind. "I'll miss you, Papa. So, so much."

"I know, Caterina. I know." Franco rubbed his daughter's back comfortingly before stepping away, floundering in his own emotions.

Why did he not see this trouble brewing and do something about it years ago? He trusted Angelina's brother and look where that trust had gotten him. He was losing his daughter today and who knew what else would happen when Luigi Saverino found out his plans to have Caterina for his own were never going to materialize. The man was involved with the Italian mafia and capable of things Franco didn't want to consider.

"We must hurry, *bambina*," Franco said, handing a light coat to Tony to wear to hide the gun. Owning the grocery store, along with an ice delivery business, the family had wagons that could get Caterina safely away from the city and out of the clutches of Luigi.

Hastily stuffing the pendant inside the neck of her dress, Caterina looked at the empty trunk waiting by the kitchen door and sighed. She hated being in close spaces. It made her skin crawl and her breath stop in her throat, but her father assured her there was nothing else to be done if his plan was going to work.

Frightened and uncertain, Anna returned wearing a dress and hat of Caterina's.

Caterina took her sister-in-law's hand in hers and kissed the girl's cheek. "Thank you for helping me."

"Anything, Rina." Anna swiped away her tears. "Anything to help."

Caterina smiled at her friend, grateful for Anna and her connections. After deciding she would be safer out of the country, Anna convinced the family to send Caterina to her grandparents in England. They would be more than happy to take her in and help her begin a new life. All they had to do was get Caterina to the docks and on a boat.

Under the guise of going to Philadelphia, the plan was for everyone to think Angelina and Caterina were going to stay with an ailing aunt for a week. After dropping Anna and Angelina at the train station, Tony would pretend he made a delivery to the docks and get Caterina on a boat as quickly as possible.

If any of Luigi's thugs were watching them, Angelina and Anna would purchase tickets and board the train with bags they packed just in case they needed them.

Angelina's sister Teresa really did live in Philadelphia, although as hearty and hale as she was, she would not only take the two women in, but also keep them safe if necessary.

"I'm sorry, Papa," Caterina said, overwhelmed with remorse and regret for letting her temper get away from her. Her irritability had caused any number of troubles over the years but nothing to equal what she'd done the previous evening.

"Hush, Rina," Franco said, knowing if Caterina hadn't angered Luigi yesterday, it would have happened another day. The man was unstable and had long ago decided Caterina would belong to him.

Franco couldn't help but smile as he glanced down at his gutsy daughter. Not everyone would dump a bowl of hot soup in Luigi's lap, smack him upside the head, and live to see another day.

Caterina loved to cook, loved the magic of making delicious food, so she begged and pleaded to go to work at her uncle's restaurant.

Franco's brother-in-law, Lazzaro, arrived in America ten years before Franco and Angelina came as newlyweds, looking to build a good life for themselves and the family they hoped to have.

It didn't take long for the couple to decide to open a store. Since Laz's restaurant was just down the street, Franco and Angelina's children grew up in both businesses, helping wherever needed.

Except Caterina. Angelina refused to expose her to the ruffians who frequented her brother's establishment.

When the girl was fifteen, she began sneaking over to her uncle's place where he taught her how to turn the secret family recipes into meals for his restaurant. Eventually, her parents gave in to her pleading and Caterina went to work for her uncle full time, becoming the head cook at his restaurant.

She was just seventeen when Luigi took note of the raven-haired beauty. From that day on, he watched her and waited for the time to be right to claim her as his own.

Five years later, he was tired of waiting. When she humiliated him, he threatened to desecrate her virtue that very night if she put him off any longer.

In an effort to keep her alive and unharmed, Lazzaro promised the raging man his obstinate niece would agree to marry him soon. He arranged for both families to meet the following evening at his restaurant to discuss the details and make formal declarations.

Franco had an urgent need to get his precious daughter out of town before Luigi had any idea he was about to be left without a bride.

Any number of potential suitors sought Caterina's hand in marriage during the last several years. Franco refused all of their requests to court his daughter.

Barely more than a boy when he married his sweetheart, Franco wanted all his children to wed for love. It was up to Caterina to decide when she was ready and whom she'd marry. At twenty-two, she'd yet to find someone who turned her head, let alone softened her heart or sharp tongue.

"You'll be fine, *bambina*, but hurry," her father said, helping her climb in the trunk. "Tony made sure there are holes in the sides so you'll have plenty of air. Be safe, my beautiful daughter."

A glimpse of her mother's tears as the trunk lid descended forced Caterina to close her eyes. Her father hooked one latch to keep the lid of the trunk closed.

Caterina tried not to panic in the enclosed space. She heard Tony and Alonzo grunt as they lifted the trunk, carrying it to the wagon. It jostled her when they set it down and slid it onto the bed of the wagon.

"Mamma, we'll miss you while you're gone. I hope Aunt Teresa appreciates the hardship we'll endure without you and Caterina here," Carlo said loudly, helping his mother and Anna into the wagon beside Tony. He wanted, quite badly, to kiss his wife goodbye, but if they were under scrutiny from Luigi's men, that would surely give away their scheme.

Convinced Luigi had someone keeping an eye on them, a careful look around didn't reveal anyone. However, when the mafia was involved, they all knew looks could be deceiving.

"Tell your sister hello for me, Angel," Franco called, using his pet name for his wife as he offered a jaunty wave to the departing group. "I'll have Laz tell Luigi to expect you back in a week or two, Rina."

Anna turned and waved at Franco, careful to keep her head down and her face shadowed.

Franco winked and strolled into his store, like he would on any regular workday. It was vital they all acted as if nothing out of the ordinary transpired. That's why they entrusted Tony to get Caterina safely on a departing ship.

Tony chatted with Anna and his mother, attempting to act as normally as he could as he guided the wagon out onto the quiet street. As they journeyed toward the train station, he occasionally glanced behind him to where several trunks and bags sat in the back of the wagon. The trunks bumped together when he hit a hole in the road, and he heard a gasp from Caterina. Praying she was fine, he didn't slow the horses, but kept on toward the train station.

He hoped Luigi's men believed Anna was Caterina. If they didn't, he had no chance of getting his sister to the docks.

None at all.

The next time he glanced back, he recognized one of Luigi's thugs riding a horse a block behind them, trying to stay out of the line of sight.

"We've got company, but don't turn around," Tony whispered as he urged the horses to move faster through the streets.

"So soon?" Angelina asked, tightening her grip on the seat of the wagon. How were they going to get her baby safely out of town if Luigi's gang was already following them? She and Anna would really have to go to Philadelphia, if they could make it on the train. Good thing they'd each packed a bag, just in case, and Franco had given her money for tickets and food.

After traveling a few more blocks, Tony noticed two of the police officers Luigi kept in his back pocket following the wagon.

With trouble dogging each turn of the wagon wheels, he kept focused on the gathering traffic and considered his options. He could make a run for it and try to get to the docks. Since Luigi's men were mounted and he was in a lumbering wagon, there was no possibility he could outrun them. He could grab Caterina and they could take off on foot, leaving Angelina and Anna to take the wagon on alone. Hastily considering the best course of action, he chose to stick with the original plan. If necessary, he could improvise.

Tony urged the team forward through the growing morning traffic and guided them expertly through the streets, glad his father invested in a strong, sturdy pair of horses.

The train station loomed ahead when the two police officers rode next to the wagon.

"Tony! Where are you taking these lovely ladies?" one of the officers asked. Tony played with Fabian and Enzo as young boys, but somewhere along the way, they ended up on the wrong side of the law despite the badges they wore.

From what he could see, their entire purpose for being on the police force was to do Luigi's bidding, not uphold law and order. He wondered how they could get up each morning with a smile on their face knowing they went against everything an officer of the law should represent.

Anna kept her head bent toward Angelina's, effectively hiding her face while Tony turned a solemn gaze to Enzo. "Aunt Teresa is terribly ill. Mamma and Rina are going to take care of her for a while."

"I thought Caterina had other obligations this evening," Fabian said, obviously aware of Luigi's plans to force her to wed.

Tony shrugged his shoulders. "Luigi understood when he heard about how sick our beloved aunt has been. He and Caterina will resume their obligations when she gets back."

"Is that right?" Enzo glanced skeptically from Tony to Anna. "Is that correct, Caterina?"

Anna nodded her head without facing the officers. With a handkerchief hiding her face, she pretended to dab at tears. "It's true."

At the train station, Tony parked the wagon and got out to assist Angelina and Anna down. Much to his dismay, the two officers dismounted and walked around the wagon.

Angelina quickly pulled Anna's face toward her, hiding it from the men, putting her arm around the girl's shoulders as Tony opened the back of the wagon.

Before he could stop them, Fabio and Enzo began unloading trunks. Tony didn't know how to refuse their assistance without drawing suspicion.

"Mamma, you and Rina go get the tickets and I'll bring your bags," Tony said, lifting down a trunk.

"How long are the ladies going to be gone?" Fabio asked, watching the two women walk off to the ticket counter as he unloaded a trunk. "Looks to me like they are planning to stay a while."

"You know women, eh?" Tony gave Enzo a friendly jab to his side. "They pack enough for months when they'll only be gone a few days. Besides, Mamma is taking medical and food supplies to Aunt Teresa."

Enzo slid the trunk that held Caterina toward him. Tony put a firm hand on the man's shoulder and grinned. "I'm sure you've both got better things to do than help me with these trunks. I wouldn't want to keep you."

"We're happy to help. You know, any friend of Luigi's is a friend of ours," Fabio declared, snagging a nearby handcart and setting a trunk on it. "We're nearly family, after all."

Grateful the noise of the busy station was enough to drown out Caterina's huff of protest along with words that sounded like "no, we're not," Tony thumped a hand on the trunk, silencing her.

Tony scooted Caterina's trunk to the edge of the wagon, fastened the second latch, and lifted it with a grunt. "I'll get you out, Rina. Stay quiet," he cautioned in a whisper as he set her trunk on the handcart.

He thought he heard her whisper "hurry" before turning to load the bags on the cart. His mother waved at him and he pushed the cart her direction.

"Got the tickets?" he asked, stepping beside her. Anna kept her head down, trying not to be obvious.

"Yes, three tickets to Philadelphia," his mother said, then wrapped her hand around his arm. "Isn't it sweet of Tony to escort us there? He's such a good boy."

Taken aback by his mother's statement, Tony tried to grasp her newly made plans for him.

"You're going, too, Tony?" Fabio asked, narrowing his eyes at Tony.

"Sure am. Can't have two lovely ladies traveling unescorted." Tony looped his arm around Anna's shoulders with a brotherly squeeze, subtly drawing her behind him, away from the prying eyes of the two police officers.

"What are you going to do with the team and wagon?" Enzo asked. Tony could almost see the wheels spinning in his head, trying to figure out what the Campanelli family hid.

"Carlo will pick it up later when he and Alonzo are finished with the morning's deliveries." Tony prayed a lightning bolt wouldn't streak down from the sky and strike him dead for all the lies spilling forth from his mouth.

"We can take it back to the store," Fabio offered, studying Tony, trying to read his face for some hint of emotion.

Tony plastered on a friendly smile. Fleeced by his brothers numerous times in card games, he finally learned to keep his face and emotions unreadable. Now, he had it down to an art. "I'd hate to put you to any bother. My brothers can take care of it."

"No bother at all." Enzo tied his horse to the back of the wagon and climbed on the seat. "I'll make sure to let your father know you all made it safely to the station."

"Thank you so much for your assistance, boys," Angelina said, smiling and waving as the two police officers gave one last glance at their little group before pulling out on the street. Anna waved her hand, keeping her face hidden in the shadows of her hat.

"We're all going to have to board that train and Caterina is going to have to stay in the trunk until we get to Philadelphia. Luigi has people watching us, so just act natural while I get the luggage loaded." Tony walked the two women to the depot door to wait for the train.

After hurrying back to the cart, he pushed it to where the baggage would be loaded and spoke in hushed, curt tones to his sister.

"Rina, don't panic. Stay in the trunk, and I'll get you out as soon as I can. I'm sorry." Tony tapped the trunk with his knuckles, trying not to grin when his sister kicked the side.

"You better be sorry, Tony," Caterina hissed through the holes in the side of the trunk. Even though she couldn't see it, she wished she could wipe the smirk off her brother's handsome face.

She loved all her brothers, but Tony was the smartest, strongest, and most fun of them all. Headstrong and stubborn like her, they often argued and disagreed. Most frequently, the two of them joined forces against their other siblings.

"Truly," Tony said, watching as the trunks were loaded. He bit his tongue to keep from asking the men loading the trunks to be extra careful with the one carrying Caterina because it was fragile. Priceless. The men would try to peep in the holes and that would bring their whole sham crashing down on them.

Instead, he watched until all the trunks were stowed then hurried to join his mother and Anna to board the train.

"This isn't exactly what I planned to do today." Tony sat in an aisle seat across from his mother and sister-in-law.

Anna performed admirably, pretending to be Caterina. As long as no one looked too closely, the deception would work.

Tony sighed as he watched one of Luigi's men board the train. He reached across the aisle and snatched a newspaper from an empty seat.

Inconspicuously handing it to Anna, he motioned for her to hold it up so it blocked her face from view.

"We've got company," Tony whispered to his mother, looking behind her at a familiar face. Luigi's thugs frequently ate at Laz's restaurant, along with Luigi's "business" associates. The Campanelli family easily recognized them.

Those men were one of the reasons they tried to keep Caterina hidden in the kitchen. She could have gotten into just as much trouble in the store, except the ruffians didn't spend much time there.

As hardheaded, beautiful, and impulsive as Caterina could be, it was a wonder she hadn't found herself in a sticky situation long before now.

What she needed was a good man with a stubborn streak wider and deeper than the one she possessed to take her in hand. Tony prayed she'd meet that man someday, if they could get her away from New York and Luigi.

Caterina couldn't breathe. The air was hot and still, and she was certain she would suffocate. Given that there was nothing to do but wait to escape her confines or die, she decided she wasn't yet quite finished living. She had so much life to experience and now she was setting off on an adventure for a fresh start.

Anna spoke with great fondness of her grandparents and their home just outside London. Grateful for the manners her mother insisted she learn, Caterina hoped she remembered everything so she wouldn't offend Anna's family.

When she pressed her eye to one of the small holes in the side of the trunk, Caterina saw nothing but shadowed darkness and shapes that looked like more baggage.

Curious where she was, she felt a moment of panic that she'd have to spend the entire voyage locked in the trunk. Didn't Tony know she'd perish without food or water? He surely wouldn't expect her to stay in the trunk for days on end. She would go out of her mind.

After trying to stretch her legs that had long ago gone numb, she found it impossible to move and wanted to weep, trapped like an animal in a cage. Determined not to give in to her fears, she sighed and rolled her neck as a jarring force began a forward motion, slamming other trunks into hers. The scrape of metal against metal ground in her ears and she sucked in a gasp as she recognized the sound of a train.

That stupid brother of hers loaded her on the train! How was she going to get to the boat? Seized with anxiety, her chest hurt and her breath came in rapid little bursts.

Afraid she might faint for the first time in her life, Caterina forced herself to calm down. Tony wouldn't abandon her. She must be in the baggage car on a train.

Rapidly piecing together the bits of conversation she heard Tony have with two of the idiot police officers Luigi often paid to look the other way, she was sure Tony put Anna and Mamma on the train to Philadelphia. She hoped Aunt Teresa was home, because she was about to have unexpected company.

Surprised Enzo and Fabio let Anna go, she wondered how Tony managed to talk them into allowing who they thought was her board the train. Caterina was certain Luigi would have made it known he was finally claiming her as his own.

Lulled by the warmth in the air and the rocking of the train, Caterina let herself doze. Awake most of the night, she alternated between packing and worrying about her future.

Heavy trunks slid into her, jolting her awake as the train lurched to a stop. A few minutes passed then the baggage door slid open, bringing in welcome air and light. Caterina prayed Tony would get her soon.

Convinced her body would never unfold from its cramped position, she supposed she should be grateful she wasn't a tall girl. Even at five feet, four inches, she still felt restricted in the enclosed space.

Finally, she felt her trunk lifted and moved from the baggage car. "Heavy on one side, isn't it," a man's voice said as he dropped the trunk on a solid surface, rattling her teeth at the impact.

"Incompetent imbeciles," Caterina started to say, then slapped a hand over her mouth, knowing life and death depended on her not giving away her hiding spot by losing her temper.

"Say, gents, I've got several other trunks that are supposed to get off here, but I'd like them to stay on a bit longer. Happen to know where this train is headed?" Caterina could have wept with relief at the sound of Tony's friendly voice. Her Mamma always said he could charm the flowers into bloom if he set his mind to it.

The men answered and Tony thanked them for their assistance.

He picked up her trunk and she tried not to slide around as he nearly dropped one end.

"Tony?"

"Hush, Rina. Just hang on a few more minutes," Tony whispered, barely loud enough for her to hear. "I'm doing the best I can."

Tony carried her trunk a short distance then set it somewhere cool. She wasn't sure if she was inside the depot or just in the shade. Carefully peeping out the hole gave her a view of Tony's legs, her mother's skirt, and little else.

However, she could hear their conversation.

"Is he still watching?" Anna asked, fear making her voice tight.

"Yes. We're going to have to get Rina out of this trunk then load it in a buggy and go to Aunt Teresa's," Tony said, matter-of-factly.

Caterina could hear the tension in his voice along with frustration. He'd warned her many times her temper was going to get her into trouble. Almost as many times as he'd warned her to stay away from Luigi. It wasn't as if she sought out the horrid man. She couldn't help it if she made the best ravioli and gnocchi in the city. Even Luigi knew enough to appreciate good food when he tasted it.

"Anna, pretend you're going to the washroom and run in to buy a ticket for this train. Just one." Tony nudged Anna toward the ticket counter. When she walked away, he turned to his mother. "Mamma, do you think you could create a distraction so we can get Rina on board as a passenger?"

"Of course, Tony. You say the word, and I'll make it happen." Angelina pulled the gloves on her fingers down firmly and brushed at her skirt.

"Good. Here's what we're going to do…" Tony lowered his voice. Caterina lost the ability to hear the conversation in the dull roar of the people passing by and wondered what crazy scheme her brother and mother planned.

The latches on her trunk slowly opened, although the lid remained closed. As quietly as she could, she moved her legs to stir some life back in them. Caterina reached up to pin her hat back in place, pulled gloves on her hands, and slipped the handle of her leather bag over her fingers. Tightly holding the strings of her reticule in one hand, she had an idea she was going to have to come out of the trunk prepared to move with haste.

Tense and ready to spring into action, she waited anxiously for Tony's next move. She heard a woman scream followed by a string of Italian that could only be Mamma. Smiling at the woman's comments about the sly trickster trying to steal her traveling bag, she heard the thumps of her mother pummeling someone with it.

The lid of her trunk popped open and Tony hauled her out in one quick motion. He closed the lid before hooking a strong arm around her waist and hustling her to the train. Anna stepped from the shadows nearby and thrust a ticket into her hand.

Afraid to draw any attention their direction, Anna squeezed her hand and disappeared back toward the building while Tony helped her onboard and settled her in a seat. After kissing her cheek, he studied the other passengers. Arriving at the conclusion no one on the train would to give his sister any trouble, he bent down and patted her shoulder.

"I wish it didn't have to be this way, Rina, but we'll see each other again someday. If you ever need me, just write home and I'll come to you." Tony held her hand and gazed one more time into her lively brown eyes flecked with gold, so like their mother's eyes. "Be safe and be strong. We all love you."

"I love you, too." Caterina bit the inside of her cheek to keep from crying. "Be careful at home, Tony. Luigi will not take this lightly."

"I know, but at least he can't force you to marry him if he can't find you."

"Tell Mamma I love her. I think she missed her calling as an actress," Caterina said, trying to lighten the moment. Before her brother left, she clutched his hand in hers one more time. "Where am I going, Tony?"

"This train will take you to Chicago. You can decide your future from there," he said with a grin, then was gone.

Caterina took a deep breath at the call for the last of the passengers to board. Although everything in her wanted to press her nose to the glass and wave goodbye to three people she dearly loved, she was careful not to sit close to the window.

From the corner of her eye, she saw Tony carry the empty trunk and two leather bags through the crowd, followed by Mamma and Anna.

One of Luigi's men walked several paces behind them. He appeared unconcerned about remaining hidden. From his smashed hat, he must be the man Mamma beat with her bag.

Tony would go to Aunt Teresa's, get Mamma and Anna settled, then travel back to New York. The two women would return home in a few days, once Luigi had calmed down. By the time he realized Caterina was gone, it would be impossible for him to find her.

Quickly praying for her family's safekeeping, Caterina embraced the excitement sweeping through her at the adventure waiting ahead. Instead of sailing to London, she was heading west.

Find Caterina and the rest of the Pendleton stories where books are sold.

Pendleton Petticoats Series

Set in the western town of Pendleton, Oregon, at the turn of the 20th century, each book in this series bears the name of the heroine, all brave yet very different.

Dacey (Prelude) — A conniving mother, a reluctant groom and a desperate bride make for a lively adventure full of sweet romance in this prelude to the beginning of the series.

Aundy (Book 1) — Aundy Thorsen, a stubborn mail-order bride, finds the courage to carry on when she's widowed before ever truly becoming a wife, but opening her heart to love again may be more than she can bear.

Caterina (Book 2) — Running from a man intent on marrying her, Caterina Campanelli starts a new life in Pendleton, completely unprepared for the passionate feelings stirred in her by the town's incredibly handsome deputy sheriff.

Ilsa (Book 3) — Desperate to escape her wicked aunt and an unthinkable future, Ilsa Thorsen finds herself on her sister's ranch in Pendleton. Not only are the dust and smells more than she can bear, but Tony Campanelli seems bent on making her his special project.

__Marnie__ (Book 4) — Beyond all hope for a happy future, Marnie Jones struggles to deal with her roiling emotions when U.S. Marshal Lars Thorsen rides into town, tearing down the walls she's erected around her heart.

__Lacy__ (Book 5) — Bound by tradition and responsibilities, Lacy has to choose between the ties that bind her to the past and the unexpected love that will carry her into the future.

__Bertie__ (Book 6) — Haunted by the trauma of her past, Bertie Hawkins must open her heart to love if she has any hope for the future.

__Millie__ (Book 7) — Determined to bring prohibition to town, the last thing Millie Matlock expects is to fall for the charming owner of the Second Chance Saloon.

__Dally__ (Book 8) — Eager to return home and begin his career, Doctor Nik Nash is caught by surprise when the spirited Dally Douglas captures his heart.

Quinn (Book 9) — Coming in 2018!

Tad's Treasure *(Baker City Brides, Prequel)* — Tad Palmer makes a promise to his dying friend to watch over the man's wife and child. Will his heart withstand the vow when he falls in love with the widow and her son?

Crumpets and Cowpies *(Baker City Brides, Book 1)* — Rancher Thane Jordan reluctantly travels to England to settle his brother's estate only to find he's inherited much more than he could possibly have imagined.

Thimbles and Thistles *(Baker City Brides, Book 2)* — Maggie Dalton doesn't need a man, especially not one as handsome as charming as Ian MacGregor.

Corsets and Cuffs *(Baker City Brides, Book 3)* — Sheriff Tully Barrett meets his match when a pampered woman comes to town, catching his eye and capturing his heart.

Bobbins and Boots *(Baker City Brides, Book 4)* — Carefree cowboy Ben Amick ventures into town to purchase supplies… and returns home married to another man's mail-order bride.

Lightning and Lawmen *(Baker City Brides, Book 5)* - *Coming in 2018!*

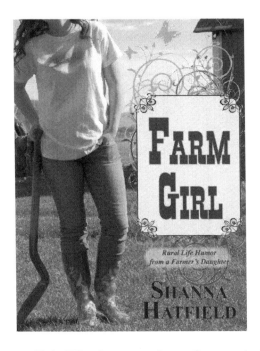

Farm Girl - What happens when a farmer who's been wishing for a boy ends up with a girlie-girl?

Come along on the humorous and sometimes agonizing adventures from a childhood spent on a farm in the Eastern Oregon desert where one family raised hay, wheat, cattle and a farm girl.

ABOUT THE AUTHOR

SHANNA HATFIELD spent ten years as a newspaper journalist before moving into the field of marketing and public relations. Self-publishing the romantic stories she dreams up in her head is a perfect outlet for her lifelong love of writing, reading, and creativity. She and her husband, lovingly referred to as Captain Cavedweller, reside in the Pacific Northwest.

Shanna loves to hear from readers.
Connect with her online:

Blog: shannahatfield.com
Facebook: Shanna Hatfield's Page
Pinterest: Shanna Hatfield
Email: shanna@shannahatfield.com

If you'd like to know more about the characters in any of her books, visit the Book Characters page on her website or check out her **Book Boards** on Pinterest.

93998179R00180

Made in the USA
San Bernardino, CA
20 November 2018